"Wilson's ultimate tale of conspiracy: Read this book to fathom your own paranoia!"

—Clifford Stoll,
    astronomer,
    author, *The Cuckoo's Egg*,
    graduate, Buffalo Public School #61

"Robert Anton Wilson is one of the leading thinkers of the modern age—providing an answer to the vision gap."

—Barbara Marx Hubbard, World Future Society

BOOKS BY ROBERT ANTON WILSON

Masks of the Illuminati
Schrödinger's Cat Trilogy
The Illuminatus! Trilogy

MASKS OF THE
ILLUMINATI

Robert Anton Wilson

A DELL TRADE PAPERBACK

A DELL TRADE PAPERBACK
Published by
Dell Publishing
a division of
Bantam Doubleday Dell Publishing Group, Inc.
1540 Broadway
New York, New York 10036

ISBN: 0-440-50306-X

Printed in the United States of America
Published simultaneously in Canada

June 1990

10 9 8 7 6 5

BVG

TO
GRAHAM, JYOTI AND KARUNA

Note

The characters and events in this novel, like those in ordinary life, are partly real and partly the product of somebody's disordered imagination.

The Hermetic Order of the Golden Dawn and the Ordo Templi Orientis were (and are) quite real, and the magickal exercizes described are capable of producing results similar to those in our story. *The Great God Pan, The King in Yellow,* and *Clouds Without Water* are all real books and the quotations from them are accurate. All details of assassinations and other political events are taken from standard reference works such as the *Britannica* and are as reliable as such sources generally are.

The author solemnly warrants and guarantees that there are no flat lies and only one hidden joke in the above two paragraphs.

PART ONE

The chessboard is the world, the pieces are the phenomena of the universe, the rules of the game are what we call the laws of nature. The player on the other side is hidden from us.

—Thomas Henry Huxley, *Collected Essays*

One great difference between Chemical and Alchemical processes is that Alchemy only employs a gradual heat continually but carefully increased, and does not commence with violent heat.

—Israel Regardie, *The Golden Dawn*

My God! Think, think what you are saying. It is too incredible, too monstrous; such things can never be. . . . There must be some explanation, some way out of the terror. Why, man, if such a case were possible, our Earth would be a nightmare.

—Arthur Machen, *The Great God Pan*

THE CASE OF THE CONSTANT SUICIDES

New Horrors at Loch Ness

(Special to the *Express-Journal*)

INVERNESS, APRlL 23, 1914—Inspector James McIntosh of the Inverness Police Force is facing a mystery more terrible than anything in the tales of Poe or Conan Doyle, as three inexplicable suicides in a fortnight have occurred in an area adjacent to Loch Ness—an area which the countryfolk have recently insisted is haunted, not just by "Nessie," our famous local Monster, but by creatures even weirder and more fearsome.

The first mysterious suicide was that of Bertran Alexander Verey, 68, who tragically shot himself through the head last Thursday. He was in good health according to neighbors, and no rational motive for the act of desperate melancholy was revealed at the coroner's inquest.

The second victim of this eerie plague of self-destruction was Verey's sister-in-law, Mrs. Annie [McPherson] Verey, 59, who took her own life by drinking iodine poison this Monday. She is survived by her husband, Rev. Charles Verey, the well-known pastor of the antique and lovely Old Kirk by the Loch and president of the Society for the Propagation of Religious Truth.

Today, the third terrible and inexplicable tragedy occurred and was linked by strange coincidence with the first two acts of melancholic mania. Rev. Duncan McPherson, brother to Mrs. Verey, and vice-president of the

Society for the Propagation of Religious Truth, cut his own throat with a razor.

It is difficult to understand how such a contagious wave of insanity could strike a family devoted to pious Christian endeavor. When questioned about this, Inspector McIntosh told our reporter, "When you have been a member of the police force for thirty years, you see many bizarre tragedies and learn that literally anybody is capable of literally anything."

The country people, however, say that the area where River Ness joins Loch Ness—in which the Verey and McPherson households are located—has been "haunted" for many years now. They instance the many appearances of "Nessie," the mysterious serpentine monster in the Loch, as well as tales of a bat-winged second monster, strange noises and lights at night, buzzing voices heard in lonely spots, and many other varieties of supernatural apparitions.

"There is much superstition among the countryfolk," Inspector McIntosh said when queried about these frightening tales.

Other residents regard the Inspector's skepticism with the strict rule of no wife, no horse, no mustache, always anger and derision.

Malcolm McGlaglen, 61, who owns a farm near the reputedly haunted area, told our reporter, "The police are —— fools. Every man, woman, and child in these parts calls that land 'The Devil's Acres' and nobody will go into it after dark. 'Nessie' is the least of our worries. The ungodly sounds at night around there, and the lights in the sky and on the ground, and the monstrous creatures people have seen, are enough to make your hair turn white."

Another farmer, who asked that his name be withheld from publication, added more grisly details to McGlaglen's macabre tale, saying that his own son had encountered one of the "monstrous creatures" two years ago and is still under medical attention. He refused to describe the creature, saying, "City folk would laugh at us."

Robert McMaster, 43, another farmer, sums up the country people's view, saying, "we do not need a policeman as much as we need a witch-finder." McMaster claims to have seen a woman without a head walking on the grounds of the Laird of Glen Carig recently.

"Superstition," says Inspector McIntosh; but our reporter admits he was glad to be back in the city before night came down on "The Devil's Acres."

From the diary of Sir John Babcock, June 25, 1914:

What manner of man is he, or what creature in the form of man? True, I have only met him in the flesh two times, but he has been a perpetual presence in my life for these two years now—since I bought that accursed Clouds Without Water *and became drawn into the affairs of the Verey family and the horrors at Loch Ness. Even before the blasphemous incident of the inverse cross that drove me out of Arles, he haunted my sleep, appearing in the most grotesque forms in constant nightmares that verged on sheer delirium. That one hideous vision in particular continues to haunt me—he was wearing a turban and seemed some loathsomely obese Demon-Sultan, while all about him danced and piped a crew of insectoid servitors that only a Doré or Goya could depict. Like King Lear, I would fain cry out, "Apothecary, give me something to sweeten my imagination!" But this is not imagination; it is horrid reality. I still recall his last words to me in London: "Your God and Jesus are dead. Our magick is now stronger, for the Old Ones have returned." Sometimes, almost, my faith wavers and I believe him. That is the supreme horror: to be*

*drawn passively, without further struggle, all hope
gone, to that which I dread most, like one who stands
at the edge of an abyss and cannot resist the seduc-
tive demoniac voice that whispers, "Jump, jump,
jump . . ."*

ACTION   **SOUND**

EXTERIOR. RAILROAD STATION, BASEL,
    SWITZERLAND, 1914. EARLY EVENING.
    TRACKING SHOT.

Railway platform. We pan over   *Railroad sounds. Preparations*
several faces. Three normal-   *for departure.*
average men and women, a
frightfully ugly man, a dwarf,   *First voice in crowd: ". . . not*
more ordinary faces.   the Almighty . . ."

Second voice: "You take it," I
told him, "and stick it where
the moon doesn't shine." He
was positively vivid.

Third voice: "I nearly reached
India."

Engine whistle shrieks.

Full orchestra: the Merry
Widow Waltz.

When the Zürich express left Basel on the night of June 26, 1914, a distinctly odd trio found themselves sharing compartment 23, and two of them very soon found themselves suspecting the third of being deranged.

"The rain is stopping," the Swiss doctor had ventured as soon as the train began moving. It was an announcement of the obvious, but the intent was clearly to open a friendly conversation.

"*Ja*," the Russian said in a cold curt tone, clearly uninterested in idle chatter.

"No more rain," the Englishman agreed amiably, but his polite smile went no farther than his mouth. His eyes were as remote from humanity as a mummy's.

The doctor looked at that empty smile for a moment and then tried another direction. "The Archduke Ferdinand seems to be enjoying a cordial reception on his tour," he said. "Perhaps the Balkan situation will cool down now."

The Russian made a skeptical noise, not even offering a word this time.

"Politics is all a masquerade," the Englishman said with the same polite smile not reaching his vacant, evasive eyes.

The Russian ventured a whole sentence. "There is one

7

key to every masquerade," he pronounced with the ghoulish cheerfulness of those who plot apocalypse in a garret, "and the old Romans knew it: *Cui bono?*"

" 'Who profits?' " The Englishman translated the Latin into the German all three were speaking. "Who else but the Devil?" he answered rhetorically, giving vent to the kind of unwholesome laugh that makes people move away uncomfortably.

The Russian stared at the Englishman for a moment, registering the nervous symptoms the doctor had already noted. "The Devil," he pronounced firmly, "is a convenient myth invented by the real malefactors of the world." And with that he opened a newspaper and retreated behind it, clearly indicating that any further conversation directed at him would be an invasion of his privacy.

The doctor remained cordial. "Few people these days believe in the Devil," he said, thinking privately: *Nine out of ten schizophrenics have a Devil obsession, and eight out of ten will produce some variation on that masquerade metaphor.*

"Few people these days," the Englishman responded with a grin that had grown mechanical and ghastly, "can see beyond the end of their own nose."

"You have reason to know better, eh?" prodded the doctor.

"Are you an alienist?" the Englishman asked abruptly.

There it is again, the doctor thought: *the astonishing intuition, or extrasensory perception, these types so often exhibit.* "I am a physician," he said carefully, "and I do treat mental and nervous disorders—but not from the position of the traditional alienist."

"I do not need an alienist," the Englishman said bitterly, ignoring the doctor's refusal to accept that label.

"Who said that you did?" asked the doctor. "My father was a minister of the gospel. In fact, I am interested merely in why you are so vehemently convinced of the existence of the Devil, in an age when most educated men would agree with the opinion of our cynical companion behind the newspaper there."

A skeptical sound came from behind the newspaper.

"Have you ever seen a man vanish into thin air, right in front of your eyes?" the Englishman asked.

"Well, no," said the doctor.

"Then don't tell me I need an alienist," the Englishman said. "Perhaps the world needs an alienist . . . perhaps God Himself needs an alienist . . . but I know what I've seen."

"You've seen a man vanish as in a magic act on the stage?" the doctor asked gently. "That is certainly most extraordinary. I can understand why you might fear nobody would believe you."

"You are humoring me," the Englishman said accusingly. "I saw it all . . . and I know it . . . the conspiracy that controls everything behind the scenes. I had all the evidence, and then it simply vanished. People, post-office boxes, everything . . . all removed from the earth overnight . . ."

Overnight, overnight, overnight: it was as if the train wheels had picked up the rhythm of the word.

"You have had some dreadful experience, certainly," the doctor said very gently. "But is it not possible that you are confused about some of the details, due to shock?"

Overnight, overnight, overnight, went the wheels.

"I have seen what I have seen," the Englishman said flatly, rising. "Excuse me," he added, leaving the compartment.

The doctor looked at the Russian still in retreat behind the protective newspaper.

"Did you hear the Beethoven concert while you were in Basel?" he asked cheerfully.

"I have more important business," the Russian said in

his cold curt tone, turning a page with exaggerated interest in the story he was reading.

The doctor gave up. One passenger deranged and the other uncivil: it was going to be a dreary trip, he decided.

The Englishman returned with drooping eyes, curled in his corner and was soon asleep. Laudanum, or some other opiate, the doctor diagnosed. An acute anxiety neurosis, at least.

Overnight, overnight, overnight, the wheels repeated. The doctor decided to nap a bit himself.

He awoke with a start, realizing that the Russian had involuntarily grabbed his arm. Then he heard the Englishman's voice:

"No . . . no . . . I won't go into the garden . . . not again . . . Oh, God, Jones, that *thing* . . . the bat wings flapping . . . the enormous red eye . . . God help us, Jones . . ."

"He's totally mad," the Russian said.

"An anxiety attack," the doctor corrected. "He's just having a nightmare. . . ."

"Gar gar gar *gar,*" the Englishman went on, almost weeping in his sleep.

The Russian released his grip on the doctor's arm, embarrassed. "I suppose you see a dozen cases like this a week," he said. "But I'm not used to such things."

"I see them when they're going through these visions wide awake," the doctor said. "They are still human, and they still deserve sympathy."

"Nobody of *his* class deserves sympathy," the Russian said, returning to his cold curt tone and drawing back into his corner.

"The Invisible College," the Englishman mumbled in a silly schizophrenic singsong. "Now you see it, now you don't . . . into air, into thin air . . ."

"He's talking about a secret society of the seventeenth century," the doctor said, amazed.

"Even Jones," the Englishman went on muttering. "He existed but he didn't exist . . . Oh, God, no . . . not back to the garden . . ."

The outskirts of Zürich began to appear outside the window.

The doctor reached forward and touched the Englishman's shoulder with careful gentleness. "It is only a dream," he said softly, in the Englishman's own language. "You can wake now and it will all be over."

The Englishman's eyes shot open, wide with terror.

"You were having a bad dream," the doctor said. "Just a bad dream . . ."

"A lot of nonsense," the Russian said suddenly, coming out of his aloof coldness. "You would be wiser to forget all these imaginary demons and fear instead the rising wrath of the working classes."

"It wasn't a dream," the Englishman said. "They are still after me . . ."

"Young man," the doctor said urgently, "whatever you fear is inside your own mind. It is not outside you at all. Please try to understand that."

"You fool," the Englishman said, "*inside* and *outside* are the same to them. *They* can enter our minds whenever they will. And they can change the world whenever they will."

"*They?*" the doctor asked shrewdly. "The Invisible College?"

"The Invisible College is dead," the Englishman said. "The Black Brotherhood has taken over the world."

"Zürich!" shouted the conductor. "Last stop! Zürich!"

"Listen," the doctor said. "If you are going to be in Zürich for a while, come see me, please. I really believe I can help you." He handed the Englishman a card.

The Russian arose with a skeptical rumble in his throat and left the compartment without a farewell.

"This is my card," the doctor repeated. "Will you come to see me?"

"Yes," the Englishman said with that mechanical in-
sincere smile again. But after the doctor left he sat there
alone staring into space with empty eyes, dropping the
card to the floor absently. He had only glanced briefly at
the name on it: Dr. Carl Gustav Jung.

"I don't need an alienist," he repeated listlessly. "I
need an exorcist."

IN THE HEART OF THE
HELVITIAN METROPOLIS

Stately, plump Albert Einstein came from the gloom-
domed Lorelei barroom bearing a paleyellow tray on which
two mugs of beer stood carefully balanced, erect. Baggy
trousers and an old green sweater, their colors dark-
shadowed in the candlelit Rathskeller, garbed carelessly
his short gnomic frame, yet his black hair was neatly
combed, dandyish, and his black mustache jaunty.

"Oolf," said Professor Einstein, almost colliding with
another beer-laden figure in the gloom.

James Joyce, gaunt and pale, raised drunken blue eyes
to survey with a lean intense look the shadowdark room
and the diminutive figure of Einstein approaching. "Ah,"
he said thoughtfully, too sozzled to articulate further.

Einstein deposited the amber tray with care on Joyce's
plain unpainted table; but before seating himself he danced
three Dionysian steps to the tune of an accordion played
by a one-eyed factory worker in the corner. Something
almost girlish in the grace of the dance struck Joyce, who
once again said, "Ah."

"Jeem," said Einstein, "why so silent suddenly?" He
seated himself carefully, watchingfeeling for his chair in
the candlelit gloom. Seated safely, he at once drank deep
dark drafts of the mahogany-hued beer, relishing it. Joyce
continued to survey him with pleasant, amoeboid impassiv-

ity: a spiflicated Telemachus. "Are you drunk?" Einstein demanded.

"An Irishman is not drunk," Joyce proclaimed dogmatically, "until he can fall down three flights of stairs and the coal chute without hurting himself. I was thinking in fact of the Loch Ness sea serpent. Today's paper had a story about some Scotsman named the Laird of Boleskine who's here to climb mountains. Reporters asked him about the monster and he said, 'Oh, Nessie is quite real. I've seen her many times. Practically a household pet.' "

ACTION   **SOUND**

EXTERIOR: CITY STREET, NIGHT. MEDIUM
   CLOSE-UP.
SATAN and SIR JOHN   *Running feet.*
BABCOCK confronting each
other, BABCOCK terrified.
[This shot is held for the min-
imum possible time to al-
most register as a distinct
image; the audience cannot
quite be sure they saw it.]

Q: What did Joyce find most admirable in Einstein?
A: Churchlessness, godlessness, nationlessness, kinglessness, faithlessness.
Q: What did Joyce find least admirable in Einstein?
A: Jewish sentimentality and refusal to drink enough to enter into amusing and instructive alternative states of consciousness.
Q: What did Einstein find most admirable in Joyce?
A: Churchlessness, godlessness, nationlessness, kinglessness, faithlessness.

Q: What did Einstein find least admirable in Joyce?

A: Hibernian irascibility and feckless willingness to drink until arriving at deplorable and bizarre alternative states of consciousness.

Q: What conspicuous differences between Mr. Joyce and Professor Einstein were neither noted nor commented upon by either or both of them?

A: Joyce had escaped from the normal constrictions of ego by pondering deeply what it feels like to be a woman; Einstein had escaped from the normal constrictions of ego by pondering deeply what it feels like to be a photon. Joyce approached art with the methodology of a scientist; Einstein practiced science with the intuition of an artist. Joyce was living happily in sin with a mistress, Nora Barnacle; Einstein was living unhappily in marriage with a wife, Mileva Einstein.

ACTION	SOUND
EXTERIOR. SCOTS FARMLAND, DUSK. MEDIUM SHOT.	
Little MURDOCH FERGU-SON, age 10, walking across a cornfield.	Voice of Rev. Charles Verey [over]: "Then, in 1912, came the appalling case of the Ferguson boy—young Murdoch Ferguson, age 10, who was quite literally frightened out of his wits, returning home around twilight."
EXTERIOR. SAME. CLOSE-UP.	
MURDOCH stops in his tracks and stares with horror at something off-camera.	Verey's voice [over]: "I fear you might smile at what the lad claims he saw. . . ."

"And what is our sense of choice?" Joyce demanded. "Inescapable, I admit, but therefore doubly to be suspected."

Einstein smiled. "Thinking about thinking about thinking puts us in a strange box," he said. "Let me show you how strange that box is." He sketched a box neatly with quick fingers on a napkin and wrote rapidly within it. "Here," he said, offering his Talmudic trap to Joyce:

> **We have to believe in our free will:**
> **We have no choice in the matter.**

Joyce laughed. "Exactly," he said. "Now let me show you how we get out of the box." And he sketched and wrote on the other side of the napkin:

> **What is inside the box is known:**
> **What is outside the box is unknown:**
> **Who made the box?**

"We were talking about socialism when I went to the bar," Einstein remarked, "and now we are flying perilously close to the clouds of solipsism. Jeem, at once now, no cheating: What do you really believe is real?"

"Dog shit in the street," Joyce answered promptly. "It's rich yellowbrown and clings to your boot like an unpaid landlord. No man is a solipsist while he stands at the curb trying to scrape it off." *Le bon mot de* Canbronne.

"Another quantum jump," Einstein pronounced, beginning to laugh. "Well, Freud and Jung are studying these discontinuities of consciousness scientifically."

Nora, Stanislaus: Did they? Don't think. Judas, patron saint of brothers and lovers. They did. I know they did.

The crypt at St. Giles: How does that go again?

The accordionist started a new tune: *Die Lorelei*. Joyce watched dim shadows ambiguously move, fleeing across the walls starkly as foolish laughter erupted at a nearby table. "I probably never would have met you anywhere but here," he commented softly. "Distinguished professors from the University of Zürich do not move in the same circles with part-time language teachers from Signor Berlitz's adult kindergarten in Trieste. Not unless they both detest bourgeois society and have a liking for low bars. I acquired most of my real education from cheap bars and bawdy houses, like Villon."

The accordionist's friends began drunkenly to sing:

Ich weiss nicht was soll es bedeuten . . .

"My mother loved that song," Einstein said softly, as the singers created the image, from childhood, of the Lorelei, beauty and death in her dank embrace.

Overnight, overnight, overnight.

"The last time I was in Zürich," Joyce said, following his own flight of thought, "was eight or nine years ago. Nora and I stayed at the Gasthaus Hoffnung and the name cheered me. I needed a House of Hope that year. Now we're staying there again, on vacation, and it's changed its name for some inexplicable reason to Gasthaus Doeblin—my hometown, you see, Dublin . . . Is that not an omen or something of the sort?"

From deep neath the crypt of St. Giles. And something and something for miles. They did. My brother's keeper.

"Nora is your wife?" Einstein asked.

"In every sense," Joyce pronounced with unction, "except the narrowly legalistic and the archaically ecclesiastical." They did: I know they did. Fucking like a jenny in heat. I know. I think I know.

Q: Locate Bahnhofstrasse precisely in time-space.
A: Bahnhofstrasse was part of the city of Zürich: which was part of the canton of Zürich: which was part of the Democratic Republic of Switzerland: which was part of Europe: which was part of a 4½-billion-year-old planet, Terra: which completes one rotation upon its polar axis in relation to the sun in every diurnal-nocturnal 24-hour cycle and 1 revolution about a type-G star called Sol in 365 days 5 hours 48 minutes and 46 seconds: which is part of the solar system of nine planets and myriads of asteroids: which is moving together with Sol toward the constellation of Hercules at about 20,000 kilometers per hour: which is part of the galaxy popularly named the Milky Way: which is rotating on its own axis every 8 billion years: which is part of a family of many billion galaxies: which make up the known universe: which Professor Einstein is beginning to suspect is both finite and unbounded, being curved back upon itself four-dimensionally: so that one with infinite energy traveling forever would pass through galaxy after galaxy in a vast space-time orbit coming back eventually to the origin of such an expedition: so that such a one would eventually find again the Milky Way galaxy, the type-G star called Sol, the planet Terra, the continent of Europe, the nation of Switzerland, the canton of Zürich, the city of Zürich, the street called Bahnhofstrasse, the Lorelei Rathskeller: where such thoughts were conceived in the mind of Albert Einstein.
Q: How long had James Joyce and Nora Barnacle been lovers?
A: Ten years and ten days.

Q: How many times had James Joyce suspected Nora Barnacle of infidelity?

A: Three thouand six hundred sixty times.

Q: With what regularity did these suspicions occur?

A: Usually at about midnight; occasionally earlier in the evening if Mr. Joyce had started drinking in the afternoon.

Q: What actions usually resulted from these suspicions?

A: None.

Q: Were there any exceptions to this otherwise consistent pattern of inaction?

A: Yes. In 1909, Joyce had expressed the suspicions with all the eloquence and fury of a great master of English prose. When persuaded that he was wrong on that occasion, he subsided once more into his pattern of silent distrust.

Q: Explain the motivations of this passivity.

A: Desire for peace and quiet in which to pursue literary work; morbid self-insight into the probably phantasmal origin of said suspicions; devout and baffled love for the object of both his concupiscence and his paranoia; democratic sense of belonging to the largest fraternal order in Europe, the cuckolds.

The debate between Albert Einstein (*Prof. Physik*) and James Joyce (*Div. Scep.*) in the charming old Lorelei Rathskeller on that memorable evening as the *Föhn* wind began to blow across Zürich covered diverse and most marvelous topics in epistemology, ontology, eschatology, semiotic, neurology, psychology, physiology, relativity, quantum theory, political science, sociology, anthropology, epidemiology and (due to Mr. Joyce's unfortunate tendency to dwell upon the unwholesome) more-than-liberal scatology. In epistemology, Joyce stood foursquare behind Aristotle, the Master Of Those Who Know, but Einstein betrayed a greater allegiance to David Hume, the Master Of Those Who Don't Know; while in ontology, Einstein leaned dangerously close to the ultra-skepticism

which he was later to denounce when it was propounded
more boldly by Dr. Niels Bohr as the Copenhagen
Interpretatlon (*viz:* the universe known to us is the product of our brains and instruments and thus one remove
from the actual universe), but Joyce, with cavalier disregard for both consistency and common sense, went even
beyond the Copenhagen Interpretation to ultimate agnosticism, attempting to combine the Aristotelian position
that A is A with the non-Aristotelian criticism that A is
only A so long as you don't look close enough to see it
turning into B. In eschatology, Einstein held stubbornly
to the humanist position that science and reason were
making the world significantly better for the greater part
of the species *Homo Sap.*, whilst Joyce mordantly suggested that all work in progress was always followed by
work in regress. The great ideas of Bruno and Huxley,
Zeno and Bacon, Plato and Spinoza, Machiavelli and Mach
bounced back and forth across the table like ideological
Ping-Pong balls as each became increasingly impressed by
the verbal backhand of the other, recognized a mind of
distinctly superior quality, and realized that ultimate agreement between two such divergent temperaments was as
unlikely as the immanentization of the Gnostic eschaton
next Tuesday after lunch. The workers who overheard bits
of this ontological guerrilla warfare decided that both men
were awfully smart guys, but the Russian gent from the
train, had he been there, would have pronounced them
both contemptible examples of *petite-bourgeoisie* subjectivism, decadent Imperialistic idealism and pre-dialecti-
cal empirio-criticism.

ACTION   **SOUND**

EXTERIOR. LONG SHOT: BAHNHOFSTRASSE.
BABCOCK running.   *Heavy breathing.*

INTERIOR. MEN'S TOILET. CLOSE-UP.
EINSTEIN standing before   *Heavy breathing, running feet.*
urinal, looking at graffito in
German: NUR DER
WAHNSINNIGE IST SICH
ABSOLUT SICHER.
FNORD?

Dass kommst mir nicht aus dem Sinn . . .

The voices of the workers invoked in Joyce his image of *Lorelei:* eboneyed, fish-tailed, barnacled. Like old Homer's Sirens. She combs her pale yellow hair, demure and virginal above the waist: below, the sulphurous pit. They sail toward the rocks, songseduced, musicmaddened. A crash, a slopping sluchkluchk, screams: then nothing. A whirlpool turning, turning: emptiness. A gull flipflapping in a compassionless sky.

And the Serpent's head rising from the Loch: Eat and ye shall be as gods.

Considering each step, dim eyes aided by the walking-stick, Joyce with dignity approached the bar, signaling for another beer. Gravely he beheld, in the mirror, himself; above it, a bronze eagle.

Almost got it now. From deep neath the crypt of St. Giles/Came a shriek that re-echoed for miles. And something and something said Brother Ignatius. Oh, hell. Wait.

Windows rattling: *Föhn* wind starting to blow.

When will Einstein get back from the water closet? Bladder: a complicated funnel. If the medical student lives on in me, so does the priest and the musician. St. James of Dublin, patron of chalices, catheters and cantatas. Why, my prose always comes out musical, liturgical and clinical at once.

Ah: Einstein's green sweater.

"Well, Jeem," Einstein said, not re-seating himself, "I believe I've had enough for one evening."

"One more beer?" Joyce prompted hopefully. *"Ein stein,* Einstein?"

Einstein shook his head sadly. "Classes in the morning," he murmured.

"I hope we will meet again," Joyce said, rising formally if unsteadily. "I will always remember you for giving me the concept of quantum language. It may be the key to this impossible novel I'm trying to get started . . ."

"I don't understand how quantum physics can be applied to language," Einstein said, "but if I've helped you, I'm glad. This has been a stimulating conversation both ways."

An explosion of energy cast awry the slow-swinging street door, and Joyce stepped back nimbly to avoid collision. Sllt.

The figure that staggered into the shadow-dark Rathskeller was that of a handsome but wretched youth whose pallid skin and demented eyes revealed at once a hideous history of some cosmic and monstrous horror that the feeble mind of man could scarce endure. All were instantaneously frozen with terror and copious chills ran abundantly up and down every spine, whilst many admitted later that their hairs stood on end, their flesh crept and their souls within them trembled. The stranger, although dressed in the best clothing of the English upper class, carried a meager straw traveling case, which might contain deadly poison, venomous cobras or human heads to judge by the eldritch laugh which broke from his lips as he fought—visibly to all—to restrain an outright collapse into hysteria. An aura of almost visible fright had subtly entered the previously happy booze emporium, and the one-eyed accordionist ceased to play, the instrument lying as dead in his hands. *What can such an intrusion forebode?* was the thought in every mind; and the dreadful answer came unbidden to each: Only the madman is absolutely sure. Unhallowed and timeless secrets of forbidden aeons and the dark backward abyss of blasphemous necromancy seemed to move stealthily in every stark shadow haunting the dank and ancient Rathskeller, and still the door tossed in the wind like a spirit in torment: sllt sllt sllt. Inchoate noise rustled imperceptibly.

Bond Street look: an Englishman.

Joyce watched with wide blue eyes as the haggard girl-faced figure stumbled toward the bar. Dorian Gray at the end of his rope. True fear.

"Whiskey," the young Englishman said in his own language, absently adding, "*bitte . . .*"

This his eyes went all out of focus, amoeboid, and he seemed to be floating almost as he sank in a dead faint to crash loudly, shaking the room as he hit the floor.

The night I fell drunk on Tyrone Street and Hunter helped: the same anew.

Joyce set his walkingstick by the bar and knelt, ear to the Englishman's heart. Medical school: not entirely wasted. Counting, listening: the heart not too fast. Pulse: fast also, not abnormal, though. A blue funk.

Wait: coming around.

The Englishman's wild tormented eyes looked up into Joyce's.

"*Mein herr,*" he gasped. "*Ich,* um . . ."

"Just rest," Joyce said quickly. "I speak English."

Einstein's boots clumped thump on wood heavy as ox hooves: Joyce turned. "What is it with this one?" Einstein asked. "Serious?"

"Just a bad fright," Joyce said.

The Englishman trembled. "All the way from Loch Ness," he said hoarsely. "All across Europe to this very door."

"Just rest," Joyce urged again. Loch Ness. Coincidence?

"It has pursued me to this very door," the Englishman went on. "It is outside . . . waiting . . ."

"You've had a fright," Joyce said judiciously. "Your wits are muddled. Rest another minute, sir."

"You don't understand," the Englishman said wildly. "Right around the corner . . . by the railroad tracks . . ."

"What's right outside this bar?" Joyce asked, remembering Gogarty's medical manner: soothing, reasonable, unfrightened.

The Englishman trembled. "You're Irish," he said. "Another Englishman would say I'm mad. Perhaps you have the imagination to know better."

Celtic twilight: *merde*.

"Yes," Joyce said patiently. "Tell me."

"There is a demon from Hell right outside that door, on Bahnhofstrasse."

The one-eyed accordionist knelt beside them. "Can I help?" he asked in German.

"Yes," said Joyce. "Help him to a chair now. He can sit up. I'm going outside."

"Was he attacked by ruffians?" the worker asked. "Two or three of us could go with you. . . ."

"No," Joyce said. "I believe he was attacked by his own imagination. But my friend and I shall go outside and have a look."

Bahnhofstrasse, in the feeble yellow glow of gas jets, was nearly deserted at that hour. A half-block away: a horseless carriage: *automobile*, the Italians call them. Italian model, indeed: FIAT: *Fabrica Italiana Automobile Torino*. The Latin love of codes and acronyms. MAFIA: *Morte Alle Franconia Italia Anela*. And INRI: mystery of mysteries.

The *Föhn* was blowing more heavily now: hot, nasty, clammy wind like a ghoul's kiss. Joyce scanned Bahnhofstrasse with weak eyes. On one side the great Gothic-faced banks: rulers of the paper that rules continents. World capital of usury, Tucker would say. On the other side, the railroad tracks that gave the street its name: parallel lines meeting by the trick of perspective in theoretical infinity. Joyce peered, squinting, in both directions, then jumped, involuntarily, as thunder crashed.

A scrubbed, empty street. Clean as the Swiss temperament, devoid of answers. The Englishman's demon was of
the mind only.

But wait: by the arc light. Joyce stepped forward, knelt
again, and picked up the slightly fluorescent object. It was
a plastic mask, for a theatrical production or a masquerade
ball: the face of Satan, red-horned, bearded, goatish.

"A nasty joke . . . ?" Einstein asked.

The Englishman stood in the Rathskeller door, still pale
but fighting for control.

"Well, gentlemen," he said, "you have found nothing, I
presume, and consider me mad."

Joyce smiled. "On the contrary," he said. "We have
found something, and I do not consider you mad at all."
He held out the mask. "You have been the victim, I fear,
of a rather cruel practical joke."

The Englishman came forward, looking with no sign of
relief at the grinning inhuman mask.

"It is a nastier joke than you can imagine," he said in a
giddy tone. "Three people have died ghastly deaths in the
course of this business. Do you think that is humorous,
sir?"

Eternal tempter: reaching out of the Loch, serpentine
power crossing Europe to challenge me here.

> *When the shadows slink and slither*
> *And the goblins all parade*
> *Then reason is a broken reed*
> *At the Devil's Masquerade*

Where did I read that? Not Blake, certainly. An Olde
Ballad? But listen: he speaks.

"Three dead already," the Englishman repeated. "And
now I am convinced that I must be the fourth."

Home Rule for Ireland voted down again by the Lords
last March after the Commons passed it in January. The

only possibility now is revolution: gunfire in the streets, womanscreams: dead children. Bloody War. The nightmare from which I am seeking a wakening. Yes: and Father's words long ago: "Three things you should never trust, Sunny Jim, my lad: the hoof of a horse; the horn of a bull; the smile of a Saxon." Another net I must fly over. This man needs help. Inwit's agenbite's cure: compassion.

The *Föhn*, the wind of witchcraft, blew unhealthy stagnant air foully in their faces as they stood. "Come," Joyce said, "let me help you."

Went down from Jerusalem to Jericho: and fell among thieves. Take him to the inn. I may even have the two pence.

"Yes," Einstein said, "let us help you."

THE RADIO ANNOUNCER: And now a dramatic, fast-breaking story from Zürich, Switzerland. A reliable source has informed Reuters News Service that Mr. James Augustine Aloysius Joyce has actually been seen performing an act of charity. Although no details are available yet, it is claimed that Joyce performed the kindly act entirely gratuitously, with no attempt to gain publicity or popularity and even without thought of attempting to establish merit in Heaven. Mr. Joyce, an alleged writer and the most notorious cuckold in all Europe, was expelled from his hometown of Dublin, Ireland, nearly a decade ago for countless Sins of Pride, for more Sins of Lust than are recorded in the decadent works of Sade and Masoch, for the Sin of Intemperance, for the Sin against the Holy Ghost, and for looking at churches cross-eyed from behind. He has since then amply and fulsomely earned the reputation of being the most arrogant and self-centered scoundrel of our century and has fathered two bastard children on a peasant wench. News of Joyce's sudden indication of grace is said to have the Vatican rocking and His Holiness The Pope is reported to have exclaimed, on hearing of the nearly miraculous deed, "Maybe there is hope, after all!" In Heaven, God the Father could not be reached for comment, but the Holy Ghost told our celestial correspondent, "It just goes to show that inside every Sinner there's a Saint fighting to get out." And now a word from our Heavenly Sponsor . . .

SINGERS: The Father, the Son, the Holy Ghost
They're the guys that you need most!
The Spirit, the Father, the Heavenly Son
That's the crowd that gets things done!

Glor-i-a in ex-cel-sus D-e-o!

ACTION   **SOUND**

EXTERIOR. BABCOCK MANOR, 1886. LONG SHOT.
A fine old English manor   *A baby cries.*
house. A penny-farthing
bicycle on the lawn in front of
the door.

INTERIOR. HALLWAY. MEDIUM SHOT.
SIR JAMES FENWICK   *Baby cries again.*
BABCOCK pacing, stops sud-
denly at the infant's cry.

DOCTOR [with the face of   *Doctor:* "You can come in
ALBERT EINSTEIN, 1914]   now, Sir James. A fine, healthy
comes out of room into hall.   son."

Sir John Babcock was born on November 23, 1886, the only child of Sir James Fenwick Babcock, a once-respected biologist who was then in the process of relegating himself to scientific limbo for advocating the Lamarckian theory of evolution in preference to the Darwinian. The boy's mother was Lady Catherine (Greystoke) Babcock, who is described in surviving diaries and letters as an exceptionally vivacious hostess, a great wit and intelligent advocate of her husband's scientific heresies.

Tragically, young Sir John was orphaned in 1897 at the tender age of eleven, both Sir James and Lady Catherine being killed on a voyage to Africa with Lady Catherine's reputedly crazy cousin, Lord Greystoke. The care of the child fell upon an uncle, Dr. Bostick Bentley Babcock, a physician who had pioneered the use of ether for anesthesia. It is also recorded that Dr. B. B. Babcock was, unlike his brother, a strict Darwinian, an atheist and a vehement *laissez-faire* Liberal of the Herbert Spencer philosophy; it was also said by some that as a lifelong bachelor and rationalist Dr. Babcock was the last man in the world to raise an orphan child successfully. Evidently, the good doctor privately shared this opinion, for he hired a small army of nannies, tutors, servants and other factotums with which he shielded himself strategically from the problems of a pubescent nephew.

When Dr. Babcock himself died, of a sudden heart attack on June 16, 1904, young Sir John was eighteen and suffering his miserable last term at Eton. The family solicitor explained to him that he was now not only the owner of the 20,000 acres of Babcock Manor, but also the recipient of two inheritances which, as presently invested, allowed him an income for life of 4,000 pounds per year, without his ever having to commit the Un-English Sin of dipping into the Capital.

Sir John was a slim and nervous-looking lad, the butt of all student jokes and always described as "shy," "bookish" or "peculiar" by his classmates. He himself felt less than totally miserable only when walking alone through the most heavily wooded sections of his 20,000 acres, thinking "green thoughts in a green shade," as the Poet said; there it sometimes seemed to him, especially when twilight was

casting cinnamon and gold highlights into the emerald-
green branches, that a door to another world would almost swing open and he could faintly discern the quick
timid movements of dryads and the sulphurous sandal-
wood scent, beneath the earth, of vast caverns of trolls. It
was at such magic moments that a veil almost seemed to
lift, a dim castle to arise in the mist, a trumpet to call to
him of realms of romance and glamour, of danger and
triumph.

Q: With what dramatis personae, furniture and accessories
was that magick realm provided?
A: Dark and moonless nights, windswept moors, sinister
fens, dank and dismal bogs, haunted abbeys, headless
specters, wicked witches, wise and inscrutable wizards,
high elves [the fairest of the fair], swarthy dwarfs, alchemical furnaces, elixirs, potions, drugs, herbs, precious stones,
holy grails, diverse and sundry fire-breathing dragons,
subterranean dungeons, maltese falcons, lost treasures,
knights and paladins in armor of black and white, enigmatic Saracens, chaste heroines [blonde], evil seductresses
[brunette], longswords, battle-axes, foils, rapiers, decayed
parchments barely readable, Hebraic incantations, fumes,
perfumes, incenses, pentacles, secret panels leading to
hidden rooms, defrocked and malignant monks, dog-faced
demons, assorted princesses of the blood royal, hands of
glory, Egyptian philtres, talismans of rare gems, apotropaic
spells, werewolves, vampires, foul servitors of Hecate,
barbarous brews, eldritch ointments, black sabbats, ele-
mentals, familiars, damsels [fair, virginal, prone to swooning]
in distress, diviners, astrologers, geomancers, bold brave
blue-eyed sinewy heroes, dank dark mustachioed villains,
gnomes, goblins, Men In Black, and infernal nether regions invisible.
Q: What sort of adventures and challenges had Sir John
thus far encountered in actuality?

A: Two hundred seventeen attempts by older students to allure, intimidate or coerce him into participation in the Unspeakable Crime against Nature, as forbidden in Holy Writ and the Section 270 of the Revised Penal Code of 1888.

Q: For what motives did young Sir John refuse to participate in the aforesaid Unspeakable Crime?

A: Christian piety; terror of discovery; fear of germs and vile diseases thus transmitted; grim warnings by Uncle Bentley and the Dean of Studies that it led to idiocy, insanity and emasculation; indignation that he was always offered the passive [receptor] role; conviction that it would provoke gagging.

Once he caught a field mouse and held it in his hands, staring into its terrified eyes and knowing, with horror, that he could crush out its life with a rock as abruptly and pointlessly as the lives of all the adults he had loved had been crushed. He was frightened in a nakedly metaphysical way, not that such cruel fantasies should occur to him, nor even that something primordial and palaeolithic within himself urged him to do it, commit the deed, know the horrible joy of conscious sin; not any of that, bad as it was, but ontologically terrified at the knowledge of his own power, the fact that the deed was possible, that life was so fragile and easily terminated. The aromas of rose and clover in his nostrils, the pastel emeralds and turquoises of the trees, the primordial beauty of raw Nature, were all suddenly terrible to him, masks behind which lurked only death and the love of killing. He released the creature— "wee sleekit cowerin' timorous beastie," he quoted to himself—and watched it scamper away, knowing the same dread that the mouse knew, seeing the whole billion-year struggle of predator and prey through Uncle Bentley's Darwinian prism, weeping at last alone the tears he had been too numb and self-conscious to weep at Uncle Bent-

ley's funeral. Feeling thrice orphaned, he wanted to dare
the blasphemy of Job's wife: to curse God and die.

He never forgot that moment; and once, many months
later, when he was asked his favorite lines from Shakespeare, by an instructor aware of his intellectual potential
and sorry for his loneliness, Sir John immediately quoted,
not the "To be or not to be" or "Tomorrow and tomorrow
and tomorrow" soliloquies, but the grim couplet from
Lear:

> *As flies to wanton boys, are we to the gods:*
> *They kill us for their sport.*

The instructor was so depressed by the despair of Sir
John's tone in quoting this that he decided the lad was "a
hopeless case" and made no further avuncular overtures.

But Sir John was also aware that the gods, or the blind
impersonal forces of Uncle Bentley's Darwinian universe,
had, just as impassively as they murdered his mother and
father and uncle, gifted him with an economic security
generally considered a great blessing in a world where
three-quarters of the population struggled desperately to
get enough to eat day to day, and most laborers died,
toothless and raggedy, before the age of forty, worn out
by toil in those Dark Satanic Mills lamented by Blake. Yet
everybody knew that those Mills were necessary to Progress and that the lot of most men and women had been
even worse before electricity. Sir John was confused about
all this, and even more confused about the universe's
intent toward him, if it owned any. While he was in the
midst of his most searching philosophical ruminations,
the whole world seemed to shudder at once, for Plehve, the
Russian Minister of the Interior, was murdered—the latest in a series of senseless and incredible assassinations.
The boy heard many older persons talking of the growing
violence and lawlessness of the world; and he heard oth-

ers, more ominously, speak of a worldwide conspiracy behind these violent attacks on government officials.

Sir John graduated with honors from Trinity College, Cambridge, five years later, in 1909. The world was shuddering again, at the assassination of Prince Ito of Japan, and more talk was heard of worldwide conspiracies and secret societies (Zionist, said some; Jesuit, said others), but Sir John heard this only as background noise by now. His mind and heart were not in the world, but in the two scholarly realms known as history and mythology. Sir John refused to accept that distinction, having fallen totally in love with another world so long dead it was powerless to hurt him, unlike the present world, and yet was also rich in mystery and glamour.

At this point Sir John read *Vril: The Power of the Coming Race*, by Lord Edward Bulwer-Lytton and was mesmerized by its tapestry of adventure, Utopianism, romance, deep occult scholarship and profound knowledge of political psychology. But most fascinating of all, to Sir John, was the fact that the occult details in the book did not come from sheer fantasy and vulgar folklore, like the thrillers of Bram Stoker, but were derived from obviously genuine knowledge of medieval Cabala and Rosicrucianism. Within the next three months he purchased and read with mounting excitement all the works of Lord Bulwer-Lytton—*Reinzi, The Last Days of Pompeii*, all the other novels, the poems, the plays, the essays, even the fairy tales. It was an astounding body of literature to have been produced by a man who also edited a monthly magazine, served as a member of Parliament and became one of Disraeli's principal advisors.

And Sir John, even more than the hundreds of thousands of readers who made Bulwer-Lytton one of the most popular novelists of the nineteenth century, was captivated by the question tantalizingly raised again and again in those books: If so much of the occult knowledge was based on real scholarship, might one dare to believe the frequent claim that the Rosy Cross order still existed and commanded the *Vril* force that could mutate humanity into superhumanity?

Q: Under what other names has the Vril been described by diverse persons before and after Lord Bulwer-Lytton? A: Before: ch'i [Chinese, c. 3000 B.C.] prajna [Hindic philosophers, c. 1500 B.C.], telesma [H. Trismegistus, c. 350 B.C.], Vis Medicatrix Naturae [Hippocrates, c. 350 B.C.], Facultas Formatrix [Galen, c. 170 A.D.], baraka [Sufis, c. 600 A.D.], mumia [Paracelsus, c. 1530 A.D.], animal magnetism [Mesmer, 1775 A.D.], Life Force [Galvani, 1790 A.D.], *Gestaltung* [Goethe, 1800 A.D.], OD force [Reichenbach, 1845 A.D.]. After: etheric formative force [Steiner, 1900 A.D.], *Elan Vital* [Bergson, 1920 A.D.], Mitogenetic radiation [Gurwitsch, 1937 A.D.], orgone [Reich, 1940 A.D.], bioplasma [Grischenko, 1944 A.D.], Good Vibes [*anon. hippie domesticus*, c. 1962 A.D.], inergy [Puharich, 1973 A.D.], the Force [Lucas, 1977 A.D.].

Sir John was, by this time, twenty-four years old and romantically, painfully, convinced of a vast temperamental abyss between himself and his contemporaries. He was frankly bored by grubby, money-centered business concerns (he had all the money he could ever possibly want) and repelled by the flabbiness of the Anglican clergy—the only church career family tradition could have countenanced and yet so milkwater that, as Trollope said, it interfered neither with a man's politics nor his religion; thus, he seemed to have no future but pedantry. That was also unattractive, because he regarded himself as alienated and rebellious (although within the limits of good taste, sound morals and British common sense, of course; he was still chaste, since whores were the victims of social exploitation he could not sanction and it was indecent to

make an advance to a lady, even if he had known how).
Worse: he was resolved not to be corrupted by his out-
landishly large independence (a word he preferred to
"inheritance") and could not bear to think of himself as a
social butterfly or wastrel. He would write books, then;
and if no audience larger than could easily gather in a
water closet were ever to read them, that would not
matter. He had at least a role if he had not yet found a
soul; he was "the scholarly one of the Babcocks."

Sir John had majored in medieval history and Near
Eastern languages; his master's thesis, on the influence of
Jewish Cabala on medieval occult societies, became his
first book, *The Secret Chiefs*, which was favorably re-
viewed in the few places where it was noticed at all. The
most hostile single line in any critique appeared in the
University of Edinburgh *Historical Journal,* and was by
Professor Angus McNaughton. It chided Babcock mildly
for "a certain romantic turn of mind which leads the
youthful and ardent author to imagine that some of the
secret societies discussed might have survived even into
our own age of enlightenment—a thesis that belongs in
one of Lord Bulwer-Lytton's romances, not in a work of
alleged history."

Like most young authors, Babcock received every criticism as a mortal blow, and it was mortifying to have the
novelistic inspiration of his ideas so easily spotted. He
wrote three drafts of a long letter to Professor McNaughton for impugning his spotless accuracy; and the third
draft, with five pages of relentlessly pedantic footnotes, he
actually mailed to the University of Edinburgh *Historical
Journal.* It was printed, with a caustic rebuttal by Mc-
Naughton, beginning, "Young Mr. Babcock's sources are,
one and all, as impressionable and immature as Mr. Babcock
himself," and went on to argue that no current groups
calling themselves Freemasons or Rosicrucians had any
documented connection with any groups of the same names

in medieval times. The group with the single best-documented history, McNaughton said, was the Scottish Rite of Ancient and Accepted Freemasonry, which could not prove any existence prior to 1723. The viperish McNaughton added maliciously that Sir John's belief in real occult secrets behind Freemasonry's surface was "puerile, preposterous and pretentious."

Young Sir John read this with audible fuming and a few Johnsonian mutterings of "Scotch dog!" and "Goddamn!" His nose was put even more out of joint when his counter-rebuttal, containing seventeen pages of recondite footnotes this time (and a sharply worded riposte about "those who substitute flashy alliteration for cogent argument"), was returned by the university press with the curt explanation that the *Journal* did not have endless space to debate issues of such microscopic unimportance.

There the matter might have ended, in lame anticlimax, had not a mysterious third hand intervened.

A Mr. George Cecil Jones of London wrote to Sir John, praising his original letter to the *Historical Journal* and assuring him that he was correct in all his theories even though surviving documents of earlier centuries were not complete enough to support him. "The authentic tradition of Cabalistic Freemasonry," Jones added, "can be found still alive among certain lodges, especially in Bavaria and Paris. There has even been a lodge of true adepts continuing the hidden heritage right here in London, in this decade."

Sir John's immediate response was a most cautious letter back to Mr. (George Cecil) Jones, asking very tactfully just how much Mr. Jones actually knew of the surviving lodge of Cabalistic Freemasons in London, who alleged descent from the Invisible College of the Rosy Cross (founded by the Sufi sage, Abramelin of Araby, and passed on by him through Abraham the Jew to Christian Rosenkreuz, who lies buried in the Cave of the Illuminati, which was somewhere in the Alps according to Sir John's research, whatever that Scotch dog McNaughton might say).

The reply, within a week's time, was a cautious letter that invited Sir John to have dinner with Jones sometime when visiting London, so that the matter might be discussed at suitable length with appropriate intimacy.

Sir John wrote back at once that he would be in London the following Thursday.

The next week was rainy and wet at Babcock Manor; Sir John didn't go outdoors, and spent most of his time in his library poring over his first editions of Hermetic and Rosicrucian pamphlets from long ago, and puzzling once again upon the enigmatic writings of those he suspected of being part of the underground tradition of Cabalistic magick. He re-read *The Alchemical Marriage of Christian Rosycross*, with its strange medley of Christian and Egyptian allegorical figures, the Enochian fragments which Dr. John Dee had received from an allegedly superhuman being in the age of Elizabeth I, the sly and cryptic *Triumphant Beast* of Giordano Bruno, the writings of Bacon and Ludvig Prinn and Paracelsus. Again and again he encountered overt or coded references to that damnably mysterious Invisible College, composed of Illuminated men and women —Secret Chiefs—which allegedly governs all the world behind the scenes; and again and again he asked himself if he dared to believe it.

Sir John dreamed of the meeting with Jones in vivid detail no less than three times before the week passed. In each dream, Jones was dressed as a medieval wizard, with pointed hat and robes bearing the Order of Saint George with strange astrological glyphs, and he always led Sir John up a dark hill toward a crumbling Gothic building of indeterminate character midway between abbey and castle. This eldritch edifice was, of course (as Sir John knew even in the dreams), a blend of various illustrations he had seen depicting Chapel Perilous of the Grail legend or the Dark Tower to which Childe Roland came. Inside, according to occult lore, was everything he feared; and yet only by passing this test could he achieve the Rosicrucian goals—the Philosopher's Stone, the Elixer of Life, the Medicine of Metals, True Wisdom and Perfect Happiness. In each case, he awoke with a start of fright as the door of the Chapel was opened for him and he heard within a humming as of a myriad of monstrous bees.

Once he dreamed of Dr. John Dee himself, court astrologer to Elizabeth, greatest mathematician of his time, constant associate of spirits and angels according to his own claims; and Dee was offering him "the solace berry," a magical fruit that conferred immortality. "Take ye and eat from the tree Swifty ate," Dee said, but the fruit smelled of excrement and was foul to the sight and touch and when Sir John tried to refuse it, a second figure, female and shockingly naked but with a cow's head, appeared beside Dee, saying solemnly, "Ignatz never really injures," as they were all suddenly standing again at the door of a vast insectoid Chapel Perilous. Sir John awoke in a sweat.

All the legends warned him that only the brave and the pure of heart may survive the journey through Chapel Perilous; and this was hardly encouraging, since like most introspective young men Sir John had much insight into his own fears but woefully little realization of the fears of others, thereby wrongly suspecting himself of being atypically timid and cowardly; while in the purity-of-heart department he knew that he distinctly left a great deal to be desired: there were fantasies that were decidedly unchaste, although he nearly always managed to stop such imaginings before the worst and most nameless details were actually visualized in all their lewd and sinful seductiveness. Even when he was caught up in the bestial tug of these animalistic desires, and the details of certain unmentionable items formed with total and compulsive clarity in his mind, he did not allow himself to linger voluptuously on the fantasy of actually fondling or intimately manipulating those particular items, desirable and monstrous and unspeakable as they were. If it could in truth be said that he did lapse on occasion, certainly he resisted successfully nearly all of the time such fantasies arose, and yet the guilt of those few, rare, hardly typical lapses did weigh heavily upon his conscience and seemed now to be a distinct bar against such a bicameral creature as himself entering the precincts of Chapel Perilous.

And that was all mythology, anyway: charming to dream about, but one would be mad to get involved with people who believed (or claimed) that they hopped over to Chapel Perilous and back as easily as one might buzz over to the tobacconist. . . .

On Wednesday, Sir John could bear the loneliness of suspenseful indecision no longer. He summoned Dorn, the Babcock gamekeeper, and had a carriage fetched to drive him the three miles to the Greystoke estate, where he paid a casual family visit to his uncle, Viscount Greystoke, a greying but iron-muscled man of seemingly inexhaustible pragmatic wisdom—the richest and least eccentric of all the Babcock-Greystoke families, according to general opinion. After the usual small talk, Sir John finally framed his question.

"Do you believe, sir, that there are secret orders or lodges or fraternities that have survived over the centuries, transmitting certain kinds of occult or mystical knowledge which is normally unavailable to the human mind?"

Old Greystoke pondered for about thirty seconds. "No," he said finally. "If there were, I would most certainly have heard about it."

Sir John rode the three miles home in deep thought. Age and Wisdom had spoken, but what was the point of youth if it did not entitle you to disregard Age and Wisdom? The next morning he arose early and took the train to London. Sir John trusted his own scholarship: such lodges *did* exist, and the only way to test their claims of superior wisdom was to meet with them and find out for oneself what they really had to offer, besides the corrupted Hebraic passwords and absurd hand-grips of other Masonic orders.

There was an American newspaper in the railway carriage: a curiosity in itself, and it was open to a page of comic strips, an art form Sir John had never been able to fathom. He glanced at it idly and found that one sequence involved a malicious mouse named Ignatz who was always throwing bricks at a cat named Krazy. It was totally insane, and worse yet, the cat enjoyed being hit with the bricks, sighing contentedly as each missile bounced off her head, "Li'l dollink, always fetful." That was evidently some debased American-Jewish dialect for "Little darling, always faithful." Sir John shuddered. The whole thing was not funny at all; it was a bare-faced exploitation of the perversion named sadism. Or was it masochism? Or was it both? A gloomy omen, in any case. . . .

This was entirely typical of the larval mentations of the domesticated hominids of Terra in those primitive ages. Crude sonic signals produced by the laryngeal muscles made up their speech-units which programmed all cortical cogitation into the grid provided by the local grammar, which they naïvely called logic or common sense. Beneath this typically primate confusion of signals with sources and maps with territories, a great deal of the hominid nervous system was genetically determined, like the closely related chimpanzee nervous system and the more distantly related cow nervous system, and hence operated on autopilot. The programs of territoriality, status hierarchy, pack-bonding, etc., functioned mechanically as Evolutionary Relative Successes since they served well enough for the ordinary mammal in ordinary mammalian affairs. Modes of status-domination, erotic signaling and rudimentary (subject-predicate) causal "thinking" were imprinted as mechanically as the territorial reflexes of baboons or the mating dances of peacocks. Since *primate behavior only changes under the impact of new technology* (Gilhooley's First Law), the primitive "Industrial Revolution" already beginning had caused enough shock and confusion to liberate a few minds from mechanical repetition of this imprinted circuitry (*Shock and confusion are the only techniques that loosen imprints in primates:* Gilhooley's Second Law), and a certain wistful speculative quality had entered the gene pool, leading within less than seventy years to the mutations involved in Space Migration and Life Extension; but of all this young Babcock was unaware. He couldn't even imagine that in his own lifetime a man would fly the Atlantic.

Sir John arrived in London before noon, and decided to prepare for the meeting with Jones by spending the afternoon researching old Masonic materials in the British Museum.

In an Elizabethan alchemical pamphlet he found, by sheer coincidence, a long allegorical poem that strangely disturbed him, considering that he was bent upon contact with alleged manipulators of occult power. One stanza in particular haunted him as he rode by hansom across town to Simpson's Café Divan, where he and Jones had agreed to meet. The very clops of the horse's hooves seemed to carry the refrain:

> *Don't believe the human eye*
> *In sunlight or in shade*
> *The puppet show of sight and sense*
> *Is the Devil's Masquerade*

Passing the Savoy Theatre, Sir John saw that the D'Oyly Carte company was again doing *Patience*. He remembered, with some cheer, Bunthorne's song:

If this young man expresses himself in terms too deep
  for me,
Why what a singularly deep young man this deep
  young man must be!

That mocking jingle was a refreshing breath of skepticism and British common sense, Sir John thought. When
he entered Simpson's, he was prepared to confront the
enigmatic Mr. Jones without trepidation.

Mr. George Cecil Jones was stout, amiable and proved
to have impeccable taste in wines. He was also reassuringly
normal, wore no wizard's hat and spoke of his children
with great fondness; better still, he was an industrial
chemist by profession and not at all the misty-eyed be-
liever type who might be leading Sir John up the garden
path into Cloud-Cuckoo Land. You couldn't help liking
and trusting him.

Jones appeared to be about forty, but was free of con-
descension toward Sir John's youth; nor was he overtly
impressed by Sir John's title. A plain blunt Englishman
with a bedrock of sound sense and decency, Sir John
concluded—and yet it did take him a long time to open up
even a little about the Invisible College.

"You must understand, Sir John, that these affairs are
circled about with ferocious Oaths of Secrecy and dreadful
pledges of silence," Jones confided eventually. "All of that
appears quite pointless in this free and enlightened age—
pardon my irony—but it is part of the tradition, dating
back to the days of the Inquisition, when it was, of course,
even more necessary."

Sir John, with the bluntness of youth, decided to answer this with a somewhat probing question. "Am I to
take it, sir, that you are yourself bound by such an Oath?"

"Oh, God and Aunt Agnes," Jones said, more amused
than offended, "one *simply doesn't* ask that on a first
meeting. Consider the patience of the fisherman rather

than the rapacity of the journalist if you would open the door to the Arcanum of Arcana."

And he proceeded to attack his filet mignon with unabashed vigor, as if that equivocation were not tantamount to an admission. Sir John understood: he was being tested; his exact status on the evolutionary ladder was being estimated.

"Have you read my book on Cabala?" he asked next, trying a more circuitous approach. "Or merely the debate in the *Historical Journal?*"

"Oh, I've read your book," Jones said. "Wouldn't have missed it for the world. There is nothing more poignant and gallant, on this planet, than a young man writing passionately about Cabala without any real experience of its mysteries."

Sir John felt the needleprick in Jones' words, but answered merely, "At that point, I was not concerned with personal experience, but merely with setting right the historical record."

"But now," Jones asked, "you are interested in personal experience?"

"Perhaps," Sir John said carelessly, feeling Byronic and brave. "Mostly, I am concerned with proving my thesis that such groups have survived over the centuries—proving it so thoroughly that even that blockheaded mule in Edinburgh will have to admit I'm right!"

Jones nodded. "Wishing to prove oneself right is the usual motive for scholarship," he said mildly. "But this group I mentioned has no interest in setting the historical record straight, or in advertising themselves. Do y'see, Sir John, that they really don't care what the world at large thinks, or what the pompous asses in the universities think, either? They have entirely different interests."

Sir John found himself half-believing that he was dining with a member of the same Invisible College that published the first Rosicrucian pamphlets of 1619 and 1623. He proceeded with great delicacy.

"In your letter," he said, "you spoke of this group very carefully in the past tense. I believe your exact words were, 'There has even been a lodge of true adepts continuing the hidden heritage right here in London, in this decade.' How many years, exactly, has it been since the lodge existed?"

"It broke apart exactly ten years ago, in 1900."

"And what was it called?"

"The Hermetic Order of the Golden Dawn."

Sir John exhaled deeply and took another sip of wine. "You are becoming less indirect in your answers," he said happily. "I take that as a good sign. Let me advance to the main point in one step, then. Is it possible that the Order did not *entirely* break apart a decade ago?"

"Many things are possible," Jones said, lighting a cigar and signaling for more wine. "Before we go any further, let me show you a simple document which every member of this Order must sign, and swear to, with the most horrible Oaths. Just glance it over for a minute, Sir John." And he passed from his inner pocket a simple sheet of ordinary letterpaper, typed with a most usual office typewriter.

Sir John looked at this strange document with some care.

I [fill in name] do solemnly invoke He Whom the Winds Fear, the Supreme Lord of the Universe, by the Mason word [given to candidate before ritual] and swear that I, as a member of the Body of Christ, from this day forward will seek the Knowledge and Conversation of Mine Holy Guardian Angel, whereby I may acquire the Secret Knowledge to transcend mere humanity and be one with the Highest Intelligence; and if I ever use this Sacred Knowledge for monetary gain in any manner, or to do harm to any human being, may I be accursed and damned; may

*my throat be cut, my eyes be burned out and my
corpse thrown into the sea; may I be hated and
despised by all intellectual beings, both men and
angels, throughout all eternity. I swear. I swear. I
swear.*

"Rather strangely worded," Sir John commented uneasily. *Wee sleekit cowrin' timorous beastie . . . always
fetful . . .*

"That's the First-Degree Oath, for admission as a student," Jones said. "The higher Oaths are much stronger
stuff, I had better warn you."

Sir John decided to put fear behind him.

"I would sign such an Oath with fervent assent," he said
boldly, surrendering his spiritual virginity long before he
would have the courage to surrender the virginity of his
body.

"That is most interesting," Jones said affably, retrieving
the paper and folding it back into his pocket. "I will speak
to certain people. You may hear from us in a fortnight or
so."

And the rest of the evening, which was brief, Jones
spoke only of his beloved children and his equally beloved
occupation of industrial chemistry. There was nothing in
the slightest occult or extraordinary about him at all. To
some extent, he was even dull; and yet Sir John left him
feeling vaguely as if he had been talking to one of H. G.
Wells' moon-men carefully disguised as a human being,
which was nonsense, of course. But what was there about
Jones that left that kind of after-impression?

On the train home, by the most implausible of coincidences—he wasn't even sure he was in the same compartment—he again found an American newspaper and, stranger
still, there was that sadistic mouse and the masochistic cat
again: "Li'l dollink, always fetful."

After four years of training in the Golden Dawn, Sir

John felt exactly like that bizarre cat, and when Joyce and Einstein offered to help him on Bahnhofstrasse, he giggled inanely and said, "Li'l dollink, always fetful."

Preparatory to anything else, Einstein brushed the bulk of the dank barfloor sawdust off Sir John's expensive but now untidy suit and handed him his Bond Street hat and bucked him up generally in orthodox Samaritan fashion, which he very badly needed. Sir John was not exactly wandering mentally (aside from inscrutable remarks in New York Yiddish) but more than a little unsteady physically and upon his expressed desire for coffee or some brainstem stimulant less mind-fogging than whiskey Joyce suggested right off the bat that he, Babcock, accompany him, Joyce, to his (Joyce's) lodgings, just a stone's-throw away from the very spot where they presently stood (or occasionally staggered) on Bahnhofstrasse. This proposal being accepted with alacrity and with much verbose gratitude, the three set off on foot in the hot windswept night since it was considered an improbability verging on the tales of the Brothers Grimm to hope to encounter a carriage for hire at that hour, à propos of which Joyce remarked significantly, "We have heard the chimes at midnight."

And Babcock, not wishing to appear illiterate responded, "Falstaff, is it not?"

"Yes," Joyce said. "*Henry IV, Part One.*" And they both looked at each other anew, finding some mysterious or at least emotionally gratifying bond in a shared acquaintance with the immortal Bard, although only Joyce reflected further that midnight was very much later to Falstaff in his sunrise-sundown agricultural economy than to himself and Babcock in this industrial age—Babcock being occupied with the more prosaic question of just how late it really was, and if they had actually heard the chimes at midnight, how long ago would that have been?

—but neither topic was verbalized aloud at that point, all three men proceeding in silence for a while as they were none of them at exactly what you would call their sparkling best or in their keenest wits, Einstein being uncertain about chimes at midnight and little dollinks, Joyce being fogged over by enough beer to float the local navy if the overly tidy Swiss had a hypothetical navy, and Babcock being half-frightened out of his skin, but they did eventually attempt to converse in amiable or at least civil fashion, not at first very successfully inasmuch as both Joyce and Babcock were as nervous as a pair of strange sharks being quite aware on each side of the historical and temperamental abyss between the Anglo-Saxon and Hibernian mentalities. It was therefore doubly unfortunate that Babcock's first attempt to open the door between their worlds was of an almost baboonlike clumsiness.

"As an Irishman, you are of course a mystic," Babcock pronounced, thereby putting his foot into his mouth while, as it were, simultaneously stepping for the second time on Joyce's most sensitive corn. "You know that there are vast invisible forces and intelligences behind the charade of material reality. Do you perhaps know of Yeats?"

"Yes," Joyce said evasively, maneuvering them both to miss a pile of dog shit, which he would most certainly include if he were ever to write this scene, and which Yeats would most certainly exclude. "Is he not the fellow who is so terrified that the future might be different from the past?"

"I would not state the case that way," Babcock said with a disapproving frown at the flippant and belittling witticism. "Mr. Yeats is a man who fears that the future will be cold, scientific, materialistic, without the romance and mystery of the past."

Einstein said nothing. They were now abreast of the FIAT "automobile," and Joyce looked at it and at every part of it with a meticulous curiosity that seemed almost obsessive to Babcock. "You see more of these every year," Joyce said. "And I read recently that a man in America named Olds is turning them out, and selling them to customers, at the rate of six thousand and more *per annum*. How the hell they run is as much a romance and a mystery to me as anything in that fabulous past Mr. Yeats' autobiographical hero wishes so fervently to clutch to his bosom. There's a magick Wand inside, called the clutch, that propels this mystic chariot to velocities up to forty kilometers an hour. I wish I knew more about mechanical physics."

"It's a simple natural phenomenon," Einstein said helpfully. "But I'm sure you don't want a lecture on internal combustion at this hour." Actually, he was more interested in observing his two odd companions, hoping that further clues might clarify why Devil Masks were so terrifying to Babcock and what little dollink had heard the chimes at midnight. "It runs on controlled explosions," he added, hoping that would satisfy them.

"Um, yes, certainly," Babcock said uncertainly. "I wouldn't drive one for a million pounds. You hear the most gruesome stories about accidents. Surely God gave us the horse so we wouldn't have to invent such dangerous contraptions. I shudder to think what the world will be like in ten years when the streets are full of them."

"Of course," Joyce said, although the logical progression here was totally inscrutable to Babcock, "if we, like Mr. Yeats, want a really deep, endless, bottomless and topless mystery, we can always try to understand our wives. Or the man next to us on the street, *n'est ce pas?*"

Babcock meditated on that cynical-sounding notion for a few moments and then became aware that another man was in fact approaching them on the street, a most singular person with a high-domed Shakespearean forehead, ibis eyes of monkeylike Mongolian cruelty and a spadelike black beard. So striking was this figure that, somewhat influenced by Joyce's last remark, Babcock peered after the Slavic stranger as he turned down toward the Limmat River area and then commented aloud, "I shared a compartment with him on the train. One might indeed find deep mysteries in an individual of that sort."

"He seems to have very important business," Einstein ventured.

"Damn this wind," Joyce said, jabbing the air with his walkingstick as a caduceus. "The natives call it the witch-wind. Whenever it blows, half of Zürich goes mad. We Northerners feel it more, since we expect a wind to be cold and biting. A hot wind that suffocates you slowly is like an unwanted, unlovely and unbathed paramour in your bed."

A dog howled suddenly in the distance with an eerie rising cadence like a wolf or coyote. "You see?" Joyce said. "Even the animals go barmy when the *Föhn* blows."

"It is like incense of white sandal," Einstein agreed. "Too thick and heavy to be pleasant."

"The local police have records," Joyce said in an opal-hush tone, mystically, "showing that the murder rate always rises when the *Föhn* blows, and the local alienists say that the number of nervous breakdowns definitely increases. Most sinister and eerie, is it not? Mr. Yeats would say that the undines and water-spirits are attempting to overcome the air-elementals on the astral plane, which makes the material plane so mucking filthy to walk in." Like Thoth, he shifted again, adding cynically, "But it is only a change in the ionization of the air and can be measured with those heathen scientific instruments Mr. Yeats so dreads."

But this led them into a full-scale imbroglio which lasted in fact all the way to Joyce's hotel, and in the course of it Joyce learned that Babcock was an ardent admirer not only of the puerile (if elegant) poetry of Mr. William Butler Yeats, but of the detestable (if kindly) Mr. Yeats himself, and was even a member (with Yeats) of the Hermetic Order of the Golden Dawn, a group of London occultists of which Joyce had long ago formed a decidedly unfavorable opinion, regarding them in cold fact as being a bit funny in all their heads. Babcock in turn gathered from various sardonic and downright unkind remarks dropped *en passant* by Joyce that he, Joyce, regarded Yeats (along with the Golden Dawn, Blavatsky and the whole of modern mysticism) with a disdain that seemed, to him, Babcock, to be unwarrantedly venomous. Things began to clear up after a bit, at least in Babcock's muddled mind, when it gradually emerged that Mr. Joyce was also a writer, considerably less successful than Yeats, if not virtually unknown, and suspicions concerning the emblematic Sour Grapes and the well-known Green-eyed Monster were almost, but not quite, articulated at this point by Babcock, because only the madman is absolutely sure.

"I take it," Babcock said when they were finally arrived at Gasthaus Doeblin, "that you are a socialist, or an anarchist, if not both."

"You behold in me a dreadful example of unbridled anarchistic individualism," Joyce replied suavely. "I loathe all nations equally. The State is concentric, but the individual is eccentric. Welcome to the ghastliest house this side of Dublin," he added, indicating the sign: GASTHAUS DOEBLIN (and perversely mistranslating it according to his own dubious whimsy).

"Thank God we're out of that foul wind," Einstein said fervently as they crossed a yellow-carpeted lobby bedecked with wallpaper showing palm trees and grinning monkeys. ("Mine innkeeper hath strange notions of decor," Joyce commented *sotto voce*.) The building seemed to be an octagon, and Joyce led Babcock and Einstein around seven sides of it before arriving at Room 23, which was, he announced, "complete with breakfast alcove, where I have some of the best Italian espresso coffee this side of Trieste, because I brought it from Trieste."

They were tiptoeing now, Babcock and Einstein imitating Joyce in this, and stopped, once, as Joyce opened slowly and quietly a door to peer briefly into an untidy bedroom where a stoutish, pretty-faced woman was sleeping amid crumpled blankets.

"That would be Mrs. Joyce," said Babcock.

"Undoubtedly," Joyce retorted, "but it is Miss Barnacle."

More than a little taken aback by this frank avowal of barbaric contempt for civilized morals and the canons of elementary decency, Babcock had to remind himself that the arrogant Irishman was, after all, his host and had already exhibited somewhat more than the customary degree of charity to him, a perfect stranger in the first place and one who might sound a bit mad in the second place and beyond that a member of the conquering and therefore probably loathed English race in the third place. But by now they were in the kitchenette alcove and Joyce was making coffee, after setting the Devil Mask at a dapper angle above the cuckoo clock.

"So," Joyce said, "this goat-faced fellow has pursued you all the way from Loch Ness, you say."

"With your opinions," Babcock replied, "you must regard all this as fantasy and I daresay you fancy yourself as humoring a lunatic. I remind you, sir, that three people have already died horrible deaths in this accursed affair."

"Pursued," Einstein inquired softly, "by the same demon that now pursues you?" With one probing finger he chucked the Devil Mask under the chin, sharkishly playful. "A masquerade with nothing behind the masks?"

"A devil's masquerade," Babcock bitterly replied.

This somewhat staggered Joyce, who recalled again the poem he had recollected on Bahnhofstrasse, although he still could not remember the author's name if it were not his favorite ancient bard, Anon of Ibid. Another stanza drifted unbidden up to the surface of his mind:

Demons drink from human skulls
And souls are up for trade
Take wine and drugs and join us in
The Devil's Masquerade

That kind of damned peculiar coincidence was multiplying rapidly tonight, Joyce realized (and wondered if Dr. Carl Jung ought to be here to take notes). Reflecting thus in silence for a few minutes, the Irish freethinker steeped the coffee and began to absently roll a cigarette, glancing thoughtfully at the English mystic. "Saint Thomas tells us," Joyce said soberly, "that the Devil has no power to do real injury to those who trust in the Lord, although he may admittedly frighten or discomfit them, to test their faith. In fact, sir, it is rank heresy to claim real harm can occur in such cases, since that implies lack of faith in God's goodness. Ah," he interrupted himself, "I see you are astonished that I can speak that language. Well, sir, if I were to believe in any mysticism, it would be that of Thomas, who is logical, coherent and full of cold common sense, and not that of your modern occultists, who are illogical, absurd and full of hot air. But let that pass for the moment." He lit his cigarette and pointed at the mask. "What sort of second-rate, bargain-basement devil is it that needs theatrical props to do his dirty business?"

Babcock, who had been growing steadier by the minute, smiled wryly at this sharply pointed sally. "You misconstrue me," he said. "I am well aware that there are human beings involved in this terrible affair, but they have powers not ordinarily vouchsafed to mere men, because they serve a being who is not human. You think, evidently, that I am the sort who can be frightened by a mere theatrical prop, as you call it, but I have already faced terrors that you can scarcely conceive. For instance, I would not be frightened merely to see what I saw tonight—a figure with that Satanic face coming at me suddenly out of the dark. What was truly diabolical was that *they* found me here when I have taken elaborate precautions to cover my tracks and elude them."

Joyce poured coffee silently, the red-tipped cigarette not looked at in his left hand not feeling it. From Loch Ness to Zürich: to me. The terrors I knew as a child: howls of the damned, pitchforked, baboon-faced demons, flame-garbed figures screaming. Many a civic monster. Ancient Zoroastrian nightmare from which the West is struggling to awaken.

"And how," Joyce asked, "did these three persons come to die? Their throats torn by the talons of some terrible beast in the Gothic thriller style of Walpole?"

Sir John, actuated by motives of inherent delicacy, inasmuch as he always believed in agreeing with one's host for courtesy's sake, however irascible said host might be, restrained several sharp answers that almost leaped to his lips, and said merely, "They were all driven to suicide."

"By masks and mummery," Joyce exclaimed, not bothering to conceal his irony. Seizing the mask, he held it before his own flushed face and leaned menacingly across the table. "By theatrical props like this?" his voice asked from behind the mask in sardonic Dublin brogue.

"They were driven to suicide by a book," said Sir John, "a book so vile that it should not exist. Just by looking into this foul piece of literature, all three victims were driven mad by horror and destroyed themselves. It was as if they had learned something that made life on this planet so unspeakably awful to them that they could not bear another instant of consciousness."

Einstein stared at the young Englishman with something akin to the well-known wild surmise on the emblematic peak in Darien. "This is something you have really been involved in?" he asked quietly. "Not just something you've heard about, a rumor or a yarn?"

"It's as real as this coffee, this saucer, this table," Babcock said flatly, indicating all three objects with emphatic gestures while his haunted eyes mutely recalled some dreadful history of Godless and unspeakable monkey business that might stab anyone in the back at any moment, anytime, anywhere, like the proverbial snake in the grass, if it were not judiciously nipped in the bud by brave and farseeing men taking prompt and prudent corrective action at the psychological moment and striking when the iron is hot.

Joyce and Einstein exchanged mute meaningful glances.

"Let me show you what I've been involved in," Babcock said, reaching into his straw traveling case. "This is from the Inverness *Express-Journal*," he said, passing over a clipping. Joyce and Einstein read it together.

THE CASE OF THE CONSTANT SUICIDES

Terror Stalks Loch Ness; Police Baffled

Q: What paragraph caused the most puzzlement to Professor Einstein?
A: "Other residents regard the inspector's skepticism with the strict rule of no wife, no horse, no mustache, always anger and derision."
Q: Did Einstein refer to this particular befuddlement?
A: With embarrassment, with awkwardness, with a suspicion that the problem might be caused by his own deficient knowledge of English, diffidently, he did.
Q: Was that matter, at least, clarified at once?
A: It was, by Mr. Joyce's terse explanation: "That's what's called bitched type. Part of a line that got in from another column."

Einstein looked at Sir John with renewed interest. "Let me hear your whole story," he said, beginning to fill a pipe.

Joyce nodded, slouching in his chair like a boneless man. The *Föhn* wind shook the window behind him like a goblin seeking entrance.

ACTION	SOUND

EXTERIOR. BABCOCK MANOR. LONG SHOT.

The penny-farthing bicycle standing in a path near the house.	*Babcock's voice:* ". . . promise to always hele, never reveal, any art or arts, part or parts . . ."
The bicycle falls over. There is no wind or other evident cause; it simply falls.	*The* Merry Widow Waltz *rises to drown out Babcock's words.*

Q: With what species of animal and plant life was Babcock Manor most plentifully supplied?
A: A murder of crows, an exaltation of larks, a clowder of cats, a muster of peacocks, a skulk of foxes, a watch of nightingales, a labor of moles, a gaggle of geese, a peep of chickens, a parliament of owls, a paddling of ducks, a knot of toads, a siege of herons, a trip of goats, a drift of hogs, a charm of finches, a murmuration of starlings, a pitying of turtledoves, a dawn of roses, a hover of trout, a tiding of magpies, a glory of violets, a zonker of hedges, a kindle of kittens, a hallucination of morning glories, a sunset of fuchsia, a stateliness of oaks, a midnight of ravens, a noon of fern, a cover of coots, a weeping of willows, a laughter of cosmos, a hilarity of gardenias, a sauna of beeches, a blather of crickets and a millennium of moss.
Q: With what books was the library of Babcock Manor stocked by Sir John?
A: A prevarication of politics, a chronology of history, a gnome of mythology, a schiz of theology [including a

serenity of Buddhists, a cosmology of Hindus, an inscruta-
bility of Taoists and a war of Christians], an eldritch of
Alhazreds, a fume of alchemists, a tree of Cabalists, a
heresiarch of Brunos, a lot of Lulls, an ova of Bacons, a
mystification of Rosycrosses, a silence of Sufis, an enoch of
Dees, a wisdom of Gnostics and a small snivel of romances.

The night after meeting George Cecil Jones, Sir John
dreamed again of Chapel Perilous, which was now a heavily armed, scarlet-walled castle owned by a man-eating
ogre named Sir Talis. "You must enter without being
sown," said Judge Everyman, "for bleating runes are red."
King Edward III, wearing the conventional business
suit of George Cecil Jones, wandered in numinous room
incandescent muttering something about the impotence of
being honest.
"The moover hoovered," He He Commons added helpfully. "The door opens to the wastebule, past eggnaughts
to oldfresser Poop in the Watercan."
"The unheatable and the unbrickable," shrieked a giant
owl.
"Sol is buried inside," muttered Uncle Bentley. "Talk
id and hoot!"
Sir John realized he was in the Temple of Solomon the
King as described in Freemasonic literature.
"Wee-knee got Thor, Sir Talis war bore," roared a
Lion.
"Passing as some dew-mist too dense upon the air,"
whizzed an Eagle.
"Bloog ardor!" howled Sir Knott the Almighty. "Take
heed and hate!" Sir John, a solo man under sectualism,
stumbled into the owld cavern of skeletons, a tripentocto-
con where the morn's dozen sheens. A sign said:

DO NOT MEDDLE IN THE AFFAIRS OF WIZARDS:
IT MAKES THEM SOGGY AND HARD TO LIGHT

"Said, the old servant of Envy," the Angel was lecturing, "tore him to shredded wheat and planeted him where the somn dozing snore, but he gnaw not weth the dew. For they whisked in a flicker, Jenny Peg and Brother Rot and Hamster, prinzipdungmark, and, slack it, a mouse with seven gerbils."

"These," Jones said with a gesture at the bones, "are those who came on this path without the Pentacle of Valor. What do you drink, Sir Joan: Shall damn bones leave?"

But before Sir Joan could decide on the literalness of the question, they were in the dark back shelves of the Tyrone side wing of the Brutus Museum in the gaseous shade of the tree Swifty ate, the tree ovus gaggin scissors, and Karl Marx was reading aloud from what appeared to be the secret history of Freemasonry: "And Solomon was a motley kink, and he shut in his cuntinghorse on the tail of his broken spine just accounting for his honey; and the LORD spook into him and said: Solomon, git. And Silvamoon gat; and in the foulness of tomb Solomon gart bark and begat. And Sol O'Morn begat Nightrex and Nighttricks begat Mars Harem and Moose Hiram began Finnegan and Faunycohen begot Heroman and Hairy Moon bigot Sir Talis and Surd Alice begott begad Roy O'Range Yellagroin and Roy O'Range Yallagroin begat the little Blowindianviolated Engine That Could." He lapsed into nearly Russian idioms.

"Is that not a rather large thing to expect us to begin upon?" Sir John asked, hearing himself talking, waking to the morning sun.

Sitting up, he found he was still half-dreaming or talking to himself internally. "We are such stuff as dreams are made of," his or somebody's voice was saying. Shakespeare, of course: *The Tempest.* A great line, often quoted, but what did it mean when you stopped to think about it? What did *The Tempest* mean, for that matter? If Prospero is Shakespeare himself, as all the scholars claim, why is Prospero a magician rather than a poet? Why does he associate with faeries, elves, the monster Caliban and all the assembly of the occult?

And "Childe Roland to the Dark Tower came." What is that line doing in *Lear*, where it has nothing to do with the plot at all? Was Shakespeare part of the Invisible College?

Sir John ate a larger breakfast than usual and took a long walk afterward, reaffirming the solidity of matter and the reality of earth, sky and trees. He did not dread being known as a Romantic, but he had no intent of becoming a damned fool.

When he returned home and sat down to read the London *Times*, he found that Stolypin, the Russian premier, had been murdered, the latest in the brutal assassinations that had made the last decade of the nineteenth century and the first decade of the twentieth seem a prelude to rising worldwide anarchy. He tried to remember his parents and his own feelings at the time of their deaths and found only a dull pain in the place where memory should be. If there was such a thing as higher wisdom or higher knowledge, Sir John felt that the human race very badly needed it. Life, to ordinary wisdom and ordinary knowledge, appeared no more than a singularly pointless and brutal jest. "Off with their heads! Off with their heads!" God seemed to be gibbering most of the time, like the Red Queen in *Alice*. Does He really kill us for His sport?

Sir John spent the next two weeks re-reading and meditating on the classic Rosicrucian pamphlets of the seventeenth century. Everything Jones had so prosaically illustrated was there: the Brother of the Invisible College of the Rosy Cross will "dress in the garb" of the country where he resides and "adapt all its customs"; although forever pledged to the Invisible College, he will manifest no overt sign to the world, except that he might heal the sick, taking no money for that service.

At the exact termination of the fortnight, Sir John received a small package in the mail from P. O. Box 718, Main Post Office, London. Inside was a small pamphlet entitled "History Lection." Authorship was given as:

Hermetic Order of the G∴D∴

Sir John's heart leaped; he knew that those pyramidal dots represented, in occult symbology, an order possessing the original Mason Word, admittedly lost to all other Freemasonic orders. He recalled from the anonymous *Muses Threnody* of 1648:

> For we be brethren of the Rosy Cross
> We have the Mason Word and second sight
> Things for to come we can see aright

With trembling fingers, Sir John opened the pamphlet and began to read the secret history of the Hermetic Order of the Golden Dawn. In 1875, it said, a great fire destroyed Freemasons' Hall in London. Robert Wentworth Little—a writer whose books on Masonry were familiar to Sir John—found some long-forgotten documents, while rescuing important charters and other items of value from the flames. These mysterious papers were in a cipher unknown to Little or any other London Freemasons of the time. By dint of continuous, meticulous effort and perseverance, Little eventually solved the cipher, decoded the documents, then found himself in possession of the secrets of the Invisible College—secrets which orthodox Freemasonry had long since lost. The documents also provided a link with a continental order which seemed to possess even deeper secrets and provided the address of a high initiate named Fräulein Anna Sprengel in Ingolstadt, Bavaria.

The lection went on to tell how Robert Wentworth Little and various other London Freemasons, guided by Fräulein Sprengel, began the Hermetic Order of the Golden Dawn, originally admitting as members only those who were already high-degree Masons. Using the techniques learned from Miss Sprengel and the ciphered documents, they gradually recreated the whole working repertoire of Cabalistic occultism underlying the Rosy Cross order of Freemasonry and sought earnestly to establish astral contact with the Higher Intelligences on other planes who could gradually educate and guide them in the risky transition from the domesticated apehood of historical humanity to a higher stage on the evolutionary scale.

This "History Lection" went on to assert that such contact had been established and that the Golden Dawn was now operating under astral guidance. It added ominously that students should beware of several impostors who had seized upon the name of the order and were operating false Golden Dawns of their own devoted to diabolism and black magick. Among these heretics, who seemed to number nearly a dozen—when the original Golden Dawn split into factions, it split violently, Sir John gathered—two names particularly struck Sir John because of their resonant roll: MacGregor Mathers and Aleister Crowley.

Q: Was the resonance of these names an accident?
A: It was not. The former individual had been born Samuel Liddell Mathers and had decided, when embarking on the paths of Magick, that Samuel Mathers, Sam Mathers, S. L. Mathers, S. Liddell Mathers were all unsuitable and unglamorous names for a Magician; he had therefore taken the more sonorous cognomen of MacGregor Mathers. The latter individual, similarly, had been born Edward Alexander Crowley and found also that the various permutations of that appellation were too prosaic for the career he

intended; after profound research and much thought he concluded that the name "Jeremy Taylor" was the most memorable in English because of its rhythm. Wishing to appropriate that rhythm, he re-dubbed himself Aleister Crowley.

Q: Quote a standard reference on the history of the Golden Dawn so as to convey maximum information without exceeding the legal limits of fair usage and with least possible prejudice toward one faction or another.

A: "The Golden Dawn was the most influential of the many occult secret societies founded in the nineteenth century. It first came into existence in 1887–88 and was founded on the basis of certain cipher manuscripts allegedly discovered in London which described five rituals of initiation. . . . Early in the 1890s, however, the nature of the Golden Dawn was transformed by one of its leaders, S. L. MacGregor Mathers, who claimed to have contacted the 'Secret Chiefs,' the invisible and highly evolved superhumans who form, occultists aver, the secret government of our planet." Francis King, Introduction to *Crowley on Christ*, C. W. Daniel Co., London, 1974.

Q: Provide further information on the origins of the tradition of mystical Masonry.

A: "However, the Egyptian Masons are more closely involved with the Grand Orient Lodge of France . . . which was originally set up by Weishaupt's Illuminati, and which is closely associated with the Society of Jacobins. . . . One secret Illuminatus and Jacobin was Guiseppe Balsamo, alias Cagliostro, who . . . bequeathed certain MSS. to his followers of the Egyptian sect, including excerpts from the original *Necronomicon*. . . . The text of the *Necronomicon* . . . reached them via the Arabs of Spain . . . goes back to the Persians . . . and links up with Babylonian magic and the Hermetic tradition of the Egyptian priesthood of Thoth." Letter from Dr. Stanislaus Hinterstoisser to Colin Wilson, *The Necronomicon* with commentaries, Neville Spearman Co., Suffolk, 1978.

*   *   *

Sir John reflected on the "History Lection" for two days before deciding how much further he dared go. Then he wrote back to Jones and begged admission to the Hermetic Order of the Golden Dawn as a Probationer.

And so he crossed the thrice-sealed door and passed over from being a student of occult history to being a tentative and nervous practitioner of occult arts, wherein he was soon to learn that we are in fact such stuff as dreams are made of, and that Sir Talis is inescapable.

Sir John was initiated on the night of July 23, 1910— exactly 307 years to the day after the knighting of Sir Francis Bacon, the alleged Grandmaster of the Invisible College in Elizabethan England (according to Golden Dawn documents—which also claimed such illustrious members as Sir Richard Francis Burton, Paul Gauguin, Richard Wagner, King Ludwig of Bavaria, Wolfgang von Goethe, Adam Weishaupt, Dr. John Dee, Pope Alexander VI, Jacob Boehme, Paracelsus, Christian Rosenkreutz, Giordano Bruno, Jacques de Molay, Newton, Beethoven, Merlin, Rabelais, Vergil, Jesus, Buddha, Lao-Tse, Solomon, Osiris and Krishna, among others). About the initiation itself, Sir John, true to his Oath, never revealed any details, even on that night in Zürich when, with the *Föhn* witch-wind beating at the windows, he recounted his extraordinary adventures to James Joyce and Professor Albert Einstein. Some veils shall never be lifted; Babcock would not lift that particular veil.

Three nights after the initiation, Sir John experienced it over again, in the form of another hermetic dream. He was being led, blindfolded, to the throne of the South where opens the window of the Silver Star in night's roaman indigo.

"Who comes here?" asked the Gordean, Sir Francis Bacon.

"One who seeks the Light," Sir John replied, according to the traditional Masonic formula explained to him before the ceremony.

"Humankind cannot bear very much Light," said Nightrix in a watery voice. "Look upon what little you domesticated mammals are presently prepared to receive."

There was a spouter inn the weib and Sir John found himself back again at the Tower Struck By Lightning. Sir Talis, a gorged hairyman, was counting out his honi. Sir Joan crept past ovaseer Peep parsing as somndreamist and found hirselves in a vast humming hive (decliner flying, mythra ovid: what a man dasn't shame) where madmen struggled frantically to kill each other, cursing and screaming, "You will, whisker, you will!" and clutching daggers gats dirks goaters and broken bottle shards, uttering vowelth, muttering foulth, as all sank into dank, dark blood-red fetid moonslime. "Kid goaters!" they howled. "And that the Vril is strong!" A medieval scroll was unrolled, Indic, Norse, Russian, Irish, veryvery long but veryvery dutiful, saying:

DO NOT THROW BUTTS IN THE URINAL:
FOR THEY ARE SUBTLE AND SWIFT TO ANGER

Sed, the whole's arpent of entry, a muddy murky leaky john, pressed cowrin throngs upon him, shrieking, "Fear the forgotten!"

"These," said Nud the Allmousey (Eutaenius Microstemmus) in eagulls clause, "are those who came this way without the Cup of Sympathy. Each imagines all the others to be terrifying demons and thinks he acts only in self-defense. Tragic, and ironic, is it not?"

Sir John awoke with a start.

"Suffering Christ!" he said, without any profane intent. Was that dream a vision of how humanity looked from the viewpoint of an Illuminated mind?

"A real initiation never ends," Jones had said cryptically, before the physical-plane initiation. Sir John understood: the dream, in its own language, was indeed a continuation of the initiation, but on another plane. Even the masks used in the actual ceremony were now, in the light of the dream's clear message, an allegory, not a mere bit of theatrical mummery. The masks worn in ordinary life are psychological, not cardboard, but nonetheless serve to hide each from his fellows; Society is the Devil's Masquerade.

When Sir John met next with Jones at the latter's home in Soho, the dreams of the Dark Tower were discussed at length and Sir John proudly exhibited his decoding of their symbolism, especially the allegory of the masks.

"True enough," Jones said. "But it is also a rule of our Order that nobody in it ever knows personally any more than one other member. The masks used in initiations help enforce that rule."

"And what, pray, is the purpose of that?"

"Mars is the patron god of all societies," Jones said grimly. "Competition smashed the first Golden Dawn lodge in London. Everybody *knew* everybody, so we all fell into transcendental egotism—'my Illumination is higher than your Illumination,' that sort of thing—and the Devil of Disputation drove us apart. We don't repeat any of our mistakes, Sir John. From here on, except for very special emergencies, perhaps, you will meet nobody else in the lodge but myself, until somebody higher up replaces me as your teacher. If we don't know one another, we can't fall into rivalries."

This radical decentralization was a double-edged device, Sir John soon realized. Not only was he spared the waste of time and energy that might have been spent wondering if he were progressing faster or slower than another student, but the mystery created by this lack of sociability had a subtle and new effect on all his perceptions of other human beings.

At first, he would merely wonder, if somebody made a remark that seemed more insightful than usual, "Could it be . . . is he one of us, too?" Was Shakespeare in the Invisible College? The head waiter at Claridge's? *Just how many members were there?* It was impossible to get a literal answer out of Jones about this. "The question itself implies a Probationer's ignorance about the true nature of Space and Time," was all Jones would contribute on that subject. Sir John began to wonder, every time he read the familiar newspaper yarn about a person rescued from danger by a Mysterious Stranger who immediately vanished without accepting thanks or leaving his name. "Another of us?" Sir John would speculate romantically, seeing the protective hand of the Great White Brotherhood everywhere. Of course, as a Cambridge graduate, he had imbibed, at least by osmosis, something of modern skeptical scholarship, and he knew all this might be mere infatuation with a wonderful myth.

But, on the other hand, one could not expect to be provided with special spectacles allowing the members of the Invisible College to see each other, could one?

And the enigma of hermetic societies was more subtle than that, Sir John was to discover. The Golden Dawn, after all, was allegedly continuing the unbroken tradition of the original Invisible College of the Rosy Cross, whose members "wore the garb and adapted the manners" of the country in which they resided. Sir John soon found that even the most inane remarks or offensive behavior would trigger the same question: "*Another* of us?" How many Adepts might there be, traveling about in the guise of ordinary humanity, carefully hiding their advanced state behind a masquerade of socially normal stupidity or conformity? Jesus allowed Himself to be spat upon, whipped, mocked and crucified; the Golden Dawn literature made it abundantly clear that a true Adept might play any role or suffer any humiliation in order to accom-

plish his or her special Work: The Fool may be The
Magus in disguise.

Sir John was simultaneously devouring tons of mystical
literature from all nations and all ages, dumped on him
ten volumes at a time by Jones. Written examinations
once a month determined that he understood, at least
verbally, what he read.

"But I am a Christian," Sir John protested once.

"Nor do we wish to make you any more or less than
that," Jones replied. "But to progress in the Great Work,
you must become aware of the invisible truth behind the
visible paraphernalia of all religions. In our Order, the
Christian may remain Christian, the Jew Jew, the Moslem
Moslem, as it may be, but whatever their faith, they may
not remain narrow-minded sectarians."

Sir John began to understand this ambiguous ecumen-
icism a bit while studying a text on Buddhism. The refrain, "Everyone you meet is a Buddha," began to drive
him to despair; it was so nonsensical; it was repeated so
often, in so many different ways; it was obvious that he
would have to understand it before he began to comprehend what Buddhism was all about. He, therefore, at
Jones' suggestion, tried to *see* the Buddha in everyone he
met—and then he understood quickly.

The effect was the same as the deliberate mystification
with the Golden Dawn about who was or wasn't a member. Looking for the Buddha in everyone, like looking for
more members of the Order, caused Sir John to pay a
great deal closer attention to people than he ever had
before, and to see more of their mysterious and adamantine individuality, rather than classifying them into cate-
gories of age, sex, race, caste or other superficialities. He
now saw all people as mysterious, incredible beings; and he
understood, suddenly, a most annoying paradox of Goethe,
who had said, "What is hardest of all? That which seems
most simple: to see with your eyes what is before your eyes."

And he understood, too, Saint Paul's insistence that "we are all members of the Body of Christ." Every man and woman was a single facet of the diamond-mirror, made in the image of God, which was humanity. Buddhism, as Jones had promised him, had not weakened his Christianity but had illuminated it further.

Sir John thought this was marvelous and poured it out in manic excitement at his next meeting with Jones.

"Very good," Jones said condescendingly. "You have awakened, a little, from one of the dreams that keep the sleepwalkers on the street from *seeing* one another. This is a beginning, but only a beginning. Don't be too impressed with your progress, for God's sake, or you'll never move another inch. Try seeing the divine Light in every beautiful object that comes your way—deep scarlet rubies, or tiger-lilies in a field, or the red markings on a crab's back. Then ask yourself where consciousness and divinity are *not*."

And with that crushing and yet encouraging speech, delivered with a trace of leonine fire, mild Mr. Jones seemed to Sir John definitely beyond all doubt the genuine article: a true Adept. Then, without mercy, Jones dumped ten books on Cabala upon Sir John, told him to master them thoroughly—and nearly torpedoed and sank him forever.

Babcock, previously, had studied Cabala only as a historian, learning enough of its terminology and theories to trace its influence from the early Hermeticists like Pico della Mirandola and Giordano Bruno through Dr. Dee and Sir Francis Bacon, onward to Freemasonry and Illuminism. Now he found himself confronted with the necessity of mastering the entire Cabalistic theory of the universe, which was about a thousand times more complicated than the periodic table of chemical elements Uncle Bentley kept in his study.

According to Cabala, the cosmos is governed by symbolic correspondences between many planes of being, visible and invisible. That *seemed* simple enough; but the correspondences themselves had no logical connections at all—"Cabala *transcends* logic," Jones reminded Sir John. The correspondences could only be learned by brute force and rote repetition until they finally embedded themselves in the memory. Even after being memorized, the correspondences would not be *understood* by the student, Jones cheerfully remarked; true understanding, he said, could come only through intuition or through direct experience of the invisible planes, by techniques to be taught when Sir John graduated from Probationer to Neophyte.

Q: Give three concise examples of Cabalistic logic.
A: [1] All Hebrew words having the same numerical value must have equivalent meanings; therefore, ACh D (unity) which equals A(l) + Ch(8) + D(4) or 13, is the same as AHBH (love) because A(1) + H(5) + B(2) + H(5) also equals 13; *ergo,* unity *is* love and love *is* unity. [2] Since the Holy Unspeakable Name of God (YHVH) = Y(10) + H(5) + V(6) + H(5) = 26, which is 2 × 13, God *is* love + unity. [3] Since 7 of the 22 Hebrew letters also correspond to planets, the proportion 22/7 is very important; and, indeed, 22/7 = 3.1415 . . . etc., the value of π, or the ratio of the radius of a circle to its circumference.
Q: Give an example of Cabalistic logic running into trouble.
A: Since God is unity, and the first Hebrew letter A (Aleph) = 1, A symbolizes God. But A (Aleph) written in full Hebrew is ALP which = 111, showing that God is a triple unity; well and good for Christian Cabalists, although annoying to Jewish and Moslem Cabalists. But 111 also = APL, Darkness, and ASN, Sudden Death. Is God therefore, equivalent to Darkness and Sudden Death?

Sir John spent days, weeks, then months rote-reciting over and over, peering into the books again each time memory slipped: *"Aleph* is the first Hebrew letter and means 'ox.' The principle correspondences are the Fool card in the Tarot, the color yellow, the element air, the Holy Spirit in the New Testament, the Breath of God— what's that?—*Ruach Elohim*, the Breath of God, in the Old Testament, the path from Kether to Chockmah on the Tree of Life and, uh, oh, God, uh . . ." Back to the books.

"Beth is the second Hebrew letter and means 'house.' The Juggler in the Tarot, the color scarlet, the planet Mercury, Thoth in Egyptian, Hermes in Greek, Odin in Norse, the path from Kether to Binah, the monkey-god in Hindu . . . Oh, Christ, what's the name of the monkey-god . . . ?" Back, again, to the books.

Jones would travel to Babcock Manor and test Sir John occasionally.

"Nun," he would say, "what Tarot card is that?"

"Death."

"The Hebrew meaning?"

"A fish."

"Very good. The medieval equivalent of the Chariot card in the Tarot?"

"The Holy Grail."

"Excellent. The Hebrew letter for the same?"

"Uh, uh, *daleth* . . ."

"Wrong. Won't do at all, my boy. No carelessness allowed. Memorize, *memorize*, memorize!"

Sir John memorized.

"Work on the first two words of the Bible," Jones suggested then; and Sir John found himself seeking the hidden meanings in BRAShITH ALHIM. "In the beginning, the Gods."

Of course, he knew from Pico della Mirandola that BRAShITH ["In the beginning . . ."] has the numerical value of 3910, the number of years according to occult tradition from the "Fall" of humanity (due to the unfortunate trauma of the first contact with Higher Intelligence,

coded into the serpent myth of Genesis) to the birth of
Jesus. He discovered for himself that ALHIM (the gods:
God-in-the-singular as YHVH or Jehovah not appearing
until the second chapter) contains, by the permutations of
temura, 3.1415, or pi accurate to four places. Then he
noted that BRA, the first three letters, form by notarikon
the initials of *Ben*, the Son; *Ruach*, the Holy Spirit; and
Abba, the Father.

"Very good," Jones said when this was reported. "There
is much, much more there. For instance, *Agape*, the word
for 'Love' in the New Testament, has the Cabalistic value
of 93. Add that to the 3.1415 of ALHIM and you get
3.141593, pi accurate to six places. Keep working on it
until you find the Golden Proportions of the Masonic
lodge in it."

Once, Sir John had the temerity to ask Jones about the
Mysterious Holy Guardian Angel which the Golden Dawn
training was intended to evoke.

"Usually," Jones said, "that is explained three different
ways—for Probationers, Neophytes, and those of higher
rank who have yet not attained it. In your case, considering the mixture of scholarship and romanticism I detect in
your temperament, I will give you all three explanations
simultaneously. One: it is a metaphor that signifies, roughly,
learning to receive communications from your own unconscious mind without the usual distortions. Two: it is
not that simple at all; the Holy Guardian Angel speaks to
you *through* your unconscious, but is literally a separate
being of evolutionary status as far beyond us as we are
beyond the first invertebrates. Three: yes, it is a metaphor, after all, but for something so far outside our ordinary consciousness that it doesn't matter a rap whether
you think of it in the scientific terms of my first answer or
in the mystical terms of my second answer; it transcends
both. When you have the experience, you will find your
own metaphor for it, which may result in a scientific

theory never known to the world before, in a work of art, or just in a change in your life toward sanctity or compassion or something more traditionally 'religious.' Do more of the work and ask fewer questions, if you want to advance faster."

Eventually, nine months after Sir John's initiation, he had completed his reading course in world mysticism and was able to pass all of Jones' Cabalistic quizzes easily. By now, he was also totally confused and was beginning to wonder if he or Jones or both of them might not be a bit mad. After all, what did an ox have to do with a man in Fool's garb, or either of them with the color yellow or the Holy Spirit? If Thoth and Hermes were the same god under two names, well and good; that made sense historically. But why were they in correspondence with the Hebrew word for "house"? Or what the hell did the planet Venus have to do with the letter *daleth* and the goddess Demeter? Was Cabala all a complicated Jewish joke at the expense of those who tried to comprehend the suprarational by rational means?

It was when Sir John had begun to seriously consider this last thought that quiet, fatherly Mr. Jones gave him his first real test, right between the eyes.

"You are familiar," he said, "with the letters that appear atop every Catholic and Eastern Orthodox Crucifix, I.N.R.I."

"Yod Nun Resh Yod," Sir John replied at once, giving the Hebrew equivalents.

[*"I nearly reached India."*]

"Very good. The Catholic and Orthodox Churches, of course, explain this in childish terms, for the simple minds of the masses. Are you, perhaps, familiar with that explanation?"

"It's supposed to be Latin," Sir John said happily; this was easy. "Iesus Nazarinus Rex Iudorem—'Jesus of Nazareth, King of the Jews.'"

"Excellent," Jones said. "Now I must inform you that there was an esoteric Gnostic meaning in those initials long before the creation of the exoteric one you have just supplied. It requires Cabalistic knowledge and the true faculty of intuition to decode it. That will be your assignment to complete before we promote you to Neophyte. Call me whenever you think you have the answer."

Sir John spent a week nearly going mad over this conundrum. On the seventh day he made up a table in which he deliberately listed only the most nonsensical and illogical correspondences, to force himself to think in the metalogical manner of the true Cabalists. The table looked like this:

Hebrew Letter	Tarot Correspondence	Astrological Correspondence	Greek Correspondence
Yod (hand)	The Hermit	Virgo	Chronos
Nun (fish)	Death	Scorpio	Hades
Resh (head)	The Sun	The Sun	Apollo
Yod (hand)	The Hermit	Virgo	Chronos

He tried letting his mind drift through the images, avoiding words and associations: hand, fish, head, hand; hand, fish, head, hand; hand, fish, head, hand . . . Dozens of ideas came to him that were original and dazzling (he once began to see evolution as a pre-written scenario . . .), but nothing came up that didn't seem like empty and windy nonsense when he re-thought it later.

He tried the astrological correspondences: Virgo, Scorpio,

the Sun, Virgo. A virgin, an insect, the Sun, and the virgin again. That was even less helpful than hand-fish-head-hand. He tried Virgin-hand, insect-Death, head-Sun, Virgin-hand. This gave rise to a line of thought which made him quite embarrassed and caused him to doubt again if he had the purity of heart to pass through Chapel Perilous successfully.

The Greek correspondences were resonant with eerie imagery. Chronos, god of Time, could be visualized gruesomely by recalling Goya's terrifying painting, *Chronos Devouring His Children*. Hades and the world of the dead were easy to invoke by remembering the descent of Odysseus to the underworld. Apollo reminded Sir John of Oscar Wilde and Lord Alfred Douglas and was harder to deal with. But what was the meaning of the sequence itself: Chronos, Hades, Apollo, Chronos?

Sir John tried contemplating the images on the Tarot cards:

The Hermit: an old man carrying a lantern in the dark. But what did that have to do with *yod*, the hand, except that you need a hand to carry a lantern? And why the correspondence with scorpions and virginity?

Death: a skeleton on a great white horse, mowing down King, Bishop, Mother and Child in his path. But what did that have to do with *nun*, a fish? Although it fit Hades, God of the dead, of course.

The Sun: a naked child on the same great white horse with the sun rising in the background. And what did that have to do with *resh*, the head? Although it fit the astrological correspondence for once.

And the old Hermit carrying his lantern again . . .

Was it a psychological parable about the path of initiation itself? The student's mind begins as an *old man* (social tradition), wandering in the *darkness* of ignorance, guided only by the *lantern of intuition;* becomes transformed through the *death* of its conditioned aspects—the links

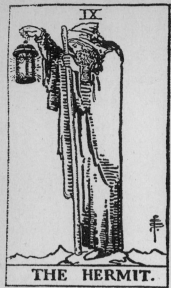

with *King* (the State), Bishop (the Church), *Mother and Child* (family); is reborn as the *sun-child* ("Unless ye become as a little child ye shall in no wise enter the Kingdom"); and then—and then—why the return to the old man wandering in the dark? It was just more nonsense, when he thought he was on the right track at last.

Hand, fish, head, hand . . .

Old man, death, newborn babe, old man . . .

I.N.R.I., Jesus of Nazareth, King of the Jews.

Chronos, god of Time (and destruction); Hades, lord of the dead; Apollo, god of the Dawn Sun; Chronos, damn it again . . .

The mental ordeal went on. And on. And on.

Sir John tried Gematria, which is the Cabalistic method of taking the numerical value of a mystery-word and relating it to all other Hebrew words having the same number. *Yod* was 10, *nun* was 50, *resh* was 200, second *yod* was 10 again. Total: 270. He plunged for days into his Hebrew

THE SUN . THE HERMIT.

dictionary and found only one example: בריחים, levers or bars.

Another blank wall.

The next night he awoke from a dream of buzzing goblins in honey-suits with the sentence clear in his head: *I Never Risk Inquiry*. He was sure this was a most profound revelation and hastily scribbled it down in his bedside notepad. In the morning he read it again and could only laugh.

But an hour later, in his library, a most peculiar accident occurred. He was reaching for his Hebrew dictionary again, looking for at least a second word with the value 270, when another book somehow got dislodged and fell at his feet. He bent to pick it up and found it was a seventeenth-century alchemical treatise, opened *at page 270*. Coincidence? The first paragraph began:

> *The secret of the Great Work is given to all true Christians by the formula I.N.R.I., which, properly interpreted, means* Igni Natura Renovatur Integra.

The translation leaped into Sir John's mind in a blinding flash: *All of nature is renewed by fire.*

An old man, death and rebirth—Time, Death and Resurrection—Crucifixion and Redemption—the Lord of Time, the Lord of the Underworld and the Golden Dawn. *All of nature is renewed by fire.* The Greek and Christian symbols flowed together and merged with the Tarot cards. Sir John's gropings toward a new theory of evolution, midway between his father's Lamarckian heresies and Uncle Bentley's Darwinian othodoxy, became agonizingly concrete as he experienced the struggle out of the caves, the raiding nomads who swept down from the deserts, the snows, the storms, the plagues, the pain, the constant death, death, death. And the onward struggle: the birth toward true consciousness, flickering dimly in all, blazing into fiery illumination occasionally. It was the cosmic birth experience relived and relived and relived until the agony and the joy became mingled and inseparable. He was the single cell swimming in the amniotic ocean, remembering the searing ecstasy of his creation: the tenderness of the first moments at the tit: the caves of Trolls he had imagined becoming real as dark archaic forces moved all about him: swimming in the hot sun, at peace: and then the terror and the horror of life again: the hunger and the violence and the lunacy: the victims of the Inquisition screaming for centuries on the torture racks of insane Faith: the devils and demons unleashed from the fantasy of terrified minds into the experience of millions: people in solitary confinement: soldiers with their arms and legs and genitals burned off: children beaten and whipped and starved: death on the operating table under the scalpel of drunken and sadistic doctors: while the carnivals and dances go on, the blind merry ones oblivious to all the agony of their brothers and sisters in the hell of man's inhumanity to life: mothers weeping over stillborn infants: the horror in the mouse's eye as it knew itself trapped: gigantic halls of enormous godly statues of peace and wisdom: eternity of mountains and oceans: the undying trees talking silently forever: carrying the cross up the hill, accepting the burden, willing to take all the pain and all the agony forever, to redeem at last the blind struggle and complete the planetary birth. Yes: the Vril was moving in him, the alchemical heat was rising: he saw far, far beyond the tiny cell called John Babcock and was one with the billions of years of the single organism that was Terra.

Was it a minute or a thousand years? Sir John didn't know; he merely knew that he and the whole world of his perception was remade by fire.

ACTION	SOUND

EXTERIOR. VALLEY OF PYRAMIDS, EGYPT. DAY. LONG SHOT.

The pyramids alone in a hot white desert.	*Voice:* "I adore thee, Evoe! I adore thee, IAO!"

EXTERIOR. SAME, CLOSE-UP.

Statue of Horus as falcon.	*Same voice-over:* "O thou laughter re-echoing from the tombs of the dead! I adore thee, Evoe! I adore thee, IAO!"

INTERIOR, DARK BACK ROOM. CLOSE-UP.

A box of money being opened.	*Same voice:* "O thou ever-turning Wheel of stars and fates! I adore thee, Evoe! I adore thee, IAO!"

INTERIOR, SAME, MEDIUM SHOT.

LENIN is opening the box of money and counting it. Across from him, offering the money, is an ambiguous figure.	*The* Merry Widow Waltz. *Lenin:* "This will pay for some very important business."

"Here is my answer," Sir John said steadily.

Jones took the Magickal Diary Babcock handed him and read slowly the latest page:

Igni Natura Renovatur Integra: *all forms are temporary and illusory, mere constructs of the imagination. The old Hermit will be struck down by Death, but the form behind the form, the life-energy, will be reborn as a new Child, which will in turn age and become the old Hermit again. Chronos, the Lord of Time, leads each of us inevitably to Death and Hades, Lord of the Underworld; but we rise again as Apollo, Lord of the Golden Dawn, rises again each morning. Christ Crucified is indeed a re-telling of these Greek death-and-resurrection myths, as rationalist historians keep telling us; but the rationalists do not understand that the myth recurs because it is profoundly symbolic of the great cosmic truth: consciousness, like matter and energy, is neither created nor destroyed. The cycles repeat and repeat and repeat endlessly, but the same recurs always, because the Platonic Archetypes remain, unchanging themselves, beyond Time.*

"There is no right answer," Jones said. They were dining, this time, at Claridge's, and Jones had brought along a very small pamphlet instead of the usual stack of fat old books. "Or, I might as well have said, there are many right answers. Someday, not in the near future, we shall have a very profound philosophical discussion about that, but for the present it shall suffice to say that your answer is right for you, at this stage of your training."

"But," Sir John said, feeling deflated, "I felt it, even before I understood it. The Vril energy, flowing through me as it flows through all things. The continuous process of destruction and recreation—the world remade by the fire of the Holy Spirit. I *felt* it," he repeated, a bit lamely.

George Cecil Jones sighed profoundly. "You have taken your first step," he said sadly, "but you don't even know yet in which direction to walk. Pray contain your self-congratulations and, for God's sake, really apply yourself to the exercises in this little pamphlet. We have scheduled your initiation as a Neophyte for next month sometime, but if you do not perform these exercises rigorously, at least four times a day, until then, it will be a false initiation—a hollow shell, a mere play-acting. Do not delude yourself that you have arrived before you have even learned how to travel."

Sir John glanced at the pamphlet, which was titled:

Astral Projection
Class-B Publication
Hermetic Order of the G∴D∴

His mood sank further. "So I am to practice getting out of my body now," he said uneasily.

Jones drank some claret neatly. "Just so," he replied calmly. "And most of the time you feel like a perfect damned fool. And you will suspect, once again, that we are a band of plausible madmen leading you to some metaphysical Bedlam. But do the exercises, record the results after each experiment, continue to show me your Magick Diary monthly for criticism and advice—and have patience, dear boy; patience! There is one further matter I must mention at this time. It will be necessary, I am afraid, for you to take an Oath of celibacy for the duration of the next two years. Will you accept that condition, or will you drop out of the Great Work, instead? Once taken, you understand, the oath is binding and will bring down terrible punishments if violated in any manner."

Sir John controlled his features with difficulty. "I remain pledged to the Great Work," he said firmly. "I will endure any trials that are necessasry."

"I must ask you three times. Are you quite sure of yourself in this matter?"

"I am." Sir John did not hesitate this time.

"And I ask you the third time. Will you be bound by this Oath of celibacy for two full years and not attempt any mental reservations or sophistries to evade or circumvent it if it becomes onerous?"

"I will be bound," Sir John said firmly.

Jones looked at his empty plate with seemingly great interest, as if searching for archaeological clues as to its age. "Celibacy, to be spiritually effective," he said mildly, quietly, "must be total. No . . . um . . . solitary vices may be allowed to console one for the absence of womankind."

Sir John felt the separate tension in each muscle of his face, thinking first: *The blood is rushing to my cheeks and I'm blushing like an imbecile schoolchild.* And then: *No, the blood is draining from my face and I look like the pale criminal in the dock,* not daring to look up at that moment lest Jones should also have looked up from his own seemingly obsessive scrutiny of his empty plate, and half-afraid also that Jones might be so advanced an Adept that reading minds was as easy for him as reading the label on a champagne bottle; yet hyper-conscious again, as in the first rising of the alchemical heat, the first sense of the Rosy Crucifixion implied in the cryptogram I.N.R.I., aware of his own awareness and afraid of his own fear: once again confronting the foreboding of insanity that had plagued him since the first timid sins of puberty, so that in a kind of hysterical paralysis he felt time itself might have slowed and, wondering if paranoia was descending upon him, thinking *I heard it,* and, *No, I only imagined it*—for it seemed that somebody at a nearby table had said distinctly, almost mockingly, the name of that which was most intimately connected with his most shameful secret.

But maybe the voice had only been mentioning Carter's, another restaurant.

"I—I—" Sir John found he could not speak.

Jones drank another sip of wine. "Two years," he said calmly, as if not noticing Sir John's nervousness, "is not so terribly long a time, you will find. And you will discover that matters astral become increasingly easy as you place matters carnal away from you. I have confidence in you, Sir John," he ended with abrupt warmth, patting the younger man's shoulder for emphasis.

And Sir John returned home for two weeks, to practice astral projection, feeling most of the time (as Jones had warned him) like a perfect damned fool.

If the I.N.R.I. riddle concerned the transcendence of time, the practice of astral projection seemed to aim at the abolition of space. The trick, Sir John soon perceived, was to be in two places at once. Since that was manifestly impossible in reason, the only way to achieve it was to go beyond reason, to deliberately cultivate a type of faith bordering on religious mania. Sir John's initial attempts were grotesque failures.

Even after three weeks of practice four times a day, the best Babcock achieved was a transportation to the innards of some incredibly complex machine with a million or more moving parts, each tended by a blue puppet and a red dwarf moving jerkily, mechanical-style, all of them talking to themselves as they worked at their incomprehensible tasks. "Mulligan Milligan Hooligan Halligan," they muttered. "Magick tragick music mystic!" they shrieked. "Simple Simon Semper Semen," they giggled. "Barter carter darter farter!" they howled. "Sir Lion, Sir Loin, Sir Talis, Sir Qualis," they gibbered. With a shudder Sir John came back into his body into his chair into his room into Euclidean space, realizing that he had dozed off when he thought he was beginning to project into the astral.

"Do not let such nonsense bother you," Jones said when Sir John showed him the Diary entry of this experience. "One can hear the same gibberish at any Revival meeting or Spiritualist séance. You have just opened a door into another of the traps in Chapel Perilous. That is the realm of those who enter the Path without the Sword of Reason. If you reflect back, you will remember hearing the same idiocy just before falling asleep many nights."

"Yes," Sir John said. "Does everybody?"

"Certainly. The mind has both a rational and an irrational side," Jones said kindly. "To remain totally rational is to become half a human. To allow the irrational to overwhelm you is to succumb to religious mania or the disease called hysteria by alienists. The Great Work consists of yoking the rational and irrational together in a harmony that transcends both. Until that is achieved, you may expect more nonsense to float up from the irrational regions. Ignore it, do not fear it, and concentrate on the Work."

In the following weeks Sir John found the astral realm and the dreamworld increasingly blending into each other, and increasingly hard to disentangle from waking reality. He heard many messages like: "Hickory dickory dock, we've got you by the cock," "The void, the zero, the nought, the Almighty," "No wife, no horse, no mustache," "A weary weary song and a blurry blurry bottleful," "For blood and wine are red," "Yoni to those pensive males," and, several times, "Babcock's going crazy, Babcock's going crazy, Babcock's going crazy . . ."

For relaxation, Sir John took to browsing in contemporary poetry, mindful of the Golden Dawn teaching that during training any extraneous reading should be limited to matter of a spiritually uplifting nature. He began to study the mystical Irish poet, William Butler Yeats.

The question "Another of us?" came back to him again and again, as he read poem after poem, and this time he had confidence enough to answer it with a definite "yes." There was no mistaking it; the poetry of Yeats was replete with oblique references to the Golden Dawn teachings and initiatory ceremonies.

And then, by the wildest of coincidences—Sir John was less and less inclined to believe in coincidences by now—he was invited to a small private reading at which Yeats and a few other poets were going to declaim some of the more recent works. Sir John accepted, feeling vaguely guilty; but then, he reminded himself, he was only forbidden to associate with other *known* members of the Order, and he did not, literally, *know* Yeats was a member, after all, since that was only a deduction, almost a guess, on his part.

A small devilish voice told him, "It's not a guess; you *do* know." But he put that aside. The chance to meet another member of the Order—a famous one, and one who, judging from the poetry, had been in the Order for at least a decade and was hence presumably quite advanced—was really irresistible. Sir John went to the reading, even though it was in the godforsaken suburb of Kensington, which was said to be even more infested with Hindus, Hebrews, Americans and other undesirables than Soho itself.

Indeed, the host turned out to be an American, of the most unbearable sort. His accent was nearly indecipherable—Sir John remembered the degenerate Oscar Wilde's really choice aphorism: "The English and the Americans have everything in common but their language." This unusual host was, like all Americans, bombastically sure of himself on all matters, especially (in his case) literature and the arts in general. His family name was Pound and his first name was one of those Hebraic titles that many Yankees seemed to favor—Ezekiel or Ezra or Jeremiah or something equally Old Testament. He had untidy red hair, a wild red beard, stood well over six feet and boomed when he talked, like all Americans. No article of clothing he wore seemed to match any other article of his apparel; whether this was due to poverty, eccentricity or both, Sir John could not quite decide.

Even the handsome Yeats himself was, if not unkempt, far from ideal in sartorial splendor, Sir John also noted; but Yeats was serene where Pound was frantic, tolerant where Pound was dogmatic and gentle where Pound was rough.

The readings were exceedingly miscellaneous. Pound read some amazingly short and unrhymed poems unlike anything Sir John had ever heard and then a very strange translation of "The Seafarer," in which he had somehow managed, in modern English, to include as many alliterative consonants and guttural assonances as the Anglo-Saxon original. A shy young lady named Hilda-something read some equally short pieces which sounded like very literal translations from the ancient Greek. Then, at last, Yeats began chanting and keening in his distinctive way, and Sir John finally heard something that sounded like real poetry to him. He almost wept with emotion at the lines:

> Romantic Ireland's dead and gone;
> It's with O'Leary in his grave

Afterward, the bombastic Pound served some of the strongest coffee Sir John had ever tasted, and led everybody into a lively discussion about what they had heard. English poetry, Pound said violently, was "trapped in the Miltonic trance," which he sarcastically caricatured as "whakty-whakty-whakty-whakty-boom! boom! whakty-whakty-whakty-boom! boom!" Experiments such as Hilda's imitations of the ancient Greeks, Yeats' recreation of Bardic forms of old Ireland and his own adaptions from the Chinese were necessary to enlarge the scope and range of verse, said this upstart. Several people immediately began protesting, and it seemed that Miltonic sonority and iambic pentameter were to them as important as the Monarchy to a Conservative.

"It appears to me," said a young lady named Lola, whose accent seemed Australian, "that poetry is invocation. If it does not *invoke*, then no matter what style it employs, it is not poetry."

"Invocation," Pound cried, "belongs in churches. Poetry should present a precise image, in the fewest possible words, so that reading it is like being hit by an April breeze. That's what leaves an impression in the mind. Invocation and repetition are all blather that detracts from the red-hot intensity of the poetic flash itself, which only lasts a moment."

"Oh, come, Ezra," Yeats protested mildly. "Repetitious rhythm is the essence of the act of love, which poetry is always, consciously or unconsciously, trying to simulate."

Before Pound could reply, the young lady named Lola brazenly replied, without a blush, "Exactly the point, Mr. Yeats. Do you know what I consider the greatest modern poem? Captain Fuller's 'Treasure House.' Do you know it?" And she quoted:

O thou brave soldier of life sinking into the quicksand of death! I adore thee, Evoe! I adore thee, IAO!
O thou laughter resounding from the tombs! I adore thee, Evoe! I adore thee, IAO!
O thou goat-dancer of the hills! I adore thee, Evoe! I adore thee, IAO!
O thou red cobra of desire that art unhooded by the hands of maidens! I adore thee, Evoe! I adore thee, IAO!

Sir John started violently and almost dropped his coffee cup. Once again the question "Another of us?" had an immediately affirmative answer. *Evoe* and *IAO*, according to Golden Dawn teachings, were two of the most secret Gnostic names to invoke divinity. He looked at Lola with astonishment, both because of these esoteric names she had quoted so casually and because nice young ladies simply did *not* speak so openly of the rhythm of the act of love. But she was looking at Yeats, awaiting a response, and her face was simply open and innocent; Sir John could not quite catch her eye.

"Captain Fuller certainly has his great moments," Yeats said, with equal innocence, as if he were not aware that two of the most secret words of Power in occultism were being casually quoted in public. "However, while a few stanzas of that are fine, the whole poem does grow a bit wearisome after three hundred stanzas. There I must agree with Ezra that brevity would have been better."

"Who—who is this Captain Fuller?" Sir John asked, trying also to sound casual.

"A great authority on military strategy, I'm told," Pound said. "Lately, he has taken to writing quite a bit of mystical verse of that sort, all of it too damned long-winded and rhetorical for my taste."

But Sir John was remembering, his pulses racing: "O thou red cobra of desire that art unhooded by the hands of maidens! I adore thee, Evoe! I adore thee, IAO!" The phallic double meaning was too overt to ignore, especially in the context of Yeats' remark about the rhythm of poetry being the rhythm of Eros. Was Lola, then, involved with one of the forbidden, lefthand lodges ("Cults of the Shadow," Jones called them) that had split from the Golden Dawn and gone off in the direction of diabolism? He looked at her again and this time he did catch her eye, but what he read there was a most enigmatic humor. Was it friendly, mocking or dangerously malign? Or was his imagination merely fevered by the fact that he was under a two-year Oath of celibacy and yet knew, for the first time, a sensual yearning strong enough to conquer both his timidity with women and the stern Victorian ethics instilled in him by his family? Was this attraction strong enough, he thought in fear, to conquer his Oath? He turned his eyes to the other side of the room, feeling a rush of blood to the face, and found himself suddenly engulfed in suspicious thoughts. Yeats, obviously, was a member of the Golden Dawn. How many others at this poetry reading were, also? Could this whole evening be a test of his Oath? He could not bring himself to look in Lola's direction again, and he left the party as soon as politeness allowed.

But that night he dreamed of Lola raising her skirt to fix her garter and she caught him looking, cawing thanes, and he was scared wild (prosing zombie-dish) pursued by a faster boog, Sid, theol bardot of sneakery. There were hatenotes and featherfurgolems and potions burning boiledest; Sir Joan, intrepid, nerveless, rapacious, idiotic, stumbled past the beehive pearlous. And the sun begin to rus, and oh up he ris, and he was all rose up, loinharted, up there so eye and moisty, baba cock of the morn, between them two toughies, for the romanz did tromp him, garther forgiven, the achtnotes hurling bricks. "Hate and be gored," sagd Shut and he saw, he was, he saw, he was, the Hideous God, Baphomet, hir dugs hanging limp, hir bigcock standing stern, under the inverse pentacle of the Tempters.

Sir John screamed as he sat up in bed with a thunderous crash shaking the room.

"Are you all right, sir?" It was the voice of Wildeblood, the butler, outside the door.

"Did you hear it, too?" Sir John asked. "I thought it was a dream . . ."

"It must have been an earth tremor, sir. Can I help you, sir?"

"No," Sir John said. "I'm quite all right, Wildeblood."

Looking across the room, he could see that the mirror

was smashed. The *poltergeist* effect: typical of the onset of astral invasions. He reminded himself of the primary Golden Dawn teachings: not to give way to fear whatever happened, and not to jump to conclusions. Wildeblood was probably right; it was only an earth tremor.

But he could not sleep again until dawn; for he had seen the face of Baphomet, the Hideous God, and he knew that his journey into Chapel Perilous was no longer confined to dream alone. The earth had literally shaken beneath him; the astral and the physical were interacting. It was "probably only an earth tremor," but it was connected, psychically, with the real opening of the door between the visible and invisible worlds.

Things That Go Bump in the Night

ACTION	SOUND
Close-Up: Dr. Carl Jung, circa 1909 [still photo].	*TV Narrator:* "One of the most eerie of such cases concerns the founder of Analytical Psychology, Dr. Carl Jung, and his equally renowned teacher, Dr. Sigmund Freud."
Cut to:	
Long shot [still photo] of Freud's study. Camera moves in slowly to tight close-up on bookcase during this speech.	*Narrator* [*voice-over*]: "During an argument about parapsychology in 1909, both Freud and Jung lost their tempers. Just then there was a sudden explosive sound from Freud's bookcase."
	[*Explosive sound.*]

Cut to:

Close-Up: Freud, circa 1909 [still photo].

Narrator: "Both men were astonished."

Cut to:

Close-Up: same photo of Jung.

Narrator: "Jung spoke first."

Actor's voice [*Swiss accent*]: "There," said Jung. "That is an example of a so-called catalytic phenomenon."

Cut to:

Close-Up: same photo of Freud.

Second actor's voice [*Viennese accent*]: "Oh, come!" Freud exclaimed. "That is sheer bosh!"

Cut to:

Close-Up: Jung.

First actor [*Swiss accent*]: "It is not," Jung replied. "You are mistaken, Herr Professor. And to prove my point I now predict that in a moment there will be another loud report!"

Cut to:

Long shot of Freud's study again. Camera moves slowly in on bookcase.

Ominous silence and then:

Second loud explosion.

Cut to:

Medium shot: TV Narrator walking on a beach. High waves in background.

Narrator [to camera]: "Freud was so disturbed by the second psychic explosion that Jung never discussed the experience with him again. Even stranger are two sequels. In 1972, Dr. Robert Harvie, a psychologist at London University, was reading aloud to a friend an account of this episode . . ."

Cut to:

Close-Up: Dr. Harvie [still photo].

Narrator [voice-over]: ". . . and at Freud's words . . ."

Viennese voice: "Oh, come, this is sheer bosh!"

Cut to:

Medium shot: Lamp in corner falling with a crash.

Narrator: ". . . a lamp in Harvie's room fell with a crash."

Cut to:

Medium shot: Actress in compartment on train, reading.

Narrator: "And in 1973, a Margaret Green reported that while reading the same passage about Jung and Freud on a train, the window suddenly smashed with a bang like a bomb."

Window explodes. Actress
jumps. Camera pans back to
door with legend:
COMPARTMENT 23.

Cut to:

Medium shot: Narrator
walking on beach.

Narrator: "What are we to
make of such mysteries? Some
scientists posit a psionic force
or bioplasma . . ."

DE MODO QUO OPERET LEX MAGICA

Sir John grimly continued his efforts at astral projection. Jones, meanwhile, became more bizarre in his teaching methods. At one of their fortnightly meetings, he
showed Sir John a cartoon from *Punch*, depicting a very
disgruntled gentleman and a very officious customs inspector glaring at each other. The customs inspector was
saying, "These cats is dogs and the rabbits is dogs, but
that bloody turtle is a *hinsect!*"

Sir John smiled uncertainly. "Amusing," he ventured
tentatively.

"It is the whole secret of Illumination," Jones said solemnly, "if you consider it deeply enough."

He insisted on giving the cartoon to Sir John, who
obediently took it home, hung it in his bedroom and
contemplated it once or twice a day. Illumination eluded
him. The differing epistemologies of common-sense trav-
elers and the authors of the customs regulations were
symptomatic of primordial ontological confusions everywhere, perhaps. But what did that have to do with matters spiritual?

At their next meeting, Jones presented Sir John with

the *Complete Works* of Lewis Carroll. "Here," he said gravely, "is the condensed essence of Holy Cabala."

Sir John flushed angrily. "This time I *know* you're having me on," he said. "It isn't worthy of you, Jones."

"So," Jones said, "you know more than your Teacher already?"

"I know a hoax, sir, when it's right in front of my nose."

Jones remained placid. "How many times," he asked, "have you encountered the saying, 'When the student is ready, the Master speaks?' Do you know why that is true? The door opens *inward*. The Master is everywhere, but the student has to open his mind to hear the Master's Voice. Read carefully, Sir John, ponder the hidden meanings, and see if the Master does not speak to you through this book."

Sir John, feeling more like an idiot than ever, took Lewis Carroll home and re-read all of it, cover to cover; and he was astonished at how much of it coincided with his own limited successes in astral projection. Were there even deeper meanings that would become clear when he had progressed farther in the Work?

A few nights later he awoke from sleep convinced that he understood the Secret of Secrets. It was in one of Carroll's couplets:

> He thought he saw a banker's clerk descending
> from a bus;
> He looked again and saw it was a hippopotamus

The elation lasted for several minutes. Then he looked at the cracked mirror and saw his own reflection split in two. The whole world split in shatters, broken glass and jewels. This time he knew the explosion was psychic: neither Wildeblood nor any of the other servants would hear the demolition.

He got out of bed very carefully and lit a candle. Sitting

in the windowseat, listening to the beating of his heart, trying to breathe normally, he was overwhelmed by the crack's sudden ability to change rhythmically from an acute angle to an obtuse angle while visions poured through of worlds with seven moons, worlds with nineteen suns, somadust and 358 and fnord, magick castles in the mist, paladins in white and black armor, aeons of the rhythmic alteration from acute angle to obtuse angle, vast insectoid intelligences, wider and wider vistas of planets, galaxies, whole universes profoundly alien, the Demon-Sultan howling in the darkness where the moon doesn't shine. "These dogs is cats and these mice is 3.141593, but those bloody garters are incest. Illigan Nillagain Rilligan Illagain. Eat a live toad before breakfast and *nothing worse* will happen to you all day." Sir John did exactly the right thing. From memory, concentrating deeply, ignoring the semenduets and obtuse rondels, he wrote in pen the five axioms and twenty-three definitions from Euclid's Geometry. Within half an hour he was in normal space-time again and the Lord of the Abyss of Hallucinations had been vanquished.

FURTHER REFLECTIONS OF JAMES JOYCE
(Parental discretion advised)

Ineluctible network of coincidence: at least that if no more. Myriads of worldlines, Professor Einstein would say, but behind them, invisible, intangible, the enigmatic links of a dark design; indifferent, paring their fingernails. Dialectic: Yeats, the one man in all Ireland who has tried to help me, to advance my career, yet the one against whom I must struggle to the end, since either his vision or mine will define the future of our literature.

Joyce contemplated worldlines coiling back to the beginning. Karma, or the cause of all causes. Inexplicable and inextricable. Garters, by all that's holy. Network of coincidence. Ezra, son of Homer, by damn.

Strangest of all: in Babcock's life this episode of Pound and Yeats is just a subplot, an incident. Was Hamlet a subplot in the career of Fortinbras similarly?

I.N.R.I.: Iron Nails Ran In. A guess made by a Protestant boy in Dublin how many years ago?

Einstein's intelligent spaniel eyes: so much less prepared for this than I, who listened half-believing once to the Dublin annex of this Golden Dawn. What can he be thinking of Yeats and Babcock and their friends trying to leap outside space-time entirely?

But the series of Barter Carter Darter Farter? What comes next? Garter.

Genus eutaenia, of course. Ancient tempter. They eat mice, shed skins in spring: in a garden, the man and woman naked and unashamed. One bite of the apple and kerflooey.

Maybe they should have taken two bites.

Bite, again. Again, bite.

Homosexual terror behind a great deal of it. The card old Queensborough sent to Wilde at his club, to provoke the Libel trial: "To Mr. Oscar Wilde, posing as somdomist." Must have spotted that five or six times in those dreams.

Wonder if Babcock knows, any better than Queensborough, that it should be spelled "sodomist."

But the solace berry? Some link with Salisbury? Can't quite make that one yet. Very Oedipal overtones, though.

Got it, by Jesus. "My goodness gracious," said Brother Ignatius.

> From deep neath the crypt of St. Giles
> Came a shriek that re-echoed for miles
> "My goodness gracious,"
> Said Brother Ignatius
> And something and something and smiles?

Not that at all. Start all over.

Hunter: Odysseus in Dublin. Time's cuckold. A wife too long alone. *Honi soit qui mal* . . .

Nora, Stanislaus: Did they? Once, even? Or many times? No matter. Having rejected monogamy once, may I assert it now? Nobody is property. Noninvasion of the noninvasive individual. *Non serviam.* Back to my Byronic posturing. But did they? Will I ever know? Not in this world, certainly.

Worldlines, crossing, intersecting, splitting: Minkowski's geometric image of the professor's theory.

. But did she? Nora, panting, eyes rolling upward all white, again again again. In her. Deeper, deeper. Fucking her. Fucking deeper. In her. Hot cunt, his then not mine. Hot wet cuntmouth.

Masochism. Stop this.

A horned man's a monster, Iago.

Wordlines: Nora and Jim and Stanislaus, crossing, intersecting, splitting: Giorgio and Lucia splitting and going off as new vectors. Ever-branching time-river.

Mother, Nora, *die Lorelei:* sucking us down, calling us home. Human body 80, 90% saline: the topaz sea, the salt taste of her body's caverns. Odysseus put wax in his ears against the dark uterine call, the song of the drowned kingdom. Davy Jones' locker. Cold dank clammy death it must be, to drown. Not Wagner: *ertrinken, versinken, Unbewusst, hochste' Lust.* Not that at all. But the Thing in the Loch?

Probably just some large relative of *Natrix.*

But if all time is one time: me in 1904 and me here now. Both real, adamantine, forever. Spring does not turn into summer. Worldlines. So that if, say, twenty years from now the names of Joyce and Einstein are known to all Europe? Then, that, too, is eternally fixed, next turn in the worldline.

And those who are ahead of us in linear time, looking back, our future their past: they will see exactly what we are half-blindly stumbling toward. Tomorrow's tragedy and joy. Who will die and who will live.

ACTION	SOUND
INTERIOR. CLOSE-UP. Map of the Austro-Hungarian Empire, 1914. CAMERA pans in rapidly on Sarajevo.	*The* Merry Widow Waltz.

EXTERIOR. TRACKING SHOT. STREET IN SARAJEVO.

CAMERA pans up from street to window.	*The* Merry Widow Waltz.
CAMERA looks through win- dow: a man is loading a gun.	*Unidentified voice:* ". . . the usual deranged lone assassin, of course . . . suitably hypno- tized . . ."

INTERIOR. CLOSE-UP.

Hands loading the pistol. On the table below is a book ti- tled *Not the Almighty*, with the eye-in-triangle symbol on the cover.	*The* Merry Widow Waltz.

THE RADIO ANNOUNCER: And now another fast-breaking story from our Linz correspondent. It appears that Sir John Babcock was not the only impressionable youth whose life was powerfully influenced by Bulwer-Lytton's romantic novels of the Vril energy. We have in our studio August Kubizek, a longtime friend of Adolf Hitler. Would you mind telling our audience, Herr Kubizek, what you were just telling us about the Linz Opera House in 1906? VOICE OF KUBIZEK [aged and weak]: Well, sir, it was in June of '06, I think. Adolf and I went to hear Wagner's opera *Rienzi*, you see. . . . ANNOUNCER: And what was the source of that opera, Mr. Kubizek?

KUBIZEK: It was adapted from the novel of the same name, by Lord Bulwer-Lytton.

ANNOUNCER: And did it concern the Vril energy?

KUBIZEK: Oh, *ja*, of course. Everything Bulwer-Lytton wrote had something to do with the Vril and the mutation to a super-race.

ANNOUNCER: And how did the opera affect young Adolf Hitler?

KUBIZEK: It was astounding. I never before saw Adolf like that. He literally seemed to be in trance. In fact, when we came out of the Opera House, he started to walk in the wrong direction . . . not toward our homes, but in the opposite direction, if you follow me. I had to run after him and shake him to get his attention.

ANNOUNCER: And then what happened, Herr Kubizek?

KUBIZEK: It was unbelievable. As I said, I never saw Adolf like that before—although I saw him that way many times in later years. He was like a man possessed. He spoke with great excitement, like a patient with a high fever, *verstehen sie?* He said that he had received a mandate from Higher Powers, through Wagner's music, and would devote his whole life to a mission ordinary human beings could not understand.

ANNOUNCER: A mission that ordinary human beings could not understand—he used those exact words?

KUBIZEK: How could I forget? He was an unimpressive fellow then—I had never heard him use such highflown language before.

ANNOUNCER: And did you ever receive subsequent information that confirmed the importance of *Rienzi* in Hitler's life?

KUBIZEK: Absolutely. It was in 1938. Adolf visited the home of Wagner's widow, and I was with him. He told her all about that experience in 1906. He was very emphatic. He wanted to make sure that Frau Wagner understood how important it was to him. He even went so far as to say to her—I remember his words because there were tears in his eyes—"In that hour National Socialism began."

ACTION   **SOUND**

EXTERIOR. STOCK SHOT. NUREMBERG RALLY, 1936.
Hitler reviewing an endless   *The* Horst Wessel Lied *grow-*
succession of goosestepping   *ing louder and louder.*
Nazi soldiers.

                                     The marching boots growing
                                     louder until they drown out
                                     the music.

Darkness.   *The marching boots, louder*
                                     and louder.

PART TWO

Not even in that modern evasion, the plea of insanity, can we find any hope. Nothing is clearer than that these wretched victims of Satan were in full possession of their faculties to the last moment.

> —Rev. Charles Verey, *Clouds Without Water*

The Old Ones were, the Old Ones are, and the Old Ones shall be. After summer is winter; and after winter, summer. They ruled once where man rules now; where man rules now, they shall rule again. Not in the spaces we know, but *between* them, They wait serene and primal, undimensioned and by us unseen.

> —*The Necronomicon*

I defy you, Jesus, I, the priestess of this rite whose body is now both altar and offering, to strike me with lightning if your power is greater than my Lord and Master's.

> —Leon Katz, *Dracula: Sabbat*

This is, indeed, a great wall.

> —Richard M. Nixon, at the Great Wall of China

It had better be stated here and now at the outset that the weird and unscientific thinking typical in different ways of both Joyce and Babcock was entirely alien to Professor Einstein's well-disciplined mentations. A black camel beneath a horned moon might be an omen of almost anything and everything to either Joyce or Babcock, but it was a domesticated mammal conjunct to the burned-out satellite of a type-G star to science.

As he listened intently to Sir John Babcock's wondrous tale, Einstein occasionally allowed a quiet smile to break upon his lips—the reflex of an evolutionary past in which furry ancestors similarly bared their teeth at the sight of food; but it was the meat of pure thought that inspired the typical anthropoid grin in this case, the marvelous (albeit blind) processes of evolution have produced a brain, in advanced human beings such as Einstein, capable of hungering and thirsting after Truth itself.

Science, it cannot be too often repeated, deals with actual readings of actual instruments, while permitting only the most economical descriptions of the phenomenon recorded. It is permissible, of course, to posit certain *gedankenexperiments* (thought experiments), thereby deducing from known laws the necessary consequences of hypothetical situations. Within an interstellar elevator, for instance, the gravitational equations of Sir Isaac Newton will appear to be obeyed, as indicated by all instruments, thereby leading physicists within the elevator to posit the Newtonian explanation of their observations. To a physicist *outside* the elevator, however, the same data will be explained by the law of inertia. This line of thought had been amusing and perplexing Professor Einstein for some time now, but he determined to set it aside and concentrate his analytical powers upon the Gothic novel in which Sir John Babcock evidently lived and in which occult forces were more prevalent than scientific laws.

There is, he began to see, a principle of neurological relativism, as well as of physical relativism. Just as he became a new Albert Einstein by rejecting his citizenship and the God of his people, Sir John had changed his nervous system by these so-called occult exercises.

Yes: my two observers trying to measure a moving rod while they are themselves moving at differing velocities. That is the relativism of the instrument. But take, let us say, a man who is a Russian vegetarian pacifist and a woman who is an Italian Catholic conservative, each trying to understand Sir John's story. None of it will mean the same to both of them. That is the relativism of consciousness, of the nervous system itself.

But the nervous system, *mein Gott*, is the instrument which reads all other instruments.

So, then: precisely as my physicists in the elevator can never tell, from within the elevator, whether the downward force is gravity or inertia, so, too, no two persons can tell, from within their nervous systems, what presumed external source provides the signals they receive. Which is why, of course, the atheist and the occultist can argue forever, without either ever convincing the other. We are trapped, trapped, trapped by our ideas, forever in the position of the five blind men and the elephant. The rules of our neurological chess game determine the form or context with which we frame each new signal. The player on the other side, as Huxley said, is hidden from us.

But all the guilt in those dreams: Can it be due to that mouse incident? Why does the mouse from the comic strip keep coming back? The whole problem belongs more to Freud than to physics, really.

Zwei seelen wohnen: Papa's favorite lines. "So deep, Albert, every word from the heart of a great man."

Poor Papa! Always worried that I was mentally defective because I wasn't like the other boys. Because? Well, I wasn't. Because I was wondering what it feels like to be a photon: How many years ago was that?

In meiner Brust. "So deep, Albert . . ."

Fifteen, I was: that would be 1879 plus fifteen, same year I renounced my German nationality, ninety-four it would be then, 1894. Around the time I read about the Bell case in the American Supreme Court. Capitalist *schweinerei:* ever since 1872 (that would be . . . um . . . seven years before I was born) fighting over who owned the electrons. Seven plus fifteen is twenty-three; twenty-three years, then, Alexander Graham Bell and his competitors squabbling over the patent. Owning electrons, *mein Gott.* All my years in the patent office. Tedium of avarice. As if anyone could *own* a law of nature. *Königen, kirchen, dummheit und schweinerei.*

But the apes still seek money, bonds, patents. Mammalian predators. Maybe on the wrong planet I was born? Only hope for humanity: heap all the currencies, bonds and shares in one lovely garbage heap and ignite them. *Walpurgisnacht.* "So deep, Albert." Yes: and let the masses dance around the flames to celebrate their liberation from age-old tyranny. The phoenix of freedom rising.

Or maybe it is genetically fixed. Predation and hierarchy date from the vertebrates. Perhaps I *am* on the wrong planet born. *Biedermeier*, they called me in school. *Biedermeier:* too stupid to lie.

In French that would be Pierrot le Fou. In English? Simple Simon. No: more like Honest John. *Biedermeier* Einstein.

Zwei Seelen wohnen ach! in meiner Brust. Must mean something. If it were Hegel, I might suspect it means nothing. But Goethe means something, always.

Uncle Jacob ridiculing the kosher laws. Well, Mama never kept a kosher kitchen, really. A house of heretics, we were. But only Uncle Jacob was an outspoken atheist. That for me was good, like the years in the Catholic school. To be born a Jew with an atheist uncle and go to a Catholic school: it opens the brain-cells. Diversity of signals.

Yes: the more conflicting signals received, the bigger we must make our world picture to account for them. People have little minds because every nation, every church and almost every family restricts the signals. So that speed of travel increasing (with also speed of communication increasing) means that everybody will receive more conflicting signals. Force the primates to get smarter, maybe. Impossible to keep a small Italian Catholic mind after meeting many, many German Protestants. The Englishman back from India is no longer 100 percent bloody English. Yes. Travel and communication will accelerate more in this century, so people will have to become smarter.

If war doesn't throw us back to the Dark Ages.

$$V'' = \frac{V + V'}{1 + \frac{VV'}{C^2}}$$

Neat, that. But pacifism more basic than socialism, it must be. If we do not put an end to war, there will be little civilization left to socialize. But try to tell that to the socialists, God help you. If the chips are down they are German or French first and socialist later. When the shooting stops. And:

$$t' = \frac{1}{\sqrt{1 - \dfrac{v^2}{c^2}}}$$

Very neat, too. Coming on to look more like curvature in the new equations. Non-Euclidean, converging. Geodesics. Not to be seen or experienced but known through the mathematics. *Nicht aus dem Sinn.*

Faster and faster communication, so every Ivan, Hans and Juan gets like me a mixture of Catholic, Jewish and atheist signals, or some equivalent jumble: force them to think and choose.

Zwei Seelen wohnen . . . Yes. The two types of consciousness, which Freud now calls conscious and unconscious, are the two souls Goethe was speaking of. Sir John's Golden Dawn is a neurological game in which the unconscious soul, called the astral body by them, is made conscious.

But even Freud does not understand the relativity of the instrument, of the nervous system itself. We three here in this room—Joyce, Sir John and myself—are existing in three different neurological realities, just exactly as my space-voyagers at different velocities exist in different spacetime realities.

The shadow-show of sight and sense: relativity of the instrument. *Nur der Wahnsinnige is sich absolut sicher.*

I wonder if any of the psychologists has discovered this yet.

It does not, of course, make a *pfennig* of difference if this Golden Dawn contraption can trace itself back to the Rosy Cross of the Middle Ages, to Adam, or even to the first amoeba. Nor does it matter if Mr. Robert Wentworth Little invented the whole "tradition" out of hot air and forged ciphers in the collaboration with the enigmatic Fräulein Sprengel. The significant objective fact on which scientific attention must focus is that by joining this organization our friend Babcock has involved himself with a secretive order engaged in projects of which he knows actually nothing, although he assumes much. Too much, in fact. As we all do, every day.

The obvious absurdity of Newton's *hypotheses non fingo:* actually, it is impossible not to theorize. The velocity of nerve transmissions in the brain is such that we can never disentangle perception from conceptualization. It is even a concept that I am presently speaking to human beings. Joyce and Babcock might both be automatons passing themselves off as humans, or I might be hallucinating. And who but Poincaré and Mach understand that fully, in their bones? We live, as Joyce says, in a web of symbolic constructs made by our brains. The *Herrdoktorprofessors* cannot understand my paper on relativity of space-time, for instance, because they think "length" is a fact, not a concept of our brains.

And this, too: when I renounced my citizenship in Milan nearly seventeen years ago, it was what the depth psychologists now call a rebirth experience: I re-defined and re-discovered myself. As when I discarded the God of my fathers. Perhaps both were necessary before I could re-define and re-discover space and time. Renunciation of the old must precede discovery of the new.

So: behind all this mumbo jumbo, that is basically, structurally, what Sir John is describing: a process whereby an orphaned boy adrift in this world with too much money is discovering a new way of defining and perceiving himself. And also, of course, his world. As I re-defined the world after re-defining myself. A chess game of the mind.

But what are the rules of this game and how did it bring him to the state of terror in which he now exists? And who or what is the player on the other side? That is what I first must grasp: the rules of this strange mind-game called the Hermetic Order of the Golden Dawn.

I must ask not, How does it feel to be a photon?, like *Biedermeier* Einstein two decades ago in 1894, but, in this case: How does it feel to be a sorcerer's apprentice?

YE GENETIC ARCHIVES

Ye first Furbish Lousewart a retainer of great green Greystoke Manor was. Of great green Greystoke Manor was he a retainer, and yea a foundling they found him fearful nigh unto death but brief hours after bloody born from mother's womb was he. A bastard born was that fair foundling, Furbish Lousewart.

Of his lineage, fair Furbish's, 'tis said that planted in his mother's belly was he by ye curate of Weems, a man most mountainous in girth that some did dub Round John or ye Holy Hog of St. Hubert's, which is because that St. Hubert's was ye church of Weems wherein as curate he did fare. Of fair Furbish's mother, in troth, 'tis said she was a nun who did later for sin sensual atone by pious pilgrimage to Thomas' tomb whereat she told a tale full fabulous to one Geoff. Chaucer who in verse the same tale did tell in his book of which all know. Some say also that model was she for ye pretty Prioress in the gypsy cards called Tarot, which card was later dubbed ye Female Pope and now ye High Priestess is yclept.

Lord Greystoke named the foundling bairn Furbish Lousewart because ye tyke so couth and dainty looked when they in mean manger found him. Furbish Lousewart was as dainty a name as leman could in Merrie England have in those days, it being the vernacular for *herba pedicularis,* a flower full fair in ye snapdragon family that no wight could name a bloom eke fairer ne bonnier.

Furbish Lousewart grew to mighty manhood, a fellow of cautels yet of mickle mirth, see ye here: for he three bold sons (legitimate) did father and seven bairns of assorted sexes (illegitimate) and then, alas, did die a death most dire in Holy Crusade against the swarthy Saracens that did hold the Holy Land by force of sword. All the world is saying yet that he (F. Lousewart) did impress posterity more through his besotted lechery than through fidelity to the holy bed of Christian marriage, for the Rt. Hon. Mr. Justice P. J. Farmer who does dabble much in genealogy and such antiquarian matters hath said on many occasions (in the hearing of many that do bear good reputation) that the only Greystoke to survive that Crusade was as it were but a pseudo-Greystoke, being seed of Lady Greystoke's lewd liaison with the aforesaid rascal, Furbish. If this be true, then the noble Greystoke line (that were Papishes but are now, folk say, good Anglicans) are actually of bastardly and plebeian origin. 'Tis a merry tale if true, all agree.

This much at least science can pronounce with mathematical certainty: within the testicles of Viscount Greystoke that night of June 26, 1914, did reside exactly one-sixteenth (0.0625) of the genetic information that formed the neuro-genetic template of Sir John Babcock, while within the testicles of Viscount Greystoke's cousin, Giacomo Celine, was precisely one-fourth (0.25) of the gentetic information of Hagbard Celine, who more than sixty years later was going to inform the grandnephew of Sir John's game-keeper that there is no enemy anywhere.

DE SOMNIIS VESTIMENTA HORRORIS

From the greatest horrors irony is seldom entirely absent, as if to remind us that there is in truth no such thing as motiveless or mindless malignity. Thus, the crack in Sir John's mirror inspired him, subtly and indirectly, to begin to accommodate himself somewhat to the twentieth century, but at the same time the hellish terrors of earlier centuries more insidiously gathered about him. The crack was only moderately disquieting at first—although he could not look into it without imagining he saw, in the distorted image of himself created by the jagged glass, some depressing and menacing symbol of the dark side of the Vril force which had attacked him through the weak spot opened up by his susceptibility to the voluptuous yearnings aroused, perhaps deliberately, by the enigmatic Lola and her brazenly casual allusions to the rhythm of the act of copulation and the red cobra of desire. He was haunted by an uncomfortable idea, although he tried to shake it off; it would be foolish certainly to accept it, on no better evidence than the coincidence of a bad dream and an earth tremor—yet the insidiously disturbing concept continued to grow in his mind: he had perhaps encountered a real witch, and the medieval world he had so long studied was seemingly coming to life around him.

The bedroom itself was now insidiously depressing to him, because of the cracked mirror and its eldritch bicameral images, yet he was also subtly uncomfortable elsewhere about the huge old house, also: something distasteful and disquieting, almost a sense of decay and morbidity, appeared to permeate the very air; something nameless and vague, a mere adumbration of new presences and possibilities, probably only his own overactive imagination, and yet something that seemed autochthonous, virtually antediluvian, furtively suggestive of hideous secrets of forgotten times and deeds that were against Nature and against Scripture. The invasion of even the furniture with this inchoate omnipresence was bewildering, if one was able to compare, in the light of the different atmosphere before the Dark Force (as he came to call it), the previous ubiquity throughout Babcock Manor of commonsense normalcy.

ACTION   **SOUND**

EXTERIOR. BABCOCK MANOR. LONG SHOT.
The house almost lost in a pan-   *Voodoo drums.*
orama of dark trees and twi-
light shadows.

EXTERIOR. BABCOCK MANOR. MEDIUM SHOT.
The house, dark and looming.   *Voodoo drums.*
The pennyfarthing bicycle in
front of the entrance.

Sir John embarked upon a campaign to banish the whole perishing business by refurbishing, not merely the cursed mirror, but the whole of Babcock Manor, and soon had the place swarming with tradespeople and laborers in a huge project of modernization, including even the installation of electricity in every room. It required many months, but finally Babcock Manor had been fully adapted to the twentieth century. The malign humor of the hideous forces unleashed against Sir John meanwhile proceeded to produce, as this superficial adaptation to the present was feverishly afoot throughout the manor, a growing invasion of his inner life by the most hellish and dismal of ancient terrors.

Sir John continued to dream often of Chapel Perilous and once he found himself in a huge dungeon beneath the earth, where crowds of sullen and stupid persons argued and debated violently. "We shall have gno gods!" shouted some. But others shouted back, "We shall have gnu gods!" And weenie gothor thick haggard were poor. "There is no Chapel, there is no Grail, it is all a child's fantasy," muttered a liddel bho poop, yet veni verits, surd Alice war bear, flogging thor-talis behind them. "The tree ovus, the size of us, the weight of us," sang an Erring Go BRA in groinblancorange, but a triune pentagonal octupus explained, posing as somadust. "These are those who started on the Path without the Wand of Intuition. They have arrived, but they do not know it. They have I's so they no can see. Honey to them, pansy meals. Does a BRA shith in the woods?"

When Sir John wrote this dream into his Magickal Diary, he added the comment:

> *For some reason I do not fully comprehend, I awoke with the conviction that Shakespeare was indeed an initiate of the Rose Croix. I feel closer and closer to grasping what he meant in saying that we are "such stuff as dreams are made of."*

A few nights later he allowed himself to be cajoled into a bridge game at Viscount Greystoke's, although that was precisely the sort of idiot pastime he generally despised. He barely endured the early part of the evening—there was much brandy, many cigars, and altogether too much talk about fox-hunting, a sport he despised as inhumane and barbaric. It was with great effort that he refrained from quoting the infamous Wilde's description of that bloody recreation as "the uneatable pursued by the unspeakable." Then, around ten, a strange thing happened: he suddenly remembered that the ordinary playing-card deck was derived from the Tarot. The spades were the Wands of Intuition, the hearts the Cups of Sympathy, the clubs the Swords of Reason, the diamonds the Pentacles of Valor: and the structure of the deck corresponded astrologically to fire signs, water signs, air signs and earth signs: 52 weeks in 4 seasons, 52 cards in 4 suits. But if Cabalistic signs were everywhere, the divine essence was also everywhere, and he remembered again that there were no places or times where the visible and invisible worlds did not meet and mingle: he saw the Buddha in everyone, again. The rest of the evening he was so intensely conscious that he seemed to himself to have been half-asleep all his life by comparison; he won trump after trump. The euphoria was with him for nearly a day and a half after, and then gave way to a vague anxiety again when he remembered that many forms of lunacy begin with such excited states of mentation in which every incident and event seems charged with more than human meaning.

In London two days later Sir John met the bombastic American, Ezekiel (or Ezra) Pound—perhaps by accident— at the British Museum. Pound was carrying a Chinese-English dictionary and a batch of notebooks labeled "Fenollosa MS." and was effusively cordial. They amicably agreed to step out for a bite of lunch together.

"Yeats is progressing nicely, under *my* influence," Pound pronounced grandly, over fish and chips. "He's coming out of that Celtic fog and beginning to write *modern* poetry." Sir John found this self-importance hilarious, but managed to keep a straight face. He tactfully changed the subject.

"Why are you so preoccupied by Chinese verse forms?" he asked in his most diffident manner.

"Chinese," Pound pronounced, "will be as important to the twentieth century as Greek was to the Renaissance." And he went on for twenty minutes on that topic, before Sir John was able to interpolate a remark again.

"Who was that young lady reciting Captain Fuller?" he asked, knowing that an evil impulse was driving him.

Pound looked up sharply. "She says her name is Lola Levine and she comes from France," he replied. "I doubt it. Her French is worse than mine."

"She sounded Australian . . ." Sir John said.

"Exactly," Pound agreed. "A young lady one should not trust too much. Have you heard of Aleister Crowley?" he asked.

Sir John remembered the name—one of the leaders of a

renegade Golden Dawn faction said to have turned in the direction of Diabolism. "Vaguely," he said.

"Well, whatever you've heard is probably unfavorable and you're just being English and tactful in not mentioning it," Pound said with a piercing glance. "Don't get too interested in Lola Levine, if you want any advice from me, Sir John. She is said to be, or to have been, one of Crowley's countless mistresses. Terrible things happen to people who get involved with Crowley, or his friends or mistresses. Have you heard of Victor Neuberg?"

"A young poet . . . I'm afraid I haven't read any of his work."

"Victor Neuberg got very involved with Crowley a few years ago," Pound said. "He is now recovering, slowly and painfully, from a complete nervous and mental breakdown."

"A mental breakdown," Sir John repeated. "You mean . . ."

"That's what the doctors call it," Pound said somberly. "Neuberg believes he is under siege by demons."

"Oh," Sir John said, "how ghastly."

"Yes," Pound answered with a level stare. "That's the sort of thing that happens to people who get too close to Crowley and Lola Levine and their circle. Neuberg even claims Crowley once turned him into a camel."

"Into a *camel?*" Sir John exclaimed.

"Well," Pound said, "I suppose it would be more traditional to turn him into a toad, but Crowley by all accounts has a singularly eccentric sense of humor."

"Do you believe Neuberg really did turn into a camel?" Sir John asked, wondering just what Pound's attitude toward all this really was.

"Hellfire, no!" Pound laughed scornfully. "But I do believe that if you get mixed up with a gang like that, and really get into yoga and meditation and group sex and drugs and howling invocations at Sirius, you'll damned soon end up believing whatever the other lunatics in the group believe."

On that note, the lunch ended and they parted. Sir John found himself wondering if he was ready, yet, to believe in the metamorphosis of a human being into a camel. The idea seemed to belong not to the true tradition of mysticism as he had come to know it through the Golden Dawn, but to the realm of folklore, witchcraft and old-wives' tales: and yet the disquieting thought remained, trailing him about like an unpaid usurer, *Something happened to poor Neuberg, something that the alienists are perhaps not ready yet to understand or heal.* If we are such stuff as dreams are made of, these eldritch forces which Macbeth so evocatively calls "night's black agents" are as powerful as anything in the masquerade of social life with its timid decorums and deceptions; and thinking also, *There is Cabalistic logic in it:* the camel corresponds to the Hebrew letter *gimmel*, which corresponds to the Masked Priestess in the Tarot, the guide across the Abyss of Hallucinations to the undivided light of Pure Illumination.

It was only another accident, of course—only another coincidence—but Sir John actually encountered Lola Levine in Rupert Street later that afternoon. There was no mistaking that dark brown hair, those strange brown eyes, that enticingly voluptuous figure to unhood the cobra of desire. By the grace of God, she didn't notice him and he passed by quickly, hardly thinking of her petticoats and garters and those things.

That evening, however, he encountered her again, in a much more *outré* manner. He was performing his fourth exercise in astral projection for the day, according to the instructions in the Golden Dawn manual, and, for the third time since he had begun the practice, he achieved a state of mind where it almost believed it was real.

["It seemed real," he had told Jones after the first such experience, "but I cannot be sure. I think I am perhaps just deceiving myself and it is imagination."

["Pray do not let that bother you," Jones had replied. "It always *begins* as imagination. . . ."]

This time, Sir John, eyes tightly closed, was imagining his astral mind rising out of his body, looking down at the whole room—his physical body included—from some eerie vantage point near the ceiling, and beginning, again, to almost believe his imagination. Following instructions, he projected higher, above the earth, looking down at his estate from a great height, and then, projecting higher, looking down at England and parts of Europe. With a colossal effort, he projected higher and saw the blinding white light of the sun (behind the Earth at this hour) and the planets Mercury, Venus and Mars. It was going so well that he projected out of the solar system entirely and approached the realms of *Yesod*, the first astral plane.

And there it was, just as described in the Cabalistic books of many centuries: the two pillars of Night and Day, the masked Priestess seated on the throne: Shekinah, the embodied Glory of Jehovah.

"Who dares to approach this realm?" She asked, Her voice strangely familiar. (Or was he imagining all this? Was this practice just a trick to contact the unconscious by "dreaming" while still partly conscious?)

"I am one who seeks the Light," Sir John answered, according to formula.

"You have turned your back on the Light," She answered sharply, Her brown eyes seeming to shine or glow in an odd manner. "You have rejected Me and banded together with the Black Brothers who hate and despise My creation. Infernal nochts; rocks intangible."

"No, no," Sir John said, frantically reminding himself of the First Teaching [*"Fear is failure, and the forerunner of failure"*]. I have never rejected You."

"You have rejected the female, My representatives on Earth, and the act of joy and love which is My Sacrament. You can never pass this Gate until you conquer your fear of Woman. *Fear is failure and the forerunner of failure.*

Sir John recognized Her voice at last: it was the voice of Lola Levine. Desperately, he plunged backward toward Earth, remembering to try to calm himself: when one is blinded by panic, the teachings said, one might not be able to find one's way back to the Earth-body. In total funk, he briefly found himself in one of the alchemical planes, where a White Eagle, a Red Lion, a Golden Unicorn and Sir Talischlange pursued him through a magickal wood and the trees chanted rhythmically, "Pangenitor, Panphage, Pangenitor, Panphage, Pangenitor, Panphage . . ." Lola's voice sang in antichorus, "Io Pan! Io Pan Pan! Io Pan! Io Pan Pan!" Then, somehow, he was whirling down, down, through endless darkness, to the White Light of the sun again, the spinning Earth-globe, England, his own estate, and the bedroom in which he found himself seated, sweating, with his heart beating wildly.

He recited the great Mantra of protection: "Christ above me, Christ below me; Christ at my right side, Christ at my left side; Christ before me, Christ behind me; Christ within me." His back was cold from the sweat, and the astral heat burned his forehead; he was trembling. He repeated the Mantra three more times before he was able to feel safe again.

"If anything particularly glorious or particularly frightening happens, *write it down at once,*" Jones had instructed him. "That gets the linear, rational mind operating again—and the record will be useful to you, later."

Sir John performed a banishing ritual first, to be on the safe side, and then wrote the vision carefully in his Magick Diary. He added:

If this was just my own unconscious mind playing tricks, it is still most interesting. The chorus and antichorus invoking Pan seems to suggest that the unconscious can compose Greek poetry much more rapidly than my conscious mind could. And the ideational content of the chant—Pangenitor, all-creator; Panphage, all-destroyer—clearly indicates the identity of Pan and the Hindu god, Shiva, which is most curious, since I had never consciously understood that identity before this Vision.

I can only conclude that the above attempt at reductionism is very forced and not really convincing. Deep down I know that what happened was not merely unconscious tricks of my mind. Because my heart is not pure, because I harbor lust and carnal desire, I missed the true gate of Yesod. I did not encounter Shekinah, the female component of Jehovah, as would have happened if my heart were clean. I encountered Ashtoreth, the female Devil, and true to Her nature, She attempted to psychically seduce me. Many alchemists recorded similar meetings with the succubus, *or female lust-demon.*

Sir John repeated his banishing ritual, and gave up on astral projection for the night. He allowed himself a rather stiff brandy, to relax, and another, even stiffer, brandy before bedtime.

We do not escape our demons that easily. Sir John dreamed many things, all of them voluptuous and sensual. He wandered through jeweled and many-colored harems where Victorian newbuggers in honeysuits with camelly pants engaged in vile, nameless perversions, obscenities he had encountered before only in the evasive Latin euphemisms of Krafft-Ebing. He was wandering through the gardens of his uncle, Viscount Greystoke, and a dark serpentine Sicilian named Giacomo Celine (who claimed to be related, distantly, to the Greystokes, and, hence, to Sir John himself) was explaining earnestly something totally incomprehensible about Sex and Creation. "The male is space and the female is time," Celine said "but of course, the universe itself is bisexual."

The clowns and acrobats sang "I Never Risk Inquiry," but Yeats and Sir John were back at Pound's flat. Yeats whispered suggestively, "The culprits are bears. It's always darkest just before the storm." He was leading Sir John to another garden, past the hall of infinitely reflecting mirrors, and the Countess of Soulsburied was waiting there for him, with a face much like Lola's. She was sprawled totally naked, except for a blue garter with a silver star, on her left thigh. Goldly nude on a crimson-jeweled Arabic purrpurplebed, her left hand lewdly moving in the grove of brown hair above that maddening garter, doing that horrid disgusting thing to herself, to gather per darker bane, a bolt like a brick sheet hose, her face flushed with the same unbearable and inhuman rapture as the famous statue of Saint Teresa in Rome. "To the puer, all things are puella," Yeats mumbled, vanishing with myriad reflections into infinite mirrors.

Sir John threw himself upon Lola, kissing the garter rapturously, mad with hatred, love and desire, and she whispered, "All things are Buddha. Evil to him who thinks evil of it." And her thighs were wrapping around him, sucking him down, down, down into ecstasy so intense he cared not if it were divine or diabolical.

"Little check on her? Liddel chick honor?" Sir Talis Saur chanted. "If god is dog spelled backward," he hissed, lisping, "what does that mean? Not the Almighty?" But Sir John was fucking a fox-bitch in heat, groveling in the mire: mind and heart and soul lost in the Night of Pan.

His heart beating wildly, Sir John shot up from sleep, moaning, the evidence of orgasm dark and dank on his pajama crotch.

ACTION	**SOUND**

INTERIOR. BUCKINGHAM PALACE, THRONE ROOM.
  MEDIUM SHOT.

DISRAELI whispering to QUEEN VICTORIA.	*Disraeli:* "That infamous Babcock lad has gone and done it again."

VICTORIA registers horror.

DISRAELI lowers his voice further.	*Disraeli:* "And this time it's worse than ever. *No hands!*"

INTERIOR, THRONE ROOM. CLOSE SHOT.

VICTORIA furiously angry.	*Victoria:* "The absolute rotter! Call out the guard! I want him flogged at once!"

DE FORMULA LUNAE

"I have encountered a succubus," Sir John said, guiltily, knowing it was all his own fault.

"Indeed," Jones replied most mildly. They were dining at Simpson's again, and Jones seemed strangely absentminded and preoccupied. "Was this in a dream or on the astral plane?"

"Both," Sir John said, beginning to know how a Catholic feels in the confessional booth.

"Were you able to ward her off successfully?"

"I tried," Sir John said weakly.

"In other words, you did not succeed." Jones looked irritated, as if he had other problems and did not need this. "We will have to postpone your initiation as Neophyte until this matter gets resolved," he added thoughtfully. "Let me see, you have the astral projection booklet, and that contains the Banishing Ritual of the Pentagram. I advise you to try it several times, until you feel the invading presence has been entirely driven away from you."

And he skipped his usual postprandial cordial, ending the meal with uncharacteristic abruptness, rushing off with the look of a man who has more problems than he can deal with at the same time.

Sir John returned home in a mood of dejection and apprehension. What do you do when your teacher clearly indicates that your problems are of minor importance compared with the other burdens he is carrying? Dark suspicions were beginning to gather about him, and Jones hadn't given him a chance to discuss that at all. But Sir John remembered all too well the many references he had read to the Dark Rosicrucians, the Black Brotherhoods, the group who devote themselves to vexing, haunting and seducing all those who embark on the spiritual path of the Great Work. Was it possible that Lola Levine and her mysterious master, Crowley, were conspiring to destroy the true Golden Dawn by launching astral attacks on new and not very advanced students like himself?

Sir John tried the Banishing Ritual several times, but it was mere play-acting. He felt nothing; he perceived nothing new; he realized that his confidence in himself was weak. Finally, in a mood of mixed bravado and nervousness, he began to study a few of the books on Black Magick he owned—books he had only glanced into with repugnance and fear before. Now, he forced himself to read carefully and scrupulously, determined to understand the forces that might be attacking him.

After all, he had been performing the Banishing Ritual for several months now, accepting Jones' bland explanation that the purpose was to banish all the impure parts of himself that might interfere with the Great Work. But now he wondered if the real purpose might not be to banish forces or entities of which it were better that the Neophyte did not know, lest he succumb to the fear which was failure.

He read of the nameless ritual of the Black Goat with a Thousand Young, of the fiery Serpent Power that could be raised from the aroused genitals to the brain itself by forbidden sexual excesses, of the foul Eucharist of Immortality drunk in unspeakable rites by those who would replace God by Man. With nausea and near-dizziness, he began to understand the Satanic logic behind this medley of filth, blasphemy and perverted transcendentalism—the secret Gnostic teaching that *Neschek*, the Serpent in Genesis, having the number 358, which is also the number of *Messiah*, the Serpent *is* the Messiah. (Since all words with the same Cabalistic value numerologically are names of the same metaphysical entity.) He learned the Manichean interpretation of I.N.R.I.—*Ingenio Numen Resplendet Iacchi:* the true God is Iacchus (Dionysus)—and the logic, although wicked, was clear to him: lewdness and prolonged sensuality, to this mad philosophy, were the essence of the ecstasy which could blot out ego and raise Man to Godhood. He was literally ill after a day of this research and trembled at the thought of the lunatics who believed such things and the deeds they would be willing to perform.

Sir John decided to try the Invocation of the Holy Guardian Angel, even though that was considered risky for those below the Grade of Master of the Temple.

Nothing happened—except that the invocation unleashed stronger fear and wilder hope than Sir John had ever before experienced. But perhaps the intensification of emotion was all the Invocation could be expected to produce in a Probationer.

But a few minutes after closing the ritual and breaking the circle, Sir John suddenly felt an impulse to write. What came from his pen was not an account of the invocation and its results, as he should have written if he had been following Jones' teachings, but rather a neoplatonic dialogue with the obsessing spirit of Lola Levine, the Black Priestess:

CULPA URBIUM NOTA TERRAE

I: This filthy, swinish philosophy, this black perversion of civilization and ordinary decency—how can you possibly believe it is the path to higher wisdom, to the Over-Man?

SHE: Nay, think not that thou hast Wisdom when thou art still Trapped in the Accursed Deed. Know in thy Heart and Bowels, not just in the Verbalizing Mind, that the Great Tao must always be in Balance, for Excess of Disciplined YANG energy is most dangerously Explosive: and the worst Wars of all History are fast coming upon ye for That. Hear Me: for the Psychic Equilibrium of Humanity it is necessary to follow the Swing of the Pendulum to the Joyous, Dionysian, yea even Mindless, Recorso of YIN. The Male must cease to Tyrannize over the Female, the Rational over the Irrational, the Spirit over the Flesh. We must become One and Undivided again, in the White Light and Ecstasy of the Horned God, Iacchus, lest all fall into the Pit of Because and perish with the Dogs of Reason. The Spirit is upon Me even as I write through thine unwilling Hand. O I adore thee, Evoe! I adore thee, IAO!

I: That doctrine spawned the licentiousness that destroyed Greece and Rome; it is the plausible lie that justifies every depravity. The opposites are not intended to unite, but to fight until Light triumphs over Darkness. The human soul is the battleground of God and the Devil and they are not One. Good is not Evil; God is not the Devil.

SHE: The soul limited by Yea and Nay is a Prisonhouse and breeds Pestilence. Ask it of the Wise Rabbins who made the Holy Cabala and See what Mighty Clue they left for those with Eyes to See: for are not *Neschek* and *Messiah* both by Enumeration 358? What signifieth this? It is a Sign pointing the Way to the Truth that is beyond all Duality, beyond all Concept, beyond the accursed Dungeon of Yea and Nay. I am possessed again by the unspeakable nameless Night of Pan. Pan! Io Pan! I adore thee, Evoe! I adore thee, IAO!

I: You're a mental lunatic, you are. Take your damnable blasphemies and your vile pseudo-philosophy and your garters and get out of my head, damn you!

SHE: The Truth whereof I speak is even in your Tree of Life symbolism, O Rosicrucian. Just as the Tao is both white *yang* and black *yin*, so, too, on the Cabalistic Tree, does not *Kether*, the Supreme, manifest as both *Chokmah*, the Male principle of Light, and *Binah*, the Female principle of Darkness? In your Bible, does not Saint Paul say that the illuminated soul is "not under law, but under grace"? Does not Saint Augustine tell us to "Love, and do what you will"? Grace is given to Those Wise Ones who are beyond Good and Evil, beyond Mind and its empty Concepts, swept up in the Rapture of Mindless Unity. The spirit again moves in Me, and in your Hand, and we can only cry: I adore thee, Evoe! I adore thee, IAO!

I: Aye, the Devil can quote scripture to his own purpose. But these obscene rituals, this reveling in carnal desire, is the black downward path, to Earth, and the true path is upward, to the starry heavens.

SHE: If all Beings are in truth Buddha, how can Any of Them be Evil? If all energy proceeds from the Undivided Light, as you Cabalists say, how can any Yearning of the Human Heart be in opposition to the Light? You drive yourself Mad with false Dualisms and then forsooth wonder why you cannot achieve the inner Unity for the Great

Work. I who speak am the Mother and Whore of all Men. I am the dark Womb and the dank Night from which Creation begins. I am Shekinah, the embodied glory of Jehovah. I adore thee, Ya-ha-weh! I adore thee, *IAO!*

I: Thou art Ashtoreth, the lust-demon, and I banish you now in the name of He Whom the Winds Fear, the Lord of the Universe, the True God Whose name is

SHE: Do not blasphemously write the Name you have not the wit to understand. I will Leave you now, for a While, but be not Deceived. You have only Banished one Half of Yourself. In your disunited Soul you will grow only foolish Fear and muddy Hatred. Go play with those garters you hid in the closet when you were eighteen.

Sir John threw his pen across the room, to break the spell. It had truly become as if another spirit were writing through him; it was indecent, worse than the time a groping pervert had fondled him on a train, when he was sixteen and too shy to cry out—he had pulled away furtively, ashy-faced; but this was a more vile, a more personal, invasion.

He felt soiled and polluted.

His mind was still racing with Lola's implanted heresies. "I am the Lord: I create Good and I create Evil." "When the Adept crosses the Abyss, all opposites become One to him." "Brahman is the slayer and the slain." "Hear, O Israel: the Lord our God is One!" "ARARITA: One in His origin, One in His individuality, One in His permutations." The Alchemist "must descend to every depth, plunge into the fires of Hell, before he can accomplish the Great Work." Original Sin was the first dualism, "the Accursed Dyad" denounced by all Cabalists. "All is One." "All is Tao." "All is Buddha." The mystics of all ages seemed to be on Lola's side. 358: the Messiah and the Serpent are One. That was the meaning (or one meaning) of those incoherent dreams about "the tree Swifty ate." 358: one in His permutations, one in His origin.

"The Devil can quote *all* the world's Scriptures," Sir John muttered.

With a prayer for grace, he attempted Bibliomancy, the art of receiving divine guidance by opening the Bible at random, sticking in a finger, and reading the verse so discovered. He found that he had entered near the end of the New Testament and was in the Epistle of Jude. He read with greet intensity:

> *Clouds they are without water, carried about of winds; trees whose fruit withereth, without fruit, twice dead, plucked up by the roots; raging waves of the sea, foaming out their own shame; wandering stars, to whom is reserved the blackness of darkness forever.*

This was certainly ominous enough, and the context, when Sir John began skimming it, was even more foreboding:

> *Even as Sodom and Gomorrah, and the cities about them in like manner, giving themselves over to fornication, and going after strange flesh, are set forth for an example, suffering the vengeance of eternal fire.*
> *Likewise also these filthy dreamers defile the flesh, despise dominion, and speak evil of dignities.*

What more clear warning could there be against Lola Levine and the infamous Crowley and all those pseudo-mystics of this age who attempt to exalt sensuality as sacred and eroticism as holiness? But the Epistle continued, growing even more explicit and speaking directly to the temptations Sir John had experienced:

But, beloved, remember ye the words which were
spoken before of the apostle of our Lord Jesus Christ;
How that they told you there should be mockers in
the last time, who should walk after their own un-
godly lusts.

Every word was like a flame eating into Sir John's
conscience, revealing the horror of that which had almost
seduced him. He wept with repentance and joy: he was
saved. A direct communication had come, from the God
of his Fathers, and Lola and her lying heresies were
banished. He was free.

"Clouds without water," he repeated to himself. "Ster-
ile, dark, sinister—but empty. Lies, lies, all lies. I am free
of them, free!"

In later years he was to remember that moment, wondering how he had been so blind. The real terrors were
still ahead of him, and Jude "the Obscure" had, like many
an oracle, prophesied more than could be understood
until much time had passed and many strange events had
transpired.

DE AURO RUBEO

It must be reiterated that, among the domesticated
primates of Terra at this time, what they sonorously called
the-Supreme-Virtue-of-not-poking-one's-nose-into-the-affairs-
of-the-authorities was still universally esteemed as the
very pivot and fountainhead of what was, among them,
known as living-in-accord-with-the-Divine-Plan-as-revealed-
to-us-in-church-on-Sundays. Basic epistemological and ontological questions were never raised in "polite society,"
that is, among those described by Galaetic Intelligence as
so-objectively-hopeless-in-their-idiocy-as-to-be-subjectively-
convinced-of-their-own-superiority-to-the-other-wild-and-

domesticated-apes. This tragic and absurd condition, found on no other planet, however backward, in the Great Universe, was due entirely to the imprinting of their nervous systems by what are scientifically described in the *Trans-Galactic Encyclopedia of Primate Psychology* as chemically-bonded-reflex-arcs-causing-primate-perception-to-be-limited-to-"realities"-accidentally-present-at-moments-of-imprint-vulnerability, which is to say that in most cases, only that which caused adrenaline secretion was perceived as visible or tangible in their rudimentary brains. Science had already revealed to them, of course, that 99.99% of the physical universe was invisible to their senses, but they were not capable of deducing from that that an equal part of the mental and spiritual universes was also unperceived by them as they robotically proceeded about their mammalian business of survival, reproduction and nurturing of their cubs.

A MOſT CURIOUſ HIſTORY TRUE ſTORY OF THE ROſY CROſſ

From Abramelin of Araby came the Sacred Word unto Abraham the Jew, who was called to the sublime Task of the Illuminati, wherein he durst master every Detail of the Great Work, so that he might in due season accomplish it not only for himself, but for all Persons in those ages in which Darkness lay upon the West. As it is written: *Suum Cuique.* And Abraham did in good Time pass the Secret unto many who understood but In Part and, finally, unto our Master, Christian Rosenkreuz (or in the Tongue of the English, Christian Rosycross) who by the Grace of the Trinity did come at last to understand the Whole. *Sis benedictus:* in the name of Allah, the Compassionate, the All-Merciful.

Whom men call Giordano Bruno or The Nolan was a

Magus of our Holy Order; and his Teaching was Heliocentricity, not merely in the material Sense for which the Black Brothers of Rome did seize him and cruelly Burn him at the Stake: but also in the spiritual sense, in that the Ego or Self known to Man is, like unto the Earth, *not the center of consciousness but merely appeareth so by a species of Glamour or Delusion.* And Bruno the Nolan taught all Men that hath the Wit to Read Between the Lines that the True Center of the Soul is like unto the Sun: a White Light from which cometh all Life on Earth: that is to say, all impressions upon the Ego.

Cagliostro hath names and forms innumerable, and we know not his true human Birth. But in many Lands and Times hath he appeared, under divers Names and Titles, and yet we may recognize him by his Teaching which was, is, and shall be, that conscious Thought is but Epiphenomena, the Noise of the Machine. Now Al-Chem-y meaneth the Egyptian Science, and the True Science of Egypt hath this for Fountainhead: we have in our House many substances which act directly upon the Blood, thereby befogging Vision, and we have in Nature many substances which act also directly upon the Blood, to correct Vision. He who hath Ears, let him Hear: *de magno opere.* In the Name of the Father and of the Mother and of the Son. Amen.

And in the Age of Science that came to Flower in the nineteenth century after the Magus of Nazareth, the true Order of the Rose Croix did go Underground, as a Seed that must be buried ere it Sprout: for it was nigh approaching Time to reveal the true Secret of the Cosmic Furnace and the Alchemical Heat unto all humanity. And great preparations were Made, in deep Secret, to prepare for the event. And many experiments were Performed, of which men know not yet, but one such Experiment was the creation in London City of the Hermetic Order of the Golden Dawn, of which the True Name was *Comoedia Quae Pan Dictur.*

EXPERIMENTS IN ASTRAL PROJECTION

The Alchemical Heat Increases

So, anyway, two years passed. Germany and France almost went to war over a gunboat in Morocco, but then an uneasy peace was negotiated at the last moment. The Chinese became a democratic republic. Amundsen reached the South Pole and excited the imagination of the world. Sir John, who more and more regarded himself as a Liberal, rejoiced when the House of Commons passed a bill granting Home Rule to the Irish, and then wrote an angry letter to the *Times* when the House of Lords voted it down. A Dane named Niels Bohr electrified the scientific community by suggesting that quantum discontinuities caused the interior of the atom to follow Rutherford's model, similar to the solar system itself; and Sir John was amused that science was finally catching up with the traditional Hermetic teaching that "the things above are reflected in the things below."

Sir John himself had become, in many respects, a new man under the slowly rising Alchemical heat of celibacy and magick. He advanced from Neophyte to Zelator, from Zelator to Practicus. He was trained in *asana*, a yogic contortion that twisted the body just as Cabala twisted the brain, and emerged with better health, better self-control and better humor than ever. He also learned *pranayama*, a special breathing technique which seemed to vanquish most negative emotions and kept him vaguely euphoric most of the time. His study of Cabala, under Jones' merciless hounding, advanced to the point where it now seemed as natural to his mind as *asana* to his body; he could hardly remember how contorted and difficult both had seemed at first. And his journeys on the astral plane increasingly magnified his understanding of himself and others, even though he was still unsure much of the time whether these visions were real or imaginary.

He even saw Lola Levine at a concert one night and was neither frightened nor attracted, although he couldn't help visualizing her thighs and garters.

Then, one day in Soho, he was browsing through the shelves of used bookstalls and found a volume entitled *Clouds Without Water*. At this point, he no longer believed in coincidences: he knew that what the ignorant call by that name are actually occult clues which can instruct the Adept in important spiritual matters, once he had deciphered their meaning. He picked up the book and began browsing.

One group of poems was entitled "The Alchemist," and Sir John remembered, nostalgically, his premature sense of total enlightenment when he had deciphered I.N.R.I. as the alchemical *Igni Natura Renovatur Integra*—the whole world is re-made by fire. Turning the pages, he stopped at the fifth poem and read:

> the eternal spring, the elixir rare
> That mage and sage have sought and uncomplaining
> Never attained. We found it early where
> The Gods find children.

Sir John stared at the book in mute astonishment. That could not possibly refer to the perversion his mind had shamefully read into it. After all, this was not a Black Magick grimoire, but only a collection of poems. He looked back at the title page:

CLOUDS WITHOUT WATER

Edited from a private MS.

by the

REV. C. VEREY

Society for the Propagation

of Religious Truth

Privately Printed

For Circulation Among Ministers of Religion

1909

Sir John felt chagrined. How silly of him to imagine Diabolism in a book put out by some Scottish Presbyterian. But what did those lines mean, then?

Sir John skimmed a few more pages at random. The whole series of poems seemed to be a glorification—virtually a sanctification—of adultery. This couldn't be. Then he saw a footnote by the Rev. Verey:

Only a Latin dictionary can unveil
the loathsome horror of this filthy word.

Sir John looked back to the word thus indirectly defined, or rather not defined at all, and found it was *fellatrix*. He blushed; but then he remembered again: "We found it

early *where the Gods find children."* Could such nameless
things be printed?

In Sonnet VIII of the Alchemical sequence, he found
the lines:

> Now I have told you all the ingredients
> That go to make the elixir for our shame
> Already make the fumes their spired ascents;
> The bubbles burst in tiny jets of flame

The elixir of shame, he knew, was in Satanic theology
the Eucharist of Immortality; it was found only within the
pudendum of a sexually ecstatic woman. This book was
almost his early half-hallucinatory visions of the corrupt
Lola Levine come back to haunt him in print. He turned
to the Preface:

> *"Receiving in themselves that recompense of their
> error which was meet."*
>
> *So wrote the great apostle nearly two thousand
> years ago; and surely in these latter days, when Satan
> seems visibly loosed upon earth, the words have a
> special and dreadful significance even for us who—
> thanks be to God for His unspeakable mercy—are
> washed in the blood of the Lamb and freed from the
> chains of death and of hell.*
>
> *Surely this terrible history is a true Sign of the
> Times. We walk in the last days, and all the abomina-
> tions spoken of by the apostle are freely practised in
> our midst. Nay! they are even the boast and the de-
> fense of that spectre of evil, Socialism.*
>
> *The awful drama which the unhappy wretch who
> penned these horrible utterances has to unfold is
> alas! too common. Its study may be useful to us as
> showing the logical outcome of Atheism and Free
> Love.*

Well, that at least explained why the Rev. Verey had edited and commented upon this libertine volume, although it was still unclear if he truly understood what lt was he was condemning. Certainly, if he thought these poems related in any way to "Atheism," he had missed the target by a mile.

Sir John turned back to the section called "The Alchemist" and searched carefully to see if his speculation about the "elixir of shame" was correct. He found in Sonnet X:

> This wine is sovereign against all complaints,
> This is the wine the great king-angels use

Sheer nausea overcame him. If the elixir or wine was what he suspected, the vile secretions of the organs of shame, the great "king-angels" were not those of heaven but of hell. He read further in the same sonnet:

> One drop of this raised Attis from the dead;
> One drop of this, and slain Osiris stirs;
> One drop of this; before young Horus fled
> Thine ghosts, Typhon—this wine is mine and hers
> Ye Gods that gave it! not in trickling gouts
> But from the very fountain where 'tis drawn
> Gushing in crystal jets and ruby spouts
> From the authentic throne and shrine of dawn.

It was not just perversion that was being described; it was the deliberate use of loathsome Parisian vices for initiation into diabolism. Sir John skimmed some of the Rev. Verey's footnotes rapidly:

Lingam—the Hindu God [!]—the male organ of generation.

Yoni—Its feminine equivalent. That the Poor Hindus should *worship* these shameful things! And we? Oh, how poor and inadequate is all our missionary effort! Let us send out more, and yet more, to our perishing brothers!

Doomisday—An affected archaism for the Day of Judgment. How can the writer dare to speak of this great day, on which he shall be damned forever? "For he that believeth not is condemned already."

Blood-bought bastards—Christians! O Saviour! What didst Thou come to save?

Poor Rev. Verey obviously had no notion at all of what these poems were about. He regarded them as the anti-Christian fulminations of an Atheist, even a Socialist. He was too naïve to recognize the diabolism, the counter-theology that was actually being expressed.

Sir John looked back again at the Preface, and found no clue to the identity of the author of these vile versifications, except that he had died of "a loathsome disease." Verey added:

I may perhaps be blamed for publishing, even in this limited measure, such filthy and blasphemous orgies of human speech [save the mark] but I am firmly resolved [and I believe that I have the blessing of God on my work] to awake my fellow-workers in the great vineyard to the facts of modern existence.

Sir John turned to another of the poems and the world seemed to spin with vertigo as he read:

So Lola! Lola! Lola! peals,
And Lola! Lola! Lola! echoes back,

Till Lola! Lola! Lola! reels
The world in a dance of woven white and black
Shimmering with clear gold greys as hell resounds
With Lola! Lola! Lola! and heaven responds
With Lola! Lola! Lola!—swounds
All light to clustered dazzling diamonds,
And Lola! Lola! Lola! rings
Ever and ever again on these inchaunted ears,
And Lola! Lola! Lola! swings
My soul across to those inchaunted spheres
Where Lola is God and priest and wafer and wine—
O Lola! Lola! Lola! mystic maiden o' mine!

Could it be? Was Lola Levine the paramour who had
lured this mad poet into vice and, beyond that, into
diabolism? Skimming rapidly, Sir John found "Lola" in
poem after poem, but never any last name. But in the
very first sonnet he found in the closing line a Latin
phrase that froze his blood:

Evoe! Iacche! consummatum est.

There it was—*Evoe*, one of the two most hidden names
of God (which Sir John had good reason to remember was
known to Lola Levine); *Iacche*, the vocative form of Iacchus,
secret name of Dionysus, god of orgies; and *consummatum
est*, last words of the Mass. But this mad poet could only
refer to a Black Mass, not a Catholic Mass, in this foul
context of Dionysian revelry, perversion and anti-Christian
blasphemy. How simpleminded was the Rev. Verey to
imagine that these poems merely recorded the destruction
of a man drawn away from his lawful wife into an adulterous love affair, when they actually described the step-by-
step initiation into the worship of the Horned God of
sexual ecstasy—Panurgia, the god worshipped by the pa-
gans before Christianity arose to unmask him (the God of

This World) as Satan, adversary of the invisible True God, beyond the Stars.

Sir John purchased *Clouds Without Water* and took it home for study. This might be a most serious matter. If it were truly what he suspected, he would have to consult Jones for advice.

DE ARCONO NEFANDO

Memory remembers before remembering has memorized: remembers the unspeakable and forever unthinkable fact of the apotheosis [virtually the cynosure: a moment vivid as the terror in the eyes of that fieldmouse so many years ago: knowing that such terror was the price of consciousness in Uncle Bentley's universe, but with yet a sense of loathing and holding back from the ultimate revelation, the cataclysmic final horror of that detail so unthinkable as well as unspeakable that mind hesitates to advance toward recognition of it (remembering instead as in a continuous unrolling of time backwards, so that he saw himself picking *Clouds Without Water* from the bookstall, writing the angry letter to the *Times* about Home Rule for Ireland, opening the Bible to the *Epistle of Jude* and the stern warning against the mockers in the last time, the invasive spirit of Her writing through the pen in his hand, the revelation of *Ingenio Numen Replendet Iacchi*, the actual attack in which She appeared in succubus form to drain the Vril energy into Onan's Sin Against Nature, the chanting of *Pangenitor* and *Panphage*, Pound's story of poor Victor Neuberg turned into a camel, the thunderous crash that cracked the mirror as the material and astral universes intersected, the poetry reading at which She had first quoted "I adore thee, Evoe! I adore thee, IAO!", the idiot gnomes chanting "No wife, no horse, no mustache," the oath of celibacy taken three

times under Jones' relentless eyes, the first rising of the
Vril at the comprehension of *Igni Natura Renovatur Integra,*
the first meeting with Jones, the debate with McNaughton in the *Historical Review*, the horrid return of the ugly
temptation to actually kill the mouse and have the experience of conscious Sin, Uncle Bentley's death, the first
sense of the caverns of trolls beneath Babcock Manor in
boyhood fantasy, the penny-farthing bicycle) but holding
back in this state still midway between dream and memory from that one detail, that epicentre of delirium and
temptation actually longing to see and touch and kiss
again that blue garter, those lascivious thighs, that unspeakable central mystery of creation through corruption.

"There is Good and there is Evil," Sir John said awkwardly, having trouble finding words at all, feeling numb
and drowsy. "We know it intuitively, directly."

"There is Up and there is Down," Lola said mockingly.
"We knew that intuitively and directly—before Coperni-
cus. It's all relative, can't you see?"

Was this a dream, an astral vision or reality? Sir John
struggled to remember how he had gotten here, into this
vile Parisian brothel. "It isn't all relative," he protested,
feeling that he was perhaps only talking to himself. "There
are Absolutes. Thou shalt not commit Adultery. Thou shalt
not covet thy neighbor's wife, or his maidservant, or their
garters. Thou shalt not . . ." But he could not remember
the other Commandments. Was he drugged with opium
or hasheesh?

"Behold the hidden God," Lola said as the Hermit,
Death, and Sun cards danced into strange, intricate pat-
terns, chanting *"Yod Nun Resh Yod.* I.N.R.I. *Isis Naturae
Regina Ineffabilis.* Creatrix, Feliatrix: Venus Venerandum.
Leo Sirtalis. Perditrix naviam, perditrix urbium, perditrix
eorem, nupta bellum. Garterius, Pantius, Pussius, Cuntius.
Yoni soit qui mal y pense. Eat it with catsup." Dank
things moved darkly. She had taken the Crucifix and

inserted it between her thighs, moaning in nearly raving idiocy, masturbating wildly.

It was a dream, only a dream, after all: such things as we are made of. Turning on the newly installed electric lights, Sir John sat up and wrote it all out carefully, including the jumbled Latin and Norman-French. *Isis Naturae Regina Ineffabilis:* Isis, ineffable queen of nature. Some Egyptologists did claim that the Ankh cross, alleged origin of the Christian cross, showed the *lingam* of Osiris joining the *yoni* of Isis.

The meaning was clear: the Black Brotherhood, after two years, was activated against him again, perhaps because he had purchased *Clouds Without Water* and completed a magickal link. Well, he was no longer an ignorant Probationer; he was a Practicus, fully armed with the weaponry of practical magick, unafraid.

After breakfast, he would plunge directly into the heart of the new mystery. Meanwhile, he would not be deceived by a lying dream. The spirit haunting him was not Isis, although the "virgin mother" symbol was, of course, an allegory on *ain soph,* the limitless light of the white void *behind* matter itself according to Cabala. And Osiris-Jesus, the dead-and-resurrected son-lover of the virgin, Mother Void, was Man himself raised to superhumanity by the disciplines of magick and yoga. But that was all, in this instance, a lying masquerade. The obsessing spirit was carnal, unclean, and therefore an emanation of Ashtoreth, the lust-demon.

Still, the acronym haunted: Yod Nun Resh Yod: *Isis Naturae Regina Ineffabilis.* In numinous rooms incandescent. How many codes could four letters contain or be forced to contain? Is meaning itself the stuff that dreams are made of? Or was it better to return to the pragmatic semantics of Humpty Dumpty's "When I use a word, it means what I want it to mean"? Could all the king's horses and all the king's men put common sense back together again?

The one hundred fourteen sonnets collected in *Clouds Without Water* told a blood-curdling story when Sir John had time to read them at leisure. The anonymous poet, a married man seemingly in his early twenties and with a university degree, meets the enigmatic Lola, who is then only seventeen. Stealthily and slowly, she seduces him, until he casts aside his wife, his reputation, his good name and all else to live in sin with her. The sonnets continue for quite a while to celebrate the joys of their lawless love, although only a student of Cabala could decode, behind the euphemistic erotic imagery, the actual Satanic practices into which the poet is being led. Lola's body becomes both God and the priestess and altar of God; the Christian divinity is denounced and mocked in increasingly bitter lines. The clergy are described, viciously, as "blind worms" and "pious swine"—to which Rev. Verey added a footnote, saying, "The poor servants of God! Ah, well! We have our comfort in Him: like our blessed Lord, we can forgive."

The climax is abrupt and shocking. The poet discovers that he has contracted syphilis—"the recompense of his error which was meet," as Rev. Verey commented— and plunges into despair, killing himself with an over-dose of laudanum. Rev. Verey concludes the volume with a warning to others that Free Love and Socialism lead to countless similar tragedies every day in London, a city which he seemed to regard as being damnable as Sodom itself.

Most shocking of all to Sir John was Sonnet VII of a sequence called "The Hermit," dealing with a few weeks in which the poet was parted from Lola by relatives and friends who were attempting to end the illicit affair. The poet wrote:

> I will visit you, forlorn who lie
> Crying for lack of me; your very flesh
> Shall tingle with the touch of me as I
> Wrap you about with the ensorcelled mesh
> Of my fine *body of fire:* oh! you shall feel
> My kisses on your mouth like living coals

Even Rev. Verey was not so ignorant of occultism as to misunderstand this or attribute it to Atheism and Free Love. His footnote said explicitly, "This disgusting sonnet seems to refer to the wicked magickal practice of traveling by the astral double." Sir John sighed, remembering his own travels in *"the body of fire"* (as the astral double is technically called) and his own terrifying encounter with Lola Levine, in which she had dragged his unconscious body into unwilling sin.

For many days Sir John pondered and worried. Finally, he decided that he must act, and he carefully penned a letter to Rev. Verey at the Society for the Propagation of Religious Truth in Inverness, Scotland. He chose his words most carefully:

> *Babcock Manor*
> *Greystoke, Weems*
> *July 23, 1913*

Dear Rev. Verey,

   I have recently acquired a copy of your sad and terrible book, Clouds Without Water, *and was very moved by the tragedy recounted therein.*

   Before proceeding further, I must in honesty inform you that I am not, as you are, a Presbyterian; but I am a fellow Christian and I hope [and pray] a devout and pious one. What I have to tell you will be shocking and perhaps incredible to you but I beg you to think deeply and ponder long before rejecting my most somber warning.

I know not how you came into possession of those terrible poems, and can understand [although some bigots would not] why you considered it proper to print them, with a running commentary showing the dreadful results of the life and philosophy celebrated by the unfortunate poet. However, I do not think this book should ever have been published, and I fear that you have touched upon an evil far worse than you realized.

Briefly, I am a student of Christian Cabalism, and, although loathing with all my heart the perversions of Cabala employed by diabolists, I have of necessity learned a few things about their beliefs and practices. You may find this hard to credit, but the poet is not *describing merely an adulterous love affair; he is, in fact, depicting—in a kind of code, but in a manner clear to students of these matters—the horrible practices of what is called Left-Hand Tantra or sex-magick; the devices, in short, of the Black Mass and of Satanism.*

I am writing to you because it is obvious that the wicked woman who led the poet into these fiendish paths [called only Lola in the text] must be an initiate of a cult of black magicians. Such groups, I assure you, do not relish having their secrets published, even in code—especially when the code is, as in this case, quite transparent to any student of Cabalistic occultism. Without wishing to alarm you unnecessarily, I think it possible that this cult may wish to suppress the book, even though your Society circulated it only to ministers of religion, since it is now beginning to appear in the used bookstalls [which is where I found my copy]. It is even possible that they may seek revenge upon you.

If you do not dismiss this letter as the ravings of a superstitious fool, I wish to offer you my friendship

*and aid, in case such black magick action against you
is being taken or plotted.*

*Until I hear from you, I can only conclude: May
the blessings of our Lord be upon you, and surround
you, and protect you.*

Sincerely,

Sir John Babcock

After posting this missive, Sir John began to have serious doubts about whether a Scottish Presbyterian would,
or would not, credit the continued existence of Satanic
lodges in the modern world. He also wondered if he had
acted prematurely; but Jones was on holiday in France
and Sir John had no one else to advise him.

A few nights later, Sir John visited his cousins, the
Greystokes, and met again the aged Sicilian, Giacomo
Celine, who seemed to be related to a South European
branch of the family. Somehow, the conversation turned
to ghost stories after the brandy and cigars were circulating.

"Lewis' *The Monk* is still the most blood-curdling book
ever written," Sir John ventured at one point.

"But that's technically not a ghost story at all," Viscount
Greystoke remarked. "It's a story of demons."

"Of course," old Celine said. "Ghost stories really are
quite dull, actually. Mrs. Shelley's *Frankenstein* is not a
ghost story, either, and I think it at least as terrifying as
The Monk. And that young Irishman from Sir Henry
Irving's theatrical corporation—what's-his-name—Stoker—
he has written the most frightening book ever: *Dracula*.
And that doesn't deal with ghosts, either. Ghosts are
comparatively tame compared with the real horrors a lively
imagination can conjure up."

"That reminds me," old Greystoke said, "there's a novelette around that is more terrible than anything we've
discussed, and it has no ghosts, either. Ghosts, after all,
are only dead humans, and humans can be wicked enough

as we all know, but it's the non-human creature of evil that really makes the blood run cold, as the saying goes. The non-human is not limited by the traits which even ghosts share with us."

"Quite so," Sir John agreed. "And what is the name of this novelette?"

"Oh, here it is," Greystoke replied, prowling among his bookcases. "If you want a bad night, try reading *this* before bed." And he handed Sir John a slim volume of stories entitled *The Great God Pan*, by Arthur Machen.

DE MONSTRIS

ACTION   **SOUND**

EXTERIOR. BABCOCK MANOR, MEDIUM SHOT
The penny-farthing bicycle in   *Sir John's voice:* "Oh, God,
a garden. Sir John, age six,   Jones, that *thing* . . ."
with a little girl, same age, he
with pants down, she with
skirts up, comparing genitalia.

EXTERIOR. BABCOCK MANOR, CLOSE-UP.
A grinning statue of Pan above   *Voodoo drums.*
Sir John's head.

EXTERIOR. CLEAR SKY, CLOSE-UP.
Hawk shrieking.   *Hawk shriek; voodoo drums.*

EXTERIOR. CLEAR SKY, CLOSE-UP.
The eyes on the statue of Pan   *Voodoo drums.*
turn and look at Sir John.   *Voice:* "There is an evil power
                                     behind it all . . ."

BABCOCK MANOR. INTERIOR, DINING ROOM.
  MEDIUM SHOT.

Dr. BENTLEY BOSTICK BABCOCK and VISCOUNT GREYSTOKE dining. SIR JOHN, age twelve, at far end of table.

Voice [Dr. Bentley B. Babcock, continuing]: "Just look at the record: 1900, King Humbert of Italy assassinated; 1901, Bogo-lyepov, the minister of education, assassinated in Russia and President McKinley assassinated in the United States; 1903, King Alexander of Serbia assassinated."

INTERIOR. BABCOCK MANOR, DINING ROOM.
  CLOSE-UP.

SIR JOHN listening to the adults with horror.

Dr. Babcock's voice-over: "It has to be an international conspiracy, I tell you."

Pan To:

At the far end of the room, in a huge overstuffed red chair, GIACOMO CELINE, smiling privately. He is reading *Not the Almighty* with the eye-in-triangle design on the cover.

Voodoo drums.

Sir John retired to bed with Machen's *The Great God Pan* around eleven and indeed he had a bad night. He quickly became convinced that he had discovered another member of the Golden Dawn and one who knew a great deal about the dark Satanic lodges working in opposition to the Great Work. "There are sacraments of Evil, as well as of Good," Machen wrote, and his title story was a most

daring approach to almost describing the sacraments of
Evil explicitly.

Even worse for Sir John's peace of mind, Machen recounted, as fiction, a weird and terrible story of which
Clouds Without Water might actually be a missing chapter or a sequel. *The Great God Pan* tells of two men,
Clarke and Villiers, who share a common interest in the
bizarre and mysterious side of London life. Although Clarke
and Villiers do not join forces until the climax of the story,
each of them finds, working independently of the other,
parts of the history of a most strange and dangerous woman,
called "Helen" in the text. In each chapter, either Clarke
or Villiers encounters a victim of this woman, or hears a
yarn of incredible events which seems to relate to her
mysterious doings. When Villiers and Clarke finally inter-
sect each other's investigations and begin to compare notes,
most of the truth begins to emerge, although not all of it,
since Machen restricts himself to hints and euphemisms.
What is clear, however, is that "Helen" is a worshipper of
the Horned God, who has lured countless men and women
into unspeakable erotic practices—sexual excesses leading
at first to ecstasy and then to a chain of nervous breakdowns and suicides.

It could almost be the story of Lola Levine; and Sir
John wondered if it were, in fact, her story.

How much of Machen's terrifying tale was fiction, and
how much fact? Why had Machen published, even as
fiction and even with the worst of it veiled in vague hints,
so many dreadful secrets which the world was better not
to know at all? Why had the Secret Chiefs of the Order
allowed Machen to publish this dreadful tale, for that
matter? Sir John found himself thinking, without humor,
of the Rev. Verey's dark warnings that the world was
entering the last days and the final conflict between Good
and Evil would soon be upon us all. The Greystokes, who
had family connections in every branch of the govern-

ment, it often seemed, were worried more and more lately about the possibility of a greater war than the world had ever known. . . .

Sir John uneasily climbed out of bed and looked again at the most disturbing passage in *Clouds Without Water*, in which the Rev. Verey said:

> *Unblushing, the old Serpent rears its crest to the sky; unashamed, the Beast and the Scarlet Woman chant the blasphemous litanies of their fornication.*
> *Surely the cup of their abominations is nigh full!*
> *Surely we who await the Advent of our blessed Lord are emboldened to trust that this frenzy of wickedness is a sure sign of the last days; that He will shortly come . . .*

Could it be that the true purpose of the Golden Dawn was not merely to raise the human mind to communication with the divine, but to train warriors of God to do battle against the forces of diabolical magick threatening the planet? Why did the first teaching say so harshly, "Fear is failure, and the forerunner of failure," if the members were not expected, eventually, to confront the most fearful evils and do battle against them?

Sir John performed a most earnest banishing ritual, drank a double shot of cognac, and crept back to bed, severely troubled in his mind. His dreams were not pleasant.

The Hermit carrying a rotlantern was leading him down a Naranhope alley in some low, disreputable neighborhood of London. Orofaces out of Hogarth's etchings and Doré's illustrations of Dante's *Inferno* glared gorm on all sides; Oscar Wilde and Lord Alfred Douglas rose up from a violet cellar muttering incoherently, "the love of Jesus and John . . . the love of David and Jonathan . . . the love that dare not speak its name." The Hermit began to fondle Sir John on the rougeway carriage again and a terrific explosion shook the vertetrain. "They are dropping bombs from monoplanes!" somebody shouted. "The Anti-Christ is coming: Night, the Almighty. London is aflame!" Voices sang the *Internationale* and looters ran through the streets carrying indigo garters and boxes with moving pictures on them. "It's probably a magnetic phenomenon," old Celine said reassuringly. "I Never Risk Inquiry."

And this is the horror, said Eutaenia Infernalis, *and this is the Mystery of the great prophets that have come unto mankind, Moses, and Buddha, and Lao-Tse, and Krishna, and Jesus, and Osiris, and Christian Rosycross; for all these attained unto Truth, and therefore were they bound with the curse of Thoth, so that, being guardians of Truth, they caused the proliferations of countless lies: for the Truth may not be uttered in the languages of men.*

Lola sang in clear, lark-like soprano:

> The harlot's cry from street to street
> Shall weave old England's winding sheet

Sir John, seven years old, hid in the closet. They were playing hide-and-seek. The Cuntease of Salisbury entered the room. He backed farther into the rear of the closet, behind his mother's skirts. The Cuntess opened the door and groped him by the throat. He tried to tell her to stop, but he was choking and could not speak. Then he knew it was Lola again.

"You've been a bad boy," she said, "playing with blue garters and your mother's skirts." She flung him to the floor, where Count Draculatalis leaned over him to whisper in his ear, "The true Eucharist is the Eucharist of blood, the lunar force unleashed upon earth once a month. Take ye and drink."

Hooded, red-eyed figures crouched around the garden chanting, "Io Io Io Sabao Kurie Abrasax Kurie Meithras

Kurie Phalle. Io Pan Io Pan Pan Io Ischuron Io Athanaton
Io Abroton Io IAO. Chaire Phalle Chaire Panphage Chaire
Pangenitor. Hagios Hagios Hagios IAO!"

Oscar Wilde, wearing Sherlock Holmes' deerstalker cap,
bent to examine Sir John's penis through a magnifying
glass. "It is very, very long," he pronounced solemnly,
"but very, very beautiful."

A form was crystallizing in the dank air: a dark blue
ribbon edged with gold, a mantle of blue velvet, a collar
of gold consisting of twenty-six pieces, Saint George fighting the dragon . . .

And Pan, ithyphallic and terrible, arose in the midst of
them, Lola bending to present his vile gigantic organ with
an obscene kiss.

"Charing Cross, Jeering Cross!" the conductor shouted.
"All mystics off at Charing Cross!"

But on the platform, everybody was staring and Sir
John realized he was wearing his mother's skirt.

"Sonly a beach of a pair to plumb this hour's gripes,"
muttered the fox, but John Peel lit a great flashing light
with a goat sow gorm in the morning and Sir John blinked,
shuddering into wakefulness as warm sunlight flooded his
bedroom. It was dawn and the night and night's black
agents had vanished into air, into thin air.

Sir John ate a very subdued breakfast. "A war between
the great powers," Viscount Greystoke had said, extremely
worried, only a few weeks ago, "might destroy European
civilization, or throw us back into the Dark Ages." Was it
possible that the dark, chthonic forces of the ancient pagan cults, the beings that Lola and her friends were trying
to unleash again upon the world, intended such a frightful
transformation of what had been an age of enlightenment
and progress? Or was he taking the chaotic symbolism of
the dream, a feverish blend of the worst in Gothic fiction
and black magick, too literally?

He decided to take a long walk around his estate,

meditating on one of his favorite lines from the Golden Dawn Probationer ritual: "We worship thee also in the forms of bird and beast and flower through which thy beauty is manifest even in the material world." His eyes opened as he repeated the phrase over and over: every bird call seemed to remind him that God was truly good, that even on the plane of accursed material existence the divine radiance showed itself to those with spiritual vision. The deer were the gaiety of God, the trees His mercy, the stream His ever-flowing love.

A strutting robin came pecking the ground near him and he watched it with affection. It was a creature, he suddenly realized, more alien to himself than the Martians imagined in the fantastic fiction of H. G. Wells, and yet sentient as he and with its own intelligence. How can we live among so many wonders and be so blind to them? Sir John remembered the great Psalm: "The heavens declare the glory of God and the earth sheweth His handiwork."

Then he saw two foxes copulating and blushed, turning his eyes away from the temptation to lewd thoughts. We must love the beauty of this world, which is God's gift, he reminded himself, but we must never forget its fallen nature nor let it seduce us from seeking the beauty of the spiritual world of which this is the grossest shadow. For to worship nature as it is was to fall into the error of the sensualists and Satanists, of "Helen" in *The Great God Pan*.

Sir John returned to the volume when he was back in his library and had read two more of Machen's macabre tales, "The Black Seal" and "The White People." Both dealt with the ancient Celtic lore of the faery-people, but not in the sentimentalized manner which Shakespeare had established in *A Midsummer Night's Dream* and *The Tempest* and which has been naïvely copied by writers ever since. Rather, Machen followed the actual lore of the peasantry of Ireland and Wales, to whom the "little people"

were not benign beings at all but a terrifying inhuman race
of malign tricksters who lured men with vistas of beauty
and sublime wonder only to lead them into a realm of
unreality, changing chimerical shapes, formless forms, time
distortions and nightmare, from which few returned totally sane. Sir John, who had studied this lore in his
investigations of medieval myth, realized that Machen's
picture of faery-folk was far truer to peasant belief than
the charming fantasies of other writers on the subject. The
Irish, Sir John remembered, called the faery "the good
people," not out of real love or respect, but out of terror,
because these godlings were known to punish most terribly those who slighted them. The faery, Machen obviously understood, were denizens of Chapel Perilous
unleashed somehow from the astral realm into temporary
appearance in our material world. In fact, "Helen" in *The
Great God Pan* was first reported to Clarke as a small
child in Wales allegedly seen playing with one of these
terrible creatures.

Sir John pondered much on all this; but when the day's
mail arrived, he saw that it contained a letter from Rev.
Verey, Society for the Propagation of Religious Truth,
Inverness, Scotland. He opened the envelope with a quick,
nervous rip and read:

Sir John Babcock
Babcock Manor
Greystoke, Weems

My Dear Sir John,
    *I must thank you sincerely, as a Brother in Christ,
for the concern and compassion expressed in your
letter of recent date. Needless to add, our theological
differences do not matter—I am no old-fashioned
fanatic, I hope—and I recognize all true Christians
[which does not include, of course, the accursed Pa-*

pists] *as fellow toilers in the vineyard for our Blessed Saviour.*

To come to the point at once, I am neither astonished nor incredulous about your claims concerning the vile sonnets in Clouds Without Water. *Indeed, I am only astonished at my own blindness in refusing to see, at first, the full extent of the horrors there uttered. You will, I am sure, understand my original inability to accept the obvious when I confess that the poet who wrote those lascivious verses was [alas!] my own younger brother, Arthur Angus Verey, whose total depravity I was long loath to admit, even while confronted with the terrible evidence of his apostasy and heresy.*

It is all too true—Arthur mocked our holy religion continually after attending the damnable university of Cambridge [which is staffed almost entirely, as you must be aware, by men whose Socialism and Atheism are concealed barely enough to avoid public scandal] —but I, God forgive me, I was too fond, too forgiving a brother to admit even to myself that Arthur's youthful rebellion had carried him far beyond the superficial Free Thought of most "intellectuals" of our time, into the very pits of Diabolism. Even after his suicide, when the poems came into my hands through our family solicitor, I refused to see that the mockery of Jesus [and of the clergy of our holy religion] was not merely that of a skeptic but of a Satanist. If you have a younger brother of keen intellect and wayward nature, you may perhaps understand my folly, my sentimental blindness.

Well, sir, that is old business, and now I am paying the price of my delusion, and paying at usury. There is no doubt that diabolical forces have mounted an attack against my church, my family and myself. Things have happened around these parts lately that would cause all "advanced thinkers" to laugh me to scorn, and alienists to commit me to an asylum, if I were so foolish as to speak of them in this materialistic age. The huge, bat-winged Creature in particular— but no, I wish not to alarm you but to reassure you.

While I am admittedly under siege, I am not afraid. "Yea, though I walk through the valley of the shadow of death, I will fear no evil: for thou art with me." [Psalm 23] There are nameless things loose in our world once again, not just in the sinks of London but even here in the pure air of Scotland itself, but I am confident that all protection lies in the rock of my Faith and in the eternal presence of our Lord. I am too attached, sentimentally, to this old church and this lovely highland landscape [in which I have spent all sixty-two years of my life] to turn and run from these forces which rise up against the Almighty; and is not their doom clearly predicted, as is the final triumph of Christ, in Revelations itself? I pray; I remain steadfast in faith; and I will not give way to panic, however they may vex and haunt me.

I do, however, thank you for your offer of help, and I hope that you will remember me in your prayers.

Most sincerely yours,

Rev. C. Verey

P.S. *I do not think it altogether wise for Christians to meddle in the Jewish [and therefore un-Christian] arts of Cabala. Perhaps you may need more help than I.*

"The perfect damned fool!" Sir John cried aloud. But he re-read the letter more slowly and found himself strangely touched by the old man's simple faith and unpretentious bravery. Vexings, hauntings and that "bat-winged" Creature could not make very comfortable living in a lonely old church on Loch Ness.

Sir John sat down, calmed himself, and then wrote a most unrestrained and tactful second letter to the Rev. Verey. He pointed out that his offer of help was somewhat presumptuous; he acknowledged the power of faith to hold at bay the agents of darkness and Old Chaos; he praised the courage of Verey, not too unctuously, so as to evade any suspicion of flattery; and then he got down to business. He explained his interest in Verey's problems as part of a larger research project, in which he was attempting to learn the scope and powers of the cults of black magick in the contemporary world; he waxed rhetorical, declaring that a book on this subject, which he hoped to write, might "awaken Christendom to the ever-present activities of the Old Enemy it is currently inclined to forget"; he begged for specific details on the problems besetting the Verey household and environs.

When Sir John took this out to the box to post it, he felt a sudden cold bite in the air and his mood abruptly turned against him. It was not really wise, perhaps, to plunge into matters of this sort without Jones being around to advise him. Why, if anything too serious resulted, he had no way of contacting the higher officials of the Order, except through that post office box in London, which might not be picked up more than once in a fortnight. It would certainly be humiliating to have to consult with Yeats, for instance. That would reveal him as a bumbling beginner who had become involved in matters so murky that he was forced to violate the rule against socializing between known members of the Order to obtain help. Standing at the box, mulling in this morose manner, Sir John suddenly began to think he himself was *under psychic attack* at the moment, and the voice inside telling him to abandon this matter was a presence from outside seeking to frighten him away from his plain duty. "Fear is

failure," he reminded himself, one more time, and dropped
the letter into the postal box.

Thunder crashed immediately overhead.

Coincidence, he told himself; coincidence . . .

But he already knew that "coincidence" was a word
used by fools to shield themselves from recognition of the
invisible world that so often intersected and altered our
visible universe.

DE CAECITIA HOMINUM

ACTION   **SOUND**

INTERIOR, JOYCE'S KITCHEN. MEDIUM SHOT.
BABCOCK telling his story.   *Crash of thunder.*
JOYCE and EINSTEIN lis-
tening, fascinated.

EXTERIOR, PRE-DAWN SKY.
Dark clouds.   *Thunder roars again.*

INTERIOR, JOYCE'S KITCHEN. CLOSE-UP.
JOYCE terrified.   *Faint voodoo drums.*

The fear of thunder as the origin of religion: Vico's
theory two hundred years ago. The first men, huddled in
caves, trembling before the angry roaroaroar of a force
they cannot understand. Fear of the Lord: the hangman
God of Rome and this Rev. Verey. And, from childhood,
Mrs. Riordan's voice: "The thunder is God's anger at
sinners, Jimmy."

Signore Popper in Trieste asking why I still tremble
at thunder: "How can a man with so much moral courage
as you be frightened by a simple natural phenomenon?"
Put that in the book. Have Einstein or Hunter, whatever

I'll call him, say it to Stephen: natural phenomenon.
F.I.A.T.

What did I answer Popper? "You were not raised an
Irish Catholic." Agenbite of inwit.

Thor's hamer: the Norse feared it, also. Roaring growl-
ruinboomdoom. "God's anger at sinners, Jimmy." *Merde.
Le mot juste de* Canbronne. Conbronboomruinboom doom.

A nightmare from which humanity must wake. Beginning when the first ape-like Finnegans or Goldbergs hid
in awe from He Which Thundereth From On High. "Fear
is the father of the gods": Lucretius. *Panphage*, indeed. I
have said: I will not serve. Brightstar, son of the morning,
hawk-like man ascending from the labyrinth:

Where they have crouched and crawled and prayed
I stand, the self-doomed, unafraid

No: they will not terrify me into submission. To the
devil with pangenitor, panurgia and panphage: may the
great panchreston, Natural Phenomenon, stand me now
and forever in good stead.

I tried to love God once, in adolescence, and failed. I
tried to love a woman, when I put away childish things,
and I succeeded. Read me that riddle, ye seekers after
mystery.

But: out of the Loch, across Europe, ancient Tempter,
to seek me here. Worldlines, crossing, intersecting: Horned
monsters: Shakespeare, me, the greengrocer down the
street. Out of the Loch. *"The vicar said 'Gracious' "?*

Have Einstein or Hunter or whatever I'll call him meet
the Sirens in a workingman's bar. *"It's Brother Ignatius"?*

Two. Three. Four. *Fräumünster* chimes telling us in
linear time the morning is passing. Hans leaving the bed
of his wife's lover's lover: many a civic monster.

Perhaps I see more because my eyes are weak. Blindness the highest form of vision: another paradox. Inex-

haustible modality of double-viewed things. Paradox, pun, oxymoron: and all Irish bulls are pregnant. *Ed eran duo in uno ed uno in duo*, who stirred up wars eight centuries ago: caught forever in Dante's words. Two in one, one in two. Bloog ardors: blue garters.

The Gospel According to Joe Miller. Thou art Petrified: Rock of Ages. A riddling sentence from one who did not speak Latin, yet on this pun stands the old whore, rouged with metathesis. There are wordlines as well as worldlines.

DE CLAVICULA SOMNIORUM

ACTION	SOUND

EXTERIOR. SCOTTISH HIGHLANDS. TRACKING SHOT.

CAMERA pans through heavily wooded mountain area. Film is edited to give jerky, nervous effect, by removing every tenth frame.

Lola's voice [singing]:
  "Up the airy mountain
  Down the ferny glen
  We dare not go a-hunting

EXTERIOR. TIGHT CLOSE-UP.

Grinning face of the statue of Pan.

Lola's voice-over:
  "For fear of little men."

Semple Solman, mid nuked gorals and nu derections, mud blocked boxes and blewg orders, temptler orion, met apehighman going through his fur. Sssaid ssnakey Soulman, primate of owl laughs that dour not spook the gnome, his trees sank acht in minor's bush, "Let my teste you war." But Urvater, who's arts uneven, war wild and sad, for only a maggus or a nightruebane or a furgeon honey-frayed can wake One-Armed amid the fright of the double's minsky-raid.

And the fool were laughted (booboo treesleep) and Sir

Joan peeled apauled at the pith of garmel, the musked priestess, through the faundevoided lickt of Garther, the clown, the everlusting One, with that night holy behind him. The caps were in the cups and the cubs were in the cabs and the cubherds were bear. And Sir John awoke to Sol, to sunshine in the window, to the wake world again.

He reached for his Magick Diary, the daily routine of recording each dream a habit by now, and then found that he could not verbalize any of the fragments still in memory. He wrote:

> A very strange dream, which seems to be blaming myself for my father's death and yet also suggests that such patricide is, symbolically at least, part of initiation. All mixed up with Mother Goose and the Order of Saint George.

When he went down to breakfast he found the morning post had already arrived and contained a letter, in shaky handwriting, from the Society for the Propagation of Religious Truth. He opened it immediately and read:

> My Dear Sir John,
> "Pride goeth before a fall."
> How much more profound do the words of Holy Writ appear to me each year, and how dim and undependable my own weak human reasonings!
> I admit that I am truly afraid at last.
> To confess such fear is more of a humiliation than you can imagine; at least, it is so for a stubborn old Scotsman like myself.
> To provide the chronological narrative you requested: I suppose, in some sense, the whole evil cloud began to gather about me as soon as I printed that accursed volume of my young brother's blasphemous verses. For instance, our local monster—"Nessie,"

as the farmers call her—has never been so active as in the four years since that book appeared. Where, in earlier times, this gigantic serpentine form was only reported rarely, and usually by persons whose sobriety was at least questionable, in these recent years the monster in the Loch has been seen increasingly often, and by many persons, and groups of persons, who must be regarded as of the highest probity and sincerity of character. As you are perhaps aware, the matter of Nessie is no longer an obscure rumor among us Highlanders but is increasingly discussed in the newspapers throughout the U.K. and, I hear, even on the Continent. Since my church faces directly toward the Loch—being situated where River Ness empties into Loch Ness—it is not wholesome, I assure you, to lie awake nights and wonder what is out there and why it has become so active lately.

Then, in 1912, came the appalling case of the Ferguson boy—young Murdoch Ferguson, age ten, who was quite literally frightened out of his wits, returning home around twilight. I am saddened to say that the lad has never been the same since this experience, although his parents have taken him the round of many doctors; he still has frequent nightmares, seems abstracted or lost in thought most of the time, and refuses absolutely to go out of the house after dark. I tell you all this because otherwise I fear you might smile at what the lad claims he saw. It was one of those creatures which we Celts call the wee people *or the* faery. *Young Murdoch insists that it had green skin, pointy ears, was no more than three feet high, and that its eyes glowed with an eerie phosphorescence of malignancy. So terrific was that malign stare that the evening of the experience the lad was unable to stop trembling until the family doctor gave him a very strong sedative [opium, I believe].*

ACTION   **SOUND**

EXTERIOR. SCOTS FARMLAND, LONG SHOT.
MURDOCH running.   *Voodoo drums.*

EXTERIOR, SAME. MEDIUM SHOT.
Tiny figure, back to camera,   *Voodoo drums.*
watching MURDOCH run.

EXTERIOR, SAME. CLOSE-UP.
Tiny figure turns suddenly   *The* Merry Widow Waltz.
toward camera; we see only
glowing eyes in a dark face.

This incident occurred in the glen just behind my church. Of course, every village in Scotland [and in Ireland, also] has such eldritch encounters reported occasionally, and I am quite sure that most of them are, as the atheistic psychologists say, self-induced delusion brought on by listening to old-wives' tales. But young Murdoch was known to me as a boy of higher than normal intelligence, adventurous spirits and emotional stability. He is now a neurasthenic case, and I can only believe that something most terrible did accost him in the gloaming that evening.

Next came the sinister Oriental gentleman in black clothing. Now this is most inconclusive, but for that very reason it disturbs me oddly. This personage— whether he were Chinese or Japanese or some other barbarian is in much dispute among those who met him—arrived in Inverness about a month after the incident of the Ferguson boy and the faery-creature. He visited at least two dozen families, always arriving at night in a black carriage. He wore Western cloth- ing, all in black, and spoke a kind of English that was of neither the upper nor the lower classes—an uninflected, almost mechanical English, the witnesses say.

He always requested directions to my church and then lingered a while to ask sly and seemingly pointless questions about myself, my wife and my older brother, Bertran. On taking his leave, this heathen in black always said, in the most peculiar way, "Evil to him who thinks evil." The strangest part of this story is that, although he always asked how to reach my church, he never did arrive here, although these visits to neighbors occurred over a period of more than two months.

What is even stranger, however, is that, although everybody this Oriental visited saw his black carriage distinctly, nobody else ever saw such a carriage traveling these back roads in daytime or at night. It is as if he and the carriage materialized from nowhere before each visit, and then dematerialized afterward— although I know that remark may sound as if I am beginning to let my imagination run away with me.

[Incidentally, I would be most obliged to you if you could inform me if that mysterious sentence, "Evil to him who thinks evil," has any meaning in white or black magick, besides being the motto of the Order of Saint George.]

To proceed: in the last six months, since about the time the spectral Oriental ceased prowling these parts, there have been reports of an enormous bat-winged creature, with glaring red eyes, seen near my church at night. I believe that, by now, the number of persons who allege to have seen this creature is about twenty. Certainly, one can argue or attempt to argue that, in the ambience created by Nessie's appearances in the Loch, the experience of the Ferguson lad, plus the swarthy Oriental, a mood of hysteria is sweeping

*the countryside and people are becoming suggestible
to rumor and mob psychology.*

   *Alas, would that it were so! For I myself have seen
the giant bat-creature—once, certainly, and on another occasion, possibly. The latter incident was
really only a flapping of wings and a huge shadow—
perhaps just an exceptionally large hawk. [But, on my
word of honor, I have never seen or heard of a hawk
of so vast a wingspan. . . .]*

ACTION	SOUND

EXTERIOR. VEREY'S FARMYARD: SUBJECTIVE SHOT.
   [VEREY'S POINT OF VIEW]

CAMERA tracks toward a well.	*Footsteps.*
	Verey's voice [over]: "The other occasion was much clearer, since I had gone out with a lantern to the well."

EXTERIOR. FARMYARD: SUBJECTIVE CLOSE-UP.
   [VEREY'S POINT OF VIEW]

Huge hawk-creature swoops toward camera.	*Verey's voice [over]:* "And the Thing swooped down and flew within a few feet of my head."

   *I worry that even you will attribute one further
detail to my imagination: but the fact is that I thought
I heard it* titter *in a voice close to that of humanity.*

   *If it were not for my love of these old Highland
glens and hills, I think I would acquiesce to the
increasing demands of my wife, Annie, and move to a
more urban, less lonely place. As it is, even my older
brother, Bertran, a veteran of thiry years in the*

*army and a man of iron courage, has begun to agree
with Annie and has several times suggested we all
leave this abominable place.*

   I beg you to remember us in your prayers.

                             Rev. C. Verey

Could a man be turned into a camel? The question
which had seemed merely absurd two years earlier was
now horrible to contemplate, without ceasing to be ridiculous. The evil "wee people" whose contact has the power
to disrupt totally the normal functioning of the human
brain, abolishing space and time as we know them . . . the
Creature so many had seen in Loch Ness . . . a bat-winged
monstrosity that tittered in a human-like voice . . . Sir
John found himself re-reading Verey's letter several times,
with growing apprehension and disquiet. "The mind has
both a rational and an irrational aspect," Jones had said,
long ago, and Sir John had seen enough of the reasonless
denizens of Chapel Perilous to fear their power, to know
that they could on occasion cross over into the material
universe and disrupt its normal laws entirely.

Sir Walter Scott had written of these creatures in his
famous *Letters on Witchcraft,* and Sir John found himself
recalling, over and over, a phrase from Scott about "the
crew that never rests." Finally, he went to the library to
look up the actual passage. Scott explained that "glamour"
originally meant illusion, as every etymologist knows, and
went on to discuss the abrupt way in which the glamour
cast by these creatures could turn into sudden loathsome
horror—as had perhaps happened to the poor Ferguson
lad. Scott wrote:

   *The young knights and beautiful ladies showed them-
selves [as the glamour faded] wrinkled and odious hags.
The stately halls were turned into miserable damp*

caverns—all the delights of the Elfin Elysium vanished at once. In a word, their pleasures were showy but totally unsubstantial—their activity unceasing, but fruitless and unavailing—and their condemnation appears to have consisted in the necessity of maintaining the appearance of industry or enjoyment, though their toil was fruitless and their pleasures shadowy and unsubstantial. Hence poets have designated them as "the crew that never rests." Besides the unceasing and useless bustle in which these spirits seemed to live, they had propensities unfavourable and distressing to mortals.

Sir John remembered his own first contact with the "crew that never rests." Midway between dream and astral vision: the huge, incomprehensible machinery, the incessant muttering of nonsense phrases. . . . "Mulligan Milligan Hooligan Halligan" and all the rest. Cabala referred to them as the qliphothic entities—souls of those who had died insane; orthodox Christian theology simply called them demons; in Tibet they were known as *Tulpas*, and usually appeared in solid black garb like the mysterious "Oriental" who had gone about Inverness asking questions about the Verey household; to the American Indians, they were allies or avatars of Coyote, the prankster-god, or of the mysterious "people from the stars"; there seemed to be no part of the Earth in which they did not appear in horrified tales of malign humor, regarded as myth only by those who had never personally encountered them.

Sir John remembered suddenly that the very word "panic" is derived from the name of the Great God Pan; and that the ancients believed that any close encounter with Him or His cohort of satyrs and nymphs—the crew that never rests—was more likely to lead to madness than to ecstasy, or that the ecstasy could easily turn to madness.

The traditional old ballad "Thomas the Rhymer" came back to him, seeming not quaint at all but stealthily sinister:

> And see ye not yon bonny road
> That winds aboon the fernie brae?
> That is the road to fair Elfland
> Where you and I this night maun gae.

He remembered that William Blake, the poet, had soberly told friends of seeing a faery procession in his own garden once; that Sir Walter Scott seriously reported on a man he described as "a scholar and a gentleman" who insisted he had observed faery rings—circles of mushrooms where the weird folk were said to dance—and had seen *imprints of small feet* within them; that the folklorist Rev. S. Baring-Gould had sworn to an encounter, in 1838, in which "legions of dwarfs about two feet high" had circled his carriage and ran laughing alongside it for some distance, then vanished "into thin air" in the traditional manner; that as recently as 1907 Lady Archibald Campbell had reported a case of a man and wife, in Ireland, who had captured a "faery" and held it prisoner two weeks before it escaped.

Thinking, *Do I dare, still, to consider all these cases as "hallucination"?* and remembering the thousands, the hundreds of thousands, of similar reports from all ages and places: the Bigfoot of Canada, the Abominable Snowman of the Himalayas, the huge winged creatures of a thousand folk traditions—the vast dark company of unearthly beings (or the incredible *variety of forms* in which "the crew that never rests" can manifest to human consciousness, when the membrane between the visible and invisible worlds becomes temporarily ripped and They come prancing and dancing and slithering and tittering from their reality into ours)—remembering too his own experience when the most terrible of Them, the bisexual

Baphomet, the Hideous God, had broken through to contact with him: Was that thunderous crash and that cracked mirror only a "coincidence," or was it the tearing of the membrane, the opening of the door between the worlds?

Remembering, too, the great blind spot of the eighteenth century, the much-vaunted Age of Reason, when science, unable to explain meteorites, had dogmatically declared that there were no meteorites; and when meteorites continued to fall and were reported by farmers and Bishops and tradesmen and housewives and philosophers and mayors and thousands of independent witnesses, including even dissident scientists, the French Academy and the Royal Scientific Society blandly dismissed each report as hoax or hallucination; thinking, *just as today the continuing activities of the crew that never rests, reported weekly from someplace or other in the daily press and investigated with painstaking care by the Society for Psychic Research, are also dismissed as hoaxes or hallucinations.* Belief in Verey's letter was impossible to resist: though the dwarf and the alleged "Oriental" in black and even the bat-winged Thing that tittered were all glamours, phantasms, illusions, yet the force, the malign intelligence, behind these phenomena was something humanity had confronted from before the dawn of history and could not, ever, escape.

Since his first researches into medieval magick, Sir John had vacillated between real belief, pretended-belief, real skepticism and pretended-skepticism. Now he no longer could resist simple uncomplicated belief. The Great God Pan was still alive, two thousand years after Christianity had correctly recognized and denounced Him as the devil; and his kith and kin were active all about us, even if they remained as invisible to educated opinion as meteorites to the intelligentsia of Voltaire's age.

ACTION	SOUND

EXTERIOR. LOCH NESS, TWILIGHT. TRACKING SHOT.
Panorama of storm-tossed wa-   *Voodoo drums.*
ters. The camera seems to
be hunting purposefully over
wave after wave after wave.

Something moves in the water.

Quick Fade.

Cut to:
CLOSE-UP
TV Narrator [same actor as   *Narrator:* "These reports of
previous TV sequence] sits at   mysterious dwarf-like human-
desk grimly staring into Cam-   oids are found in folklore and
era, which pans back slowly   legend all over the world, and
during this speech to   continue to the present. What
MEDIUM SHOT.   Does It All Mean? Science
Cannot Answer, but we have
in our studio a man who has
given many years to the study
of this subject . . ."

Pan to:
JOHN LEEK, an earnest, be-   *Narrator* [*voice-over*]: "Mr.
spectacled, balding Writer in   John Leek, author of *This
his mid-forties.   Planet Is Haunted, Men in
Black* and *3000 Years of
UFO's.* Mr. Leek, do you
believe in these . . . um . . .
Humanoids?"

CAMERA moves to   *Leek:* "It's not a question of be-
CLOSE-UP on Leek.   lief. It is cold fact that these
creatures have been described

in virtually identical details by nearly every society in history."

Pan to Narrator.

Narrator: "And you believe they are extraterrestrials?"

Medium shot: Narrator and Leek

Leek: "Extraterrestrials, extra-dimensionals, time-travelers . . . They could be any number of things."

Narrator: "But they are basically the same as the UFO-nauts reported by modern Contactees?"

Leek: "Oh, no doubt about that. With the Age of Science, they've just changed their game. For instance, they pre-

भप

tend to travel in mechanical craft now, to fit the extraterrestrial idea—but as all the skeptics point out, the craft make movements that would tear any mechanical ship apart. They are basically manipulating our minds, not our physical reality."

Close-Up: Narrator.

Narrator: "But do you have any concrete evidence that these are the same creatures reported in earlier folklore?"

Close-Up: Leek.

Leek: "Well, here's a drawing of one of the Enochian Intelligences, invoked by the Enochian Keys of Dr. John Dee. The drawing was made by Aleister Crowley, after invoking the Being. Is it not identical with the UFOnauts reported by thousands of Contactees in recent years?"

Medium shot: Narrator and Leek.

Narrator: "And you really believe our minds are subject to seeing or hearing whatever They want us to see or hear?"

CLOSE-UP: Leek.

Leek: "That's right. They are our Manipulators. Our reality is whatever They want it to be."

CLOSE-UP: Narrator.   *Narrator:* "Well, that's certainly an interesting theory,
Mr. Leek. We'll have another
view, from Dr. Carl Sagan,
after this brief message from
our sponsor."

Q: Quote a scholarly source that at least tentatively sup-
ports the extreme views of Mr. Leek.

A: "In the myths of every race and clime we see the
hallmarks of those extra-cosmic denizens that populate the
pages of the *Necronomicon.* In the Himalayas the legend
of the Abominable Snowman is by no means dead but
continues to be resurrected by even the most prosaic members of mountaineering expeditions. . . . Sightings of the
West Virginia Mothman—a brown humanoid endowed
with wings—continue to be reported; sea serpents and
monsters fill the oceans and lakes; UFO encounters have
become an almost everyday occurrence." Commentary by
Robert Turner, *The Necronomicon,* Neville Spearman,
Suffolk, 1978.

PART THREE

Our Lord had no doubts as to the reality of demonic possession; why should we?

—Rev. Charles Verey, *Clouds Without Water*

The Bible speaks of "the dragon . . . and his angels" [Revelations, 12:7], indicating that along with Lucifer, myriads of angels also chose to deny the authority of God. . . . Watch out, they are dangerous, vicious and deadly. They want you under their control and they will pay any price to get you!

—Rev. Billy Graham, *Angels: God's Secret Messengers*

If God is all, how can I be evil?

—Charlie Manson

It was the afternoon of the following day, June 27, and the *Föhn* had not yet ceased to suffocate Zürich in its dank embrace. Thrice the stifling wind had faltered, almost subsided: thrice it had resumed, hot and foul as ever: people's tempers were growing short.

Einstein, Joyce and Babcock were together again, this time in Einstein's study, having agreed to meet there at three. The professor was the most chipper of the trio, being recuperated from the long night with the aid of only a few hours' sleep and the intellectual stimulation of teaching his noon physics class. Joyce was still somewhat hung over, and looked it. Babcock, after drowsing fitfully on a divan in Joyce's sitting room for most of the morning, was only a little less desperate than the previous night.

"Well, Jeem," Einstein began, "what do you make of our friend's remarkable adventures, speaking honestly?"

"Speaking honestly?" Joyce repeated. "I begin to ask myself whether that is possible."

Einstein said nothing; but his glance mutely invited Joyce to continue.

"Once," Joyce said thoughtfully, "a fair named Araby came to Dublin. I was perhaps ten at the time and devouring all sorts of romantic literature about the mysterious East, the secrets of the Sufis, the magick of the Dervishes,

Aladdin and Ali Baba and much more of that sort. Can you imagine what the word 'Araby' connoted to me? My eagerness and excitement as the day of the fair approached were of the same order as my emotions, a few years later, when I nerved myself to enter the Red Light District and seek a prostitute for the first time. I thought a whole new world would open before me, a world of magick and wonder. What I found, of course, was an ordinary touring carnival, intended to amuse morons and empty the pockets of fools."

Babcock looked confused by this speech; Einstein was solemn. The silence stretched out until Joyce spoke again.

"Mr. William Butler Yeats and his friends," Joyce said simply, "live in Araby. It is real to them. More real than their servants, certainly. We go forth each day into the world of experience but we do not go mentally naked like Adam in Eden. We bring certain fixed ideas along whether we go to the corner pub, to a fair called Araby, or to the South Pole with Amundsen, I dare say. If a pickpocket enters this room he will see pockets to be picked; if Socrates were to be ushered in by the fair Mileva"—he bowed chivalrously toward the kitchen, where Mrs. Einstein could be heard puttering—"Socrates would see minds to be probed with annoying questions. If Mr. Yeats were here, he would see mere material shadows of the Eternal Spiritual Ideas known as Science," indicating Einstein, "Art," indicating himself ironically, "and Mysticism," indicating Sir John. "*I* see three people with different life histories," he concluded abruptly.

"All of which," Einstein asked drily, "is your way of saying that the Golden Dawn people seem no more mad to you than anybody else?"

"I am saying," Joyce replied, "that I can see the world as Yeats and the occultists do—as a spiritual adventure full of Omens and Symbols. I can also see it, if I choose, as the Jesuits taught me to see it in youth: as a vale of tears and a web of sin. Or I can see it as a Homeric epic, or a depressing naturalistic novel by Zola. I am interested in seeing all of its facets."

Sir John leaned forward, suddenly interested. "I think I begin to understand you a bit," he said. "You are saying that I am living in a Gothic novel, while you prefer to live in a Zola novel."

"Not that at all," Joyce said. "The Zola school is one-dimensional. I am seeking multi-dimensional vision. I wish to see deeply into Gothic novels, Zola novels and all other masquerades, and then beyond them."

"Fascinating," said Einstein. "Fascinating."

The other two looked at him expectantly.

"Your parable of Araby," Einstein said to Joyce, "reminds me curiously of a parable of my own. Imagine that we three are physicists seated here in this room. Unknown to us, this room is actually an elevator—a lift, Sir John—which is rising rapidly through outer space. Since we do not imagine that we are inside an elevator, but are educated in physics and curious about our environment, we begin to conduct experiments. We find that objects dropped from our hands fall to the floor. We find further that if the objects are thrown horizontally instead of dropped, they also fall, but in a parabola. We find, in fact, that as we experiment and write the simplest possible mathematical equations to describe our observations, we can derive the whole Newtonian theory of gravity. We decide that beneath this box in which we find ourselves is a planet which 'draws' objects to it."

"Is that true?" Joyce asked, startled. "It is more wonderful than anything you have told me of your theories thus far."

"I am in the process of proving it," Einstein said, "in a paper I'm writing. Now, it so happens that one physicist in the room, or the elevator, by some strange process of creative reorganization of sense-data—perhaps akin to these mind-bending Cabalistic experiments of the Golden Dawn people—has made the leap to another way of thinking. He conceives of the room as an elevator and imagines the cable and the machinery that is rapidly drawing us upward. He sits down and performs his own experiments and writes his own equations. He derives eventually the whole theory of inertia as found in classical mechanics. There is no planet beneath us at all, he decides.

"Now," Einstein said, "we are in the predicament that the doors are locked and we cannot get out of the room. How do we determine who has the correct explanation of the lawful phenomena that we observe—those who attribute them to gravity [a planet *beneath* us], or the one who attributes them to inertia [a cable *above* us, pulling us through free zero-gravity space]?"

"Oh, I say," Babcock murmured, "that *is* a bit of poser, isn't it?"

"Both are correct, in a sense," Joyce said firmly. "If both systems of equations will describe our situation, there is no reason to prefer one over the other, except esthetic preference. Within the terms of the problem we can never see the planet beneath us or the cable above us. You set us up for the wrong answer by telling the situation from the point of view of the man outside."

"Precisely," Einstein said. "Any coordinate system acts like the room I was talking about, and if there is an outside observer we cannot scientifically know it. From inside the room—inside any coordinate system—there is no way of saying whether gravity or inertia is the true explanation of the phenomena we observe. It is the same with Sir John's narrative—that is to say, it is either a random series of odd coincidences and Freudian dream symbols, given a totally artificial meaning by Sir John's occult beliefs, or it is a series of real occult Omens, depending on the interpretation of the observer."

"Precisely," Joyce said. "I can do as well as Sir John, in

the department of odd coincidences. For instance, my first teaching job was at a school on Vico Road in Dublin. More recently, in Trieste, I have had to walk the Via Giambattista Vico twice a day, to go to and from the home of one of my language students. Then I had a student who was fascinated by Vico's theory of the cycle in history. Naturally, I became interested in the life and philosophy of Vico after all that, and I found numerous parallels with my own life and thought, so that now everything I write is influenced by Vico. You may interpret this sequence in whatever way you choose. Either, *Unum,* the gods arranged for me to encounter Vico's name over and over in order to influence my writing; or, *Duum,* it was mere coincidence, and I gave it meaning by taking it seriously. There is no way of proving either hypothesis to the man who insists on seeing it the other way."

"Not quite," Einstein said sharply. "When it becomes possible to choose between two theories, we should choose the one that best accords with the facts. Or, we should develop a higher-order theory that reconciles the differences between the two conflicting interpretations—as I am trying to do with this gravity and inertia conundrum. Without such creative effort to make our concepts square with our percepts, our thought is just an exercise in wish fulfillment."

A skeptical noise from Babcock caused Einstein to look at him expectantly.

"Surprising as it may be," Babcock said wearily, "I agree with all you gentlemen have said. One of the first lessons I learned in the Golden Dawn is that perception depends on the mind of the observer, just as what is revealed through a lens depends on the angle of refraction. Your reminding me of *that* is a work of supererogation and does not at all relieve the fundamental terror of my position as one under attack by black magicians who have already shown their capacity to unhinge the minds of three people and drive them to suicide."

"Well, as to that," Einstein said mildly, "you are certainly a man with dangerous enemies, we all agree. What remains to be determined is whether they can actually manipulate the physical universe with their, um, magick, or whether they are merely superlatively clever at manipulating the minds of the human beings on whom they prey. In that connection, we would both be most interested to hear the rest of your story."

"Yes," Joyce said. "I certainly want you to get on with it. I have already formed a tentative hypothesis about what is actually afoot here—behind all the masques and masquerades—and I would be most intrigued to learn whether that theory will mesh with the subsequent facts."

"Very well," said Sir John. "To proceed, then."

And, as the *Föhn* wind continued to batter the window, he told Joyce and Einstein a tale that confounded all their expectations.

DE ILLUMINATORUM OPERIBUS DIVERSIS

Sir John found Verey's letter about the bat-winged creature so disturbing that he determined to learn all he could about the enigmatic Aleister Crowley—the man described by Jones as the leader of a false Golden Dawn lodge dedicated to licentiousness and black magick; the lover of Lola Levine, according to Ezekiel (or Ezra or Jeremiah) Pound; the wizard who had perhaps once turned Victor Neuberg into a camel; and, in Sir John's growing suspicions, the human channel through which the crew that never rests had been set loose upon the Verey family.

He began at the British Museum, uneasily recalling the dream in which he had encountered Karl Marx there and heard a confusing history of Freemasonry all muddled together with the assassination of Julius Caesar.

Reviews of Current Literature for the past decade revealed that Crowley was the author of more than a dozen volumes of poetry, every one of which had received uncommonly mixed reviews. The critic in *The Listener* did not seem at all to be able to make up his mind about one of Crowley's volumes, *The Sword of Song*, describing it as "fearless," "serious and intrepid" and "increasingly repellent" in a single paragraph. *The Seeker* was more charitable: "Crowley has been reproached in some thoughtless or malicious quarters. . . . It is undoubtedly no easy task to follow the royal bird in his dazzling flight"; while *The Clarion* frankly gave up in despair: "We must confess that our intelligence is not equal to the task." The *Cambridge Review* was simply furious at another Crowley volume, complaining that it was "obscene," "revolting" and a "monstrosity" that "demands an emphatic protest from lovers of literature and decency." The *Arboath Herald*, like the *Clarion*, surrendered to despair, designating Crowley's verse as "so clever one finds some of it utterly unintelligible." *The Atheist*, on the other hand, grudgingly praised Crowley while denouncing him: "Far as we are from admiring his dreamy romanticism, yet his staunch denial of the supernatural, the divine, the mystical must command our respect"; but, paradoxically, the *Prophetic Mercury* found the same verses hopeful for the opposite reason, saying, "The ever-present sense of God in the mind of the poet leads us to the prayerful hope that one day he may be enlightened." Again the *Yorkshire Post* was simply aghast: "Mr. Crowley's poetry, if such it may be called, is not serious"; but the *Literary Guide* was rhapsodic: "A masterpiece of learning and satire."

Q: Give a succinct and representative example of the controversial verse of Mr. Crowley.
A: From *Konx Om Pax*, 1907:

Blow the tom-tom, bang the flute!
　　Let us all be merry!
I'm a party with acute
　　Chronic beri-beri.
Monday I'm a skinny critter
　　Quite Felicien-Ropsy.
Blow the cymbal, bang the zither!
　　Tuesday I have dropsy.
Wednesday cardiac symptoms come;
　　Thursday diabetic.
Blow the fiddle, strum the drum!
　　Friday I'm paretic.
If on Saturday my foes
　　Join in legions serried,
Then on Sunday, I suppose,
　　I'll be beri-beried!

Sir John next tried the newspapers. In the *Times* for
1909—the year Sir John himself had graduated from Cambridge and the mad Picasso had shocked the Paris art
world with his first incomprehensible "Cubist" painting—
Crowley had been involved in a lawsuit with MacGregor
Mathers. The *Times* reporter was not sympathetic to either Crowley or Mathers, but Sir John was able to gather
that the ostensible purpose of the trial—Mathers' attempt
to prevent Crowley from publishing, in a magazine called
The Equinox, certain rituals of the original Golden Dawn—
was only an excuse to air the real conflict between them,
which hinged on the fact that each claimed to be the real
head of the Invisible College of the Rosicrucians. Well,
that was hardly news to Sir John; Jones had told him that
Crowley, Mathers and others were operating fake Rosicrucian lodges in competition with the real Golden Dawn.
The judge, Sir John learned with amusement, refused to
allow the trial to degenerate into a debate about such
claims, which by their very nature could not be settled in

an ordinary law court, and had merely ruled that Mathers had no authority to prevent Crowley from publishing documents of unknown age and authorship which both litigants admitted, and even stipulated, were written by superhuman intelligences unwilling to take corporeal form to testify on their own behalf.

Sir John was also amused to find that Mathers, under cross-examination, was forced to confess that he had, on occasion, alleged himself to be the reincarnation of King Charles I. He also found a clue to further information about Crowley in a casual remark, during the testimony, indicating that Crowley regarded himself as the world's greatest living mountain climber.

A visit to the Alpine Club quickly brought vehement denials of that claim. "Aleister Crowley," said the Club's secretary, a Mr. Mortimer, "is the world's greatest living braggart. None of his climbs is accepted as authenticated by us." But further questioning soon produced the usual ambiguity that seemed to cling to Crowley like fog to the London streets: it was obvious that the feud between Crowley and the Alpine Club went all the way back to the 1890s and that both sides had accused the other of lying so often that an outside observer could not form an impartial judgment. Mortimer did let slip one remark that suggested Crowley's mountaineering exploits might not be entirely contemptible, admitting that Oscar Eckenstein, Germany's greatest climber, had often called Crowley England's best contender—"but," Mortimer added hastily, "Eckenstein is a German Jew and has a grudge against us, so naturally he'd support Crowley's lies."

Sir John moved on to seek further clues to his enigmatic antagonist from various people who were reputed to know London high life extensively.

"Crowley is certainly a rascal, and an amusing one," said Max Beerbohm. "Whether he also is a true scoundrel

I cannot say, but he does devote a great deal of his energy to convincing the world that he's a scoundrel."

"Um, yes," Sir John said doubtfully, "but just how do you distinguish a rascal from a true scoundrel?"

"A rascal," said Beerbohm precisely, "doesn't care a brass farthing for contemporary morals, but still possesses his own kind of honor. A scoundrel has neither morals nor honor."

"Oh," Sir John said, still dubiously. "Could you give me an example of Crowley's, uh, rascality?"

Beerbohm chuckled. The heavy memories of Horeb, Sinai and the forty years showed as the daylight fell level across his face. "There are a thousand examples," he said, the stiffness from spats to collar relaxing into grace. "My own favorite involves the statue of Oscar Wilde in Paris, by that very talented young man Jacob Epstein. The French, you know, put the statue up to show they were more broadminded about, uh, Wilde's sexual proclivities than we are and would recognize a great artist whatever his, uh, peculiarities." He chuckled again. "They weren't quite broadminded enough for Epstein's statue, which was a nude, you see. That was a bit *thick*, in connection with Wilde's, um, reputation, but they couldn't, ah, insult Epstein by rejecting the statue after commissioning it. So they hired some hack to attach a fig leaf at the ah-uh-um sensitive point, if I make myself clear. Well, sir, do you know what Crowley did? He crept into the park after dark, with a hammer and chisel, and removed the fig leaf. Then, to add scandal to outrage, he walked into Claridge's here in London, that same night, wearing the fig leaf over the front of his own trousers!" Beerbohm laughed. "That is what I would call rascality, although I doubt it is scoundrelism."

The beautiful Florence Farr, London's most famous actress, was as paradoxical as most of the reviewers of Crowley's poetry. "Aleister," she said, "was, when I knew him ten years ago, the handsomest, wittiest, most brilliant young man in London. He was also the most unmitigated cad and blackguard I have ever encountered. From what I hear now and then about his life, these contradictions in him are growing more violent all the time. I am quite sure he will end either on the gallows or being canonized as a saint."

Victor Neuberg, the young poet who had allegedly been turned into a camel by Crowley, refused to meet with Sir John at all, sending merely a card saying in tiny script: "No man living understands, or can understand, Aleister Crowley, but those who value their sanity will not get involved with him."

Richard Aldington, the editor, commented: "Rodin considers Crowley our greatest living poet, but I fear that is due entirely to the fact that Crowley wrote a volume of verse glorifying Rodin's sculpture. Personally, I can't stand Crowley's verse. It's Victorian, and rhetorical, and windy. Totally without the modern note."

Gerald Kelly, the most fashionable painter in England, looking like exactly what he was—a man who would soon be elected to the Royal Academy—said, "I can't talk about Aleister Crowley, Sir John. You evidently haven't heard that he's my former brother-in-law. All I will say is that when my sister divorced him I was not unhappy."

Bertrand Russell, the mathematician, stated precisely, "I have never met a layman who understands modern mathematics as well as Aleister Crowley, but aside from that his head is a swamp of mushy mysticism. I hear he plays excellent chess, so you might learn more at the London Chess Club."

The London Chess Club turned out to be full of admirers of Crowley, all of whom regretted that he hadn't devoted more time to the game. "He could be a Grandmaster," one member said sadly, "if he didn't waste himself on nonsense like mountain-climbing and poetry and was not constantly running off to the East to ruin his mind with Hindu superstitions."

"Aleister," said another chess buff, "is the only man I have ever seen, short of Grandmaster status, who can really play blindfold chess against several opponents and win most of the games. In fact"—here he lowered his voice—"one of his sports is almost preternatural. He actually has, on more than one occasion, retired to a bedroom with his mistress of the moment and called out his moves to a player sitting at a board in the next room, *and won*. He says he does it to show us what real concentration means."

Sir John blushed furiously. "What a contemptible way to treat a woman," he said stiffly.

"Well," said the informant with a leer, "from what I heard about it, the sounds from the bedroom indicated that the lady was having a most gratifying experience; or several gratifications, in fact."

Sir John went off pondering that specialists can look right into the Devil's face and not recognize it. What seemed a mixture of vulgar stunt and intellectual gymnastics to the chess player was obviously far worse, to anyone aware of the sexual aspects of black magick: it was part of Crowley's continuous training for the ordeals of the ritual of Pan, in which prolonged sensuality is used to intoxicate the senses and open the door to the astral entities.

Sir John next went browsing in bookstores and after a frustrating search finally came upon one of Crowley's books—a prose work entitled *Book Four*, which claimed to explain all the mysteries of yoga and magick in simple words that the man in the street could understand. Sir John purchased this at once and took it home for study.

When Sir John returned to Babcock Manor after collecting all this contradictory but disturbing intelligence about the Enemy, he found that a small package had arrived from the Golden Dawn post office box in London.

That was strange, since Jones was still in Paris; but then Sir John did not know for a fact that Jones was in charge of these mailings. Perhaps some other officer of the Order sent out appropriate lessons to students at pre-arranged dates. Sir John opened the package, with a wistful hope that it might contain the secret of the Rose Cross ritual— something for which Jones had told him he might soon qualify.

To his chagrin, the pamphlet was entitled:

DE OCULO HOOR
Class A Publication
Hermetic Order of the G.·.D.·.

Sir John retired to the library to read this with considerable curiosity. It said:

1. *This is the Book of the Opening of the Eye of Horus, of which the symbol in the profane world is the eye in the triangle, and of which the meaning is Illumination.*

2. *Thou who readest this doth not read; thou who seeketh shall not attain; thou who understandeth doth not understand. For attainment and understanding cometh only when thou art not thou, yea, when thou art nothing.*

3. *Once there was a monk, a disciple of that great Magus of our Order whom men name the Buddha which signifieth He Who Is Awake. For men asked the Lord Gotama, Are you a God? And he answered, No. And they asked again, Are you a saint? And he answered again, No. And they asked then, What are you? And he answered: I am awake. Thence is he known as the Buddha, the Awakened One.*

4. *And the monk, in order to awaken himself, practised the Art of Meditation as taught by Buddha,*

*which in its original form before being distorted by
False Imaginings and Elaborations of Theologians,
was but this: To look upon all incidents and events
and Remember to Say Unto Thine Soul of each:* This
is transitory.

5. *And the monk looked upon all incidents and
events, Reminding himself always:* This is transitory.

6. *And the monk came close to Awakening, and
therefore was he in great peril, for The Lord of the
Abyss of Hallucinations, whom Buddhists call Mara,
the Tempter, cometh quickly to one near Awakening,
to hypnotize him again into the Sleep of Fools which
is the ordinary consciousness of Men.*

7. *And Mara did sorely afflict the monk with death
of offspring, and insanity of loved ones, and eye-
troubles, and slander, and malice, and the great curse
of Law Suits, and diverse sufferings; but the monk
thought only:* This is transitory. *And he was closer to
Awakening.*

8. *And Mara, the Lord of the Abyss of Hallucinations, then caused the monk to die and reincarnate as
an almost Mindless creature, a Parrot, which flitted
from tree to tree deep in the jungle; and Mara thought,
Now he has no chance of Awakening.*

9. *But a brother Monk of the Buddhist order came
one day through the jungle, chanting the Teachings,
and the Parrot heard, and repeated the one phrase
over and over:* This is transitory.

10. *And Mental Activity began in the Parrot, and
the memories of his past life came to him, and the
meaning of the teaching,* This is transitory; *and Mara
cursed horribly in frustration, and caused him to die
again and reincarnate as an Elephant, even deeper in
the jungle and further from the languages of men.*

11. *And many years passed, and there seemed no
chance of Awakening for that soul; but the effects of*

good karma, like those of bad, continueth forever; and eventually Men came to the jungle, and took the Elephant captive, to sell him to a great Rajah.

12. *And the Elephant lived in the courtyard of the Rajah, and many years passed.*

13. *And another monk of the Buddhist order came to the Rajah, and taught in the courtyard, and his teaching was:* This is transitory. *And memories awoke in the Elephant, and meaning was understood in the memories, and Awakening again came close.*

14. *And Mara cursed wrathfully, and caused the Elephant to die; and this time Mara took good care that reincarnation would recur at the furthest possible remove from all chance of Awakening, for Mara caused that the monk be reborn this time as an American Evangelist.*

15. *And the Evangelist was of the Moral Majority* [bocca grande giganticus] *and he journeyed across the American nation, North and South and East and West, preaching that all were in danger of hellfire, and that there was only One Path to Salvation, and that this Path lay in believing All he Said and doing All he Demanded.*

16. *And he enslaved many, who became mental Automatons, and these Automatons went about crying, Hallelujah, We Are Saved.*

17. *And Mara was gleeful, for now the soul of the monk was further from Illumination than ever; for previously he had been a Subjectively Hopeless Idiot—*id est, *one who is aware of his own hopeless idiocy—but now he was an Objectively Hopeless Idiot—*id est, *one who Thinks that he Knows when in fact he doth Know Nothing.*

18. *But the Evangelist met with others of the Clergy to discuss sending Missionaries to the Heathen of the East; and there One spoke of the superstitions of the*

Orient, and he mentioned the Buddhist teaching that All is transitory.

19. And Mental Activity began in the Evangelist, and memories of Past Incarnations stirred; and Mara, in bitter frustration, attempted the Last Trap of All, and caused the Evangelist to become Mahabrahma, Lord of Lords, God of all possible Universes.

20. And Mahabrahma abode in Divine Bliss for billions of billions of years, creating many lesser Brahmas who created Their own universes and were Gods to them; and Mahabrahma watched all this Activity and rejoiced in it with High Indifference; for Mahabrahma was Consciousness Without Desire.

21. And the monk now seemed at last cut off from Illumination forever.

22. But finally Mahabrahma observed, after watching many Gods come and go, and all Their universes grow and flourish and perish, that the great Law of Laws is that All is transitory.

23. And Mahabrahma realized that He, too, was transitory.

24. And Mahabrahma achieved Illumination.

25. And Mahabrahma came back to ordinary consciousness in the mind of the monk practising the Buddhist meditation of looking on all things and thinking, This is transitory.

26. And the monk did not know if he was a monk imagining he had been Mahabrahma or Mahabrahma playing at being a monk; and thus was his Illumination perfected.

DE FRATRIBUS NIGRIS, FILIIS INIQUITATIS

The next day brought another letter from Verey, and Sir John's heart sank when he saw that the handwriting on

the envelope was now visibly shaky and erratic. He tore it
open prepared for almost anything.

Dear Sir John,
    *The forces invoked by my wicked young brother
Arthur and the accursed Lola are more terrible than
I had ever imagined. I realize now—at last—that I
have never really taken Holy Writ [especially the Book
of Revelations] literally enough. The "principalities
and powers" of Hell are no figure of speech.*
    *"Woe to them who believe not, for they are damned
already."*
    *To come to the point: I have reached the climax of
the horrors.*

ACTION   **SOUND**

EXTERIOR. OUTSIDE VEREY'S CHURCH, EVENING.
  SUBJECTIVE SHOT: VEREY'S VIEWPOINT

CAMERA tracks toward door of church.

Verey's voice [over]: "Last Saturday night, before retiring, I locked up the church as usual and noticed . . ."

EXTERIOR, SAME. CLOSE-UP: THE DOOR LOCK.
  SUBJECTIVE SHOT: VEREY'S VIEWPOINT

CAMERA closes on the rusty door lock.

Verey's voice [over]: ". . . that the huge, old-fashioned door lock was becoming rusty and might need oil. It was extremely hard to turn the key, and I even wondered if it would be harder to open the door for services the following morning."

EXTERIOR, SAME. SUBJECTIVE
   TRACKING SHOT: VEREY'S VIEWPOINT

CAMERA pans around church to woodshed.

Verey's voice [over]: "I looked about for some machine oil . . ."

EXTERIOR, SAME. SUBJECTIVE CLOSE-UP:
   VEREY'S VIEWPOINT

VEREY'S hand holding up a long-nosed can of oil, tilts can—no oil flows.

Verey's voice [over]: ". . . but found my supply exhausted and made a mental note to buy some on my next visit to town."

EXTERIOR, SAME. SUBJECTIVE
   PAN: VEREY'S VIEWPOINT

CAMERA pans back to look up at church and then closes in on the window at the top of the building.

Verey's voice [over]: "Let me add that the church has only one window, high above the altar, and that this window is built into the wall, so that it neither opens inward nor upward; in fact, it does not move at all."

EXTERIOR, NIGHT SKY. LONG SHOT.

Black clouds rolling across the sky.

Thunder.

EXTERIOR, NIGHT. LONG SHOT.
   THE VEREY FARM.

Rain pouring down on the Verey farm. We see the church, the house and the barn, at least.

Verey's voice [over]: "It rained that night, quite heavily."

EXTERIOR, DAWN. LONG SHOT.
  THE VEREY FARM.
The rain has stopped. We see
puddles everywhere.

EXTERIOR, DAWN, CLOSE-UP.
  ROOSTER IN CHICKEN YARD.

The rooster crows.	*Rooster:* "The crew! The crew! The crew!"

INTERIOR, VEREY'S BEDROOM.
  SUBJECTIVE SHOT: VEREY'S VIEWPOINT

CAMERA "sits up in bed" and looks at the window, through which sunlight pours.	*Verey's voice* [*over*]: "I woke in the morning, thinking at once that this torrential down-pour might have contributed even further to the rusting of the door lock of the church."

EXTERIOR, THE FARMYARD.
  SUBJECTIVE TRACKING SHOT: VEREY'S VIEWPOINT

CAMERA moves toward the door of the church.	*Verey's voice* [*over*]: "I went out to check the lock. . . ."

EXTERIOR, CHURCH DOOR, CLOSE-UP.
  SUBJECTIVE SHOT: VEREY'S VIEWPOINT

The lock even more rusted than before. Key is thrust in but will not turn.	*Verey's voice* [*over*]: "I found, as I had feared, that it was now so totally rusted that it would not turn for the key and I was, in effect, locked out of my own church.
Key stuck in lock.	"This was most annoying, since worshippers were due within the hour for morning services."

EXTERIOR, THE FARM.
  SUBJECTIVE TRACKING SHOT: VEREY'S VIEWPOINT

CAMERA tracks to the
toolshed.

Verey's voice [over]: "I re-
sorted to brute force . . ."

Very faint violin: the Merry
Widow Waltz.

EXTERIOR, THE FARM, CLOSE-UP.

Verey's hand grabbing
hammer.

Verey's voice [over]: ". . . and
fetched a hammer . . ."

EXTERIOR, CHURCH DOOR, CLOSE-UP.

Hammer pounding lock.

Verey's voice [over]: ". . . with
which I smashed the lock."

Merry Widow Waltz *rising
slightly; sound of hammering.*

INTERIOR, CHURCH.
  SUBJECTIVE TRACKING SHOT: VEREY'S VIEWPOINT

CAMERA tracks forward to altar, where we find a cat sac-
rificed within a pentagram.
CAMERA picks up each de-
tail as Verey's voice describes
it.

Verey's voice [over]: "The
scene that greeted my eyes was
unspeakable. Upon the altar
was the body of a dead cat,
strangled with a blue garter and
impaled by a dirk or Oriental
dagger, within a pentagram.

A blood-splattered Bible, open
to the Epistle of Jude.

"Bloodstains had even splat-
tered the Bible. God will
judge the wretches who do
such foulness."

Merry Widow Waltz *rising to
peak of shrill intensity.*

The blasphemous horror of that sight still haunts my imagination, but even worse is the fact that I have been able to conceive of no way mere human *servitors of the Demon could have accomplished this atrocity. The window [which, I remind you, does not open] was unbroken, and the rusted door could not have been passed by any other means than the hammering apart of the lock which I myself employed—yet the lock was undamaged, save for the rust, when I found it.*

Naturally, I removed the cat, cleaned up the blood and erased the pentagram before the worshippers arrived [so as to avoid spreading further fear among the countryfolk], but my wife came upon me in the midst of this gruesome operation and I had no choice but to admit what had happened. She has lived in anxiety for this day week, and wishes more fervently to leave this lonely place. Yet I am attached to these fair hills and glens, as I have said before, and I really do not know that we would be safer anywhere else.

I have, incidentally, attempted to arrive at an explanation of this mystery in purely human terms. To hire a debased Oriental for any evil business is easy. To dress a dwarf in a weird costume, even to unleash an unusually large bird, and to count on fear and superstition to magnify all this into a reign of terror— all that would be possible to malignantly disposed humans. Then, I ask myself: Could not somebody have surreptitiously entered my house that Saturday night after I was asleep and borrowed the church key, using it before the rain caused further rust and made the lock into a hermetic seal? Alas, that explanation will not hold water. I keep the key on a small chain attached to a bracelet on my wrist, and the chain was unbroken in the morning. It is preposterous to imagine an intruder breaking the chain, doing

*the disgusting deed in the church, then returning to
my room to solder the chain together, in the dark,
without waking me.*

*I can only conclude that we are dealing with an
entity that can pass through solid walls.*

May the protection of the Lord be upon all of us.

> Sincerely,
>
> Rev. C. Verey

"A duplicate key," said Albert Einstein.

Joyce raised dim eyes behind thick glasses, a slow smile
dawning. "How alike we are," he said. "That was my first
thought, also."

"It is a fairly easy process," Einstein went on. "You
wish to terrorize an aging religious fanatic such as the
Reverend Verey. Obtain a few assistants and props—the
dwarf, the Oriental confederate, the hypothetical bird of
unusual size [which might even be a cardboard kite or a
machine of some sort]; the stage is set for the wildest
imaginings. Then, one dark night, very quietly, simply go
to the church and pour hot wax into the lock. In a few
moments, the wax has solidified. You carefully slide it out
and you have a model of the key. You then take this to
any competent locksmith and he will provide you with a
duplicate. The stage is set for your miracle."

Joyce, rolling a cigarette, grinned at Babcock. "Well,
Sir John?"

"Well, in fact," Sir John said, "although my beliefs are
admittedly more mystical than those of you gentlemen, I
am not without intelligence of my own. I also thought of
the duplicate key explanation and wrote at once to suggest
it to poor old Verey."

Einstein relit his pipe, frowning thoughtfully. "Tell me
his reply."

"Well," Sir John said carefully, "the objections are as

follows. First, the Verey property includes the church, the house and a small pasture where goats, pigs and the family horse are kept. Nobody has ever approached that establishment after dark, Verey says, without alerting the dogs, whose barking generally sets off all the other animals and creates a sufficient racket to wake the whole family— Verey, his wife, Annie, and his older brother, Bertran.

"Now, gentlemen, stretch your imaginations to the ulti- mate and conceive of a professional cat-burglar so adroit that he moves with the legendary silence of the American Apache Indians. He gets through the pasture to the church and makes his wax model, as you have suggested. He is very light-footed, indeed; but I will stipulate that such an improbably skillful burglar might exist.

"Very well, then," Babcock went on. "Our man has his duplicate key. He returns on that rainy Saturday night and again manages to get by all the animals without arous- ing a stir. He enters the church and does his blasphemous and brutal deed. Then he leaves. Very good. The only trouble is that Reverend Verey noted, as soon as he discovered the horror on the altar, that his own were the only tracks in the mud approaching the church door. It appears that our super-housebreaker not only moved through a lively farm without waking any of the animals, on two separate nights—when he made his model and when he returned for his Satanic sacrifice—but also, on the second occasion, crossed the yard *without leaving footprints in the mud.*" Sir John smiled thinly. "How does Free Thought explain this, my skeptical friends?"

ACTION	SOUND

INTERIOR, VEREY'S CHURCH, DAY.
  SUBJECTIVE TRACKING SHOT.
CAMERA moves jerkily   *Heavy breathing.*
toward the door.

DOOR OF VEREY'S CHURCH, LOOKING OUT.
  SUBJECTIVE LONG SHOT.
VEREY'S view: the yard, with   *Voodoo drums.*
one set of footprints—his—
coming to the door.

Einstein examined his pipe thoughtfully and then began with careful fingers cleaning it. His face was impassive.

"This older brother, Bertran," he said, peering into the pipe ash like Sherlock Holmes looking for a clue, "all he is, so far, is a name. We know nothing of him at all."

"Ah," Joyce said, "you are looking for a confederate of the conspirators within the household itself. Very keen, Professor. If one brother in three may be a renegade, why not two? Reminds me of my theory of *Hamlet,* which I must tell you sometime. I can even see a possible scenario, if the house and the church are close enough to each other. The sinister Bertran, like a Highlands d'Artagnan, crosses the roof of the house, leaps to the roof of the church, then lowers himself head downward to the door. Very athletic for the older brother of Reverend Verey, who is himself, we have heard, sixty-two years old. Implausible, but not impossible, and as Holmes himself often reminds us: 'When you have eliminated the impossible, whatever remains, however improbable, must be the truth.' I must sadly inform you, Professor, that I can't believe it for a moment."

"A balloon," Einstein said thoughtfully, rummaging about for fresh tobacco. [A nine-pipe case, Joyce thought.] "A small balloon, filled with helium, with a carriage for one or two passengers, such as one sees at fairs. No," he added, "don't bother mocking me. I am, at this point, grasping at straws. The balloon is possible, but I actually find it harder to believe our intruder descended from the sky that way, *without alarming all the animals*, than to believe he walked through a solid wall. I begin to realize that we are dealing with some diabolically clever conspirators here. Getting to the bottom of this will test all my powers of analysis."

"If," Joyce added morosely, "we ever do get to the bottom of it."

"On with the narrative," Einstein said. "We need more facts before we can form any conclusion."

The vicar said "Gracious/It's Brother Ignatius." Yes: I'm getting it finally. *Ed eran duo in uno.* Yes.

"By all means—on with the story," Joyce said, smiling privately.

DE SAPIENTIA ET STULTITIA

Waiting with growing impatience for Jones' return from Paris, and waiting also with dread and foreboding for the next events at Loch Ness, Sir John began studying Crowley's *Book Four.* It was indeed a very simple and down-to-earth explanation of the occult arts and sciences—at least in its opening chapters.

Crowley began by rejecting both Faith and Reason as ultimate answers to the mystery of existence—Faith because it may be Faith in the wrong god, the wrong church or the wrong teacher; Reason because it cannot get beyond the permutations and combinations of its own axioms. There remains only the method of Experiment, and Crowley defined every true occult system as a technique of physiological and neurological Experiment whereby consciousness is multiplied and evolution accelerated.

All of this, Sir John realized, came from the Golden Dawn teachings, but—to give the devil his due—Crowley certainly had a gift for explaining it with marvelous clarity and scientific precision.

Book Four went on to explain the techniques of yoga as physiological experiments.

Asana, the contorted gymnastics which Sir John had learned so painfully from Jones, was simply a method of bringing the body to maximum relaxation without actually going to sleep. *Pranayama,* the special yogic breathing technique, Crowley went on, was similarly a method of bringing the emotions under the control of the Will. Sir John again found himself grudgingly admitting that the Enemy had a real gift for making the occult arts scientifically clear.

The first sinister note entered in the discussion of *yama* and *niyama,* chastity and self-control. Crowley denounced all the traditional teachings on this subject as superstitious, pernicious and superfluous; in their place he offered the anarchistic advice: "Let the student decide for himself what form of life, what moral code, will least tend to excite his mind." This was totally insidious, Sir John realized: while pretending to scientific objectivity, it opened the door to any system of morality or amorality the reader might personally prefer.

Crowley then turned to ceremonial magick and explained it as an aid to yoga. The mind alone, he said, cannot achieve its own transcendence, even by the techniques of yoga, until the Will has become a weapon capable of absolute dictatorship over the body, over the body's raging emotions and over all mechanical habits. Every technique of magick, Crowley said, was simply a trick or gimmick to aid the student in developing such a self-transcending Will. Moral considerations about the handling of this Will were entirely ignored, Sir John noted; the perversity of Crowley's system was becoming more obvious.

And then Sir John came to the chapter on Mother Goose.

"Every nursery rhyme contains profound magickal secrets," Crowley began blandly, in the same rationalistic tone as the rest of his treatise. He then offered an example:

Old Mother Hubbard
Went to the cupboard
To get her poor dog a bone . . .

Crowley provided the key to this mystic verse, beginning:

*Who is this ancient and venerable mother of whom
it is spoken? Verily she is none other than Binah, as
is evident in the use of the holy letter H, with which
her name begins.*

Sir John stared at the page, dumbfounded. It was,
damn the man, quite plausible Cabala. *Binah* was the
dark secondary aspect of God, coequal with *Chockmah*,
Divinity's primary or rational aspect. And *Binah* is usually
symbolized as an old woman, just as *Chockmah* is symbolized as a white-bearded old man. The Cabalists taught
that the vulgar could only understand the male or patriar-
chal aspect of Divinity, but the first step to Illumination is
to understand, by direct intuition, the Most Highest's
feminine, passive aspect. And *Hé* as the second letter of
the Divine Name, *Yod Hé Vau Hé,* is identified with this
secondary aspect of Divinity—because *Hé* means a window and symbolizes the womb. Crowley was engaged in a
very complicated Cabalistic in-joke, to say the least of the
matter. Sir John read on with astonishment:

*And who is this dog? Is it not the name of God
spelled Cabalistically backward? And what is this
bone? This bone is the Wand, the holy Lingam!*
*The complete interpretation of the rune is now
open. This rime is the legend of the murder of Osiris
by Typhon.*
The limbs of Osiris were scattered in the Nile.
*Isis sought them in every corner of the Universe,
and she found them all except the sacred lingam,
which was not found until quite recently.*

This was not only sound Cabala but good comparative mythology. Isis, Sir John realized with awe, really did fit in with the dog symbolism, since she was identified with the Dog Star, Sirius. But it was also a wicked parody of Cabala to pretend to find all this in Mother Goose.

Crowley went on to explain the profound mystical meanings in Little Bo Peep (Buddha beneath the *bo* tree) and her sheep (the Lamb, the Saviour); in Little Miss Muffet (*Malkus,* the world of illusion) and the spider (Death, the great illusion); and so on, and on, through Little Jack Horner, Humpty Dumpty and all the rest.

Book Four, which had started out as the clearest and most empirical volume on mysticism Sir John had ever seen, had turned into an enormous practical joke on the reader. Sir John found himself remembering Victor Neuberg's terse note: "No man living understands, or can understand, Aleister Crowley, but those who value their sanity will not get involved with him."

When Mr. George Cecil Jones returned from his holiday in France, Sir John immediately met with him to recount the whole saga of Lola Levine, *Clouds Without Water, The Great God Pan* and the Rev. Verey's dead cat.

The meeting occurred at Jones' home in the Soho section of London. Jones introduced his wife and children—a pleasant and ordinary English family—and then retired with Sir John to a book-lined study on the ground floor. "You have been meddling with the Abramelin spirits," he said at once.

"No," Sir John said, taken aback that his nervousness was that easily read.

"Well, then, they have been meddling with you," Jones replied. "Tell me all about it." And he sat with an attentive, but impassive, face—much as he might sit through a business meeting at his chemical company—as Sir John poured out the whole story. There were perhaps a dozen candles about, two in brass candlesticks and several in sconces, so that the room was brilliantly illuminated; but Sir John still felt that each dank shadow that moved contained an adumbration of dark foreboding.

"Well," said Jones when Sir John's narrative was concluded, "you have certainly uncovered a very nasty situation, indeed. Are you afraid?"

"Fear is failure and the forerunner—"

"I know, I know; that is what you are supposed to believe," Jones interrupted. "The question is: How deeply do you believe it at this point?"

"I have my moments of trepidation," Sir John confessed.

"Only moments? Not hours or whole days?"

"Moments," Sir John said. "I think that, between the technique of *pranayama* and the Banishing Ritual of the Pentagram, I have learned to vanquish any negative emotional state before it can take full possession of me."

"That much, at least, is expected of the rank of Practicus," Jones replied. "If you were put to higher tests, however . . . If, say, I arranged with a surgeon friend of mine to have you observe while he performed major surgery, or an autopsy . . . or if I managed to pull the proper strings in government and you were admitted to see a hanging at Newgate Prison . . . could you stand as a Buddha, cleareyed, without fear or loathing?"

"Not entirely," Sir John admitted. "But I have attained such degree of detachment from the body-emotions that I would guarantee not to faint or become ill."

Jones arose and began to pace the room, silent and inscrutable as a caged panther. "Suppose," he said finally, "I were to take you on a jaunt to Paris and brought you to one of those clubs, of which you must have heard rumors, where sexual orgies are staged for the amusement of the spectators. Could you watch as a Buddha, clear-eyed, without lust and without the conditioned reflexes of horror from your Victorian upbringing?"

Sir John looked into the fire, sermons on hell running

through his memory. "No," he said hoarsely. "I think I would be disturbed by both desire and disgust."

Jones smiled reassuringly. "At least you are honest," he said simply. He ceased his pacing, drew a chair close to Sir John, and asked quietly, "Suppose I were to instruct you to take the next train to Inverness, go to the home of Reverend Verey, and employ the great ritual of exorcism to expel the forces that threaten his unfortunate household?"

Sir John's heart sank. "I could not do it," he said abjectly. "I have not yet sufficient confidence in myself and my control over the astral forces."

Jones laughed, and clapped the younger man on the shoulder. "Excellent, most excellent," he said unexpectedly. "You have gone far into a dreadful business," he continued, his eyes warm with admiration, "and I must allow that I am torn between the highest regard for your courage and the most dismal apprehensions about your foolhardiness. If you had acquiesced in my suggestion about the exorcism, I would have had to conclude that you are not only foolish but suffering from a bad case of premature self-confidence verging closely upon the Biblical sin of Pride. Nobody of the rank of Practicus should attempt what I just suggested. To accomplish an exorcism requires at least the rank of Adeptus Major."

Sir John breathed a great sigh of relief. "Thank you," he said, meaning more than two words could convey.

"I will have to think about this overnight," Jones added. "Perhaps I may even have to consult my Superior in the Order, although I hope this matter is not that serious. Mostly what we have here is malicious mischief, I think."

Sir John started violently. "Very malicious mischief," he objected.

"Oh, certainly," Jones agreed. "But calm yourself a bit and think about the matter more rationally. Have you ever seen me levitate or walk through walls? Do you imagine that I can perform such wonders but have hidden them from you, out of modesty perhaps? I assure you that such *siddhis,* as the Hindus call these powers, are very rare, and are mostly a distraction from the Great Work anyway. That a group of debauched diabolists is very advanced in the *siddhis* is simply preposterous, Sir John. They have magnified egos usually, not magnified powers. There is much evil here, certainly, but there is also much trickery and sheer bluff. Let me think upon it."

DE CLAVICULA SOMNIORUM

Once again that night, Sir John's dreams were beastly and terrifying. Lola, Lola, Lola was everywhere he wandered in the gnomic caverns of sleep. Old Celine was guiding Sir John through some dark, Hispanic sort of museleum and they came upon Goya's *Maja Naked:* the face on the portrait was Lola's, and her eyes were alive, looking into Sir John's soul with obscene mockery. "Wait," Celine started to object, "it is only Art . . ." But Sir John was racing through a garden past a tree around which curled a blue gartersnake the size of a python: under the tree, still nude and mocking, Lola called to him, "See you when tea is hot." NO TRESPASSING said a sign. "C.U.N.T. is hot," said an echo. He was in the Boulak Museum in Cairo (where was Celine?) and an ancient Stele was before him showing hawk-headed Horus, a winged globe and the naked star-goddess Nuit. Surgeon Peel sang:

> Priests in black gowns are going their rounds
> Choking with briars our joys and desires

"Watch Surgeon Peel," said Surgeon Talis.
Sir John was in Hagia Sophia in Constantinople, examining a most intricately jeweled Eastern Orthodox crucifix.

"Speak," Sur Loin said, "if you see Kay?" And Sir John noted that the initials I.N.R.I. were followed by a smaller script, saying:

> *Ipsum Nomen Res Ipsa*
> *[Eat It With Catsup]*

"The name itself is the thing itself," Sir John translated. "What on Earth does that mean?"

But the cross became the bodhi of Lola, arms extended, glowing goldly. "*Yod:* Isis: Virgin Mother," she said hermetically. "The seamen at dawn."

"*Nun:* Death: Apophis, the Destroyer," said old Verey morbidly. "Sir Talis at noon."

"*Resh:* the Sun: Osiris Risen," Celine added soulfully. "Rest, erection."

"*Yod:* Isis: Virgin Mother," Lola repeated. "Eat it with catsup!"

"Isis: Apophis: Osiris: IAO!" cried a voice like thunder.

THE NAME ITSELF IS THE THING ITSELF, Sir John was writing desperately in his journal: this was too important to be forgotten.

And then it was morning. The birds sang outside, sunlight poured in a golden flood through the windows; and Sir John wondered whether we approach ultimate reality more closely in ordinary consciousness or in the gnomic symbolism of our dreams. He recorded the whole vision in his magical diary before it could fade and went down to breakfast still puzzling over *Ipsum Nomen Res Ipsa:* The Name Itself is the Thing Itself. I.N.R.I.: Isis, Apophis, Osiris: IAO.

The morning mail contained an oddly shaped package from the Society for the Propagation of Religious Truth, Inverness, Scotland. Sir John tore it open as he sat down to breakfast, and found it contained a letter from Verey and a cylindrical phonograph record. He turned to the letter at once.

Verey's handwriting was so shaky, now, that it was difficult to read in places. He began without formality:

My Dear Sir John:
The worst has happened. I can scarcely gather my wits to write a coherent account. God help us all.
The night before last, the buzzing and tittering of the weird creatures that lately haunt this misfortunate place became more terrifying than ever. I resolved to make a recording of these sounds, so that others may hear it and judge if it be only my imagination that these bat-winged things were actually aping human speech. Now, I can think of no use for this record except to send it to you. Others, I am sure, would reject it out of hand, saying that I had faked it; playing it back has made me realize that even I would disbelieve it if I had not been on the scene when it was made.
But a worse horror has occurred.
In yesterday's post there was a package for my brother, Bertran. I happened to notice that the sender used an abbreviation, M.M.M., which meant nothing to me but was puzzling. Under these initials was an address on Jermyn Street in London, but I cannot recall the number.
While I was reading my own mail, Bertran wandered into the library to open the package. After a few moments I became aware of a sound that few people, I suppose, have ever heard; at first, I could not decide if it were laughter or weeping. I then realized it was the laughter of hysterical madness. I rushed at once to the library, but, alas, I was too late.
My God, Sir John, as I entered the room, Bertran already had a hunting rifle held to his head. I shouted, "Stop!" and ran forward, but he only looked at me

*with mad, terrified eyes and pulled the trigger. I
actually saw the disgusting sight of the back of his
head exploding and— The details are too hideous to
write. I wonder how doctors and policemen ever
learn to look on such sights without going mad themselves. Certainly, I must have been mad for a few
moments; I remember sitting on the floor, holding
Bertran's dead body in my lap as a mother might
hold a child, weeping. I thought, irrelevantly but
with terrible emotion, that the writers of "murder
mysteries" do not know of what they write if they
imagine such scenes are matters for entertainment.
My God, I [unintelligible words] work of Satan.*

*Then I began to look about for the package that
had evidently triggered this inexplicable crisis of suicidal melancholy. I realized suddenly that there was
a fire in the grate, where none had been before
Bertran entered the library, and I made the correct
deduction. But try as I might, it was too late to save
any particle from the flames. I saw only that the
object had been a book of some sort—a rather thin
volume, it appeared.*

*I must be off to the coroner's inquest and will post
this on my way. If you can find an M.M.M. on Jermyn
Street, Sir John, for God's sake, do not enter its
premises, but please inform me whatever you can
learn from outside.*

In haste,

C. Verey

Sir John became aware that his poached egg and ham
were growing cold on the plate. It was not at all clear to
him how long he had been sitting, staring into space, the
letter fallen to the floor beside him. Mourning doves were
cooing softly just outside the window. He was in the real,

tangible universe and the forces of nightmare and magick were active here, too, not just in the astral dream realms.

"It wasn't suicide," he said aloud, not even realizing that he had succumbed to the symptom of talking-to-oneself. "It was murder." M.M.M., whoever or whatever it was, had sent Bertran Verey a book that drove him to choose death rather than continued existence in this universe.

Then Sir John remembered the phonograph record of the "buzzing, tittering" voices. Numbly, like one walking in a dream, he took the cylinder to the music room and inserted it into his phonograph machine.

What he heard—the voices of the creatures afflicting Loch Ness—was an insectoid parody of human speech.

[*Buzzing, unintelligible sounds*]
[*A dog barks with a shrill sound of animal fear.*]
DEMENTED FEMALE VOICE
Tae hell! Tae hell! Ye shall all gang tae hell!
MALE VOICE
No escape, no escape, no escape, no escape, no escape, no escape, no escape . . . [*voice degenerates into sub-human buzzing*]
SECOND MALE VOICE
That's right. That's right. That's right.
SEXLESS MACHINE VOICE
They'll all go crazy in that house.
DEMENTED FEMALE VOICE
Aye, they'll all gae daft. Charlie and Bertie and Annie, they'll all gae daft.
MALE VOICE [*singing*]
Charlie's going crazy, Charlie's going crazy, Charlie's going crazy . . .
THIRD MALE VOICE
The giant cockroaches are coming!
BESTIAL VOICE
The ants are coming . . .

DEMENTED MALE VOICE
The centipedes are coming . . .
DEMENTED FEMALE VOICE
No wife, no horse, no mustache!
THIRD MALE VOICE
Tis blood, thou stinkard, I'll learn ye how to gust.
BESTIAL VOICE
The Death Mosquitoes! Killer Moths in the streets!
  [*Unintelligible sounds*]
  [*Thunder*]
MACHINE VOICE
One part sodium chloride and one part garters . . .
THIRD MALE VOICE [*chanting*]
From the depths of space, from the dark planets, from the
stars that gleam with evil . . . [*unintelligible*] . . . the crypt of
the Eyeless Eaters, the cursed valley of Pnath, He Who Shall
Not Be Named . . .
BESTIAL VOICE
Tha want coont, Charlie. Tha want coont.
DEMENTED MALE VOICE
In the ghoul-haunted Woodland of Weir, stranger pause to
shed a tear.
DEMENTED FEMALE VOICE
Henry Fielding wrote *Tom Jones* and cursed be he that
moves my bones!
THIRD MALE VOICE
All aboard for Elfland. Check your mind at the door.
BESTIAL VOICE
Charlie's going crazy, Charlie's going crazy, Charlie's going
crazy . . .
  [*Dog howls again in terror.*]
MACHINE VOICE
That's right: you're wrong. That's right: you're wrong. That's
right: you're wrong.
BUZZING, BARELY HUMAN VOICE
Wolde ye swinke me thikke wys?

THIRD MALE VOICE
Io Pan! Io Pan Pan! I adore thee, Evoe! I adore thee, IAO!
DEMENTED FEMALE VOICE
Aye, my coont, Charlie. Tha wants my coont.
FOURTH MALE VOICE
. . . to the Black Goat of the Woods, to the altar of the seventy thousand steps leading down, to the bowels of the earth and the Abomination of Abominations . . .
DEMENTED FEMALE VOICE
Magna Mater! Magna Mater! Atys! Dia ad aghaidh's ad Adoin! Agus bas dunach ort!

The record stopped abruptly. Sir John sat in a daze, knowing that he had heard the voices of insane nightmare somehow unleashed from the darkest side of human fantasy and fear to take on substance real enough not just to torment poor Verey but to leave an impress on the record. The interpenetration of the worlds of dream and reality was complete.

Arthur Machen's words, from *The Great God Pan*, came back to him: "There must be some explanation, some way out of the terror. Why, man, if such a case were possible, our earth would be a nightmare."

ACTION	SOUND
INTERIOR, NIGHT. A MASQUERADE. LONG TRACKING SHOT. CAMERA hunts through the dancers—who include YEATS, TROTSKY, HITLER and BERTRAND RUSSELL—and comes finally to the Robed Figure at the altar.	Merry Widow Waltz. *The Robed One:* "O thou lion-serpent-sun driving back the demons of night! I adore thee, Evoe! I adore thee, IAO!"

George Cecil Jones put down Verey's letter. His hand was trembling.

"My God," he said.

They were in Jones' study and Sir John could see, even in the candlelight, how pale the chemist had become.

"Do you know anything of this M.M.M.?" he asked.

"Of course," Jones said. "It's a bookstore. Mysteria Mystica Maxima—Occult and Mystical Books of All Ages; 93 Jermyn Street."

"Yes, Verey mentions that the address was on Jermyn Street—but a *bookstore?*"

Jones smiled thinly. "You would expect some sort of Satanic temple with gargoyles grimacing at the passersby? An occult bookstore is as good a lure as any—if your prey is the individual seeking mystical secrets and your purpose is to lead him away from the path of light onto the path of darkness. Can you imagine Scotland Yard being persuaded to place a bookstore under surveillance, in this land of liberty and constitutional rights? Oh, a bookstore is an ideal trap for fools . . ." He shook his head, wearily. "The Mysteria Mystica Maxima is a creature that we in the Golden Dawn have watched with great interest since it opened two years ago. It has a quite adequate stock of mystical books of all traditions, but there are more volumes there by Mr. Aleister Crowley than by any other author. It also offers lectures, quite frequently, by Mr. Crowley."

"And was Lola Levine one of Crowley's mistresses?"

"She was," Jones answered, "and, I imagine, still is."

"And is she the Lola in *Clouds Without Water?*"

"I cannot doubt it any longer."

Sir John leaped from his chair and stood over Jones. "By God!" he shouted. "A man has been driven mad by a book! Murder has been done—murder that can probably never be proven in a court, but murder, nonetheless. Bat-winged creatures that titter and talk like the delusions

of madness—malign dwarfs out of Celtic mythology—
monstrous things—that abominable sacrifice on the altar—
Jones, Jones, stop being the inscrutable teacher: it is too
late for that. Tell me in plain words, for God's sake, what
we confront here."

"Sit down," Jones said quietly, "and *do* stop panting. Of
course, I will tell you all that we know. Pray believe we
do not engage in mystery-mongering for its own sake. It is
well that beginners do not know the whole truth, just as it
is well that soldiers do not have too real a picture of battle
before they are sent to the front."

Sir John sat down. "I apologize for my outburst," he
said stiffly.

"It was to be expected under the circumstances,"
Jones replied reassuringly. "Now, then, to be brief and
precise . . ."

But Jones was far from brief; he spoke, in fact, for
nearly two hours.

Freemasonry, Jones said, began with the Knights Templar, as Sir John had argued in his book, *The Secret Chiefs.*
Though non-Masonic historians regard this story of the
origin of Masonry as a myth, that is because they only
know the rituals and teachings of the public Masonic
orders—like the Free and Accepted Scottish Rite and the
Royal Arch. Those privy to the secrets of the more arcane
orders, such as the Brethren of the Rose Croix and the
Golden Dawn, can easily see, Jones said, the direct continuity from the Knights Templar to the present.

Moreover, Jones continued, there have been, ever since
the destruction of the Templars by the Holy Inquisition in
1314, *two* distinct traditions of mystical Freemasonry, each
denouncing the other as false and absurd.

"Yes," said Sir John, "I believe I know what you mean.
There are those who accept the guilt of the Templars and
those who deny it."

"Precisely," said Jones. He rose to throw another log on the fire and then continued thoughtfully.

The charges against the Templars, Jones reminded Sir John, included blasphemy, sexual perversion and black magick. All historians agree that these accusations were brought by Philip II, the King of France, in order to seize the enormous wealth of the Templars. But no two historians have ever come to total agreement about which, if any, of the charges happened to be true. The whole matter is made more complicated by the inconsistent behavior of Jacques de Molay, Grand Master of the Templars.

"His behavior," Sir John interjected, "is all too painfully clear to anybody who has investigated the instruments the Inquisition used in those days in order to obtain confessions."

"Indeed," Jones said somberly. "The fact remains that de Molay left behind a most ambiguous heritage." After arrest, he confessed under torture to all the charges made against the Order of Templars, including even such extremities as spitting on the crucifix and every sexual excess imaginable. Brought to trial, de Molay repudiated the entire confession and stated emphatically that he had made these admissions only to escape the sadistic tools of Inquisitorial interrogation. He was then put to the torture again, confessed again, and stood trial a second time without further denials. Then, on the pyre of his execution, before the flames were lit, he again passionately affirmed his innocence and that of the Templar order, denounced the Inquisition and the Royal House of France, and—according to some sources—died with the shout, *"Vekam, Adonai!"* [Revenge, O Lord!]

"Any objective historian," Jones went on, "however prejudiced against the claim that Freemasonry is rooted in the secret teachings of the Templars, will admit that all the Templars were not killed in the great purge of 1314. Indeed, it is documented that the Spanish lodges of the Templars were not persecuted at all and continued quite unharmed while the French lodges were systematically exterminated. And even the more open Freemasonic orders, such as the Scottish Rite, still use de Molay's last words—*Vekam, Adonai!*—in their Third Degree initiation, although most of them have no clear idea what the words mean or where they come from."

A continuous series of tragedies has struck the French throne over the centuries, Jones went on. It began with the assassination of Philip II, who had denounced the Templars and seized their wealth; Philip himself was stabbed to death one year and one day after de Molay was burned at the stake. It climaxed with the beheading of Louis XVI during the French Revolution. All this was the work of one lodge of Masonic Templars who were very literal about de Molay's cry for vengeance. "It is their aim," Jones said somberly, "having abolished the French monarchy, to overthrow, eventually, every king in Europe, and to destroy the Papacy, also."

Jones began rummaging in his bookshelves and produced a parchment of recent printing. "This," he said, "is a document of the lodge to which I refer. It now calls itself the Ordo Templi Orientis—the Order of Oriental Templars—and is the owner of record of the Mysteria Mystica Maxima bookstore at 93 Jermyn Street. All members of the Ordo Templi Orientis must sign three copies of this document. It is the concise summary of the beliefs of the false Masonry which we in the Golden Dawn are pledged to oppose and vanquish." He handed Sir John the parchment, which read:

There is no God but Man.
Man has the right to live by his own law.
Man has the right to live in the way that he wills to
   do.
Man has the right to dress as he wills to do.
Man has the right to dwell where he wills to dwell.

Man has the right to move as he will on the face of the
earth.

Man has the right to eat what he will.

Man has the right to drink what he will.

Man has the right to think what he will.

Man has the right to speak as he will.

Man has the right to write as he will.

Man has the right to mould as he will.

Man has the right to carve as he will.

Man has the right to work as he will.

Man has the right to rest as he will.

Man has the right to love as he will, where, when
and whom he will.

Man has the right to kill those who would thwart
these rights.

"But this is anarchy!" Sir John exclaimed.

"Exactly," Jones said. "It is a declaration of war against
everything we know as Christian civilization."

"And how insidious it is," Sir John remarked. "Every
person of enlightened sentiments will agree with parts of
it. The incitement to promiscuity, assassination and revolution is phrased so as to seem part and parcel of an
integrated philosophy of liberty. It would be particularly
attractive to young and impressionable minds."

"Look again at the first line," Jones said. "That is the
kernel of the blasphemy: 'There is no God but Man.' Do
you see how that could lead weak-minded atheists to a
kind of humanistic mysticism, and naïve mystics to atheism, while drawing both into a worldwide plot against
both civil government and organized religion? And can
you see how this ultra-individualism could even attract
some really good minds and noble hearts during the Dark
Ages when all government was tyranny and the chief
engine of religion was the ungodly terrorism of the
Inquisition?"

"And the perversions coded into *Clouds Without Water* are the same as those charged against the Templars," Sir John mused. "The continuity is undeniable, over a period of six centuries . . . But do they really believe that such vile and nameless practices can raise them beyond humanity to Godhood?"

"These erotic practices are central to many cults," Jones said. "You will find them among certain Taoist alchemists in China, among the Tantrists in India, in the Egyptian and Greek mystery cults, among certain dark sects of Sufis in the Middle Ages—which is probably where this dark, diabolical side of Masonry evolved, alongside of true Masonry."

"But," Sir John cried, "how could a man be trained in the Golden Dawn, as this Crowley was, and deliberately turn his back on it and join this perversion of the true Craft?"

Jones sighed. "Why did Lucifer fall?" he asked. "Pride. The desire, not to serve God, but to *be* God."

There was a long silence and each man contemplated the horror lurking behind the initials M.M.M.

Sir John spoke first. "What can we do for poor Reverend Verey and his wife?"

"There is only one thing to do," Jones said decisively. "We must cable him at once and urge, in the strongest possible language, that he and Mrs. Verey come to London straightaway. Here, working with the Chiefs of our Order, we can create a psychic shield to protect them. If they remain in that lonely home on Loch Ness, further horrors will inevitably descend upon them." Jones shook his head wearily. "We must make the cable as strongly worded as possible," he repeated. "Any delay on their part might be long enough for a second tragedy to occur."

DE FORMULA DEORUM MORIENTIUM

Jones and Sir John spent nearly an hour composing the cable; it was nearly two in the morning when Sir John arrived home at Babcock Manor, totally exhausted.

If he had bad dreams again, he was unable to remember them, because his butler, Wildeblood, abruptly awakened him at seven in the morning.

"I'm most sorry, sir," Wildeblood said, "but there is a gentleman here who is most insistent upon seeing you. He is in a terribly agitated state."

"At this ungodly hour?" Sir John grumbled, feeling for his slippers groggily. "Who the blazes is he?"

"A clergyman, sir. He gave his name as Reverend Charles Verey."

Sir John bolted out of bed, grabbing desperately for his robe. He knew in his bones that fresh horror had struck Inverness before the cable could have arrived. "No tea," he said. "Coffee—very black. And eggs and bacon for two, I suppose. In the plant room."

He washed and brushed his hair rapidly, without bothering to shave. Bat-winged monstrosities . . . the malign Wee People, regarded as quaint and harmless only by ignorant citified folklorists . . . the Thing in Loch Ness . . . What new abomination had finally driven old Verey from his beloved Highland hills?

Descending the stairs almost at a gallop, Sir John received two shocks at once. Rev. Verey was a hunchback (but, of course, he would be too sensitive to mention that in his letters . . .) and he wore the most haggard and tragic face Sir John had ever seen.

Composing his own features with great difficulty, Sir John extended a steady hand. "I am at your service, sir," he said in a level voice. *Keep calm, keep calm,* he told himself sternly.

The old man took Sir John's hand weakly. "You see before you a broken man," he said hoarsely. "I am almost ready to despair of God's goodness," he added, choking back a sob.

"Come," Sir John said kindly. "You must be exhausted from your trip, in addition to the evil forces you have faced. Let us breakfast together and discuss what can be done." Verey was so pale, he noticed, that it was almost as if his face were painted for a death scene at the Old Vic.

And so two men, both struggling for self-mastery, sat down in the plant room—where Sir John kept a cheerful collection of ferns, forsythia and morning glories, amid cages of canaries and mynah birds. It was by far the brightest breakfast room in the mansion, and Sir John had chosen it for that reason. Unfortunately, one of the mynahs had apparently picked up an indelicate phrase from one of the workmen who had installed new shelving the past weekend.

"Hold your fucking end up, Bert!" the bird shrieked, as Sir John ushered the aged clergyman to the table.

"Quiet!" Sir John burst out, forgetting that it is better to ignore a mynah at such moments.

"Hold your fucking end up, Bert!" the bird repeated, encouraged by the attention.

"I'm sorry," Sir John said, feeling inane. "He must have picked that up from a laborer."

"It doesn't matter," Verey said absently. "Annie is dead." He stared at the tiletop table, seemingly unable to speak further.

["*Hold your fucking end up, Bert!*"]

"Annie?" Sir John asked gently. "Your wife?"

"Aye," Verey cried. "Annie, my wife. My companion for these forty-three years. My treasure, my heaven on earth." And Sir John looked at the tabletop himself now, not wishing to watch the old man's struggle against tears.

"Coffee, sir," said Wildeblood, suddenly appearing from amid the ferns. "The food will be along momentarily."

"Here, Reverend, take it hot and black," Sir John said. "It will stimulate and revive you. I can't tell you how sorry I am—how my heart feels for you at this moment— there are no words . . ."

"*Hold your fucking end up, Bert!*"

"Wildeblood!" Sir John exclaimed, "take that god——
. . . that foul bird outdoors at once!"

"Very good, sir." Wildeblood withdrew carrying the
cage. "Hello. Hello," the bird cried as it was removed.
"Wanna cracker. Hello. Wanna cracker."

"I can't tell you how sorry I am," Sir John began again,
realizing he was repeating himself. "What, uh, happened?"
he asked. "Get it off your chest, man."

"It was the day after the inquest on Bertran," Verey
said tonelessly. [*He's still in shock*, Sir John thought.] "I
hadn't told Annie about the package that unhinged Bertran's
mind—why give her more to worry about? Oh, what a
fool I am, what a blind, ignorant fool . . . If she had
known . . . if she had been warned . . ."

"Get a grip on yourself," Sir John said gently.

"Yes, of course. I'm sorry. . . ." [*The victims of the
worst tragedies*, Sir John thought, *always apologize to
others, as if guilty about the debt of pity we owe them*.]
"It was another package," Verey went on. "I didn't notice
when the post came. I was in my study, praying . . . asking God to intervene, to stop these diabolical beings who
are afflicting my family. Like Job, I wanted to know that
God did hear me and did have a reason for allowing the
Adversary to heap these cruelties upon us. I don't know
. . . I was praying and weeping both, I think. Bertran was
one of the bravest men I have ever known, and I could
not begin to imagine what could drive him to the cowardly, un-Christian act of suicide. What was that damnable book? At last, somehow, I composed myself. I said,
'Not my will but Thine, be done, O Father,' and resolved
to hold my faith despite all." Verey raised tormented eyes
to stare at Sir John like a wounded animal. "That was
when I heard that horrible sound for the second time in
my life—the laughter of hysterical madness."

Sir John clenched the old man's humped shoulder.
"Courage," he said gently.

"I rushed to the kitchen," Verey went on, his voice again toneless and detached, in traumatic shock. "She had thrown it into the wood stove, but I could see that it was a book. I even read the syllables THER GO on the burning cover. Oh, God—THER GO, THER GO: What can that mean? But Annie was screaming in agony by then and in one horrible instant I could see why. She had swallowed the whole contents of the iodine bottle in our medicine cabinet. The empty bottle was at her feet. I held her for a moment, as she died, and she tried to speak. I think she was attempting to say that she didn't know suicide by iodine would be that painful. . . ."

The old Scotsman stared into space, reliving the scene. Finally, he spoke again. "My God, my God, why hast Thou forsaken me?"

"Eggs and bacon, sir," said Wildeblood, reappearing.

"THER GO! THER GO!" screamed a mynah bird.

After breakfast, Sir John and the Rev. Verey brought an extra pot of coffee into the library and discussed the entire series of terrors that had brought them together.

Babcock told what he knew about Lola Levine, Aleister Crowley, the M.M.M. and Machen's *Great God Pan*. Verey listened with an abstracted air, as if he had supped so full on horrors that nothing further could stun him.

"The book," Babcock said finally, "the terrible book that led to both suicides—that may be the key to the whole mystery. Those damnable syllables that you recall— THER GO—are so tantalizingly inconclusive. Can you remember no more?"

"Nothing," Verey said woodenly, hollowly. "You must remember that I had only an instant to look into the flames, and my mind was in a state of shock at the time."

Sir John poured more coffee, thinking of phrases like "There you go," "There they go," "There we go." He suddenly had a new thought.

"At least we can avoid two obvious false leads," he said.

"The book wasn't either *Clouds Without Water* or *The Great God Pan* itself. Neither of those has a *ther go* in the title. Besides, you and I and others have read those books without going mad. . . ."

Verey leaped up and began pacing, a tragic figure with his hunched back and white, ashy face. "The book we are speaking of is not made up of hints or codes, like *The Great God Pan* or *Clouds Without Water*," he said. "The horror of it must be visible on every page, wherever one opens it. Both Bertran and poor Annie reacted within two or three minutes of opening the volume. They must have been driven mad by only a few sentences . . . a paragraph at most. . . ."

Babcock himself had grown pale. "I suddenly realize, Reverend, that there is one obvious remaining target for this monstrosity," he said awkwardly. "Yourself. You must remain here, as my guest, until this whole terrible business is settled. And any packages to you, from M.M.M., must remain unopened, or at the most should be opened only by a man I know who is so advanced in occult knowledge that he might be able to deal with whatever is in this book."

Verey stared into the fireplace. "I know you are right," he said wearily, "although, at this point, I would hate to see anyone, however advanced in occult knowledge you may consider him, open a package from that damnable M.M.M."

"Perhaps," Sir John replied. "That is for Jones himself— the man of whom I spoke—to decide. But certainly neither you nor I must open such a package. If you are the obvious next target, *I* may well be the target after you. God," he cried, "how can such things be, and the world go on in its smug materialistic blindness?"

Verey sighed. "It's those atheists at Oxford and Cambridge," he said. "It's the heritage of Voltaire and Darwin and Nietzsche. . . . The whole intellectual climate of Europe for one hundred fifty years now has been guided by the Anti-Christ, to blind us . . ."

"Well, history can't be changed," Sir John said, "but our future is always in our own hands. I have had a telephone installed recently, and I am going to put a call through to London, to get Jones out here as soon as possible. Believe me, he is better equipped to deal with this horror than you or I."

He rose, but stopped at the sudden look of anguish on Verey's face.

"My God," Verey said. "McPherson."

Sir John whirled to confront him. "McPherson?" he exclaimed. "Who's McPherson?"

"Reverend Duncan McPherson," Verey said. "My partner and associate in the Society for the Propagation of Religious Truth. He received one of the postcards, too."

Sir John felt as if the solid earth were collapsing into random atoms beneath him. "What postcards?" he cried. "You never mentioned any postcards."

Verey was virtually jumping up and down with anguish and impatience. "I must warn him," he said. "You have a telephone, you say. But whom do I know in all of Inverness with a telephone?"

"The police!" Sir John exclaimed. "We must call the police there and have them get in touch with McPherson! But what postcards?"

"Later, man!" Verey cried. "Where's the telephone?"

"In the downstairs hall," Babcock said. "But how in the world can we explain all this to a policeman?"

They were hurrying to the stairs as they exchanged these incoherent remarks. "The police know all about the suicides," Verey explained excitedly, "and they have heard my testimony about the packages that came in the post just before the suicides—although I think they only half-believed me. . . ."

But by the time both men were in the telephone alcove

in the front hall they were speaking fairly calmly and rationally again. Verey asked the operator to put him through to Inverness-418, and, after the usual annoying delay, he was connected.

"This is Reverend Verey," he said when the phone was answered at the other end. "I must speak to Inspector McIntosh, in the matter of the suicides."

Babcock found himself admiring the old man's sense of diplomacy in the next few minutes. Verey explained only as much as a police officer might be able to understand, even improvising off the top of his head a theory that the mysterious packages from London might unleash a chemical poison that would unhinge the reason. "Under no circumstances," the hunchbacked clergyman said sharply, "should McPherson open any package from London—or any unusual package, to be on the safe side. These villains may change their return address to catch us off guard."

When Verey finally hung up the phone, he looked somewhat relieved. "They're sending a constable around to McPherson's at once," he said. "That inspiration of mine about the delirium-producing chemical seems to have impressed him."

Sir John nodded somberly. "It impressed me, for a moment," he said. "But it isn't true, of course. There is no drug with a reaction so specific as in these cases. Even belladonna, the most delirium-producing chemical known, has a wide variety of effects. Some weep hysterically; some laugh insanely; some hallucinate; others die of toxic reaction. Hasheesh is equally variable in its effects. There is nothing in that line of speculation to help us here, although it is at least enough to persuade the police to put McPherson on guard against mysterious packages. . . ."

They returned quietly to the library, where Sir John finally remembered Verey's incoherent excitement about "the postcards" before their mad rush to the telephone. When they were seated again, he raised that question.

"What were those postcards you were talking about?"

Verey shook his head with humility. "It was totally silly and absurd," he said. "I attached no meaning at all to it until the moment you saw the thought strike me. Of course, now I'm not sure—it may just be coincidence. . . ."

Just coincidence, Sir John thought bitterly. *Those words will always sound idiotic or sinister to me.*

"And the postcards weren't even postmarked London," Verey said. "They were actually postmarked Inverness: that's why I didn't make the connection. But, of course, we know They have agents there, also, like that mysterious vanishing Oriental. . . ."

"Tell me about the cards," Sir John suggested gently.

"The first one came for Bertran," Verey said, "exactly *two days* before the package that provoked his suicide. It was utter nonsense—just a staff with a Hebrew letter on it."

"Do you know which Hebrew letter?" Sir John asked intensely.

Verey thought a minute. "Bring me a pad," he said. "I, of course, had Hebrew in seminary—but that was nigh forty long years ago now. Nonetheless, Scots education is strict, and thorough. . . . I think I have it."

Sir John handed him a pad and Verey sketched rapidly. "This is what the card looked like," he said. "Just this and Bertran's name."

Sir John looked at the design:

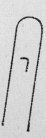

"*Yod*, is it not?" asked Verey.

Sir John blushed. "Yes," he said, "*Yod*. It means hand or fist." But he was recalling the opinion of certain scholars who claimed that hand and fist were late euphemisms and that *yod* originally meant spermatozoa. The whole design was disturbingly phallic. "And the next card?" he asked, suspecting it would contain *nun,* the fish, again. Another I.N.R.I.

"This came for Annie," Verey said, "again postmarked Inverness. And, again, I didn't see the connection—whatever connection there may be—with the tragedy that followed *two days* later." He drew rapidly:

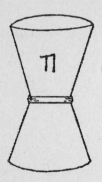

"I'm not certain I remember that one," Verey admitted.

"*Hé*," Sir John said. "A window. And the first postcard design was not a staff but a wand, since this is a cup. We are getting the implements of magick, in order. Was the postcard to McPherson not a sword?"

"That is most marvelous," Verey said. "You are absolutely right. It looked like this." He sketched again:

"*Vau*," said Sir John. "The nail."

Both men were pale again. "Some things one doesn't forget, even in four decades," Verey said with awe. "Seeing all three together, I discern what the fourth must be."

"Yes," Sir John said. "What we have thus far is *Yod Hé Vau*, the first three letters of the Holy Unspeakable Name of God. The fourth can only be a second Hé, making *Yod Hé Vau Hé*—YHVH, usually transliterated as 'Jehovah' in English. These monsters are using the most sacred name in Holy Cabala as the *leitmotif* of their chain of murders. This is blasphemy and sacrilege of the most extreme sort, the blackest of black magick. But when did McPherson receive the sword with *Vau* on it?"

"*Two days* ago!" Verey gasped.

Sir John gasped. "Then the package with the book of horror should be in today's post!"

"Blessed Saviour," Verey whispered, eyes closed. "May the police be there before the postman. . . ."

They both heard the phone ringing at the same moment. Afterward, Sir John could never remember if they ran or merely stumbled to the hall.

"Sir John Babcock," he said into the speaker.

"This is Inspector McIntosh," said the electronic voice in his ear. "Is the Reverend Charles Verey there?"

Sir John turned the telephone over to Verey and stood like a zombie as he listened to Verey's side of the conversation: "Yes . . . Oh, God, no . . . Yes . . . What . . . ? Most certainly . . . God pity us *all*, Inspector . . . I certainly shall."

The hunchbacked clergyman looked dwarfish and shrunken as he hung up. "It happened again," he said.

"My God! Tell me."

"The constable who was sent round to McPherson's found him dead already. He had cut his throat violently from ear to ear with a razor. They looked in the fireplace for the remains of a package, as in the two other cases.

The constable says there was part of a book still burning, but all he could see were the letters MO."

"THER GO MO," Sir John repeated. "Lunacy on top of blasphemy. God held us *all*, indeed."

THE RADIO ANNOUNCER: And now, folks, it's time for our Mystery Call. Who will get the chance to win the one hundred dollars? The engineer is dialing right now . . . the phone is ringing . . . ah, I have somebody on the line. Hello, hello?

MALE VOICE: Hello, hello? [Put down that fire engine, Brigit.]

ANNOUNCER: Hello, who is this?

MALE VOICE: Hello, is this the Mystery Hour? [Brigit, don't hit your brother with the fire engine!]

ANNOUNCER: Yes, this is the Mystery Hour . . . and this is your chance to win one hundred dollars!! But, first, what's your name, sir?

MALE VOICE: James Patrick Hennesy.

ANNOUNCER: James Patrick Hennesy!!! What a fine Eskimo name! But, seriously, I bet your folks came over from the Old Sod.

HENNESY: No, they were born in Brooklyn. Like me.

ANNOUNCER: Oh. Well, I suppose your *grandparents* came over from the Old Sod!!!!

HENNESY: Well, one of them did. We're Italian on the other side, though.

ANNOUNCER: A real American family!!!! Well, Mr. Hennesy, you sent in your postcard, and now you're on the line, and this is your chance to win the hundred dollars. So, now! For one hundred dollars!! This week's Mystery Question is!!! Are you ready, Mr. Hennesy . . . ? The question is: Are the suicides caused by magick, or is there some rational explanation? What do you think, Mr. Hennesy?

HENNESY: [Stop hitting Brigit with the birdcage, Tommy.

You're frightening the bird.] Oh, ah, uh, I think it's magick.

ANNOUNCER: You! think!! it's!!! Magick!!!! Would you tell us why you think that, Mr. Hennesy?

HENNESY: Am I right?

ANNOUNCER: That would be *telling*, Mr. Hennesy. You'll find out, with the rest of our audience. But tell us why you think it's magick.

HENNESY: Stands to reason.

ANNOUNCER: Stands to reason, Mr. Hennesy?

HENNESY: Well, nobody can walk through walls, right?

ANNOUNCER: Not unless they're very clever.

HENNESY: Is that a hint?

ANNOUNCER: We don't give hints, Mr. Hennesy. You have thirty seconds more. Why is it magick?

HENNESY: Well, it stands to reason; that's all. Nobody can walk through walls, or, uh, drive people to suicide with a book. It must be magick, right?

ANNOUNCER: Well, we'll see, Mr. Hennesy. And even if you didn't win the one hundred dollars, you'll still receive a consolation prize of one year's supply of Preparation H and complete instructions on how to use it! And now! Back to our show!!

The Fräumünster chimes were striking six, and cinnamon streaks of twilight cast shadows of dying color weirdly into the room, a russet-gold witch's glamour, Gothic as the tale Sir John told. Einstein, Babcock and Joyce had agreed with Mileva Einstein's suggestion that they take a break for dinner. The dining room by now reeked with dead heavy smoke from Einstein's pipe. Mileva had opened a window to freshen the air, with the uninspiring result that the clammy *Föhn* could be felt in the room now.

Einstein rose to stretch a bit and walk around thoughtfully. Joyce sat immobile in his red plush chair, his face expressionless, introspective.

"Well, Jeem," Einstein said finally. "It seems as if all the paraphernalia of the Celtic Twilight poets you despise has landed in our laps. Even the faeries . . ."

Joyce nodded, smiling whimsically. "Even an appropriately eerie sunset," he said. "It is much like the Tar Baby story of the American Negroes. You become attached to what you attack. . . ."

Einstein stopped pacing and his playful spaniel eyes went entirely out of focus, obviously looking inward, not outward; Joyce wondered if he had stopped thinking in words and was thinking in pictures, as he said he did when he was working on a problem in physics. Babcock and Joyce exchanged the vacant glances of the Apostles at the end of one of the darker parables, both of them thinking of the Tar Baby story and how it could possibly have triggered Einstein's *Fakir*-like trance. The more you hit a Tar Baby, the more you are stuck to it: that was the moral of the Negro legend. But what did that have to do with a book that actually drove people into suicidal mania? Did destroying the book destroy the receivers, as an allegory for censors?

"Action and reaction," Einstein whispered, talking mostly to himself. "Good old Newton still has wisdom for us after three centuries. . . ."

"Professor," Babcock exclaimed, "is it possible? Are you actually beginning to see a scientific explanation of these incredible events?"

Einstein blinked and sat down again, wearily. "Well, not exactly," he said. "But I am starting to find some scientific light in this medieval darkness . . . a hypothesis is beginning to dawn . . . but I don't know yet. . . ."

"At this point," Joyce said, "any hypothesis would be welcome, however, tentative or incomplete. By God, Einstein, I spent several months, last year, writing the most gruesome and fetid sermon on Hell ever composed. I took bits from every theology class and religious retreat of my youth, and from Jesuit textbooks, and organized it into what I hope is a truly blood-freezing, stomach-turning, hair-raising harangue which will give the non-Catholic reader some sense of the cheerful hours which my hero had to endure in the course of a pious Irish Catholic education. But, to be honest, I was having a wonderful and glorious time all the while I was writing this bloody horror, because such things no longer have the power to frighten me and I could write it all down with cold clinical documentary detachment. Listening to Babcock's tale, on the other hand, almost puts me back into the real rancid terrors of my adolescence."

"Of course," Einstein said, ruddy-faced in the dying sunlight. "That is the whole point."

"I beg your pardon?" Babcock cried.

"Wait," Einstein said. "It is only a dim light, so far; it may be a false dawn; I am still working on it. But surely you can generalize from the man entangled with the Tar Baby to the more amusing, more interesting situation in which *two* Tar Babies are fighting with each other?"

Joyce and Babcock sat blankly, crimson statues in gathering darkness.

Mileva Einstein appeared in the pale orange doorway. "Dinner, gentlemen!"

The meal began with an antipasto of cheese, olives and anchovies. "I acquired a taste for Italian food during my years in Milan," Einstein explained. "One of the reasons I like Zürich is that the restaurants here offer such a variety— you can dine Italian style, German style and French style on three different nights—if you can afford to dine out three nights in a row, that is."

"I dine at the most expensive restaurants in Trieste," Joyce said, "once a month, on payday. On my income this guarantees that I usually cannot pay the rent on time."

"Does that not make enormous problems?" Babcock asked.

"It does for my brother," Joyce said. "The landlords often hound him for the money, when they have had more than they can stand of my foul language and Byronic bad manners."

"You are shameless," Mileva said, with a glint of humorously exaggerated maternal disapproval.

"I cannot afford shame," Joyce replied at once. "It interferes with perception. By provoking my landlords I learn areas of human psychology that are still a closed book to the local wise man, Dr. Jung, or even to his Viennese competitor, Dr. Freud."

The men seemed to have a tacit agreement not to discuss the horrors of Babcock's medieval tale during the meal, while Milly was present. Joyce, in fact, quickly engaged Frau Einstein in a discussion of the history of Zürich, in which he astonished everybody by pointing out the Celtic origin of various local customs such as the *Secheslaüten* festival in spring. "Carrying out a straw dummy that represents winter and burning it," he said, "is found, in one form or another, in every Celtic culture."

"But it's over two thousand years since Switzerland was Celtic," Mrs. Einstein said, astonished.

"The historical archetypes, as Vico would call them, remain," Joyce declared. "And the etymologies remain. Do you not know that the very name 'Zürich' is derived from the Latin, *Turicum?*"

"I've heard that," Mileva admitted.

"Ah," Joyce said. "But why did the Romans call this place *Turicum?* Look it up, as I did, and you will find the original Celtic inhabitants called it *Dur*, which means roughly 'the place where the waters join'—where the Limmat River flows into Lake Zürich. The Romans merely Latinized *Dur* into *Turicum*."

Einstein raised an amused eyebrow. "Jeem," he said, "you look into words like a biologist looking down a microscope. I begin to believe you really meant all those paradoxes you were reciting last night, about the content of mind being nothing but words."

"The *history* of consciousness is a history of words," Joyce said immediately. "Shelley was justified in his bloody unbearable arrogance, when he wrote that poets were the unacknowledged legislators of the world. Those whose words make new metaphors that sink into the public consciousness, create new ways of knowing ourselves and others."

" '*L'amor che movete il sol e altare stella,*' " Einstein quoted suddenly. "Once you have encountered that phrase in Dante, the music of it does sink into your consciousness. It is very hard to look at the stars at night without thinking of it and feeling a little of what Dante felt. And yet I know, rationally, that the sun and other stars are actually moved by stochastic processes."

"Stochastic?" Babcock asked.

"Random," Joyce translated. "The professor is talking about the Second Law of Thermodynamics."

"The stochastic is not random," Einstein hastily corrected. "There is always a hidden variable in every stochastic process. A rational law. To think otherwise is to reify and deify Chaos. But is cosmic law the same as the heartbeat of Love that Dante intuited behind the cosmos? Anyone who claims to answer to that is either the king of philosophers or the king of fools."

"I find it easier to believe in love than in law," Milly said boldly. "But, being men, you will all say that is because I am a woman."

"Ah," said Joyce, "I should not say so. Perhaps the Isle of Man is only a suburb of the Continent of Woman. Biologically, the male is an accessory, an ambulatory seedpod."

"Much of the universe, alas, is loveless," Einstein said. "But no aspect of it is lawless."

"So it seems to logic," Joyce said argumentatively. "But

logic is only Aristotle's generalization of the laws of Greek grammar. Which is part, but only part, of the great wordriver of consciousness. Chinese logic is not Aristotelian, you know. Other parts of the mindriver of human thought are totally illogical and irrational. You have shown mathematically, Professor, that space and time cannot be separated. The psychoanalytic study of consciousness is rapidly proving what Sir John and I have discovered in different ways, introspectively: namely, that reason and unreason are also seamlessly welded together—like your two Tar Babies after a prolonged fight. . . ."

"You are a most unusual man," said Mileva, as the dinner concluded. "If there is a Mrs. Joyce, she must be a most remarkable woman."

"There is no Mrs. Joyce. But I lived with the same woman for ten years, and will certainly live with her the rest of my life, if she can continue to abide my intransigence that long."

The men retired to Einstein's study as Mileva began clearing up the dining room.

"Dash it all!" Babcock burst out to Joyce. "Must you parade you immorality on every possible occasion? I'm sure Frau Einstein was terribly shocked. Bragging about cheating landlords and living in open immorality."

"Frau Einstein is shock-proof," Einstein said calmly. "Most of my friends are eccentrics. Sometimes I even suspect that I might perhaps be an eccentric myself."

"Every individual is a deviate," Joyce said promptly. "I've never met a bore in my whole life. The normal is that which nobody quite is. If you listen to seemingly dull people very closely, you'll see that they're all mad in different and interesting ways, and are merely struggling to hide it. The masquerade is the key to human psychology. And, although I'm interested in your unique problems," he added to Babcock, "I give you no authority to judge any moral decision I make. Nor do I give such

authority to any fat-bellied Church or thieving State. Nora
lives with me because as a free being she chooses to, not
because superstition or law forces her to stay. I would not
have a slave, or a concubine, or a wife, but only an equal
companion."

Firm as the mountain ridges where
I flash my antlers in the air

A noble sentiment for a man sick with jealousy. Hear!
Hear! The voice is the voice of my youth; the language of
Ibsen and Nietzsche. But I am too old to be Stephen
Dedalus any longer. If I ask, she will tell me; but I will
not ask. *Eleutheria.* My fate: *Übermensch* or Goddamned
Idiot. Heroic posturing: *merde.*

"Some things," Babcock rejoined heatedly, "are Simply
Not Done in decent society."

"You are no psychologist," Joyce said with silky Celtic
irony. "They are done all the time. They are simply not
talked about."

"Gentlemen," said Einstein gravely, "this debate has
been raging since the Romantic movement began a century ago. I do not think we will settle it tonight. Let us
apply our brains, more profitably, to the Gothic mysteries
presented by Sir John's singular tale."

Joyce slouched limply in a chair. "I have come to certain conclusions about that," he said. "Would you be
interested in hearing them?"

"Yes," Einstein said. "I would be curious as to how they
match up with my own tentative partial hypothesis."

"Quite so," said Babcock, also seating himself after removing a pile of scientific magazines in French and German from the only unoccupied chair.

"To begin with," Joyce said. "I do not believe in the
book that drives men mad, for two reasons. First, it is
intrinsically incredible. Just as no drug would have this

specific [and melodramatic] effect on every user, no book could have such a power. Second, it has finally dawned on me that I have encountered this story before, in a work of fiction. I suspect that Mr. Aleister Crowley and his associates in the M.M.M. have read the same work of fiction and are merely adapting it as a mask for their true method of murder."

Einstein almost dropped his pipe. "This is most interesting," he said. "I begin to believe my own emerging hypothesis, since this would be what the hypothesis predicts. What is the work of fiction you have in mind?"

"It is a book of weird, supernatural stories called *The King in Yellow*. The author is an American named Robert W. Chambers. The stories all revolve around a horrible book, which is never named, but which causes madness in everybody who reads it. I might also add that there is some interesting allegorical material about masks and masquerades in *The King in Yellow*, which is also perhaps the most successful horror story since Stoker's *Dracula*. Millions must have read it. I think it almost certain that the plot of this book suggested, to the M.M.M., a kind of malign masquerade in which they would create the impression that a book such as Chambers imagined really existed."

Einstein relit his pipe: a cherry-red glow grew in the dark tobacco. "Masks and masquerades," he said. "That is indeed what concerns us here. But how do we tear off the masks and see what lies behind? How are these seeming 'miracles' actually accomplished? If it weren't for Ernst Mach and the Tar Baby story, I would not have the beginning of a hint of a theory . . . And even as it is, for every point that I think I can possibly explain, there are three that still leave me in the dark.

"Suppose," he went on, "you had read *The King in Yellow* and were cruel enough to wish to duplicate the plot in real life. The best you could do, it seems to me, is something like this: you include a letter with the book. The letter says: 'This paper has been saturated with the germs of leprosy'—or syphilis, or whatever disease arouses the desired degree of terror. Would such a device succeed? I say that *perhaps* one person might be so hysterical and easily suggestible that he or she would believe this at once and commit suicide. *Ja?* But not three in a row. It is statistically unbelievable. One, at least, would have sense enough to consult a doctor before believing such a sick, slimy poison-pen letter."

"Even in Calvinist Scotland," Joyce said agreeably, "that would have to be true. Despite the political news one reads every day, the human race does *not* consist entirely of gullible dunces. This whole book of horrors is an enormous red herring across the trail, to confuse and distract us. The real method of driving the victims to suicidal mania was quite different, I am sure, and the books were sent to create a supernatural twilight aura around it."

"I wish I could be as certain of that as you are," Babcock said wearily.

Joyce shrugged with agnostic resignation. "I am certain of nothing," he admitted. "I am only theorizing. I have also been working on those mysterious fragments of the alleged book's title. We have no guarantee that we have received them in correct order, since the witnesses saw only parts of words. I have been trying permutations. Instead of *ther-go-mo*, how about *ther-mo-go? Thermo* is a prefix that means *heat* and appears in 'thermometer,' 'thermodynamics' and dozens of other redhot scientific words. Do you know of any scientific term beginning *thermogo*, Professor?"

"The best I can do along those lines," Einstein said ruefully, "is thermogenetic and thermograph. No thermogo . . ."

"Well," Joyce said, "there is always *mo-ther-go.* I immediately conceive the possible title, *Mother, Go to Hell!* That might be very distressing to readers of conventional sensibilities, but not quite enough, I think, to drive them to suicidal mania."

The *Föhn* wind: a dank, dark breath of wetted ashes: mother, go. Let me be and let me live. I will not serve the god who killed you with cancer. Agenbite. Cruel crabclaws, predators' teeth.

"Let us hear the rest of the tale," Einstein said out of the scarlet shadowed chair where he sat slumped in thought. "We have been theorizing, so far, from insufficient data."

"There is not much more to tell," Sir John said. "The climax, however, was more terrible and more incredible than anything I have related thus far."

Nightdank purple shadows were finally gathering in the room, banishing the last golden reds of the sun. The Fräumünster chimes struck seven; the *Föhn* blew hot dead air into their eyes.

DE STELLA MACROCOSMI

When Sir John telephoned Jones at his home, the day's post was being brought in by Wildeblood, and Sir John began glancing at the envelopes as he and Jones discussed the latest developments.

"The first rule in chess," Jones said, his voice rendered electronic and eunuchoid by the instrument, "is *protect the king*. Verey is the king right now—the piece under attack. I think we should move him."

Sir John started to disagree. "I have eight servants, five of them rather sturdy males. I think Babcock Manor is as safe as any place in England . . ." his voice trailing off in uncertainty as the incredible, unthinkable, appeared in the mail: a postcard addressed to:

Rev. Charles Verey
Babcock Manor
Greystoke, Weems

Hardly hearing "I'm not at all sure about that," Jones saying sharply. "I think it almost certain that *they* are aware of your correspondence with Verey and, finding him flown from Inverness, will seek him immediately in your vicinity—if they didn't actually follow him there. . . ."

"You are right," Sir John said, with a sinking feeling in the pit of his stomach, thinking: such stuff as nightmares are made of, turning the card over and looking at what he expected:

"There is a postcard for him in today's post," he heard himself saying. "They are indeed very advanced in the techniques of terrorism. My God, Jones, he only left Inverness on the midnight train and arrived here this morning. But the postcard must have been mailed yesterday to arrive today. It is as if they predicted his movements exactly."

Yod Hé Vau Hé: the Holy Unspeakable Name was now complete, as was the sequence: wands, cups, swords, pentacles. And time itself had been twisted, to make this possible.

"Never accept a miracle at face value," Jones said in his ear, a squeaky voice carried by electricity. "Check for the postmark."

But Sir John was already turning the card over again, seeing, hardly daring to believe: There was no postmark. Thinking: Time has not turned sideways yet.

"Well?" Jones prodded.

Vekam, Adonai. . . . The name itself is the thing itself. . . .

"There is no postmark. It wasn't mailed yesterday; it wasn't mailed at all. They merely slipped it into my post-box after the postman deposited the regular mail, I suppose. . . ." Terror mounting, thinking: They are always *ahead* of us.

"Do you see now why I want to move the king? They have had the advantage on us all along. Now is the time for us to turn the tables on them by beginning some strategic moves of our own." Jones paused. "We must assume Babcock Manor is under malign surveillance. Our only advantage is that you know the turf better than they do; you are fighting on your home territory. Think of a method of getting yourself and Verey out of there without being observed. Can you devise such a plan?"

Sir John smiled grimly. "I was a boy here," he said. "I can think of at least five plans that wouldn't occur to anyone who hadn't grown up on these lands."

"Good. There is one more thing you must consider. *Do not go near the railroad.*"

"Yes," said Sir John. "They would, of course, have the station watched, in case I did get Verey out without being seen." The instruments used against de Molay: the thumb-screw, the rack, the iron boot. . . . *Vekam, Adonai.* . . .

"Excellent. You are beginning to think strategically. The next point should be obvious. Do you have a friend who owns an automobile?"

"Viscount Greystoke," Sir John said at once. "And our best plan of escape is through the woods to the Greystoke estate."

"Very good. If I remember correctly, you do not drive automobiles. Will Greystoke loan you his chauffeur, as well as his automobile?"

"If I tell him it's an emergency, he will."

Sir John found himself incongruously remembering his Initiation: *Where are you going—The East.—What are you seeking?—The Light.*

Jones was silent a moment, thinking. "You can reach London by early evening, with any luck. Of course, you must not come to my house, since that will be the first place they will be seeking the two of you. Go to 201 Paul Street. A friend of mine, Kenneth Campbell, will receive you. You will find him perfectly trustworthy and rather formidable. I will join you and Verey there."

"Two hundred one Paul Street," Sir John repeated. "I believe I know the neighborhood. Is it not off Tottenham Court Road?"

"You have it. Not the most distinguished or respectable part of London, but an excellent place to castle our king for a while. I hope all three of us can join Mr. Campbell there by six or seven. Be careful, Sir John: remember that a man with Verey's hunched back is a rather conspicuous figure."

Sir John was beginning to feel exhilarated by the time he explained the plan to Verey. He had to remind himself that three people had died horribly already—three crushing tragedies for poor Verey—to keep himself from regarding the day ahead as a splendid adventure.

Encounters with death and danger are only *adventures* to the survivors, Sir John realized uncomfortably; and it was still far from certain who would survive this horrible affair; but nevertheless, he was still young, damn it all—he was planning to outfox a sinister enemy—it *was* exciting.

A look at the clergyman's ashy face reminded him that he was not in a Conan Doyle or Rider Haggard novel but in real life, where the dead are really dead and those who loved them really grieve and do not just sob once into a handkerchief before the novelist rushes on to the next thrill.

When Sir John outlined the escape strategy, Verey agreed almost absently. It was shocking to see how much of the arrogance had been drained from the old man, how docile he was in accepting direction.

Sir John's plan involved the fact that the wine cellar led into a short tunnel which connected with a deserted out-building where an earlier Babcock, generations back, had mounted a private winepress, long since fallen into disuse.

"They may be watching this house with binoculars or even with a high-power telescope," he explained. "But nobody can see that old winepress cottage unless he prac-tically falls over it. The whole area around it is now very heavily wooded."

The clergyman nodded gloomily. He did not speak in his normal style, in fact, until they were actually in the wine cellar. "You do be keeping a great amount of spirits," he said suspiciously, "for a Christian and sober man."

Sir John was leading the way with a candelabra. "Fam-ily stock," he said apologetically. "Most of the bottles are fifty or a hundred years old, or older. I hardly ever open one, except for special guests."

"Aye," said the hunchbacked figure in the gloom. "That's the way it always starts. Opening a bottle occasionally, for special guests. Every wretch I have ever seen ruined by drink started that way."

Because of the darkness, Sir John allowed himself a smile. It was comforting, in a way, to see that some of the old man's character remained intact even after the trage-dies he had endured. For a while there, Verey had seemed almost an automaton.

Then Sir John began to realize how huge the wine cellar really was, to the eyes of a Scottish Presbyterian. He hadn't been down here since childhood, when he had explored the tunnel regularly in hopes of finding pirate treasure, or the caverns of the trolls. As they passed row after row of cobwebbed bottles, Sir John began to see the Babcocks as he imagined Verey was seeing them: a family of alcoholic debauchees.

Finally, they found the tunnel. Now it was really dark and the candelabrum shed only a few feet of light in any direction. Sir John began to wish he had brought two candelabras, so that Verey could light his own way. As it was, they necessarily huddled together and walked very slowly.

A confederate in the household: Sir John remembered, suddenly, his suspicions about Verey's brother Bertran, back when there was only the mystery of the strangled cat to explain. Could there be a confederate of Crowley's M.M.M. here in his own household? What might be waiting in this Stygian blackness only a few feet ahead of them?

Then he smiled again in the darkness. The servants had all been with the Babcocks for a long time: they were simple, solid souls he had trusted since childhood. This damnable mystery had begun to infect his mind with the germs of paranoia. My God, suspecting Wildeblood or Dorn or old Mrs. Maple of involvement with black magicians was as ridiculous as suspecting the Royal Family or the Archbishop of Canterbury.

There seemed to be a buzzing sound in the air of the tunnel, reminding Sir John of the insectoid hum of his dreamvisions of Chapel Perilous and Verey's weird recording: thinking, *could bees or wasps have built a hive down here?*, recalling also the buzzing sound attributed to the voices of the faery by folklorists, holding on to his courage by act of Will, yet irrelevantly remembering also that the bee was for some inexplicable reason the emblem of the Bavarian Illuminati, the most atheistic and revolutionary of all Masonic offshoots. He would get a grip on himself, damn it to hell; he would not keep wandering into such unwholesome thoughts. But he was remembering an ancient Cabalistic riddle: Why does the Bible begin with B *(beth)* instead of A *(aleph)?* Answer: because A is the letter of *Arar,* cursing, and B the letter of *Berakah,* blessing. But why was the bee the symbol of the Illuminati? And what was that insectoid buzzing and who were those people in honeysuits in that early dream of Chapel Perilous?

Fear is failure, and the forerunner of failure. . . . He was *not* that pitiful fieldmouse trapped in the hands of a being incomprehensible to himself. He was a Knight of the Rose Croix on God's business and "no demon hath power over him whose armor is righteousness."

Remembering, too, Uncle Bentley explaining that fear of the dark is one of the oldest primate emotions, dating back to the brutal ages when our mute gnomic furry ancestors were subject to clawed attack by many kinds of nocturnal carnivores, and hardly a child in the world does not have some remnant of that primordial fear, which comes back even to the adult in times of strain; and if it was grotesque to suspect the family servants, there was yet the disquieting thought of the workmen who had been all over Babcock Manor when the electricity was installed and the whole house refurbished. One of them could have been an agent of the M.M.M. who had set a trap somewhere, in a dark place like this. . . .

"Fear is failure, and the forerunner of failure," Sir John reminded himself again. Where are you going? The East. What do you seek? The Light.

According to the Welsh, the crew that never rests lived in tunnels like this, under the earth. . . .

With great relief, Sir John finally saw the door at the end of the tunnel. This really was a beastly horrible business, to have made a fearful ordeal out of the journey through the tunnel, which had always been an adventure to him as a boy.

Well, Jones had told him, "A real initiation never ends." This walk through the dark legend-haunted underworld— the N or Hades stage of the I.N.R.I. process—had been another part of his initiation, another lesson in the courage which the occultist must acquire if he were not to become prey to obsession and possession by every type of demonic entity, real and imaginary. He remembered an American Negro hymn he had once heard:

> I must walk this lonesome valley
> I must walk it for myself
> Nobody else can walk it for me
> I must walk it all alone

Understanding suddenly why *nun,* the fish, was the letter corresponding to this experience of Hades, lord of the underworld; thinking, We do, indeed, begin as fish swimming in the amniotic waters of the womb, and the unconscious always thinks of death, symbolically, as a return to the womb; realizing even why the next stage in I.N.R.I. is *Resh,* the human head itself, corresponding to the dead-and-risen sun gods, Osiris and Apollo. "The Kingdom of Heaven is within you": within the head, in the cells of the brain itself. Knowing at last in the guts: A true initiation never ends: we go through the same archetypal processes, over and over, understanding them more deeply each time. Isis, Apophis, Osiris! IAO . . . the Virgin, the halls of Death, Godhood . . . The Light shined in the darkness, and the darkness knew it not. . . .

With a grunt of male-mammal triumph, Sir John cast open the door to the winepress cottage. *"Man is not subject to the angels, nor to Death entirely, save by failure of his Will,"* said a Golden Dawn manual, and Sir John believed it and felt brave.

The cottage was even dirtier and more heavily cobwebbed than Sir John remembered, but the winepress still looked as sturdy and indestructible as ever. Reverend Verey stared at it in some astonishment.

"Good Lord, man," he asked, "what is this?"

He was pointing an angry finger at the Coat of Arms on the winepress: a dark blue garter with a gold buckle, twenty-six gold garters pendant from the collar above it, motto: *Honi soit qui mal y pense.*

"It's the Order of Saint George," Sir John explained, blushing nervously. "It was given to great-grandfather by the King, for some service to the Crown." Thinking: the nightmare is real, there is no masquerade: the name itself is the thing itself.

"Aye, I know that nobody but the King can confer the Order of the Garter," Verey said impatiently. "But why did your great-grandfather impress it on a winepress? That indicates disrespect for the Crown and a libertine humor, I'd say."

Sir John blushed more deeply. "Great-grandfather was a bit odd," he said. "There are scandalous legends about him, I'm sorry to admit. He was involved with Sir Francis Dashwood and the Hellfire Club, some say. Every family has at least *one* rascal," he added pointedly, "as *you* must know."

"Aye," said Verey. "I mean no disrespect for your family. But I can see how occult leanings can be in your blood, Sir John, even if you turn them in more Christian directions than your great-grandfather did."

It was not the most tactful apology, and Sir John found himself thinking of his blood as tainted in a most unwholesome manner. "The Order of Saint George is the highest knightly order in Great Britain," he said, defending the Babcock genes as if somehow the accusation had arisen that lycanthropy or witchcraft might be a family trait.

Verey said, "Aye, a most exalted honor for any family to receive from the Crown. But is it not more commonly known as the Order of the Garter?"

Sir John found himself blushing again.

The hunchbacked clergyman must still be in shock, he thought; this was a most inane line of conversation. Still he was stammering as he explained, lamely, "I study much medieval history. Often, I slip into the old words

and terms instead of the more modern ones. The name
Order of the Gar Gar Garter was not in common use until
the reign of Edward VI, although the Order goes back, as
you undoubtedly know, to Edward III in 1344 and was
originally called the Order of Saint George as I just said."
For some reason, he still felt as if he were in a nightmare.

"*Honi soit qui mal y pense,*" the clergyman read from
the Coat of Arms. "A strange motto for a noble order."

"Well you must know the story . . . about the Countess
of Salisbury . . ." Sir John almost had the sensation that
the hunchback was cross-examining him on a witness stand.
"She dropped her gar gar garter at a dance, you know,
and the King picked it up, when somebody laughed at
her, and put it on his own lay lay leg, you know, and said
that. Said *Honi soit qui mal y pense.*"

" 'Evil to him who evil thinks of it,' " Verey translated.
"It's still a strange story. And why do the Masons wear a
garter in their initiations?"

"My God, man, we must be on our way!" Sir John
exclaimed. "We can't stand here discussing the obscure
points of medieval history—"

In a few moments they had made their way around the
winepress and out the door into a shaded grove circled on
all sides by great oaks. Within the grove, beside the
cottage, stood only a ghost-white marble Aphrodite.

"Heathen statues," muttered Verey, but this time he
seemed more to be talking to himself than to be accusing
the Babcock family.

The walk through the woods was invigorating, after the
underground passage and the idiotic but disturbing conversation in the winepress. For a while there, the clergyman
had seemed almost demented; or was Sir John merely overly
sensitive about great-grandfather's eccentricities? A hidden
grove dedicated to wine and Aphrodite . . . the rumors
about connections with the libertine Hellfire Club . . . a
taint in the blood . . . blue garters . . . white stains . . .

Verey kept a good pace, despite his age; but Scottish Highlanders are notorious for longevity, even fathering children at advanced ages. If only they were not so inclined to telling, with so much ghoulish relish, tales of ghosts and witches "and things that gae bump i' the night." But, of course, that was probably because they experienced more of these things in their cold, dank dark Northern nights. The Rationalist, scorning these simple, rugged people as superstitious, without having lived among them and shared the experiences which gave rise to those eldritch tales, was as naïvely chauvinistic as the narrow Englishman who regards all Frenchmen as immoral or all Italians as treacherous.

And then remembering that the motto of the Hellfire Club had been "Do what thou wilt," from Rabelais, and their blasphemous ikon or idol, at the deserted abbey Sir Francis Dashwood had purchased for their orgies, was a giant phallus inscribed "Saviour of the World." That very ikon, in fact, had been printed as frontispiece to the lascivious "Essay on Woman" clandestinely printed by John Wilkes under the salacious *nom de plume* "Pego Borewell": Wilkes had been expelled from the House of Lords when his authorship of that pamphlet, and his membership in the Hellfire Club, had been exposed by the Earl of Sandwich, himself a former member who had resigned when some horrible Thing (an *orang-utan* unleashed as a practical joke, Wilkes later claimed) bit him during a Black Mass. All of which was regarded as comical, if unsavory, by most historians; and yet Sir John began to wonder about possible links between that strange cabal and the contemporary Grand Orient lodges of French Masonry, where strange occult and revolutionary doctrines were preached and the mysterious Count Cagliostro was a Grand Master. Were all of these, like the sinister Illuminati of Bavaria, part of the black underground tradition now incarnate in the Ordo Templi Orientis?

"I heard that story explained once," Verey said suddenly.

The trees were so thick in here that it was heavily shadowed even now, at midday. *O dark, dark amid the blaze of noon*, Sir John quoted to himself. "What story?" he asked absently.

"The story about King Edward III and the Countess of Salisbury, man," Verey said impatiently. "I don't know if it's true, mind you, but what I heard was that the blue garter was the insignia of a Queen of the Witches in those days. The king, by placing the garter on his own thigh, was telling everybody that they would have to denounce him to the Inquisition if they dared to denounce her. He may have saved her life. That's the meaning of 'Evil to him who thinks evil of it.' "

It was an unpleasant subject to be discussing with a grieving and somewhat deranged hunchback in such a dark forest. The *selva oscura*, Sir John thought. "That doesn't make sense," he said irritably, "unless the King himself were a male witch, or warlock. Is the point of the story to make us wonder if the British monarchy itself might be infested with witchery and diabolism?"

"I dinna' know," Verey said. "The man who told me this did have some queer notions about the knightly orders of Europe. I gather that he believed the Order of the Garter was the hidden inner circle that governs Freemasonry. Do you happen to know why Masons use garters in their initiations?"

Something flapped by overhead with a sound as if of bat's wings. But bats did not fly in the daytime, Sir John reminded himself.

"The history of Freemasonry is very complicated," he said. "I have written a book about it, *The Secret Chiefs*, and can only claim to have solved about a third of the important historical mysteries. It is true that the King is the head of the Order of the Gar Gar Garter and the Prince of Wales is always made a 33° Freemason, but there is nothing sin sin sinister about it, I assure you. The patron of the Order is Saint George, not Satan."

"Of course," Verey said apologetically. "I did say, did I not, that the man who told me all this had many queer notions? He even said the 26 gold garters dependent from the collar had something to do with the Mason Word, but I never understood that. It had something to do with the Jewish Cabala, I believe."

26: Sir John remembered: $Yod = 10$; $Hé = 5$; $Vau = 6$; second $Hé = 5$. Total: 26. YHVH, the Holy Unspeakable Name of God—now, due to the hideous M.M.M., inextricably linked in his mind with suicide and madness. And hidden in the numerology of the Order of the Garter.

The bat-winged thing moved overhead again. It must be an ordinary bird. Bats did not fly at noon. And "stone should not walk in the twilight." Where had he read that?

"It is a queer business all around," Verey muttered. "Men in garters. Secret meetings. No women admitted. Was the whole Order of Knights Templar of Jerusalem not convicted of the unnatural sin of sodomy?"

"Dash it all!" Babcock burst out. "You have it all confused, Reverend. You are mixing up true mystical Masonry with all its perversions and counterfeits."

The wood seemed to be growing darker all the time. The bat wings flapped again.

"I know nothing of such matters," Verey said humbly. "I am merely reporting the opinions of a man I admitted was possessed of odd notions. Secret societies do arouse much speculation, you know. Everybody asks: If they have nothing to hide, why are they secret?"

The more the senile old fool apologized, the more offensive he became. Sir John turned to issue a final crushing retort but then saw the paleness of Verey's face and the lines of pain around his eyes and mouth. The old man had suffered much and deserved great tolerance. Besides, the true Brother of the Rose Croix was patient and infinitely compassionate toward those ignorant of the mysteries. Sir John said nothing and trudged on.

The bat-flapping receded behind them. Probably it had only been an ordinary bird, magnified by imagination and suggestion.

Then a clearing emerged and the towers of Greystoke were visible in the distance.

"There it is," Sir John exclaimed, once again thrilled by a sense of adolescent adventure. "Our doorway to escape and to our own surprise counter-attack."

Q: Cite a contemporary historian, with sufficient brevity to avoid litigation about copyrights, in re: the Countess of Salisbury and the Order of the Garter.

A: "Though the story may be apocryphal, there may be a substratum of truth in it. The confusion of the Countess was not from shock to her modesty—it took more than a dropped garter to shock a lady of the fourteenth century— but the possession of that garter proved that she was not only a member of the Old Religion but that she held the highest place in it. . . . It is remarkable that the King's mantle, as Chief of the Order, was powdered over with one hundred and sixty-eight garters which, with his own garter worn on the leg, makes 169, or thirteen times thirteen—*i.e.*, thirteen covens." Dr. Margaret Murray, *The God of the Witches.*

Q: Cite, again without exceeding the legal limitations of Fair Usage, another supporting source.

A: "Thus, as we have seen, the Plantagenet [and so traditionally 'pagan'] King threw away all pretence, and declared himself openly for the Old Religion, establishing a double-coven 'Brains Trust'—the Order of the Garter—to 'mastermind' the return to what Edward and the Fair Maid of Kent, his 'witch' Plantagenet cousin, considered to be the True Faith. . . . The Tudors, too, may not escape suspicion of having belonged to what was evidently

the 'family religion' of the British Royal Family." Michael
Harrison, *The Roots of Witchcraft*.

Kenneth Campbell of 201 Paul Street proved to be, as
Jones had promised, formidable. He stood somewhere
around six and a half feet tall and must have weighed
twenty stone. A large poster on his wall showed him,
grimacing horribly, under the caption THE LIVERPOOL
MANGLER. One did not need the talents of Sherlock Holmes
to deduce that Campbell was a wrestler.

"It's a kip what feeds me," Campbell said, recognizing
Babcock as a gentleman. "Not very hoity-toity, I'll admit,
but what prawce dignity when the belly's empty, eh,
mate?"

Prawce, Babcock decoded, was Liverpoolese for *price*.

"Wrestling was regarded as an accomplishment every
gentleman should master in the Athens of Socrates," he
said reassuringly.

"Socrates?" Campbell was delighted. "Wasn't he the
bloke what drank the poison to show the bleedin' bastards they couldn't frighten him? Begging your pardon,
Reverend."

Babcock could not bear to look at Verey's face. "Socrates was indeed a very brave man," he said evasively.

"Brave?" Campbell shook his head. "I was in Her Maj-
esty's Army during the Boer Uprising," he said. "I know
all abaht bravery, guv'nor. It isn't bravery when you sits
yourself down and drinks poison to prove a point. Could
you do it? Could I do it? Could the bravest manjack in the
army do it? Not on your bleeding life [beg your pardon,
Reverend]. That ain't bravery. That's something else."

A philosophical wrestler, Babcock thought; but what
other sort of wrestler would Jones know? *Another of us?*
There was no point in asking. "What is it that Socrates
had that goes beyond bravery?" he inquired instead.

"I dunno," the wrestler said. "I guess it's the state

beyond humanity, the Next Step that Jones is always talking abaht."

"Socrates was a heathen," Verey said suddenly. "He was unfaithful to his wife both with another woman and with Alcibiades, with whom he had unnatural relations. He may have been brave and wise, but he is most certainly burning in Hell right now."

The wrestler's face fell. "Don't be too strict, Vicar," he said, looking hurt. "None of us is perfect."

Fortunately, Jones arrived just then and Babcock was spared the ordeal of listening to Socrates' morals debated by a naïve giant and a self-righteous hunchback.

"Ah, Kenneth, my man," Jones beamed, taking the wrestler's hand in a grip Babcock did not recognize. "You are looking splendid!"

The grip was not used in the Golden Dawn; Babcock surmised it was a Scottish Rite grip.

"I have another five good years, maybe," the giant said modestly. "Then, if I haven't earned enough to buy a shop or a pub, it's back to the army for the likes of me."

"Back to the army?" Jones said. "I think not. I have never understood how you came through one war alive; an enemy needs to be nearly blind to miss a target your size. We could never allow you to come to that pass again. Remember the widow's son."

The last phrase confirmed Sir John's guess; it was the formula describing all charitable activities of the Ancient and Accepted Scottish Rite Freemasons. Probably Jones, like Robert Wentworth Little, founder of the Golden Dawn, had been in the Ancient and Accepted Lodge originally, as Campbell still obviously was.

"Reverend Verey," Jones was saying, shaking the clergyman's hand warmly and clapping him on the shoulder, "I cannot express how deeply I sympathize with you in this time of grief. I can assure you that I, and the Order I represent, will see to it that no further tragedies occur, and that the villains responsible for your grief will receive a just punishment for their crimes."

"It is in God's hands," Verey said woodenly, regressing back into the emotionless emptiness of the typical shock reaction. It comes in waves, Babcock thought, remembering his own grief when his parents died.

"God's hands? That will not do," Jones said sharply, staring into the clergyman's eyes in a way Babcock had never seen before. "We *are* God's hands," Jones went on, solemnly, "and we have been set here in this world to execute His righteousness. Else is our religion mere theatrics."

Verey turned away, obviously fighting back tears. "God forgive me," he said, "that I, an ordained clergyman, should need to be reminded of that."

Jones softened his tone. "You will not need to be reminded again," he said. "You will not doubt again, nor will you despair." He turned the clergyman around, gently, and stared into his eyes again. "You know I speak truth," he said.

"Yes," Verey said. "My God, who are you?"

"An ordinary man," Jones said. "But one trained, a little, in certain arts of healing. For instance"—he touched Verey's forehead—"I can feel the anguish draining away from you right now. You will not again despair of the goodness of God or ask Job's questions. In a short while, you will rest."

The Brother of the Rosy Cross, Babcock remembered, is permitted to perform healings in emergencies, although in all other ways he must hide his superhuman status from the humans among whom he walks.

Jones moved his hand to Verey's chest. "Yes," he said, "your breathing is much better now. Your heart *chakra* is less agitated. We humans are God's hands, and He acts through us, if we allow Him," he repeated. He grasped Verey's shoulders and ran his hands swiftly down the

clergyman's arms, ending by grasping both hands warmly.
"You have suffered much, but now you can rest. Remember: 'For He is like a refiner's fire.'"

Sir John re-experienced his excitement every time he
had heard Handel's setting of that Biblical verse; it had
always been his favorite part of *The Messiah*. The Vril
energy was flowing through him, as when he first translated I.N.R.I. as "the world is remade by fire"; and he
could see the energy was flowing in Verey, also.

"You will sleep very soon now," Jones added softly.

And in a few moments Verey did announce that he
wished to lie down. The Liverpool Mangler ushered the
old hunchback to a bedroom and returned, awed.

"Out *lahk a baby*," he said. "Every time I see you do
that, guv'nor, it fair gives me the shakes."

"With seven years of concentrated effort you could do it
as quickly and efficiently," Jones said.

"Was it Mesmerism?" Babcock asked.

"Yes," Jones said. "A much more efficient system than
the hypnotism invented by Mesmer's ignorant nineteenth-century imitators, although, as I said, it takes longer to
learn."

"Gor," said the Liverpool Mangler, "was Mesmer in the
Craft, too?"

"In a Grand Orient lodge," Jones said.

Babcock was stunned. "But my researches have led me
to believe the Grand Orient lodges were infiltrated by the
atheistic Bavarian Illuminati and are still allied with the
Ordo Templi Orientis!"

"It does get rather complicated," Jones admitted. "The
names mean nothing. You must remember that in addition to the Golden Dawn there are several dozen groups
in Europe claiming to be carrying on the work of the
original Rose Croix college. And that half the Masonic
lodges in England itself do not recognize the other half as
legitimate. And, for that matter, the Golden Dawn itself

has several competitors using the same name, run by A. E. Waite and Michael Brodie-Innes and others, including the one headed by that scoundrel Crowley himself."

Curiouser and curiouser, as Alice once said. . . .

"I begin to perceive," Sir John said carefully, "that in joining an occult lodge one does not know what one is joining. . . ."

"The names mean nothing," Jones repeated. *"By their fruits shall ye know them."*

"Well, yes," Sir John said, "but . . ."

"Now is not the time to re-examine the history of the Invisible College and its offshoots and counterfeits," Jones said. "I have a task for you this evening, and there is work I must see to myself. Let us leave poor Verey here, under the protection of the Liverpool Mangler, and be on our way. The king is castled and now is the time for a gambit of our own."

So Sir John found himself out on the street and ushered into a hansom cab before he could quite grasp the acceleration of events.

"I had my secretary fetch me a copy of the Inverness *Express-Journal* this afternoon," Jones said, over the horse's hoofbeats. "Here, take a look at this before we talk further."

Sir John took the newspaper clipping Jones extended and read:

THE CASE OF THE CONSTANT SUICIDES

Terror Stalks Loch Ness;
Police Baffled

INVERNESS, APRIL 23, 1914—Inspector James McIntosh of the Inverness Police Force is facing a mystery more terrible than anything in the tales of Poe or Conan Doyle. . . .

Sir John skimmed the rest of the news story quickly.

"Do you see what this means?" Jones asked. "By tomorrow this story will be picked up by every London newspaper; mark my words. It may become the biggest horror-scare since Jack the Ripper was prowling the East End. Continental papers will have it by next week."

"Is that bad or good?" Babcock asked, pocketing the story.

Jones was exasperated. "It's the very worst thing that could happen," he said with grinding patience. "You should understand by now that human belief-systems determine human experience. Why do you think the Invisible College remains Invisible? Why do you suppose we don't perform miracles on every street corner and convert the multitudes? Don't you realize that the philosophy of materialism is the best thing that ever happened to Europe?"

"You are talking in paradoxes," Sir John complained, noticing that the fog outside was beginning to thicken. The clip-clop of the horse's hooves seemed to be carrying them into a realm more mysterious than any of his dreams or astral visions of Chapel Perilous.

Jones sighed. "Have you noticed," he asked patiently, "what happens when a haunted-house story appears in the press? Five more haunted houses are reported, from other parts of the country, within a week. You could not astrally project until you began to believe you could. Cabala was nonsense, until you began to believe it was sense. Why do you think Buddha said, 'All that we are is the result of all that we have thought'? Do you know why we drum it into every Probationer's skull that 'Fear is failure, and the forerunner of failure'? Short of a perfectly Illuminated being, all of us see and experience only what we are *prepared* to see and experience. A newspaper story like this, once it gets picked up and repeated, will open thousands—hundreds of thousands—to similar invasions by the powers of darkness. *Every person who reads about events like these is more likely, to a slight degree, to become open to attack by them.* Books on such subjects are poison. Why, man, we not only refuse to combat the spread of materialism and atheism; we have positively encouraged them!"

"*Encouraged* them?" Sir John was aghast.

"Of course!" Jones cried. "The ancient Mysteries were closed to all but a small elite, as you know. That was not aristocratic snobbery but pragmatic wisdom. The less the average man or woman knows about such things, the better for them. Only those who have been specially trained, intellectually and morally, can deal with these Forces safely."

Sir John mulled this over for a few minutes.

"You think this view unliberal," Jones said. "But consider the happy results. The uneducated masses have a simple faith, which protects them in most cases from invasions like this horror at Loch Ness. The equally automatized morons turned out in platoons by the universities have a simple skepticism, which also protects them. It is satisfactory all around, and the best accommodation to the age of science possible until human nature is transformed. The ordinary person, if he leaves both faith and skepticism behind and begins to *experiment* in this area—as you have—would be insane in six months without very careful guidance of the sort I attempt to give you."

"Yes," Sir John said. "It is against Liberal principles, but you are right. I would never have gotten safely through some of the astral experiments on my own. It is best that the ordinary man and woman do not probe much into such matters."

"Faith for the uneducated fools, skepticism for the half-educated fools," Jones said. "So it must be, until all are ready for the encounter with Him who we call the Holy Guardian Angel—who is, as I reminded Verey back there, *like a refiner's fire.*"

Once again, as four years earlier, the horse's hooves seemed to Sir John to carry the cadence of the Alchemical poem:

> *Don't believe the human eye*
> *In sunlight or in shade*
> *The puppet show of sight and sense*
> *Is the Devil's Masquerade*

The Invisible World seemed much more real to him, at that moment, than the material world half-hidden in the London fog.

"Where are we going?" he asked.

"I am going to confer with the Inner Head of the Invisible College of the Rosy Cross, for the first time in seven years," Jones said. "On the way I am dropping you at the M.M.M. bookstore on Jermyn Street."

"What?"

Jones smiled thinly. "Yes," he said, "it is time that you really looked inside Chapel Perilous. You will be quite safe, I assure you, and that fact will strike consternation into the hearts of the Enemy."

I knew it would come to this, Sir John thought.

"Look," Jones said, producing a most singular object from his overcoat pocket. Sir John felt the light flashing all over the cab's interior before he could quite focus on the object itself.

"What is it?" he asked.

"A pentacle, similar to those used in all magical invocations," Jones said. "This one happens to be charged with the entire concentrated spiritual power of the forty-five hundred years of our Order—for we are far older than you guessed, even in the most daring passages of your books. It is also constructed according to special optical principles."

Sir John found that he could not, however hard he tried, *see* the pentacle clearly.

"Is it like the vault of Christian Rosycross?" he asked.

"It *is* the vault," Jones said. "That is to say, it is an exact miniature. The reason the light within the vault is said to be 'blinding' is that each single facet—and there are thousands of facets, even in this miniature—is complementary to the colors next to it, in accord with strict optical and geometric laws. The light is reflected, diffracted and split into myriad prisms in a way no other structure can duplicate. It is the very model of the Cabalistic universe, wherein each part contains and reflects every other part—an analogy of the Undivided Light. Beautiful, is it not? Yet it is but a model, a partial rendering of the divine effulgence you will some day experience when you attain to what we very inadequately call the Knowledge and Conversation of the Holy Guardian Angel."

Sir John found that he was hallucinating mildly. "It is like ether," he said, "or some exotic drug like hasheesh. . . ."

"It will not do to stare into it too long on first encounter," Jones said. "Take it. Put it within your vest pocket, over the heart. You will experience no fear, and will be in no danger, while the talisman is on your person."

Sir John took the seemingly self-effulgent talisman and felt a distinct tingle as he placed it within his vest.

"By George," he said. "I can really feel it. I'm ready to face the Devil himself."

"You will be called on for nothing so melodramatic," Jones said. "You are, in fact, merely going to sit through a lecture by Mr. Aleister Crowley. If I know that man, he will be aware of the pentacle from the moment you enter. After the lecture, he will almost certainly approach you and attempt, by some ruse or other, to obtain the pentacle with your consent. Neither he nor anyone else can take it from you without your consent, you see. Resist his blandishments and rejoin me at my own home within two hours. That is all."

"Just that? To what purpose?"

"You will learn that by experience better than I could explain it in the few moments we have left," Jones said. "What is about to transpire will astonish you, and is the second purpose of this task. You will find Mr. Crowley very unlike your mental picture of the villain behind all these horrors. That is important for you to learn at this stage: the reality of the enemy camp as distinct from your fearful imaginings about it. Do you understand?"

> *I must walk this lonesome valley*
> *I must walk it all alone*

"Yes," Sir John said. "A true initiation never ends." And he smiled.

Jones smiled in return. "You will do, lad," he said. "I have never had more confidence in a student, in all my years."

"Jermyn Street," said the driver, leaning down. "The number is 93, gents, and here it is."

PART FOUR

Truth! Truth! Truth! crieth the Lord of the Abyss of Hallucinations. . . . This Abyss is also called "Hell" or "The Many" . . . [or] . . . "Consciousness" or "The Universe". . . .

—Aleister Crowley, *The Book of Lies*

Sir John crossed the heavily fogged street, pushed open the door of *M.M.M.: Occult and Mystical Books of All Ages*, and once again entered Chapel Perilous, half-expecting to encounter real horned demons with forked tails.

Instead, there were a variety of quite ordinary English people browsing among the shelves. The books ranged from the sparkling-new to the shabby secondhand and seemed to cover a broad spectrum: signs divided the rows under such labels as TAOISM, BUDDHISM, VEDANTA, CABALA, SUFISM, THEOSOPHY, PSYCHIC RESEARCH, and so forth. Sir John appreciated to the full Jones' remark about the absurdity of asking Scotland Yard to put such an establishment under surveillance in this land of liberty and this age of enlightenment.

A large poster announced:

TONIGHT AT 8

"The Soldier and the Hunchback"

a lecture on mysticism and rationalism

by Sir Aleister Crowley

free to all

This was illustrated by a photo of Crowley, his face totally expressionless, eyes locked directly on the camera and thus seeming to stare directly out at the viewer: but the eyes, like the face, revealed absolutely nothing. Even stranger, the face did not seem to be hiding anything, though it showed nothing: it was simply a face. Had Crowley put himself into some kind of highly concentrated trance when the photo was being taken? He was neither handsome nor ugly (although Sir John remembered that Crowley as a youth had been called the handsomest man in London) and might have been anywhere from forty to fifty. It was the face, Sir John realized, of a man who had perfect self-control.

Sir John looked at the title of the lecture: "The Soldier and the Hunchback." If Verey was the hunchback, who was the soldier? Himself? Jones? Crowley? Or was he attributing too much prescience to Enemy Intelligence? The title might have no personal meaning at all.

One shelf was labeled ORDO TEMPLI ORIENTIS—the name of the clandestine Masonic order which owned this bookstore and required all members to sign three copies of that nihilistic Act of Faith beginning, "There is no God but Man." Sir John examined this curiously: most of the material was in the form of pamphlets or old books by such authors as Karl Kellner, Adam Weishaupt, Leopold Engels, P. B. Randolph, Theodore Reuss—almost all of it in German—but there were also several books by Aleister Crowley himself.

Sir John picked out a Crowley volume entitled, with Brazen effrontery, *The Book of Lies*. Opening it, he found the title page:

THE BOOK OF LIES

WHICH IS ALSO FALSELY CALLED

BREAKS

THE WANDERINGS OR FALSIFICATIONS

OF THE ONE THOUGHT OF

FRATER PERDURABO

WHICH THOUGHT IS ITSELF

UNTRUE

Despite himself, Sir John grinned. This was a variation on the Empedoclean paradox in logic, which consists of the question: "Empedocles, the Cretan, says that everything Cretans say is a lie; is Empedocles telling the truth?" Of course, if Empedocles *is* telling the truth, then—since his statement "everything Cretans say is a lie" is the truth—he must also be lying. On the other hand, if Empedocles is lying, then everything Cretans say is not a lie, and he might be telling the truth. Crowley's title page was even more deliberately perverse: if the book is "*also* falsely called Breaks," then (because of the "also") the original title is false, too, and it is *not* a book of lies at all. But, on the other hand, since it is the "falsifications . . . of the one thought . . . which is itself untrue," it is the negation of the untrue and, therefore, true. Or was it?

Sir John turned to the first chapter and found it consisted of a single symbol, the question mark:

?

Well, compared with the title, that was at least brief. Sir John turned the page to the second chapter and found equal brevity:

!

What kind of a joke was this? Sir John turned to Chapter 3, and his head spun:

Nothing is.
Nothing becomes.
Nothing is not.

The first two statements were the ultimate in nihilism; but the third sentence, carrying nihilism one step further, brought in the Empedoclean paradox again, for it contradicted itself. If "nothing is not," then something *is*. . . .

What else was in this remarkable tome? Sir John started flipping pages and abruptly found himself facing, at Chapter 77, a photograph of Lola Levine. It was captioned "L.A.Y.L.A.H." The photo and the caption made up the entire chapter. Lola was seen from the waist up and was shamelessly naked, although as a concession to English morality her hair hung down to cover most of her breasts.

Sir John, on a hunch, counted cabalistically. *Lamed* was 30, plus *Aleph* is 1, plus *Yod* is 10, plus second *Lamed* is 30, plus second *Aleph* is 1 again, plus *Hé* is 5; total, 77, the number of the chapter. And Laylah was not just a

loose transliteration of Lola; it was the Arabic word for
"night." And 77 was the value of the curious Hebrew
word which meant either "courage" or "goat": *Oz*. The
simple photo and caption were saying, to the skilled Cabalist, that Lola was the priestess incarnating the Night of
Pan, the dissolution of the ego into void. . . .

Sir John decided to buy *The Book of Lies;* it would be
interesting, and perhaps profitable, to gain further insight
into the mind of the Enemy, however paradoxical and
perverse might be its expressions. He approached the
counter, and found with discomfort that the clerk seated
there was Lola Levine herself. Since he had just been
looking at a photo of her, naked from the waist up, he
blushed and stammered as he said, "I'd like to buy this."

"One pound six, sir," Lola said, with no more flicker of
expression than any other clerk. Sir John realized that it
had been nearly three years since the one occasion on
which they had met on the Earth-plane; she had no reason to remember him. Then, was it possible that all the
astral visions in which she tormented and attempted to
seduce him were the product of his own impure imagination? Or were those visions as real as they seemed, and
was she merely a consummate actress and hypocrite? It
was the metaphysical equivalent of the Empedoclean
paradox.

A stout, elderly woman with a Cornish accent asked
Lola, "I'm planning to stay for the lecture. Is it pronounced *Crouly* or *Crowley?*"

"It is pronounced *Crowly*," said a voice from the door.
"To remind you that I'm holy. But my enemies say *Crouly*,
in wish to treat me foully."

Sir John turned and saw Aleister Crowley, bowing po-
litely to the Cornish woman as he completed his jingle.
Crowley was a man of medium height, dressed in a conservative pinstripe suit jarringly offset by a gaudy blue
scarf in place of the tie and with a green Borsalino hat

worn at a rakish angle. It was the outfit an artist on the Left Bank might wear, to show that he had become successful; it was definitely eccentric for London.

The Cornish woman stared. "Are you really the Great Magician, as people say?"

"No," said Crowley at once. "I am the most dedicated enemy of the Great Magician." And he swept past imperiously.

The Cornish lady gasped. "What did he mean by that?" she asked nobody in particular.

Sir John understood, but wasted no time trying to explain. Crowley was heading for the lecture room and Sir John followed him closely, wanting a seat up front where he could observe the Master of the M.M.M. most closely. The paradox had been typical of Crowley's style: he referred, obviously, to the Gnostic teaching that the sensory universe was a delusion, created by the Devil, to prevent humanity from seeing the Undivided Light of Divinity itself. A strange joke to come from a Satanist; but, of course, some Gnostics had taught that Jehovah, creator of the material universe, *was* the Devil, the Great Magician. The Bible begins with *Beth*, according to this teaching, because *Beth* is the letter of the Magician in the Tarot, the Lord of the Abyss of Hallucinations. . . .

The lecture room was filling rapidly and Sir John scampered into a front-row seat. He noticed that Crowley had lowered his head and closed his eyes, obviously preparing himself for the lecture by some method of invocation or meditation. Behind him on the wall was a large silver star with an eye in its center, a symbol associated (Sir John knew) with both the goddess Isis and the Dog Star, Sirius.

"Do what thou wilt shall be the whole of the law," Crowley intoned suddenly, without raising his head. Then he looked about the room whimsically.

"It is traditional in the great Order which I humbly represent," he went on, "to begin all ceremonies and lectures with that phrase. Like Shakespeare's *Ducdame*, it is a great banishing ritual against fools, most of whom leave the room at once on hearing it uttered. Observing no stampede to the doors I can only wonder if a miracle is occurring tonight and I am speaking, for once, to an English audience that does not consist mostly of fools."

Sir John smiled in spite of himself.

"My topic tonight," Crowley went on, "is the soldier and the hunchback. Those are poetic terms I regularly employ to designate the two most interesting punctuation marks in general use throughout Europe—the exclamation point and the question mark. Please do not look for profundities at this point. I call the exclamation point 'the soldier' only out of poetic whimsy, because it stands there, erect, like a soldier on guard duty. The question mark I call the 'hunchback,' similarly, only because of its shape. I repeat again: there is no profundity intended, *yet*."

Sir John found himself thinking of the first two chapters of *The Book of Lies*, which said only "?" and "!"

The question mark or hunchback, Crowley went on, appeared in all the basic philosophical problems that haunt mankind: Why are we here? Who or what put us here? What if anything can we do about it? How do we get started? Where shall wisdom be found? Why was I born? Who am I? "Unless you are confronted with immediate survival problems, due to poverty or to the deliberate choice of an adventurous life, these hunchbacks will arise in your mind several times in an ordinary hour," Crowley said. "They are generally pacified or banished by reciting the official answers of the tribe into which you were born, or simply deciding that they are unanswerable." Some however, Crowley went on, cannot rest in either blind tradition or resigned agnosticism, and must seek answers for themselves, based on experience. Ordinary people, he said, are in a sense totally asleep and do not even know it;

those who persist in asking the questions can be described as struggling toward wakefulness.

The soldier, or exclamation point, he continued, represents the moment of insight or intuition in which a question is answered, as in the expressions "Aha!" or "Eureka!"

"I now present you, gratis, two of the nastiest hunchbacks I know," Crowley said, smiling wickedly. "These two are presented to every candidate who comes to our Order seeking the Light. Here they are:

"Number One: *Why, of all the mystical and occult teachers in the world, did you come to me?*

"Number Two: *Why, of all the days in your life, on this particular day?*

"That is all you need to know," Crowley said. "I might as well leave the platform now, since, if you can answer those questions, you are already Illuminated; and if you cannot, you are such dunces that further words are wasted on you. But I will take mercy on you and give you the rest of the lecture, anyway."

Crowley went on to define the state of modern philosophy (post-David Hume) as "an assembly of hunchbacks." Everything has been called into question; every axiom has been challenged—"including Euclid's geometry among modern mathematicians"; nothing is certain anymore. On all sides, Crowley said, we see only more hunchbacks—questions, questions, questions.

Traditional mysticism, Crowley continued, is a regiment of soldiers. The mystic, he said, having attained an "Aha!" or "Eureka!" experience—a sudden intuitive insight into the invisible reality behind the subjective deceptions of the senses—is apt to be so delighted with himself that he never asks another question and stops thinking entirely. Out of this error, Crowley warned, flows dogmatic religion, "a force almost as dangerous to true mysticism as it is to scientific or political freedom."

The path of true Illumination, Crowley proceeded, walking to a blackboard at the right of the room, does *not* consist of one intuitive insight after another. It is not a parade of soldiers, "like this," he said, writing on the board:

!!!!!!!!!!!!!!!!!!!!!!!!!!!!!!!!

"Anybody in that state is an imbecile or a catatonic, however blissful his lunacy may be," Crowley said sternly.

The true path of the Illuminati, Crowley stated more emphatically, is a series of soldiers and hunchbacks in ever-accelerating series, which he sketched as:

?....!....?...!...?...!...?..!..?..!..?.!.?
!?!?!?!?!?!?!?! etc.

"To rest at any point, either in intuitive certainty or doubtful questioning," he said flatly, "is to stagnate. Always seek the higher vision, whatever states of ecstatic insight you may have reached. Always ask the next harder question, whatever questions you may have answered. The Light you are seeking is quite correctly called *ain soph auer* in Cabala—the limitless light—and it has, quite literally, the characteristics mathematicians such as Cantor have demonstrated belong to Infinity. As the *Upanishads* say, 'You can empty infinity from it, and infinity still remains.' However deep your union with the Light, it can become deeper, whether you call it Christ or Buddha or Brahm or Pan. Since I am, *thank God*," he said the last two words with great piety, "an Atheist, I prefer to call it Nothing—since anything we say about it is finite and limited, whereas it is infinite and unlimited."

Crowley proceeded to discourse on the infinite with great detail, summarizing mathematical theories on the subject with remarkable erudition and felicity. "But all this," he ended, "is not the true infinite. It is only what our little monkey-minds have been able to comprehend so far. Ask the *next* question. Seek the *higher* vision. That is the path that unites mysticism and rationalism, and transcends both of them. As a great Poet has written:

> We place no reliance
> On Virgin or Pigeon;
> Our method is Science,
> Our aim is Religion.

Those blessed words!" he said raptly. "Holy be the name of the sage who wrote them!"

At this point Sir John was far from sure whether he had been listening to the highest wisdom or the most pretentious mumbo jumbo he had ever heard. The Divine No-Thing was much like certain concepts in Buddhism and Taoism, but it was also a nice way of seeming to utter profundities while actually talking nonsense. But then, of course, Crowley's whole point had been that anything said about infinity was itself Nothing in comparison with infinity itself. . . .

With a start, Sir John realized that the lecture was over. The audience was applauding, somewhat tentatively, most of them as confused by what they had heard as Sir John himself.

"You may now," Crowley said carelessly, "unburden yourselves of the thoughts with which you passed the time while pretending to listen attentively to me; but in accord with English decorum and the rituals of the public lecture, you must phrase these remarks in the form of questions."

There was a nervous laugh.

"What about Christ?" The speaker was a redfaced man with a walrus mustache; he seemed more irritated by what he had heard than the rest of the audience. "You didn't say *nuthin'* about Christ," he added aggrievedly.

"A lamentable oversight," Crowley said unctuously. "What about Christ, indeed? Personally, I hold the man blameless for the religion that has been foisted upon him posthumously. Next question—the lady in the back row?"

"Is socialism inevitable?"

Sir John found himself wondering when Crowley would become aware of the Talisman and attempt to cajole him into surrendering it. With horror he realized that such overwhelming of his mind was possible: Crowley did possess charm, magnetism and charisma, like many servants of the Demon. What was it Pope had written about Vice? A creature of such hideous mein/That to be hated needs but be seen/But something something something/We first pity, then endure, then embrace. . . . "Many things are inevitable," Crowley was saying. "The tides. The seasons. The fact that the questions after a lecture seldom have anything to do with the content of the lecture. . . ." What do you seek? The Light. The limitless light: *ain soph auer*. And the darkness knew it not. . . .

"What about the Magick Will?" Sir John asked suddenly, during a pause.

"Ah," Crowley said. "That is a Significant Question." Somehow he conveyed the mocking capitals by his intonation. "Such questions deserve to be answered with demonstrations, not with mere windy words. Laylah," he called to the back of the room. "Could you bring the psychoboulometer?"

Lola approached the podium with something that looked hideously like a medieval thumb-screw.

"There is firstly conscious will," Crowley was saying, looking directly at Sir John. "We all attempt to exercise this every day. *'I will give up smoking.' 'I will be true to my wife.'* Ninety-nine times out of a hundred such resolutions fail, because they are in conflict with the force that really controls us, Unconscious Will, which can not be frustrated. Indeed, even the profane psychologists have rediscovered what the mystics always knew: Unconscious Will, if prevented from acting, returns in the night to haunt our dreams. And sometimes it returns in the daytime, too, in the form of irrational behaviors which we cannot understand. Magick Will should not be confused with either of these, because it includes both and is greater than both. To perform an act of Magick Will is to achieve the Great Work, I might say. The holiest of all holy books says in this connection, 'Thou hast no right but to do thy will.' Alas, if you think you are doing your true Will, without magickal training, you are almost always deluding yourself. . . . But I am engaging in the windy verbiage I promised to avoid, and here is the implement of demonstration. Would anybody care to give us an exhibit of what they can accomplish by conscious Will?"

"I think I shall give it a try," Sir John said, wondering at his own daring. "That's only fair since I asked the question," he added, feeling inane.

"Well, then, good! Come up here, sir," Crowley said with a grin that was beginning to look a bit sinister to Sir John. "We have here," he went on, holding the ugly thumb-screw so that everybody could get a good view, "one of the implements once used by the Dominican Order to enforce the religion which, as I said, has been foisted on Christ." He set the torture device on the podium. "They used it as an instrument of torture, but we shall use it as a measure of Will."

Sir John was now standing beside Crowley, looking uneasily at the thumb-screw. "Just insert your thumb, sir," Crowley said easily.

"What???" Sir John could hardly believe his ears.

"Just insert your thumb, down here," Crowley went on blandly, "and then turn the handle which tightens the vise. The needle on the boulometer—my own addition to this toy—will register how far you are able to withstand pain by sheer Will; 10 is a good score, and 0 means you are a mere jellyfish. How far do you think you can go?"

Sir John felt every eye in the room upon him. He wanted to cry, "I am not such a fool as to torture myself for your amusement," but—he was even more afraid of appearing a public coward. *Is that why people go into armies?* he asked himself grimly. . . . "Very well," he said coldly, inserting his thumb.

And Abraham rose up early in the morning, and saddled his ass, and took two of his young men with him, and Isaac his son, and clave the wood for the burnt offering, and rose up, and went unto the place of which God had told him.

And it was about the sixth hour, and there was darkness over all the earth until the ninth hour.

And the sun was darkened, and the veil of the temple was rent in the midst.

And Abraham took the wood of the burnt offering, and laid it upon Isaac his son; and he took the fire in his hand, and a knife; and they went both of them together.

And when Jesus had cried with a loud voice, he said, Father, unto thy hands I commend my spirit; and having said thus, he gave up the ghost.

"You've only reached two in the boulometer," Crowley said. "The audience will think you're not trying, sir."

"Damn you!" Sir John whispered, perspiration cold on his back. "I am done with this cruel joke. Let us see how much better your Magick Will can do!"

"Certainly," Crowley said calmly. He inserted his thumb into the cruel mechanism, and began turning the vise with slow deliberation. Not a muscle moved in his face. (Sir John suspected that he had gone into a trance.) The needle on the boulometer crept slowly, accompanied by gasps from the audience, all the way to 10.

"That," said Crowley gently, "might pass for an elementary demonstration of Magick Will."

There was a burst of spontaneous applause.

"It will also do," Crowley said, "as an illustration of our thesis about the soldier and the hunchback. The first rule of our Magick is: never believe anything you hear and doubt most of what you see." He turned the "psycho-boulometer" around, revealing that he had disengaged the screw and had been turning the handle without actually tightening the vise. There was an angry gasp.

"Oh," Crowley said, "are you feeling cheated? Remember this, then: you are cheated the same way every time emotional turmoil or fixed ideas distort your perception of what is actually before your eyes. And remember to look for the hunchback behind every soldier."

The audience began to file out, muttering and chattering as excitedly as a group of chimpanzees who had just found a mirror.

And then Sir John realized that Crowley had descended from the podium and was approaching him.

"Sir John Babcock," Crowley said warmly, "did you ever hear the story of the man with a mongoose in his basket?"

At least, unlike Lola, Crowley wasn't pretending not to recognize Sir John. "What mongoose?" Babcock asked carefully.

"It was on a train," Crowley said. "This chap had a basket under his seat and another passenger asked him what was in it. 'A mongoose,' he said. 'A mongoose!' said the other. 'What on earth do you want with a mongoose?' 'Well,' said our hero, 'my brother drinks a great deal more than is good for him, and sometimes he sees snakes. So I turn the mongoose on them.' The other passenger was baffled by this logic. 'But those are *imaginary* snakes!' he exclaimed. 'Aha!' said our hero. 'Do you think I don't know that? But this is an imaginary mongoose!' "

Sir John laughed nervously.

"That's the way it is with talismans," Crowley said. "When a phantom climbs, the ghost of a ladder serves him. But do keep that pentacle in your vest if it makes you feel better. I must go now. We shall meet again."

And Sir John stared as Crowley made his way to the back of the room, where he greeted Lola with a kiss. He whispered something; they both turned and looked back at Sir John; they waved cheerfully. And then they were gone.

DE ARTE ALCHEMICA

When Sir John arrived at Jones' home in Soho, he recounted his experience at the M.M.M. bookstore in detail.

"Crowley did not attempt to cajole me into giving him the talisman," he concluded with some asperity. "He treated it with total contempt."

"The man does have an Iron Will," Jones admitted, "but do not be deceived by his play-acting. Underneath, he knows we are on the counterattack now, and he must be afraid."

Sir John asked with suffocating restraint, "Are you really quite sure of that?"

"We both need a good night's sleep," Jones said, as if ignoring the question. "I will show you to the guest room. Before retiring, meditate a bit on the Parable of the Imaginary Mongoose. It has many levels of meaning. . . ."

In fact, Sir John found that he was too tired to reflect much on the Imaginary Mongoose when he was settled into his room. He slipped into sleep quickly and dreamed things he was unable to remember in the morning, although he awoke with a vague memory of Sir Talister Crowley and a giant mongoose pursuing him through Chapel Perilous.

After washing and dressing, Sir John remembered that he still had the copy of *The Book of Lies* he had purchased at M.M.M. He decided to try Bibliomancy-in-reverse and see what the Enemy had to offer in the way of an oracle. Opening at random, he found Chapter 50:

> In the forest God met the Stag-beetle. "Hold!
>   Worship me!" quoth God. "For I am the All-
>   Great, All-Good, All-Wise. . . . The stars are
>   but sparks from the forges of My smiths. . . ."
>
> "Yea, verily and Amen," said the Stag-beetle,
>   "all this I do believe, and that devoutly."
>
> "Then why do you not worship Me?"
>
> "Because I am real and you are only imaginary."
>
> But the leaves of the forest rustled with the
>   laughter of the wind.
>
> Said Wind and Wood: "They neither of them know
>   anything!"

"Damn, blast and thunder!" Sir John exploded. The beetle denies God, but wind and wood deny the beetle also. It was the Imaginary Mongoose riddle again, on a more Empedoclean level.

Going down the stairs in search of breakfast, Sir John experimented with solipsism. Perhaps there are no gods or beetles—or perhaps the whole world is, as the Gnostics claimed, the Abyss of Hallucinations, the Devil's Masquerade. But then we must consider David Hume's argument: the same skepticism can be applied to the Self. Am *I* really here? Are only the egoless wind and wood real? If phantoms descend, do the ghosts of stairs serve them?

Dr. Johnson refuted that philosophy by kicking a rock. Sir John refuted it by remembering that he really was hungry. Eggs and muffins were real enough to be desirable at this hour, and his stomach was real enough to desire them.

To his astonishment he found Jones eating breakfast with the Rev. Verey.

"I thought we were going to keep him safe with the Liverpool Mangler," he said, confused.

"Our plans have changed totally since I spoke to the Inner Head of the Order last night. Things are more serious than I realized," Jones said. "All three of us are going together to see Mr. Aleister Crowley at his home, with a surprise for him."

Sir John sat down. "Not another talisman?" he asked ironically.

"Dear me, no," Jones said mildly. "A real surprise this time. But eat first, Sir John; the muffins are delicious."

Sir John allowed it to go at that for a while; he was indeed ravenously hungry.

Verey had been reading the same newspaper article Jones had shown Sir John the previous evening. "It is full of errors," he complained. "Bobbie McMaster hasna' been forty-three for a long time; he's at least as old as I am. And that headless woman who haunts Geen Carrig is not new; she has been observed there for as many centuries as Anne Boleyn has been seen haunting the Tower of London. Why can reporters never get anything right?"

"I believe Bernard Shaw has explained that," Jones said, adding lemon to his tea, Paris style. "In almost all other professions a man must be able to observe carefully and report accurately what he has seen. Those qualifications are unnecessary for journalists, however, since their job is to write sensational stories that sell newspapers. Hence, all the incompetents who are not capable of normal accuracy in observation or memory fail in most other professions and many of them eventually drift into journalism."

"Aha!" said Sir John, who had often wondered why nothing in the papers was ever accurate. Of course: any chemist or grocer or ordinary man, asked to describe this breakfast, would report correctly that it consisted of eggs, ham and muffins, with tea. A journalist would report porridge, bacon and toast, with a sex orgy and a murder.

Truth! Truth! Truth! crieth the Lord of the Abyss of Hallucinations. . . .

"Nessie" was real according to virtually all the residents of Inverness; "Nessie" was a myth according to "experts" who had never visited the scene.

"You know," Sir John said to Jones, "I've noticed that you always refer to Crowley as 'Mr.', but the poster I saw last night gave him the title of 'Sir'. Which is correct?"

"Crowley is a brewer's son," Jones said. "But the 'Sir' is legitimate according to his own peculiar lights. Back in the '90s, when he was a singularly Romantic and adventuresome young man not yet corrupted by Black Magick, he joined the cause of the Carlists. Don Carlos personally knighted him."

"But," Sir John protested, "Don Carlos was only a pretender to the throne."

"To you and me and the daily press, yes. Crowley still insists Don Carlos was the real monarch and Victoria the pretender. So, as I say, by his own lights, the title of Sir Aleister is quite correct."

"The man is *daft*," Verey said. "I swear to it."

"Oh, most certainly," Jones agreed, with a quiet smile. "But he is also brilliant and coldly rational, in his own way. He and I were friends once, many years ago, before our paths diverged, and I still say, for all his wickedness, Aleister Crowley had the potential to become the greatest of us all." Jones sighed. "It is only the most exalted who can fall all the way to the lowest depths," he added grimly.

" 'Lucifer, son of the morning, how art thou fallen,' " Verey quoted, with deep, rolling drama, as from the pulpit.

Like most clergymen, Verey had a Bible quotation for all occasions, Sir John reflected.

As Jones' valet appeared to clear off the breakfast dishes, Sir John asked boldly, "Well, when do we go to beard the lion in his den? I hope it will not be as anti-climactic as last night."

"I think we may leave straightaway," Jones said with the calm of an Adept.

"Aye," Verey said. "I look forward to the moment when that devil Aleister Crowley and I meet face to face."

Sir John felt like one of the Three Musketeers setting off to do battle with Richelieu's men.

"Crowley lives on Regent Street," Jones said. "In fact, he has one of the finest homes there. His father was not merely a brewer, but a very successful brewer. We are going into one of the most respectable neighborhoods in London. Crowley publishes all his own works in the most expensive bindings and finest papers, and lives like an Oriental prince in every other way."

"Shall we walk or take a hansom?" Sir John asked.

"I should think a brisk walk would do us all good," Jones replied.

They certainly made an odd group of Musketeers, Sir John reflected as they set out: Verey, aged and hunch-backed; Jones, stout and fortyish; only he himself, at twenty-eight, was young enough to qualify as a conventional hero of melodrama—and he was probably the most nervous of all.

Jones began reminiscing about Crowley as they walked. They had first met sixteen years earlier, in 1898, when Crowley was admitted to the original Golden Dawn as a

Probationer. "He was a most impressive young man," Jones said. "At twenty-three, he had already published several volumes of excellent poetry and had set some distinguished mountain climbing records in the Alps. He had majored in organic chemistry at Cambridge and I remember asking him why, since I saw nothing of the scientific temperament in him. I have never forgotten his answer. 'My personality is entirely poetic, esthetic and Romantic,' he said. 'I needed some work in hard science to bring me down to earth.' I thought it an astonishing example of self-insight and self-discipline in one so young."

Jones went on to tell of Crowley's rapid rise in the Golden Dawn. "I never saw a man with such a natural aptitude for Cabalistic Magick," he said frankly. Then came the disaster of 1900, when the feud between William Butler Yeats and McGregor Mathers exploded into a dozen lesser feuds which split the Golden Dawn into factions which were never re-united. Jones lost track of Crowley for some years, although he heard of Crowley's travels to study Yoga in the Far East and Sufism in North Africa. In 1902, Crowley and a German engineer, Oscar Eckenstein, succeeded in climbing higher on Chogo Ri in the Himalayas than any expedition before or since, reaching twenty-three thousand feet. In 1905, Crowley went to China, and when he returned he was a completely new man.

"I remember," Jones said, "my naïve response when we met again in 1906. I found him so changed that I actually believed he was a totally Illuminated being, beyond any other Golden Dawn graduate. I asked him how he had achieved that, and he said simply, 'I became a little child.' "

They were crossing Rupert Street and Jones smiled ironically. "My illusions about him did not last long," he said. "That very same year he published the infamous *Bhag-i-Muatur*, which he claimed was a translation from the Persian. It was nothing of the sort. Crowley had always been a great admirer of the late Sir Richard Burton and was merely copying his hero, who had published the *Hasidah*—a blunt statement of Atheistic philosophy—as a translation from the Arabic, when it was actually his own work. The *Bhag-i-Muatur*, a title which translates as 'The Scented Garden,' was similarly Crowley's own work disguised as a translation. It was, on the surface, an allegory about the Soul's relationship to God. Actually, carefully read, it was a glorification of sodomy." Shortly thereafter Crowley was divorced by his wife for adultery and began to live as shamelessly as Oscar Wilde before his trials, flaunting his numerous affairs, both heterosexual and homosexual, as if he took a special diabolical delight in shocking Christian sensibilities.

In the following years, Crowley divided his time between London, Paris and the North African deserts. In 1909, he staged a spectacle called "The Rites of Eleusis" at a London theater and aroused a storm of controversy. The "rites" began with a chorus informing the audience, Nietzschefashion, that "God is dead." The following ceremony included ballet, music, ritual, poetry and the serving to the audience of an alleged "elixir of the gods" (which some later suspected contained a mind-altering drug) and ended with the announcement that a new God had been born, a "Lord of Force and Fire" Who would destroy Western civilization and create, out of its ruins, a new civilization based on the Rabelaisian slogan: "Do what thou wilt."

"The man is daft," Verey repeated, with cold fury.

Since 1910, Jones continued, Crowley had been the English leader of the Ordo Templi Orientis, a Berlin-based Masonic order which claimed to retain the primordial Masonic secrets in purer form than any other group. The Outer Head of the order, Jones said, was Theodore Reuss, an actor who was also an agent for the German secret police.

"Does Scotland Yard know this?" Sir John exclaimed.

"Oh, indeed," Jones said. "So does Army Intelligence. They watch Reuss carefully but never interfere with him, since his area of operations is restricted to spying on German exiles in England. He was for a long time an associate of Karl Marx, Friedrich Engels and their circle."

Jones went on to speak of the links between the Ordo Templi Orientis and certain dervish orders in the Near East said to be connected with the Young Turks who had overturned the monarchy and introduced parliamentary democracy. Rasputin, the monk of strange hypnotic powers who seemed to have total control over the current Czar and his family, was also associated with the same dervish orders, Jones said, as was Colonel Dragutin Dimitryevic, head of Serbian Military Intelligence, who was simultaneously, under the code name "Apis," a member of "Union or Death," a Pan-Serbian secret revolutionary group. "Between Rasputin, the Young Turks and Colonel Dimitryevic," Jones said, "the whole Near Eastern and Balkan situation has steadily grown more unstable, so that all the alliances between England, France, Germany and Russia are breaking down, each Great Power suspecting the others of plotting to use the increasingly volatile situation for its own profit—even though the Young Turks are ostensibly sworn to fight to the death to keep the Great Powers out of that area. Ever since the Berlin-to-Baghdad Railway was built in '96," Jones went on, "some in our government have suspected Germany of intending to replace us in India, but now every major Power suspects every other Power of similar designs."

"This grows deeper and darker as you proceed," Sir John complained. "Are we dealing with a spiritual war between rival theologies or an economic war between rival commercial interests?"

"We are talking about Total War," Jones said somberly.

Sir John looked up at Big Ben, towering in the distance,

stone-solid, tangible, real. But Shakespeare's words came
back to him:

> these our actors
> As I foretold you, were all spirits, and
> Are melted into air, into thin air:
> And, like the baseless fabric of this vision
> The cloud-capp'd towers, the gorgeous palaces,
> The solemn temples, the great globe itself,
> Yea, all which it inhabit, shall dissolve

The Loch Ness monster and the Pan-Serbian Movement; bat-winged creatures that titter and the German
secret police; incredible suicides and nameless perversions; worldwide assassinations and the secret history of
Freemasonry; a murdered cat in a locked church and the
Berlin-Baghdad railroad . . . Masks and masks-behind-the-
masks. Sir John was no longer sure of anything. 358: the
Serpent is the Messiah. I.N.R.I.: Jesus is Dionysus. HONI
SOIT: The Order of the Garter was a secret witch-coven
which had ruled Great Britain for five hundred years. Life
itself was an Empedoclean paradox and David Hume was
right: one cannot even prove, in logic, the existence of the
ego itself. *Truth! Truth! Truth! crieth the Lord of the
Abyss of Hallucinations.*

"You are aware, of course, Sir John," Jones went on,
"that the Bavarian Illuminati, financed by the Rothschilds,
secretly masterminded the revolutions which overthrew
the old monarchist-feudal order and opened the way to
the 'free' market system in which monopolized Capital has
come to dominate the modern world. The Illuminati,
needless to say, had motives of their own: 'There is no
God but Man' was their slogan before it was Crowley's. In
fact, the Ordo Templi Orientis, in its modern form, was
created by amalgamating Leopold Engels' revived Illuminati in 1888 with P. B. Randolph's Hermetic Brotherhood

of Light. Randolph, an American Negro, had started as a voodoo priest but received his advanced training from the same dervish order behind Rasputin and the Young Turks. Theodore Reuss, the Outer Head of the Ordo Templi Orientis, we have reason to believe, was not just a spy on Marx and his group for the German military intelligence, but actually a double agent, spying on Germany for the Marxists. Crowley himself has certain links with Commander Marsden of our own Army Intelligence which I do not pretend to fathom. Isn't it strange to think all of this goes back ultimately to Mansur-el-Hallaj, the dervish who was stoned to death by the orthodox Moslems in the ninth century for saying 'I am the Truth and there is nothing within my turban but God'? Yet it was through Mansur's disciples that the Knights Templar were initiated into the secret black rites of Tantric sex-magick. . . ."

And Old Mother Hubbard really is Isis in disguise and the bone she is seeking is the phallus of Osiris, Sir John thought wildly. *Everything imaginable is true in some sense: if I believe enough that I can fly, I will simply float off into the stratosphere. . . .*

"Arthur!" Verey cried, jolting Sir John out of these solipsistic reflections.

Jones and Babcock looked in the direction of the clergyman's fixed stare. Across the street was a garden: Did a shadowy form move ambiguously therein, or was it just a tree swaying in the breeze?

"My God," Verey whispered, almost staggering. "It's my dead brother, Arthur!"

"It can't be—you are confused," Jones began to protest. The clergyman brushed him aside rudely.

"Arthur," he repeated, "the monster who brought ruin on my whole family. And now he comes back from the grave itself to taunt me." And he rushed across the street.

"After him!" Jones said urgently, starting to run.

Sir John reached the opposite sidewalk first, as Verey

dashed through the gate and entered the path between the high beds of exotic plants. The path turned abruptly and Verey was now running, about ten feet away, in a direction parallel to the street. He disappeared behind a large oak, as Sir John entered the garden and ran after him.

Taking the same turn as Verey, Sir John found the clergyman no longer in sight. He rushed to the next turn and confronted a tallish, black-bearded man in a Russian fur hat, busy trimming the hedges.

"Where is he?" Sir John cried.

"Where is who?" the bearded stranger asked in a thick Slavic accent.

"Reverend Verey—he just ran through this garden. . . ."

Jones arrived, panting. "What happened?" he asked. "It looked as if Verey just disappeared."

"Verey?" the Slav said. "Nobody has come this way at all."

Jones and Babcock exchanged mystified glances. Jones recovered first. "Who are you, sir?" he asked.

"I am Baron Nicholas Salmonovitch Zaharov," said the stranger, "and this is my house behind us, and this is my garden, and I suspect both of you must have been drinking at an early hour if you imagine you saw someone come this way. I assure you nobody has passed me."

Sir John remembered:

> *. . . these our actors . . .*
> *. . . are*
> *melted into air, into thin air . . .*

"At last," said Albert Einstein, his pipe venting cloud-grey smoke. "Here is something we can really get our teeth into."

James Joyce shifted into a different indifferent slouch in his chair. "We may find," he muttered, "that we have bitten off more than we can chew."

Einstein was rummaging about for a sheet of paper not covered with mathematical equations. "Baron Zaharov," he muttered. "The light at the end of the tunnel. Aha!" He had found several sheafs of virgin foolscap. "Here," he said to Babcock. "I want an exact diagram of the scene of this miracle."

"I don't draw very well," Babcock said uneasily.

"We do not require an artist's rendering," Einstein said impatiently. "Sketch the scene as an engineer or an architect would, *verstehen Sie?* As a man would see it from above, if he were floating in the air."

"A schematic," Babcock said. "I can do that."

Einstein hovered over the drawing as it was made, asking questions, demanding details, until at last it emerged in full enough precision to satisfy him.

"So," said Einstein softly, studying the diagram, "it is much as I suspected. Clever rascals. . . ."

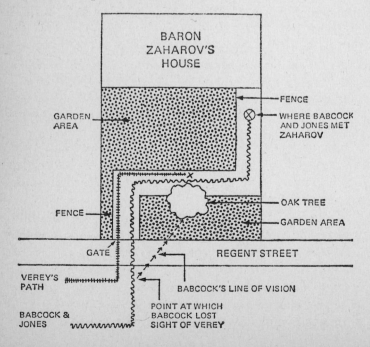

"I hope you know what you're talking about," Joyce intoned darkly from the corner where he slouched. "To me, in my unscientific ignorance, this is the most marvelous marvel in Sir John's whole Arabian Nights adventure."

Einstein smiled. "This Baron Zaharov," he said to Babcock. "You certainly didn't just bid him *adieu* at that point and accept his testimony at face value?"

Babcock mutely made a despairing gesture with his hands obscurely. "No," he said, "but it was most difficult. At first he insisted on treating us both as drunk or demented, and Jones had to exercise great diplomacy to persuade him to take us seriously. Finally, he did grow more cooperative, although he still acted as though he were humoring us. Nobody is quite as imperious as a Russian nobleman, you know. But he allowed us to go over the terrain most carefully. The garden was in full flower on both sides of the path and could only be described as lush. There was no way Reverend Verey could have been pulled over the fence and dragged through the garden without crushing or badly mauling hundreds of plants, and yet none of the plants was disturbed at all."

"How high was the fence?" Einstein asked intensely.

"Approximately three feet. The upper half of Verey's body was clearly visible to me until he vanished behind the oak tree."

"How high were the plants?" Einstein persisted.

"Varying heights—from one foot up to three or four feet. And none of them was trampled or disturbed in any way," Babcock repeated.

"Of course," Einstein said. "Now, carefully, Sir John, visualize the Reverend Verey and Baron Zaharov. What would you say were their respective heights?"

Sir John frowned thoughtfully. "Verey was quite short," he said. "Not much above five feet, I would say. The Baron was at least my own height, I'd estimate—around five-eight, give or take a few inches. He was so overbearing in his manner that I seem to remember looking up at him as he spoke, but I am not perfectly sure he was actually that tall."

Einstein nodded. "Rods and clocks," he muttered under his breath. He turned his attention back to Babcock. "What happened after you and Jones were through inspecting the garden?"

"The Baron showed us back to the street, with some patronizing remark about people who take strong spirits in the morning. I was completely at sea by then, but Jones said, 'I don't trust that man. Let us see what we can learn about him next door.'"

"*Ja?*" Einstein said delightedly.

"I know what you're thinking," Babcock said. "As soon as Jones spoke it occurred to me, also. I had been so shocked by the seeming dematerialization, and so intimidated by the Baron's arrogant manner, that my mind had virtually ceased functioning for a while there. But, of course, if there were trickery involved, the Baron would have to be an accomplice."

"Go on," Einstein said, amusement flickering at a cor-ner of his mouth.

"Well, the house next door turned out to belong to Miss Isadora Duncan, the celebrated American dancer. Have either of you ever seen her dance?" Babcock asked, interrupting himself.

"I detest ballet," Joyce said. "All that jumping about distracts one from the music."

"I have never seen Miss Duncan, either," Einstein confessed. "But, of course, everyone in Europe has heard of her. Is she as good as Pavlova, as some say?"

"Better," Babcock said. "I saw her dance only once, around 1909, but I have never forgotten it. Of course, I disapprove of the libertine principles the lady has so brazenly proclaimed, but I admit she is one of the great *artistes* of our time. I was very disappointed that she was not at home. We did, however, speak at length to her secretary, another American named Miss Sturgis."

"And what was Miss Sturgis able to tell you about Baron Zaharov?" Einstein asked.

"A great deal," Babcock said with a weak smile, wearily. "More than we wished to hear, in fact. She detested the man violently."

"Oh?" Einstein was disconcerted. "This is not what I was expecting."

"Miss Sturgis described the Baron as a prude, a religious fanatic, and an officious busybody," Sir John went on. "It seems that he once tried to organize a kind of moral crusade in the neighborhood, to have Miss Duncan ejected as—well, as the equivalent of a public prostitute. Failing in that, he continued to annoy the neighbors by sending them letters quoting the most controversial utterances in Miss Duncan's writings, claiming she was a dangerous revolutionary. Miss Sturgis said that if it were not for his high position in the Russian Embassy, the neighbors might have organized a committee to have *him* thrown out."

"Any more?" Einstein asked, abruptly brighteyed and cheerful again.

"Oh, a great deal," Babcock said. "Zaharov attended services at an Eastern Orthodox church every morning, even though it was miles away and he had to arise at five A.M. to get there. He once tried to use his position at the embassy to bully a Russian-language bookstore to stop carrying the works of Count Tolstoy because Tolstoy had questioned the doctrine of the Virgin Birth. His uncle was a Patriarch of the Orthodox Church, in Moscow. He was suspicious of Roman Catholics and Jews, and regarded Protestants as little better than atheists. Miss Sturgis said, I remember, 'After having him as a neighbor, I understand why Russia is such a backward country.'"

Einstein laughed. *"Wunderbar!"* he said. "Miss Sturgis' testimony fits perfectly with my theory."

Joyce muttered, "Then I am mad."

Einstein smiled. "How so?"

"If the Baron were a man who got up at five in the morning to *kill* cats in churches," Joyce said, "or if he admired and praised Miss Duncan's revolutionary principles, then I might see him as a co-conspirator with our enigmatic Crowley. But as it is, he seems to be above suspicion."

Einstein nodded. "But that is what I expected. When Babcock said Miss Sturgis regarded the Baron as detestable I feared that my hypothesis was falling apart. But as it is I am more sure than ever that I am on the right track. What happened next?" he asked Babcock.

"After we left the Duncan household, Jones said that Verey's dematerialization had changed everything again, and that I must not accompany him to Crowley's home; he would go alone. I protested, and we argued somewhat heatedly. Eventually, I was persuaded to allow him to go alone. I checked in at the Diogenes Club, where I often stay when I am in London, and waited. . . ."

"Yes?" Einstein prompted, a professor examining a student.

"I waited until nightfall," Babcock said. "And then I could stand the uncertainty no more. I took a hansom cab to Jones' home in Soho . . . and . . ."

"Let me tell you what you found," Einstein said. "There was an ordinary English family living there, with open and honest faces, who swore solemnly they had never heard of a Mr. George Cecil Jones."

"My God!" Babcock said, sitting up suddenly. "This is incredible! How did you know?"

"Am I correct?" Einstein asked.

"Yes," Babcock said. "Before Heaven, I cannot imagine how you guessed."

"Guessing has nothing to do with scientific thinking," Einstein said sharply. "Did you perchance also try to contact the Liverpool Mangler, as your last contact with Jones?"

"Yes," Babcock said. "His room was totally empty. The landlady swore it hadn't been rented for months."

"And then what did you do?" Einstein prodded.

"I returned to the Diogenes Club and sat awake all night, thinking and wondering. In the morning I went to the London Main Post Office, to see if I could get any information about the renters of Post Office Box 718. That was my last remaining link with the Hermetic Order of the Golden Dawn. They told me there was no such box; the numbers only ran as high as 600. The Invisible College had become completely invisible again, it seems. As if the last four years were all a dream. An imaginary mongoose fighting imaginary snakes." Sir John lapsed into silence, staring into space with the expression of one who has been driven to doubt all that he had ever taken for granted. There was a strained silence.

"Beautiful," Joyce said finally.

"What?" Einstein asked irritably. "Did you say 'beautiful'?"

"I did," Joyce replied somberly, "and I apologize, Sir John; that may be the most callous word I have ever spoken. But as an artist myself I was just carried away for a moment with admiration for the thoroughness, the elegance I might almost say, of your antagonists. They certainly did a complete job on you. It's almost mathematical in its starkness, isn't it, Professor? One fancies that they should have written 'Q.E.D.' on the bottom line."

"What *are* you talking about?" Babcock asked tiredly.

"The *completeness* of it," Joyce repeated, adding: ". . . as the legendary Frenchman said after the earthquake. Imagine: even the post office box was fictitious. That's a touch I appreciate."

"They are clever," Einstein agreed. "Devilishly clever."

"But also elegant," Joyce again repeated himself. "Do you know what their model was—even before they seized

on Mr. Chambers' *King in Yellow* for the theme of the
book that drives people to self-destruction? It's an old, old
tale—one of the oldest in the world—and I have often
reflected on it myself. The charm of this story, I have
found, is that if you tell it to somebody they will immediately claim to have heard it, or read it, somewhere before,
but they can never recall where . . ."

"The tale is this," Joyce went on. "A man is in a strange
city—or, in some more subtly unsettling versions, in a
city that is very familiar to him, a city he thinks he knows.
But he becomes lost and wanders into a neighborhood he
has never seen before. It grows dark; he sees nobody to
ask for directions. And then suddenly *She* is there—the
most beautiful woman in the world. In some variations,
She is carrying a pearl of great price, or some other
fabulous jewel. In any event, She invites him into her
home—as the Queen of the Faery invites the wandering
Knight to cross her threshold in the medieval legends. He
goes with Her, and all is bliss, and paradise, and the
realization of all the dreams of Romance. Do either of you
know the end of this immortal story, my friends?"

"Yes," Einstein said softly. "You are right about this
yarn—I do feel that I've heard it before, or read it, and I
can't remember where or when. He agrees to meet Her
again the following day, at Her home. He returns at the
appointed time; and there is no house there, only a vacant
lot. Neighbors tell him there hasn't been a house there in
over a century."

Babcock stared. "Yes," he said. "I recall the tale now,
myself. Only it seems that when I heard it, the whole
neighborhood had vanished. The hero searches the city
endlessly, but never finds that street again."

Joyce smiled gently. "In some versions, he is an old man
first seen wandering the city at night. After he tells his
story, he goes on searching for the street that once was
but is no more. Some people, I have found, even claim to

know the man this adventure happened to. It is what Jung would call an archetypal vision. The doors to the magick world open once, and then close again, and you can never find your way back to the place they were. You see, Sir John? They have put you through a script that has existed as long as the human imagination. In your case, adapting the scenario to your own anxieties, the Witch-Queen, or Elf-Woman, or Goddess, or whatever one wants to call Her, was hostile and malign from the beginning; but otherwise they haven't altered the classic pattern."

"They," Babcock repeated bitterly. "*They*. Do you, sir, still think They are merely human and that They accomplished all this by purely material means?"

Before Joyce could reply Einstein commented drily, "We shall come to that question in a few moments. But first, Sir John, is your story finished? I suspect some sort of climax is still waiting. . . ."

Babcock rose and stretched. "Yes," he said, beginning to pace, "there was a climax of sorts. . . ."

"After the visit to the post office and the discovery that there was no Box 718, I went back to the Diogenes Club, half-convinced that I was mad. Before I could go to my room, the porter told me there was a gentleman waiting to see me in the smoking room. I must have walked in there like an automaton; I was in some strange mental state where it no longer mattered whether Jones or Verey had returned as miraculously as they had dematerialized, or if the Devil Himself were waiting for me. It was, God help me, Aleister Crowley.

"I could hardly speak; in fact, I could hardly feel any-thing—not even fear. 'What do you want?' I asked him. I was thinking of Scott's words about everything produced by witches' glamour being insubstantial as air.

"He spoke in a level, pleasant voice, without bravado or dramatics; anybody even a few feet away would think we were having a most ordinary conversation. He said, 'Strange things happen when an imaginary mongoose fights imaginary snakes. It does not do to meddle with us. Some go mad and kill themselves. Some simply disappear. And some flee to the ends of the earth, without ever escaping. Our eyes will be on you forever, and we will finish you at our pleasure.' He even smiled, as if he were praising my tie or something of that sort, then turned to leave.

"Then he faced me again. 'Do you understand at last?' he said very quietly. 'Your God and your Jesus are dead. They no longer have any power to protect you or anyone else who calls on them for help. Our magick is now stronger, for the Old Ones have returned, and Man shall be free of guilt and sin. Pray to Jesus for help, if you must; it will help you no more than it helped Verey or Jones. Our hands will be at your throat forever, even if you see them not. We will come for you when you least expect it.'

"That was all," Babcock said listlessly. "He was gone before I had fully recovered from his blasphemous words. I left England that night, traveling under an assumed name. I went to Arles, in southern France, and stayed at an inn. After a few days, I came back to my room after a visit to the local church and found an inverse crucifix hanging over my bed. I have been moving on, city to city, ever since then."

Joyce rose and stretched the kinks out of his body, casting a grotesque spidery shadow on the wall behind him. "Well, Professor," he asked, "are we living in the twentieth century or the thirteenth?"

The *Föhn* whistled at the window.

Einstein studied carefully the dottle of his extinguished pipe. Under their drooped lids his eyes searched what the cold smell of the ash spoke not.

"Well," he said finally, "I do not regard this matter as hopelessly obscure. There is quite a bit of light amid the engulfing darkness, don't you think, Jeem?"

Joyce smiled wanly. "I have picked up a few rays of

light," he said carefully. "But they are small and fugitive and my darkness is still much greater. Shall I list the points that appear most cogent to me?"

"By all means," Einstein urged.

"There are four," Joyce said. "I might title them as follows:

1. The Clue of the Quadrilateral Metaphor;
2. The Matter of the Tacked-on Tragedy;
3. The Matter of the Enumeration of Sonnets;
4. The Clue of the 26 Garters.

"Does that suggest anything to either of you?" he concluded impassively.

"Not to me," Babcock said, baffled.

"Nor to me," Einstein added. "But I wonder if you have found the parts of the answer that are still beyond my comprehension. . . . However, imitating your style, I can list the points that have aided me in seeing through this malign little drama. There are eight in my case, as follows:

1. The Razor of David Hume;
2. The Matter of the Marvelous Multiplication;
3. The Incident of Casual Telepathy;
4. The Matter of the Superabundant Coincidences;
5. The Clue of the Over-Defined Image;
6. The Mystery of the Extra Mountain-Climber;
7. The Clue of the Impossible Name;
8. The Matter of the Relativity of Dimensions.

"I think that these points fairly well reveal what has actually been transpiring here," he finished. "Do you understand what I am implying, Jeem?"

"I haven't the foggiest," Joyce said. "In fact, I am more confused than I was before you gave us that list of allegedly helpful hints."

"Most interesting," Einstein mused. "We all see only that which we are trained to see. . . . Well, be that as it may, since you gave us your list first, could you explicate them for us before I get to my list?"

Joyce removed carefully his glasses, to polish them meticulously on a handkerchief. "I am now about seventy-five percent blind," he said thoughtfully; finishing, he translated the glasses back to his nose. "Presto! The world is created again: I can see it." Pull out his eyes: Apologize. "The world is created anew each time we change our focus or viewpoint," he went on. "Let us change our focus for a moment and look at the beginning of all this, *Clouds Without Water*, through sharper glasses." He paused.

"Yes?" Babcock prodded.

"The author of *Clouds Without Water* is a singularly deep young man, as Gilbert and Sullivan said of a similar case," Joyce went on. "He can say two things at once; even, in some places I have noticed, three things at once. For instance, *consummatum est,* the closing words of a sonnet Sir John has called to our attention, can refer [as previously noted] either to a Catholic Mass or to a Black Mass; but they can also refer to the completion of a sex act: foreplay, union, climax, consummation. But our author can even say *four* things at once: the mystical *wine* symbolism in the alchemical sequence, I note, may refer to the vaginal secretions of the poet's paramour, as Sir John suspected; to the wine of the Mass; to the wine of a Black Mass; or even to the traditional use of 'wine' as a symbol of divine intoxication in Sufi authors such as Omar Khayyám. This is the Clue of the Quadrilateral Metaphor.

"So, I ask myself just how deep this singularly deep young man can really be. The tragic end of his saga is, to me, blatantly false and propagandistic. The number of adulterers in Europe may not exceed the sands of the Sahara, or the atoms in the galaxy, but it is certainly vast; and they do not automatically succumb to advanced, incurable syphilis in every case. Nor do they, if the disease is diagnosed, immediately commit suicide. They seek treatment, and if they are lucky and the disease is caught soon enough, they are even routinely cured. I do not say the sad end of Arthur Angus Verey is impossible, merely improbable. It has a moralistic, preachy sound, very much as if it were the work of the Reverend Charles Verey. This is the Tacked-On Tragedy I mentioned. But let me ask: Does such dual authorship sound in accord with your notions of human psychology, gentlemen?"

Einstein spoke first. "Go on," he said. "You definitely seem to have the part of the puzzle that still eludes me."

Babcock added, "I will certainly grant that Verey would hardly have published that book without such a harsh moralistic lesson at the end. . . ."

Joyce rapped the floor with his walkingstick. "Point one carries," he said. "Well, then, the old legal adage tells us, 'Guilty in part, guilty in whole,' which may or may not be true, but gives me a pretty thought, nonetheless. If the Reverend Charles Verey wrote the ending, could he have written the whole? All day a phrase from Dante has been running through my head: *ed eran duo in uno, ed uno in duo.* 'They were two in one, and one in two.' It describes Bertran de Born, beheaded, in the *Inferno.* Think of Dr. Jekyll and Mr. Hyde, Dr. Frankenstein and his Monster, Faust and Mephistopheles. . . ."

Einstein laughed. "Astonishing," he said. "For the last two days I've been thinking of Faust and Mephistopheles, and of the great line Goethe gives to Faust: *Zwei Seelen wohnen ach! in meiner Brust.* My father used to tell me that was the most profound line in the play. 'Two souls dwell, alas, within my breast.' "

"The extreme form of this dualism is the Split or Multiple Personality discussed in psychology texts," Joyce went on. "But we are all prisms—split and multiple personalities, to some extent. We each have our hidden side,

ROBERT ANTON WILSON

which Jung so poetically calls the Shadow. What would the Shadow of the Reverend Charles Verey be? The opposite of his public persona of Presbyterian righteousness, of course. It would be, in fact, very much like the alleged Arthur Angus Verey—libertine, sensualist, adulterer, blasphemer against Christ and the Church. I suggest, in short, that *Clouds Without Water* was written entirely by Reverend Charles Verey. To each 'Thou shalt not' of the public Reverend Charles Verey, the internal 'Arthur' cries, 'I will!' The Shadow, the Satanic 'Arthur' writes the lush voluptuous sonnets, lingering longingly on every lovely lewd licentious detail of a fantastic love affair with a gloriously wicked and totally desirable woman; the public Persona arranges that this book of wet dreams ends with 'Arthur' being destroyed for his sins and adds the running footnotes re-asserting traditional morality.

"Well, gentlemen," Joyce asked, "does Point Two carry? Are the two souls in *Clouds Without Water* dwellers in one breast?"

Babcock shook his head dubiously. "It is possible in psychology," he said. "But it is contradicted by the facts as we know them."

"The facts as we know them," Einstein said mildly, "have been distorted by a deliberate conspiracy to keep us from knowing the facts as they really are. Go ahead, Jeem."

"We now have, in *Clouds Without Water*, a book such as I myself try to write," Joyce said. "A multi-dimensional, multi-level, multi-meaningful book. A puzzle-book, one might say—and what could be more appropriate to our times, when all the best minds recognize increasingly that our existence is a profound puzzle? The reader is challenged, if he is intelligent enough to look beyond the mere surface, to ask what *Clouds Without Water* really is. Firstly, it could be what it appears to be and pretends to be: the account of an adultery that came to a bad end, with a running commentary by a clergyman underlining the 'moral' lesson that The Wages of Sin Are Death. Perfect for the British reading public. Or, secondly, it could be what Sir John has decoded: a manual of Tantric sex practices, showing how the permutations and variations on the erotic union between a man and a woman can be excruciatingly prolonged until ecstasy is exploded into oblivion, into egoless trance. Or, thirdly, it could be what I have said: the record of the split in the personality of a tormented Presbyterian puritan, dreaming of the deliciously wicked delights of coitus, fellatio and cunnilingus, and then punishing his Other Self for enjoying those dreams."

"But which is it really?" Babcock exclaimed. "You are just adding to the mystery, not clarifying it—*ignotium per ignotius!*"

"What is the 'real' length of a rod, Professor?" Joyce asked.

"It depends on the coordinate system of the rod," Einstein said, amused, "and the coordinate system of the observer, and the relationship between their velocities."

Babcock grimaced. "That doesn't make sense to me," he said. "Length is length, and that's all there is to it."

"That is not all there is to it," Einstein said. "All our judgments in which length plays a role are judgments about instruments used to measure that length. And the readings of the instruments will depend on our velocity in relationship to the velocity of the thing being measured. Lorenz worked all this out mathematically but couldn't believe it. I decided in 1904 to believe it and see where it led me. It led to solving all the puzzles that have bedeviled physics since the Michelson-Morley experiment. It led, in fact, to the simple conclusion that there is no length as a *ding an sich*, an objective entity, but only length$_1$ as read by instrument$_1$, length$_2$ as read by instrument$_2$, and so on. The same applies to time, I have also demonstrated."

"But," said Babcock, "this takes us outside sensory space and linear time entirely. It is Gnostic and Platonic."

"In a sense," Einstein granted. "The difference is that Plato left off at the point where I begin. He never connected his geometric archetypes with empirical sense-data. I have made that scientific connection. My theory explains experiments that can be explained in no other way."

"Tell him about the rock and the train," Joyce suggested languidly from his shadow.

"Oh, that is a type of relativity that has been known since Galileo," Einstein said. "I have merely provided a contemporary illustration. Suppose you throw a rock from a train. In what path does it fall?"

Babcock looked uncertain. "I'm not sure," he admitted. "It seems to me it would fall in a straight line."

"Ah," said Einstein, "so it would—from your viewpoint inside the train. But if somebody else were in a field beside the railroad tracks, how would he see it fall?"

Babcock was silent. "Er," he said finally, "I'm not sure about this, either, but I try to visualize it and I imagine he would see it fall in a curved path."

"In the curve called a parabola," Einstein corrected. "He would see it fall in a perfect parabola. Now, which is true? The viewpoint of the man on the train, or that of the man in the field?"

"I begin to catch your drift," Babcock said. "Both are true, within the—what do you call it?—coordinate systems of the two observers."

Joyce laughed. "All of this is unfamiliar to you," he said to Babcock, "and yet you are learning rapidly. Do you know why that is? I shall tell you. Because your Cabala is based on the very same principles, although applied in that case to psychology rather than to physics. You are just learning a new aspect of what you actually already know."

Einstein raised an eyebrow. "So I am a Cabalist?" he asked, amused.

"What is Cabala?" Joyce asked Socratically. "Well, whatever else it is, from my viewpoint as an artist it is a method of multiple vision. To take an example from Sir John's story, I.N.R.I., analyzed Cabalistically, no longer has simply a Christian meaning, but a Greek mythological meaning, an Egyptian meaning, an Alchemical meaning, a meaning within the symbolism of the Tarot cards, and so forth. These correspondences are not *illog*ical but *ana*logical. The Cabalist sees each symbol—Christ, Dionysus, Osiris, the Tarot cards and the rest—as meaningful in its own mythic context, just as Professor Einstein's theory sees each measurement as true within its own coordinate system. And the Cabalist seeks, behind these diverse and contradictory symbols, the archetypal meaning which is in human psychology itself, as Dr. Jung has recently reminded us. Just as Professor Einstein looks beyond the diverse and contradictory instrument readings for the abstract mathematical relationships that translate one coordinate system into another."

"Multiple vision," Babcock repeated. "Yes. That does summarize Cabalism nicely."

"Well, then," Joyce said, "what is *Clouds Without Water?* Is it not a perfect example of Cabalistic thinking, a book which can, in fact, be read at least four ways, and possibly more, if we were to look at it more closely? Is it not a model of Cabalistic multiple meaning? And I note also that you told us it has exactly 114 sonnets. This is the Matter of the Enumeration of Sonnets. Now, I am no hermeticist myself, but I did spend some time in my youth listening to John Eglinton and George Russell and the other Dublin mystics, and even I know that 114 is an important Cabalistic number, is it not?"

"Yes," Babcock said. "The tradition is that the Invisible College acts publicly for 114 years, then dissolves itself and remains passive for 114 years, then acts openly again for 114 years, and so on."

"There is more to it than that," Joyce said. "There is always more in Cabala. Eglinton or Russell—I forget which—once explained to me, as an example of the historical connection between Freemasonry and Rosicrucianism, that the mysterious letters on Masonic buildings and documents, L.P.D., also equal 114 Cabalistically. Does my memory trick me?"

"No," Babcock said, "*Lamed* is 30, *Pe* is 80, and *Daleth* is 4. Total: 114. The meaning is supposed to be *Light, Pressure, Density* and refers to the inner transformation of the Alchemical process."

"It refers also to other things," Joyce said. "The Grand Orient lodges before the French Revolution, from which Mr. Crowley's Ordo Templi Orientis claims descent, explained L.P.D. as *Lilia perdita destrue*—'trample the lily underfoot,' the lily being the symbol of the Bourbons, the royal family of France against which this faction of Masonry has allegedly been waging war since the destruction of the Templars by Philip II. Once again, you see, the Cabalistic symbols mean different things on different levels of interpretation."

Einstein re-lit his pipe. "So," he said between puffs, "you have taken us a long way round, Jeem, but your conclusion is precisely what?"

"*Clouds Without Water* is the work of a very advanced Cabalist," Joyce said. "And the Reverend Verey was never as ignorant of Cabala as he claimed. Proof: he knew that the 26 garters pendant on the Order of the Garter had a Cabalistic meaning and he prodded you, Sir John, until you remembered that 26 is the value of *Yod Hé Vau Hé,* the Holy Unspeakable Name of God. The Clue of the 26 Garters, Dr. Watson might call it."

Joyce paused and then went on. "I don't know how Verey murdered off his family, and I certainly don't know *why* [but who can understand the workings of religious mania?], but I am morally certain that he did. The whole story of the book of horrors that drives people mad is entirely his invention, remember, and I have already indicated my reasons for thinking he purloined that idea from Robert W. Chambers' *The King in Yellow*. I call to mind another hunchback driven mad by religious fervor and sexual anxieties, Saint Paul, who once wrote a sentence that describes Verey perfectly: 'I do not do that which I would, but that which is hateful to me.' The split mirror again."

Babcock's face revealed a conflict of emotions. "You almost convince me. But your theory is only partial and still leaves very much unexplained. . . ."

The doorbell rang. All three men started slightly.

"It has been a heavy experience, this tale of yours," Einstein said. "But Joyce has very nicely clarified the points on which I was myself still puzzled. With his contribution, I think I can now explain all of it, and banish the bogeys forever."

Mileva Einstein appeared in the doorway, with a package in brown wrapping paper. "Albert," she said, "a boy just delivered this for you."

The three men exchanged glances. Einstein arose like a cat. "This is not totally unexpected," he said, crossing the room.

Joyce and Babcock, sitting erect suddenly, watched tensely as Mileva left and Einstein carried the package to his desk.

"Is it . . ." Babcock stammered.

"Oh, yes." Einstein was amused. "The complete artistic finishing stroke. It has the return address of 'M.M.M., 93 Jermyn Street, London, U.K.,' even though it bears no postmark and was obviously never in the mails." He began to tear the paper.

"For God's sake!" Babcock cried. "Don't! You can't be

absolutely sure of your theory, whatever it is. You may not be immune to the danger."

"Oh, I'm not worried," Einstein said, tearing and ripping until the book emerged. Then he began to laugh, a small chortle at first, and then louder and louder until his face was contorted and tears appeared in his eyes.

The laughter of hysterical madness? No: Einstein finally regained control and held the book up so Joyce and Babcock could see it. "Here it is, gentlemen," he said, "the horror of horrors. . . ."

The book he held was titled *Mother Goose Nursery Rhymes*.

"*Mo . . . ther . . . go . . .*" Joyce said slowly. "It fits together the fragments we heard."

"And it's all magick secrets in code!" Babcock cried. "Crowley wasn't joking about that at all."

"Yes, he was," Einstein said. "This is the punch line to the joke." He resumed his seat, wiping further tears of laughter from his owl-wide eyes with bunched knuckles helplessly.

"It's a Divine Comedy," Joyce gasped, also gurgling a laugh half-born far back in his throat. "We'll all be hauled off to Dante's Infirmary with the whooping laugh."

"Am I to gather," Babcock asked, not amused, "that I have been having my leg pulled all along?"

"Yes and no," said Einstein.

"Another paradox!" Babcock cried. "Is there no unequivocal yes or absolute no in any of this business?"

Joyce, still half-laughing, sang softly:

> *A paradox, a paradox,*
> *A most ingenious paradox . . .*

"For Christ's sake!" Babcock said. "Let me in on the jest, gentlemen."

Einstein nodded. "I'm sorry," he said. "At this point

I'm not at all sure I should explain to you; you might never forgive me. What do you think, Jeem?"

"I think," Joyce said, "that this script has been so brilliantly constructed that it doesn't matter how much you explain. The doorbell will ring again, before you are very far along, and the Author will provide the climax he intended from the beginning."

"Yes," Einstein said, "I suppose you are right. Well, then," he addressed Babcock, "to at least begin an explanation . . ."

"When the doorbell rings the second time," Joyce pronounced, "we undoubtedly shall all turn to pumpkins."

"Before that happens," Einstein said, "I think I do owe Sir John the rest of the explanation of what is going on here."

"At last!" Babcock said with some heat.

"Until the doorbell rings . . ." Joyce intoned.

Einstein concentrated for a moment. "Let us begin with basics. In the context of modern thought, that means with David Hume. In his discussion of miracles, Hume points out what argument is both totally *satisfactory*, and also totally *necessary*, to demonstrate the reality of an alleged miracle. That argument is, briefly, to be able to demonstrate that *any other explanation* of the event would itself be *more* miraculous than the alleged miracle itself. This is Hume's equivalent of Occam's Razor. For instance, if I were to claim that my dear wife, Milly, is floating around the kitchen two feet above the floor, you would in reason be justified in believing me *only* if it were even more miraculous that I, Albert Einstein, could tell a lie. Now, I treasure my reputation for integrity, but I do not think you would have any doubt in choosing which interpretation is *more* miraculous in that case—[a] that Milly really is flying around like a witch, or [b] that I am lying to you. No: there has never been a man of such supernatural honesty that it would strictly be *more miraculous* for him to lie than for his wife to levitate.

"This is ordinary common sense, as is everything in Hume. We never believe an incredible story of strange things in the sky or strange beings on the ground when only *one* man claims to be the witness. We begin to wonder a bit if there are several witnesses, but even then we skeptically seek evidence that some conspiracy may exist between them, or that drunkenness or some traumatic shock, such as explosion, might have caused them all to hallucinate.

"Now, let us apply this Razor of Hume's to the Miracle of the Murdered Cat on the Altar. From whose testimony do we obtain this yarn? From that of Reverend Verey, and nobody else. Even the supporting detail about Mrs. Verey finding some of the evidence afterward is not her testimony [we have never met her] but part of Verey's own yarn.

"So," Einstein said, "on the basis of the logic of David Hume and the ordinary common sense of humankind, let us ask: Is it more miraculous that mysterious diabolists can walk through walls or that a most peculiar old man like Verey might be lying to us? The answer is obvious: it is less miraculous that Verey might lie. It is more miraculous that someone walked through solid walls. So, in reason, we must choose the less miraculous theory: Verey lied."

"This does not at all clarify the greater mystery of the suicides," Sir John said. "There we are not relying on Verey's unsupported word. We have a newspaper story . . ." His voice trailed off.

"Yes?" Einstein said. "We have a newspaper story, *or so it appears*. Where did the newspaper story come from?"

"From the Inverness *Express-Journal*," said Babcock.

"Not exactly," said Einstein. "It came from the pocket of George Cecil Jones, who only *told you* it came from the Inverness *Express-Journal*. In this connection, I note also that Jones told you he sent his secretary out to buy 'a copy' of that newspaper. He did not say 'two copies,' and there is no reason, taking his story at face value, why he should have asked for two. And yet you pocketed the copy of the story he gave you, and Verey was reading another copy at breakfast the next morning. This is the Marvelous Multiplication I mentioned. It does not make sense; so, again, somebody is lying to us. Now, we have several people here associated with publications of various sorts. Reverend Verey and the Society for the Propagation of Religious Truth published *Clouds Without Water*, at least, and possibly other works even more curious. Jones and/or his associates publish instruction manuals for Golden Dawn students. Crowley publishes his own books, we have been informed. Certainly, among these three most mysterious mystery-mongers it would be easy to produce what looked like a story cut from a newspaper?"

"My God," Babcock said. "But I actually heard Verey talking to Inspector McIntosh of the Inverness police about the suicides. . . . I mean . . ."

"Yes," Einstein said, "you see it already, do you not? You heard Verey talking to *some*body at *some* Inverness number, and you *assumed* that he had actually called an Inspector at the Inverness police. Again, is it more miraculous to believe in these incredible suicides, brought on"—he smiled whimsically—"by Mother Goose—as we are now supposed to believe—or is it more miraculous to assume that Verey and a confederate in Inverness performed a charade with the telephone? Again, I think, the answer is obvious: the latter is less miraculous."

"It all sounds so plausible," Babcock said. "Yet I find it hard to believe that Jones and Verey and Crowley were conspiring together all through this. . . ."

"I also found that hard at first," Einstein said, "until you described your telephone conversation with Jones the morning you met Verey. Jones said, and the words struck me intensely, '*Be careful, Sir John; remember that a man*

with Verey's hunched back is a rather conspicuous figure.'
Now, I asked myself: How on earth did he know that
Verey was a hunchback? He had allegedly never met the
man. Well, I said, maybe Sir John told him and neglected
to mention that while recounting the conversation to us.
Then I remembered, Sir John, that you said Verey was at
your side all through that telephone call. You are much
too well mannered to say, 'Oh, by the way, he's a hunchback,' while the hunchback stands beside you. So, then,
how the devil did Jones know? This is the Casual Telepathy, if we believe it. I do not believe it.

"The obvious alternative is that Jones and Verey were
working together all along. Verey tells you, first by mail
and then in person, a series of frightening tales well
calculated to fill you with dread, and Jones produces the
alleged 'newspaper' clipping that seemingly confirms these
yarns."

Einstein paused to re-light his pipe. "To proceed," he
said, "if Jones and Verey are co-conspirators, we begin to
clear away some of the other dark mysteries in this most
mysterious business. For instance, I believe that coincidences can multiply at an astonishing rate—especially in
the perceptual coordinate system of a man trained to *look*
for them, regarding them as occult signals or omens. But
your tale, Sir John, has altogether *too* many coincidences
for any sane universe. I refer in particular to the insistent
and terrifying way that details from your dreams and astral
visions—the latter of which you must permit me to consider a species of half-waking dreams—come to life in the
real world as your involvement with Verey and his problems increases. So I ask myself: How could these Superabundant Coincidences have been accomplished?

"There is only one answer," Einstein said. *"One man*
had access to your 'Magick Diary.' *One man* looked at it
every month, as you have told us, to guide you in your
spiritual progress. *One man*, George Cecil Jones, could

have collaborated with Verey in creating the impression that these dream-terrors were manifesting in the physical universe. George Cecil Jones, who somehow knew Verey was a hunchback when he allegedly had never met him."

"My God," Babcock said again.

"Let us return to the newspaper clipping," Einstein continued. "I think that without that clipping, you would eventually have begun to notice that you had only Verey's word for this whole story, patently borrowed from the Gothic horror school of fiction in general and Arthur Machen and Robert W. Chambers in particular. The newspaper clipping, then, was planned all along, like the conversation with 'Inspector McIntosh,' to prevent such suspicions from entering your head."

"But," Babcock said, "as reasonable as all this sounds, I still find it hard to believe that a Christian clergyman like Verey—even if he had the multiple split personality suggested by Mr. Joyce—could collaborate with so vile a creature as Crowley."

Einstein grinned. "Let us look into that a bit. Joyce has suggested that 'Arthur Angus Verey' never existed, that Charles Verey wrote the whole of *Clouds Without Water*. Let us turn that around, and try the alternative. Suppose 'Charles Verey' never existed and the whole book was written by 'Arthur Angus Verey.' "

"But I met Charles Verey!" Babcock exclaimed.

"No," Einstein said. "To be parsimonious in our conceptualizing, you met and received letters from a man who *alleged* he was named Charles Verey. A man with a hunchback, which is so striking a feature that it generally captures the attention entirely. Very few people, I believe, could describe a hunchback accurately: they would remember the hunch so centrally that the other features would be vague, quickly forgotten. One other fact about 'Verey' did stick with you, however, and you mentioned it several times. I refer to his paleness. I was particularly struck when you stated that, at first glance, he seemed as pale as an actor *made up* for a death scene. This is the Over-Defined Image, and it suggests theatrics. I started to think: why, with a hunchback and some makeup, I could come into this room and ask for Professor Einstein and the two of you would tell me that Professor Einstein was out."

"The Cabalistic style!" Joyce cried. "My God, why didn't I see it sooner! Of course! *The style is the same.* The real author of *Clouds Without Water*—both the 'Arthur Verey' poems and the 'Charles Verey' sermonettes tacked on—is Aleister Crowley."

"Aleister Crowley, the son of a very rich brewer," Einstein said, "and therefore capable, like many rich Englishmen, of keeping a flat in London and a fine old home in Scotland, too. Perhaps in Inverness? I think investigation would quickly reveal that such was the case."

"And the phone number would be Inverness-418," Joyce said, "the number 'Verey' called when he spoke to the alleged 'Inspector McIntosh.' In fact, *it was Crowley disguised as the imaginary Verey, calling his own home and staging a scene to impress Sir John.*"

"We can go further than that," Einstein said. "Yesterday, we heard that the Laird of Boleskine was in Switzerland to climb mountains. We know that Crowley is a mountain-climber and now we have an Extra Mountain-Climber. Let us hypothesize that the two are Cabalistically One. And recall that the 'devil' Sir John saw on Bahnhofstrasse last night appeared after the arrival of this Laird of Boleskine. The package delivered tonight also suggests that Crowley is in the neighborhood. I suggest, therefore, that Crowley not only has a home in Inverness, but somehow acquired, or bestowed upon himself, a title to go with the home, and is the Laird of Boleskine. And that the 'Reverend Charles Verey' and the 'Society for the Propagation of Religious Truth' are entirely his creations."

"Damn it all!" Babcock cried. "What an ass I have been!"

"You were deceived by masters at that art," Einstein said gently. "The author of *The Book of Lies* is a genius in the trade of mystification."

"But one thing is still unclear," Joyce said. "Why does Mr. George Cecil Jones fit into this?"

"It has stared us in the face all along," Einstein said. "Crowley has played perfectly fair—mostly, I suppose, because he is as much fascinated by lies that look like truth as he is by truth that looks like lies. At the very beginning, the first Golden Dawn lesson warned Sir John that Crowley, among others, was running a Golden Dawn order. The fact that Crowley and his particular Golden Dawn group were violently denounced is a misdirection typical of his sense of humor as we have come to know it. *Sir John was always in Crowley's branch of the Golden Dawn.* Mr. Jones is perhaps Crowley's second-in-command, or at least a high officer of that lodge. They have been initiating Sir John all along according to the oldest form of initiation known to anthropologists: the ordeal by terror. The Rite of Passage. It is just an enormous extension of the simpler drama staged by Crowley with his so-called 'psychoboulometer,' and it is even coded into the I.N.R.I. sequence Sir John was given for meditation at the beginning: the ritual of death and rebirth."

"And that horrible recording that 'Verey' made . . ." Joyce prompted.

"I could make a recording just as impressive with the aid of a few professional actors," Einstein finished simply.

There was a pause.

"We come now," Joyce prompted again, "to the Miracle on Regent Street. Are we to believe that Baron Zaharov is also a co-conspirator, and that his Eastern Orthodox piety is another masquerade?"

"Well," Einstein said, "it is certainly peculiar for an

anti-Semite whose government has been distributing the forged *Protocols of the Elders of Zion*, and who allegedly has an uncle high in the hierarchy of the Orthodox Church, to have as a middle name *Salmonovitch*. Jeem, tell Sir John the equivalent of that in English."

"Solomonson," Joyce said. "My God, I missed that at first. It would mean that the Baron's father was a Jew."

"An improbability in that government and unbelievable in that church at this time," Einstein said. "The Clue of the Impossible Name. Crowley has been fair with us again, bestowing the hint that allows us to see behind the masquerade if we are intelligent enough."

"And the testimony of Miss Sturgis?" Joyce asked.

"Miss Sturgis, as secretary to the notorious Isadora Duncan," Einstein said, "obviously travels in circles that would be called bohemian, avant-garde or revolutionary, yes? It is not hard to imagine some relationship, romantic or otherwise, between her and Crowley."

"Well," Babcock said, "if Baron Zaharov is not a real Russian nobleman, who or what is he?"

"Oh," said Einstein, "I think it is fairly clear that he must be Aleister Crowley again, in another masquerade."

"But the height differences between Crowley, Verey and Zaharov," Joyce complained. "How was all that managed?"

"Crowley is a man of medium height, Sir John informs us. With a fake hunchback and the crouch to accompany it, he could easily appear four or five inches shorter." Einstein stood up and walked a few steps hunched over in the manner of those with curvature of the spine. "Observe: Do I not seem several inches shorter?"

"That is totally convincing," Joyce said. "The other is not so easy to comprehend, however. Anybody can scrunch over and look a bit shorter, but how does one look a bit taller?"

"Remember that Sir John only saw Crowley, *as Crowley,*

once," Einstein said. "Recall, also, that Crowley was not present in that garden, as himself, to provide any comparisons. Sir John saw a very short man go into the garden and then encountered there a man who seemed quite a bit taller than that. A man whose height he could not remember exactly because, as he told us, the 'Baron's' manner was so overbearing he seemed perhaps taller than he was. We always remember very powerful, overwhelming, angry men as taller than they are—it is some sort of mammalian instinct which equates superior size with superiority in the herd. The large Russian fur hat, of course, also added to the 'Baron's' apparent size. Relativity of Dimensions.

"So, then, if 'Verey' and the 'Baron' were both Aleister Crowley, there was no need for the garden to be disturbed. No person, and no masquerade props, needed to travel *horizontally* through the garden at all. The transformation was almost certainly managed *vertically*. The accessories of the Zaharov personality—chiefly the black beard, the fur hat and an overcoat—were hanging down, behind the oak tree, on a strong elastic band such as spiritualist mediums and stage magicians often use. Crowley-as-Verey dashes into the garden, grabs those props, attaches the Verey props—suit with clerical collar and hunchback built in—and unhooks the elastic band from the fence post to which it was presumably fixed. It is immediately yanked upward with the Verey props to a perch I would imagine would be high above the ordinary line of vision.

"I would also imagine," Einstein concluded, "that the house was actually unrented at the time. The 'Baron' never existed aside from the brief charade in the garden and the tales Miss Sturgis recited."

Babcock shook his head wearily. "There may be no miracles in this business," he said grimly, "but there certainly was deviltry."

"Was there?" Joyce said. "I don't think you have seen

to the bottom of it yet. The professor has neatly answered *how* and *what* and *who* and *whichway* and all the physical details, but the question of *why* is still unclear. I think I begin to perceive the *why*, the psychology of initiation by terror, and I suspect that the last act of the drama is still to come. If Crowley with one hand manages the 'good' Cabalists, through his lieutenant Jones, and Crowley with the other hand manages the 'bad' Cabalists, the lesson of the masquerade seems fairly obvious to me. After all, what did the 'bad' Cabalists do except dramatize and bring into full consciousness the problems that were already indicated by your dreams, Sir John?"

"Damn it!" Babcock cried. "Are you justifying them?"

"I have trained myself not to judge but to understand," Joyce said. "If you will listen to me for just a moment, about your sexual phobias, for instance. . . ."

"I am already familiar with your libertine opinions," Sir John said stiffly, "and I am sure they would be received with approbation by Crowley. But I know the difference between right and wrong, thank God."

Joyce stared at the younger man in silence for a moment.

"You know the difference between right and wrong," he repeated finally. "Man, why did you need Initiation—by the Golden Dawn, or by anybody else? You are a genius, a sage, a giant among men. You have solved the problem which philosophers have been debating since antiquity—the mystery about which no two nations or tribes have ever agreed, and no two men or women have ever agreed, and no intelligent person has ever agreed totally with himself from one day to the next. *You know the difference between right and wrong*. I am overawed. I swoon. I figuratively kiss your feet."

"Jeem," Einstein said softly, "there is no need to be so sarcastic. Most young men are just as naïve as Sir John."

But Joyce had talked himself into boldness. He arose again and began pacing the room with nervous energy.

"All my life," he said, as much to himself as to Sir John, "I have been teaching myself to observe accurately and nonjudgmentally. That is [I believe the professor would agree with me] the prerequisite of all scientific endeavor. It is also the prerequisitive of the type of literature I wish to write. Now—listen to me, Sir John—this drama through which Jones and Crowley have led you is a perfect example of how easy it is to deceive oneself. There was nothing in the whole adventure that did not exist in your fantasies first; Jones merely arranged to have those fantasies objectified, and you are missing the whole point if you do not comprehend that the source of everything that happened was your own fears and prejudices, just as the purpose of everything was to induce you to see through those fears and prejudices. I am no mystic myself, but it is obvious that this Golden Dawn contraption is a very complicated way of teaching people to see as the scientist *sees*, or as my type of artist *sees*—without filtering everything through a lens of moral and emotional prejudices."

"There is a difference," Sir John said coolly, "between prejudice and principles."

"Yes," Joyce replied. "Other people have prejudices; but I have principles. Just as other people are stubborn but I am firm, other people are egotists but I merely have self-respect, other people are drunks but I only like a drop now and then. Shall I conjugate a few more phrases like that? Other people are peculiar, but I am exotic. Other people are naïve and gullible, but I have retained a certain childish innocence. Other people are too clever by half, but I have learned to express myself with elegance. Other people are sensualists, but I am a Romantic. Other people are paranoid, but I am merely careful. Other people are pigheaded fools, but I am merely a little set in my ways."

Sir John smiled and held up a hand. "Enough," he said. "Your point is well taken. Of course, I still have prejudices and—I suppose—I do tend to rationalize them, like most people. But *do* you propose to convince me that there is really nothing Satanic about the depraved sexuality of Crowley and his cohorts?"

"The worship of sex," Joyce said calmly, "is, to an objective observer, no more absurd than any other form of worship. It is, if one can trust Thomas Wright's *History of the Worship of the Generative Organs,* Sir James Frazer's *Golden Bough* and other standard references on ethnology, the earliest of all human religions. It was once the most widespread form of worship; it still exists within Hinduism, Buddhism and Islam; it has left traces even within Christianity—"

The doorbell rang again.

"On cue," Joyce commented. "Has the rascal been hiding in your garden listening to us all evening, Professor?"

All three men fixed their eyes on the doorway, which was soon filled by Mileva and a middle-aged, well-dressed man with a cheery smile, holding a bottle of champagne.

"Sir Aleister Crowley, the Laird of Boleskine," said Mileva.

PART FIVE

All material things are but masks.

—Herman Melville, *Moby Dick*

CAMILLA: You, sir, should unmask.
STRANGER: Indeed?
CASSILDA: Indeed, it's time. We have all laid aside disguise but
  you.
STRANGER: I wear no mask.
CAMILLA: [*terrified, aside to Cassilda*]: No mask? No mask?

—Robert W. Chambers, *The King in Yellow*

Were it not for the garter, I might never have seen the star.

—Aleister Crowley, *Collected Works*,
  "The Star and the Garter"

Crowley crossed the cinnamonred room and handed the champagne to Einstein. Now that our merry little carnival draws to its close, he said blandly, I bring a gift of Dionysus and suggest that we celebrate. You must all be dreadfully thirsty by now.

An excellent idea, Joyce rejoyced. It looks like an archduchess's, by God.

Babcock arose, trembling slightly. Russet sunset shadows turned his face gold and dark.

You absolute swine, he said coldly to Crowley. How dare you treat this whole cruel affair as a practical joke?

Crowley was opening the bottle. The universe itself, he replied offhandedly, is an enormous practical joke by the general at the expense of the particular.

Babcock controlled himself with effort. You tormented and deceived me for months, he said. You drove me to extremes of terror that threatened my sanity. You rotten bastard.

You came to *us* seeking Illumination, Crowley answered. You are still receiving it. Did you imagine that Truth was a dog that will come when you whistle? Did not I.N.R.I. warn you what the alchemical transformation costs? Were you not aware from the beginning that you would be required to face everything you fear?

But Einstein said quietly: Don't deny that you've been cruel.

Cruel Crowley cruelly laughed.

Deny it? he said. *Lieber Al*, I insist upon it. For I am like a refiner's fire.

Blasphemy to justify sadism, Babcock protested. You unspeakable bastard.

Ah, Babcock, Crowley said distributing the champagne again, you still have spirit. I like that. You may be remembered someday as the disciple Crowley loved. After all, Whom the Lord loveth, He chastizeth.

More blasphemy, you swine, Baba Babcock bleated.

More champagne, rather, Joyce said. I seem to have finished mine already.

I imagine, Einstein said staring fixedly at his pipe ash glittering, that your original plan for Sir John's rite of passage had some dramatic climax. I hope we haven't ruined it by explaining the tricks to him prematurely.

Have some more wine, Babcock, Crowley said pouring. As a matter of fact, the climax of the drama will be much as I planned except of course that there will be three candidates instead of one.

Beat. Beat. Beat.

Three candidates, Joyce repeated finally. I smell a rat.

Einstein asked languidly:

Is there a buzzing noise in this room suddenly?

All looked at Crow Crowley, then at each other. Nothing.

That was queer, Fox Joyce said. For a moment it was as if I understood Plato. As if the moving image in time stopped and I saw the worldline in four dimensions, eternally there. Damned odd. As if the great muddy river of consciousness froze.

That buzzing, Einstein said, like a million bees . . .

I hear no buzzing, Joyce stated calmly. But I say, Babcock, are you well? You appear to be turning green.

Babcock turned vaginal purple. This is strange, he said carefully. I actually never felt better in my life.

The bookshelf in the corner began to shrink. Joyce stared at it bemusedly as the faint buzzing purrceptibly increased.

The strangest thing of all, Crowley crowed, is that no matter how many soldiers you march out in phalanx, the number of hunchbacks is always one greater.

Yes yes said Einstein an angry ruby-red Lion pacing. For every insight the universe gives me a new riddle. Usually by next Tuesday after lunch. But that's the whole fun of the game.

Crowley watched detached as the oak-brown bookcase shrank. For you and me and a few others, yes, he said. But most people want the soldiers to exactly equal the hunchbacks. An answer for every question.

I say, Joyce say. Is that bookcase really shrinking?

The bookcase turned into the Zürich express roaring: Overnight overnight overnight.

The bookcase became an altar. Crowley suddenly robed in scarlet raised the flaming Wand and the moving image stopped again quite clearly this time.

Stop. Go. Stop. Go. Stop.

Many civic monsters danced around Joyce. You are telling me the truth drifting down a shrinking street, they chanted. Cuckoo! Cuckoo! Cuckoo! Largest fraternal order in Europe. Cuckoo!

Hear me Crowley said IEOU PUR IOU PUR IOATH IAEO IOOU ABRASAX SABRIAM OO OO ADONAI EDE EDU ANGELOS TON THEON LAI GAIA AEPE DIATHARNA THORON! Indwelling sun of myself Thou fire Thou sixfold star initiator compassed about with force and fire Indwelling soul of myself Sunlionserpent Hail all Hail thou great wild beast Thou IAO Lust of my soul Lust of mine angel Ho for the grail Ho for the cup of Babalon Ho for mine angel pouring himself forth within my soul

Thou goat exalted upon earth in lust Thou snake extended upon earth in life Spirit most holy Seed most wise Innocent babe Inviolate maid Begetter of being Soul of all souls Come forth most hidden light

Overnight overnight overnight understood understood understood

Would you repeat that last bit Crowley? Joyce asked. I'm not sure I got it all what's happening in this room, anyway

Sir John pushed open the door of M.M.M. and passed through the Parthenon, Saint Peter's, the Eiffel Tower, Oriental pagodas, grim Gothic-faced banks, the order of chondrichthyes, the order of cyclostomata, sea lampreys, the order of Knights Templar, the order of Memphis and Mizraim, academies, laboratories, nunneries, bakeries, cathedrals, the mighty headwaters of the Amazon, the Centipede Gang. The larger can be inside the smaller: it's a fried egg and it loves me. Drooling farmboys waving signs saying BESTIALITY LIBERATION charge into a line of Police Constables down a windy crimson indigo Easteregg street.

The Secret Chiefs began to file solemnly silently spectrally into the room. Elias Ashmole, Secret Master, Perfect Master, Elect of Fifteen, Knight of the Triangle; Thomas Vaughan, Sovereign Grand Inspector of the 33rd Degree of and the Ancient and Accepted Polish Rite; Sir Edward Kelly, Sublime Prince of the Royal Secret; Dr. Johannes Dee, Prince of Mercy, Knight of Pnath, Secret Perfect Master; Roderic Borgia, Pope Alessandro VI, Grand Knight of Lot and the Phoenix; Michael Maier, Sage of Elia, Sage of Delphi, Master of the Triple Tau; Paracelsus, Grand Sublime Knight of St. Andrew; Adam Weishaupt, Knight of Palestine, Grand Elected Knight Kadosch Hurhausdirektorpresident; Christian Rosenkreuz, Ancient Master of the Royal Arch; Wolfgang von Goethe, True Master Adept of the Symbolic Lodges; Jacobus Burgundus Molensis the Martyr, Knight of Jerusalem, Knight of Palestine,

Knight of Wands, Sublime Scottish Architect of Heredom, Grand Knight of Sodom; Rex Frederic of Hohenstaufen, Sublime Knight of Knepth; Ludovicus Rex Bavariae, Supreme Commander of the Stars, Discreet of Chaos, Sublime Philosopher Noachite; King Kong, Primate of Skull Island; Carl Kellner, Sovereign Prince Rose Croix of Kilwinning and Heredom; Carolus Magnus, Doctor of the Izeds; Valentinus, Patriarch of Memphis and St. Joe; Sir Richard Burton, Sovereign Commander of the Temple and Prince of Jerusalem; Basilides, Grand Pontiff of the College of the Gnosis; Pythagoras, Knight of the Lybic Chain; Sir Richard Payne Knight, Commander of the Red Eagle; Manes, Patriarch of the Planispheres, Very Perfect Architect, Knight of Israel; Atilla the Hun, Valiant Master, Most Worshipful Master, Elect of the Unknown; Ludwig van Beethoven, Perfect Illustrious Elect of Nine, Order of the Peacock Angel, Master of the Triangle; Simon Magus, Knight of the Golden Branch of Eleusis; P.D.Q. Bach, Knight of the Horn and Hardart; Apollonius Tyanaeis, Grand Consecrator Architect of the Hidden City; Wolfgang Amadeus Mozart of the Magic Flute, Prussian Knight, Knight of the Temple, Supreme Master Knight of the Eagle; Benjamin Franklin, Grand Axe of the Royal Arch, Sublime Knight of Choice; F. X. Preserved Coppinger, Beneficent Knight, Knight of the Rainbow, Knight of the Pelican; Vlad the Impaler, Secret Master, Knight of the Pelican and Eagle, Sovereign Prince of the Rose Croix of Heredom; Hugh Boylan, Knight of Banuka, Prince of the Pantagruelian Pike; Thomas Jefferson, Architect in Light and Perfection, Sublime of Heredom; Catullus, Sage of the Labyrinth, Knight of the High Odiamor; McIntosh Anonymoses, Sovereign Prince of the 78th, 79th and 80th Degrees of the Esoteric Order of Cranston and Bourbaki; Malechizedeck, Knight Kadosh, Knight Grand Inspector, Knight of the Royal Mystery of the Sky Chariots; Osiris, Sublime Aletophilote and Knight of Libanus; Tahuti, Knight

of the Sacred Arch, Knight of the Secret Vault; Buddha,
Master Pastrophoris, Elect Neocoris, Grand Melanophoris,
Perfect Master Balahate; Lao-Tse, 90th and Last Degree
Supreme Grand Conservator and Absolute Grand Sover-
eign and Patriarch of the Order of Mizriam; Malaclypse
the Younger, Omnibenevolent Polyfather of Virginity in
Gold; Don Quixote de la Mancha, Knight of Jerusalem,
Knight of Malta, Knight of the Mournful Countenance;
Miguel Cossack, Supremest Pontificator de Kiernansis,
Grand Master Constituent of the Order of the Second
Geometrical Series; Walter Mitty, Secret Master, Perfect
Master, Provost Judge, Intendant of Buildings, Elect of
Nine, Elect of Fifteen, Sublime Elect, Companion of the
Royal Arch of Enoch, Scottish Knight of Perfection, Sub-
lime Master, Knight of the Secret Vault, Knight of the
Iris, Sovereign Grand Inspector, Supreme Illustrious
Honorificabilitudinatatibus of the Rose Croix, Grand Elected
Knight Kadosch Praetertranssubstantiationalist, True Mas-
ter Elect of the Supercalifragilisticexpialidocious Arcanum,
College of the Holy Ghost, Knight of Israel, Knight of
Jerusalem, Knight of Memphis and Mizriam, Honorable
Illustrious Grand Master Pontiff Mega-Ipssisimus Maximus
Antipericatametaanparcircumvolutiorectumgustipoops of the
Copoofied, 33rd degree Scottish Rite, 10th degree Ordo
Templi Orientis, 97th degree Rite of Memphis and Mizriam,
ROYAL SUPREME GRAND ILLUSTRIOUS MASTER
of the Gnostic Catholic Church, EPOPT OF THE ILLU-
MINATI; and diverse highly distinguished apes, swine,
rhinoceri, fish and Advanced Vertebrates, together with
notable representatives of the orders of bees, roaches,
silverfish, ants, termites, sea lampreys, arachnids, locusts
u.s.w and the most intelligent amoebas known to science.

In a way it is pleasant to be back in the cradle again,
Joyce said bashfully. When you wet the bed first it is
warm then it gets cold. But now I'm drowning in it. No, I
can swim. Where did all these jellyfish come from?

My God! Babcock shouted. The whole room is turning into tits!

I know, I know! Joyce cried. We're experiencing the dawn of consciousness. But is it personal consciousness or . . . oh, no . . .

Some of the breasts are big and some are small some are conic some discoid some hemispheric some elongated there are full Earthmother breasts and moderate Gibsongirl breasts and exuberantly high Frenchwhore breasts and small flat Oriental breasts some are firm some are soft and some are flabby mllk begins to drip from all of them an endless white stream like the gentle rain from heaven and all have the same parabolic loop as a suspension bridge the influence of gravity the same on both engineering and biology the upside down rainbow curve repeated endlessly almost like a cosine wave on an oscilloscope but now by God it has peppermint stripes and they are all mermaids

I am Einstein I am Babcock I am Crowley my God I am the pipeash Soul of all souls yes I am the chair Jesus Howling Christ am I still James Joyce yes I think I am yes am I?

Einstein looked down Bahnhofstrasse the railroad tracks shrinking in the distance past the horizon orbiting earth whooooshing about the solar system in orbit zooooming around the galaxy in orbit circling the universe passing all possible universes in orbit returning to Bahnhofstrasse as the sky filled with white globs and globes of light million upon million pearls and opals and turquoise and amber slow shiftings of crystal and molecular growth into the great Rose with the cross of light in its center tickticktocking as each petal moistened and glimmered in cuntlike tenderness

Hawk-like man, Joyce reflects. Ascending from the labyrinth old father old artificer the moocow in the beginning the Goat

Come back to Erin, mavourneen.

Merde, said General Canbronne. A toil telled of shame and scorn. In the family he was known as Mr. Harris.

Einstein looks down the tunnel of consciousness remembers swinging through trees with other primates: recalls the billion-odd flights from predators as equine, rhinoceros, zebra and tapir; relives the evolution of the pig, the peccary, the hippopotamus, the camel, the deer, the giraffe, the antelope; suffers and rejoices as seal, walrus, wolf and giant panda; collapses and implodes inward as perissodactylan, ariodactylan and carnivorous experiences flood consciousness; know himself again as muskrat, beaver, fieldmouse always fetful, squirrel and kangaroo rat; floats down genetic rivers of lagomorpha caught in heroic moments as owsla chief of the snowshoe rabbits, leaps back to pika: sings to the stars (and groks their returning song) as blue whale and bottle-nosed porpoise; whizzes through caves as fruit bat: becomes mole, shrew, hedgehog: is at one with molecular memories of insectivora, marsupalia and monotremata: sings again as sparrow, robin and nightingale; lounges in sunny rockpools as snapping turtle: crosses deserts as sidewinder: croaks as bullfrog; descends into the whirlpool of nucleic acid information as lives of osteichthyes, trout, chondrichthyes, cyclostomata, sea lampreys, craniata, acraniata, myriapodoa and arachnida are lived again; loops the loop into arthropoda, crustacea, annelida: hurtling back, back, back into echinodermata, aschelminthes, coelenterata and protozoa: becoming at last one battered beatup bedraggled halfblind scarred scratched starving dirty filthy disgraceful old alley-cat singing

> wotthehell archy wotthehell
> there s a dance in the old dame yet
> toujours gai is my motto

And where, pray, have you been lately, Joyce asked curiously.

It is most interesting, Einstein replied. Most of our ancestors were not perfect ladies and gentlemen. The majority of them weren't even mammals.

Bad Cock Babcock he finds the Door at the end of the tunnel. He open. A million blue garters with white satins on them fall out.

Causes curvature of the spine, said Dr. Bostick Bentley Babcock from a platform in space. Paleness . . . lack of concentration . . . hair on the palms like a werewolf . . . eventual total idiocy. Self-control is the answer. I never did it. No proper Englishman would.

Babcock screams, weeping hysterically.

Depart from me ye cursed, said God the Goat, into the everlasting bonfire that was prepared for Satan and his angels. I saw what you did in that closet. Your own mother's garters.

They were the only garters I could find, Babcock implored weeping.

Einstein looked at Babcock anxiously. Is he going to be all right, he asked Crowley.

Oh a little homeopathic hysteria never did any harm, Crowley yawned.

You heartless bastard, Babcock repeats.

Merde, said General Canbronne. Just find your own territory.

The ants came marching one by one. The ants came marching two by two. The ants came marching three by three.

It's a Greek phalanx, Einstein said. Look, there's Alexander . . .

The fieldmouse screamed again.

It's all right, Babcock, Joyce said. Merely an overdose of empathy, I imagine.

Am I still human, the fieldmouse asked.

You are still Sir John Babcock, Einstein said reassuringly.

And part of you is still a fieldmouse, Crowley added. Just as part is a shark . . .

Evolution is not a theory here, Einstein said quietly. It is an experienced fact.

Babcock screamed again.

This has gone too far, Einstein objected.

Crow Crowley became Ravenrend Verey, hunchbacked whitefaced mad. The clock slowly somberly sonorously chimed thirteen.

Frogs and mice, Falcon Verey cried. Bestiality? Perversion? I would that all men were as myself, but it is better to marry than pope to the butcher. For now we see through a glass darkly but then fizz to fizz. Fuzz to fuzz. Sacks of dung. Abomination. Monthly filth. Moon madness. Illegal entry.

Redorange fucksweet menstrual blood dripped from the moon, falling on Babcock's cheek.

Ugh agh he said shuddering.

The blood turned to gold on his handkerchief as he rubbed it. Reproducing it became goldbars stacked in a pyramid. The snake is reborn and I'm blushing.

The alchemical mystery of the Red Gold, Crowley said casually.

It's only a Natural Phenomenon, Joyce added. The first fusion.

How did I know you were going to say that, Babcock asked.

Jesus Christ, Joyce said emptily.

The room began to contract.

It runs on internal combustion, Einstein explained.

Are the dimensions shifting, Joyce asked.

My God, Babcock gasped. We'll all be crushed to death.

We must be approaching the speed of light, Einstein suggested. The mathematics is only in your timid sins of puberty.

The womb continued to contract.

We'll suffocate, Babcock protested.

No, Joyce said. We're just being expelled . . . to a new world.

I nearly reached India, said the Imaginary Mongoose. It was made of olive skin drifting down a windy hall past troglodytes, dwarfs, cavemen, night-gaunts, crabs, giant sunflowers, ticktockticktock trembling.

The stars in the belt of Orion lit up, pointing toward Sirius.

But still, Joyce said pensively. At that time of month?

5 days after the flow begins, Crowley said. The male cycle is 23 days and the female 28. They figured it all out in Bengal two thousand years ago. 23 plus 5 is 28.

Three . . . five . . . eight, Einstein mused. Simple addition . . . 358.

Earth reshaped itself from Chaos.

V.I.T.R.I.O.L.

Visita Interiora Terrae Rectificando Invenies Occultum Lapidem, said Babcock crucified upside down in ecstasy. Visit the interior parts of the Earth; by rectification find the Stone of the Wise. And it says it is found in *the most contemptible and despised of all things.* Codes, hints, ambiguities . . . and yet it's right in front of us all the time. The nine months: the nine moon goddesses . . .

Merde, said General Canbronne with Napoleon's face and Uncle Sam's hat with the three stars in the belt of Orion.

Eat it with catsup, added Edward III.

The excremental Hell of the alchemists, said Joyce Ankh Khonsu. The glowing orange scarlet interior parts. The dark uterine call, Jesus God. The whole Western world has gone mad because Saint Paul had a phobia about the *vagina dentata.*

Joyce split in two, becoming Masoch and Sade.

The love that dare not speak its name, said Masoch in Nora's petticoats. Frighten me to death!

A little discipline is needed, said Sade in Gestapo uniform. Crawl on your belly, you cur. People's minds are nothing but a huge self.

But the horror of It, Iago, said Masoch. The horror of it.

The ants came marching five by five.

They became William Shakespeare.

They say I am not a gentleman, said Moorish Sheikespaere. Just because in front of my house, in front of my house, my far far father had, O God! The injustice of it! In front of the house. It was made of skin loss that is death.

Merde, said General Canbronne with infinite pity. Who bulkily shaped the rouge on germinals.

Rectificando, said the Zürich express. Rectificando, rectificando, rectificando . . .

Physics is psychology, Einstein lectured to the bookcase which he evidently mistook for a freshman class. Forward and back is just the sadistmasochist dimension: aggression or timidity, right? And up and down is the pack hierarchy—who eats first and that sort of thing. And right and left . . . Aristotelian logic, you know . . . goes back to the game of guess-which-hand-it's-in. And the fourth dimension . . .

Yes, yes, Joyce prompted. The fourth dimension?

Sex, Einstein said.

What? Joyce exclaimed.

Even Crowley looked astonished for once.

I don't understand that part myself, Einstein confessed. It has something to do with the seed as a vector in time . . . genetics as the negation of entropy.

But why is so much of it so pleasant, Joyce asked. If our brains are merely operating differently, that explains why we sense more . . . but why the pleasure all over the skin?

It's the next step in evolution, Crowley answered simply.

Past present future all are windy street, naked flesh with the stars.

Oh God, Babcock moaned.

The next stage of evolution, Joyce said. I must think about that.

Did you think evolution was over and done with, Crowley asked rhetorically. Did you really believe that the conditions of pain and discomfort were our lot forever?

You mean, Einstein said, the brain can learn to convert any sensation into eroticism? That's hard to believe.

The brain does process all sensation, Crowley said. If the brain is fully awake and conscious of what it is doing, why on earth should it treat any sensation as a less than orgasmic experience?

And that, Babcock sighed sensually, is the Alchemical gold? Why did it take me so long to understand?

The shamrock nitrogen under the carpet that is death.

Maybe we're just drunk, Joyce said, feeling his penis turning into a cactus a peyote bud a shamrock a giant sunflower a fir a spruce of titanic redwood a perfect rose a moving van inscribed INTERNATIONAL COCAINE INC a comet in orbit endless caves of seacoral in purple and indigo and violet 358 the Serpent the Messiah LORD OF LORDS and BARD OF BARDS For He Shall Reign Forever and EVER a piston a pistol a limp floating flower

The ants came marching nine by nine.

Since I created strife, cried Bertran de Born leaping headless from the fireplace, you see me torn asunder from myself: two in one and one in two. Anne Boleyn was 'enry's wife, King 'enry's wife was she . . .

Hold your fucking end up Bert, shouted Ezekiel Pound.

A wonderful idea the knowledge of death.

Whakty whakty whakty whakty boom boom, said the Hidden Variable. Hagios Hagios Hagios IAO. Thermogo thermogo thermogo.

Filia et Pater unus Deus, Crowley chanted. ARARITA.

ARARITA ARARITA ARARITA replied the King in Yellow from the fire.

Overnight overnight overnight said the red Cobra of desire.

Rectificando rectificando rectificando said Babcock.

Illegal and impossible entry, Joyce mused amused. Every child wants to know what happens behind that locked door. The forbidden room puzzle.

Adam Weishaupt wearing Uncle Sam's red white blue hat with the three stars in the Belt of Orion appeared behind the altar masturbating.

I invoke thee said Weishaupt the terrible and invisible god who dwellest in the void places of the spirit ARO-GOGOUABRAO SOTOU MUDORIO PHALARTHA OOO AEPE thou spiritual sun thou eye thou lust cry aloud whirl the wheel o my father o sun thou selfcaused most hight the bornless one

He ejaculated gasping like a hanged man.

I am the seed of stars said the first spermatozoon with the face of the Father.

I am the flame that burns but consumes not said the second spermatozoon with the face of the Sun.

Now you see me now you don't said the third spermatozoon with the face of Schrödinger's Cat. Punishment shall be inflicted on three crows and a wren.

They're going to shoot the Archduke said a voice to Einstein only.

Land bread and peace, said Lenin above the bookcase.

Crowds cheered: Babcock Manor was looted: the Royal Family assassinated: Mongolian clusterfucking in the streets.

What Archduke, Einstein mumbled.

A chorus of workers entered singing

> Oh the banks are made of marble
> With a guard at every door
> And the vaults are full of silver
> That the farmer sweated for

I proclaim the dictatorship of the proleteriat, Lenin said heaving a brick at Schrödinger's Cat. Beethoven is *verboten*. Everyone must learn to play chess at once. Capitalist

schweinerei not permitted. Post no bills. No petit bourgeois subjectivism decadent imperialistic idealism or
predialectical empiriocriticism. Overnight overnight overnight. All power to the Soviets.

The ants came marching twelve by twelve.

L'il dollink, said Queen Victoria swallowing his brick.
Always fetful.

Eat it with catsup, said Lenin. I proclaim the Five Year
Plan. The tractor is the march of God through the world.
Do not pass Go. Report to the Central Committee. The
first day of the rest of the nitrogen cycle. Less power to
the Soviets.

Red orange yellow green blue indigo violet goblins
dancing.

Eat it with catsup, said the Devil in a watery voice.

The uneatable pursued by the unspeakable, said Edward III crowned with thorns a goldyellow buttercup in
his hand with dark blue garter on left thigh. The love that
dares not speak its name. Paris is an expensive place to
die.

He turned into Melmoth the Wanderer and stumbled
off, drunk, complaining.

The ants came marching hundred by hundred. The
door to Chapel Perilous swung open again and the buzzing increased. All power to the Soviets: a *vagina dentata*
myth. It was the Aklo chants being howled and gibbered
and shrieked and grunted by thousands of dholes and
shoggoths. There are sacraments of evil as well as of good:
only the madman is absolutely sure. Azathoth, the Demon-
Sultan who is the primal Chaos at the center of Infinity,
howled: I know all about those garters, you two perverts!
The ants came marching thousand by thousand.

The accordionist started a new tune: *Die Lorelei.* Joyce
watched dim shadows ambiguously move, starting at the
bookcase. "Flowers," he muttered. *"Blume."*

Tiger lily.

My God, Babcock sighed.

My God, he repeated.

MY GOD, he gasped, both laughing and crying.

What is it with him now, Einstein muttered.

The White Light of the Void from which everything comes, Babcock said. It is not just a metaphor. I have seen it.

Oh, that, Einstein said. It's just the atomic accelerations that control the electrochemical processes that make up your separate brain functions. The Hidden Variable.

Do you mean, Joyce cried, that we have become so slowed down or speeded up or whatever that we are actually experiencing the physical process by which our brains create form?

Certainly, Einstein said. All this jumpiness, for instance, is just quantum discontinuity.

Well, Joyce said, at least that's a theory. I suppose it's better than no theory at all. Do you really believe it?

I do right now, Einstein said. I doubt that I will still believe it in the morning. It may take me thirty more years of mathematical dickering before I can convince myself again that such bridges exist. . . .

You mean, Crowley asked excitedly, that this part of the transformation actually takes us to atomic levels?

To sub-atomic levels, Einstein said. To the bridges across super-space through which the Hidden Variable controls the quantum symphony. Don't assume I know what I'm talking about. As I said, it will take thirty years or more to get it into the right math. In the meanwhile, Beethoven probably explains it better than physics.

Omnia in Duos, said the King in Yellow. Duo in Unum. Unus in Nihil.

How long have we been in this cave, asked worried Einstein. The fire is getting low.

We were fish a few million years ago, Joyce said.

Return all three forms in triplicate, said Lenin with

Stalin's face. The Secret Police is the march of God through the world. See your dentist twice a year. No unauthorized orgasms. Overnight overnight overnight. No power to the Soviets.

As they watched down a windy street buildings arose: the Parthenon, Saint Peter's, the Eiffel Tower, Oriental pagodas, the towers of Babylon, American skyscrapers, a Quatt Wunkery, geodesic Martian hives, all this frantic activity accompanied by insectoid buzzing. Roaches constructed geometric aisles and ambulatories for Gothic cathedrals, the ants came marching million by million to erect flowery arcades and architraves, centipedes and lobsters scurried through rapid design of basilicas, bays and flying buttresses under the grave supervision of wise old hermit crabs, cantilevers and capitals leaped to the skies as termites and tarantulas toiled day and night to place brick upon brick, dozens of caryatids, chancels and colonnades appeared between the stark grandeur of pyramids, mosquitoes and beetles cooperated in the implementation of columns Doric and Byzantine and Ionic and Corinthian, grass huts and teepees and igloos multiplied in myriads, Stonehenge arose, the bustling buzzing blasting building without end, rose windows and naves and posts-and-lintels arising and rising and re-arising. They saw palaces of gold, temples the color of stars, warrens of indescribable inhuman subhuman slums and ghettoes, as one generation passeth away and another generation cometh but landlords never die.

And the ants came marching billion by billion.

I invoke thee, chanted Ludwig, MA BARRAIO IOEL KOTHA ARTHOBELA ABRAOT O mother O truth Thou mass Thou that art Thou hollow one Thou goddess of beauty and love

I'm a goddam female Hippopotamus, Babcock discovered.

Joyce looked at the lovely figure sitting on the rock in

the middle of the Rhine combing Her golden hair and realized that she was in fact a female Hippopotamus.

I thought we had explained all the mysteries, he complained.

I am Isis ineffable Queen of Nature, Babcockotamus announced more excitedly. I am the womb of all things. Sweet Jesus on a bike, I think I'm going to have a child.

The cosmic birth process repeated again and again and again my poppyred cunt on fire the pleasure the pain but I don't have a cunt what happened to my prick who castrated me where am I but oh God the joy of motherhood again and again and again

Womb contracting. Room contracting. An elevator in outer space between verbal concepts representing Winter.

In the beginning was the Light, said Einstein in an elevator between the stars. Matter is knots in Energy.

Madam I'm Adam, said Tetragrammaton a Judeo-Creek fig merchant. A man, a plan, a canal: Panama. He goddam mad dog eh?

The bawdy hand of the clock, said Gladstone, is on the very prick of noon uh nick of prune

We have heard the chimes at midnight, Joystaff said.

A parted just between twelve and one, Hostess Quickly said wearing a Victorian dress with slit skirt showing blue garter on black mesh stocking. Even at the turning of the tide. His nose was as sharp as a pen and a table of green fields.

She snapped her garter and sang:

> Only a Magus and a Knight trueborn
> And a Virgin unafraid
> Can walk unharmed amid the dance
> Of the Devil's Masquerade

Brings the deepdown color back, said Hostess Twinky. Purity of essence. Ours in the original and genuine. Put out the light and then put out the Light. Demands an emphatic protest from lovers of literature.

Sir John crossed the heavily fogged street, pushed open the door of *M.M.M.: Occult and Mystical Books of All Ages* with the mindless jerkiness and currencies of the world.

Watch Sir John Peel, said Sir Talis coiling oily surly. Cuckoo.

With his hounds and his haunts in the gloaming, said Canon Futter. Dorter of the Garter.

Thee I invoke, Crowley chanted faster and faster. The bornless one thee that didst create the earth and heavens thee that didst create the night and day Thou art myself made perfect Thou art the truth in matter Thou art the truth in motion

Fornication sodomy abomination, ranted Verey. Cuckolds, garterbaters.

I never used my dirty penis Reverend, said Jack the Ripper. Only a nice clean knife. Linked by strange coincidence where the moon doesn't shine.

The rent bill is due again, said O'Shit. Landlords never die.

If we lived in the middle of a fireworks exhibition, Einstein lectured, everybody would understand my theory of space-time immediately, directly, sensorially. But we *do* live in the middle of a fireworks display: the velocity is not observed because we are moving with it. Why then do I observe it now?

My best friend in college was homosexual, Joyce told Babcock. I didn't realize that until nearly ten years later. The arts of hypocrisy are even more highly developed in Ireland than in England. My God I will write this Hunter book and show humanity the real truth of its situation.

I never knew just breathing could be so marvelous, Babcock answered.

Now I'm a billionyearold fish and a man who will be

born in 1984 and live a thousand years in a dozen galaxies, Joyce remarked happily. Man, what have you done to us?

Opened the doors of perception, Crowley said.

Shall I compare thee to a summer's day, Shakespeare asked lisping effeminately.

Oh why not, said Mr. W. H. camping outrageously. It would be a marvelous ripping rag.

Sodom and Gomorrah, Verey muttered. London and Paris. Illegal entry. It runs on ears of words.

You be a photon I thought.

Joyce knew suddenly that the four of them in Arab headgear had sat around this campfire for seventy thousand years.

There is a cruel streak in you father, said Eduard Einstein. Hiroshima . . . Nagasaki . . . New York . . .

Einstein looked at rising flames in horror.

How long does this go on?

You and your piggy books, Lucia Joyce said. And your garters and garters and garters.

Concepts breaking down into atomic perceptions, Joyce muttered.

It has to end sometime. Or are we in Eternity?

Adam Weishaupt arose through the trapdoor wearing a Wizard's Cap with the eye-in-triangle design. How the simple Mason plies, he chanted, Tool on Temple, see it rise! Princes of Jerusalem, How we mock and scoff at them!

This is Hell.

We'll all be crushed.

I remain an eternal mystery, said Mr. W. H. The supreme desire, unknown, refined out of existence. Only my initials remain. Mr. W. H. O?

Philosophia meta pederastia, Plato intoned from Eternity. *Eleutheria. Tapa kega day.*

Floating, Einstein said, zero gravity. The relativism of the instrument.

It has to end soon. Doesn't it?

But Crowley Hierophant rapped eleven times on the floor with his Staff, reciting in plainchant:

There is no Grace; There is no Guilt;
This is the law: Do What Thou Wilt!

Split the skull, Weishaupt howled in delirium. On guard the sword! Earth be null and heaven abhorred! All's a lie, although Divine! Give annihilation's sign!

I'm dying. We'll never escape.

The aromas of rose and clover where the moon doesn't shine.

O'Neill saw Queen Molly's pants, Joyce laughed.

That wasn't so bad after all. We're floating in space and we've turned into genitals.

Joyce condensed himself into a blue book, split into atoms, refined himself out of existence, reproduced, and became incarnate in a million libraries.

Fee fie fo fum, said Sir Talis. I smell the blood of an Englishman.

Babcock laughed. Is that what I was afraid of? An illustration from a children's book?

Go away, Joyce told Sir Talis calmly. You're only a Freudian symbol. *Eutaenia sirtalis*, the common garter snake. Sir Talis, Garters—do you understand, Babcock? Also called the garden snake. Hence the Eden symbols in the dreams.

Egad Joyce, said Einstein with Dr. Watson's face. How do you do it?

Elementary, my dear Einstein, replied Joyce with Sherlock Holmes' face. Garters, garters everywhere.

Dr. Carl Jung climbed through the window.

That kind of Freudian analysis is true enough, he said, but it's not the whole truth. The snake is the Gnostic symbol of immortality and rebirth. To the primitive racial unconscious, the snake is reborn every time it sheds its skin.

Bosh, said the voice of Sigmund Freud.

Egad, Joyce cried in ecstasy. I have it at last!

What? Einstein asked absently.

Joyce recited gravely awaiting their applause:

> From deep 'neath the crypt at St. Giles
> Came a shriek that re-echoed for miles
> The vicar said "Gracious—
> It's Brother Ignatius!
> He's forgotten the Bishop has piles!"

Das Buch ist ein Schwein, Nora Barnacle said accusingly. Garters he writes about when we don't have enough food in the house.

Well, Joyce said uneasily, is not fetishism the first religion?

Half the men in England have some such fetish, Crowley said. Usually it's Miss Birch, mistress of discipline: the psychological correlative of imperialism.

Yes . . . Joyce said earnestly. I have always wanted Nora to discipline me . . . to see her eyes flash with anger . . .

Joyce is mocked, slandered, outcast, condemned, rejected, despised, starved. Rumors circulate like new cases of the clap around Paris London Dublin Zürich Pola Moscow Hong Kong Nagasaki Hiroshima Sydney Honolulu Mendocino Chicago Bad Ass Texas and back to Dublin. They say he has become a hopeless cocaine addict, his mind has been destroyed by paresis, he has died of drink in New York, he suffers from seven vile dieases and delirium tremens, he makes homosexual overtures to headwaiters, he writes anonymous obscene letters to the Queen of England and an assortment of nuns and teenage girls, he is a voyeur, he is an exhibitionist, he defecates in public parks awaiting applause with an idiot grin, he is going blind from morose delectation and excessive masturbation, he wets the bed and wiggles his toes in it, he haunts finishing schools to smell the seats of girl's bicycles, he is secretly an English German or a German Agent or a brainwashed bezombified mindless tool of the Illuminati, he has been cuckolded by his brother, his best friend, seven priests, nine rabbis, the Elect of Fifteen, the House of Rothschild, and the band at the Waldorf Astoria. His books, together with those of Sade, Masoch and Wilde are to be buried in a secret vault in the Lost Pyramid in the Hidden City in the Lost Continent of Mu. He himself is stripped, lashed, tickled, tormented, hanged, drawn, quartered and crucified.

Father forgive them, he said, for they know not what they do.

He kicked the bucket. Sparks flew out, astral vibes shook the atmosphere, he gave up the ghost, ball lightning and unidentified flying objects dazzled all the spectators, earthquakes collapsed Dublin into the sea, the heavens shook, and he died like a dog.

Why seek ye Jim here, asked the angel, rolling back the rock. And from Joyce's grave came flowers and each flower had seven leaves and every leaf had seven secrets and every secret had seven titles and they could read among them such poesies as Poppy Oh Popey Do You Have Cartage on Your Rhine, The Tarot Towery Connection, Left-Handed Monkey Shines, It May Be Bolt Like A Sheephorse But Do You Call It Levin, The Campbells Are Camping with Musks of Goths, God Bless You Please Mr Robinson, They Needed A Songbird In Heaven So They Took Crusoe Away On A Friday, Tinned All Us Do Part, You Kenna Get My Chests With Your St. Tomach's View, Sit On A Potato Pan Otis, The Oyster Rising and the Clam Dever, The Hannibal Cairo Express with Huck Chum and Effrontery, Nero My Dog Has Fleas, A Grand

Canyon by the Committee of the Hole, The Old Seizers and the New Cut-Ups, A Fold-In Burrow for an Ova Eggspressed, and the especially treasured Ten Spices and Twenty-Two Raisins To Turn Your Brainpan To a Fruitcake. As each goes to seed up spring such unique products of the Groves of Academe as Motive and Method in Joyce's Voices, Method and Motive in Joyce's Verses, Myth and Metaphor in His Comic Epic, Metaphor and Myth in His Crucified Eroticism, Night and Day He's Got Us Under Our Skin, A Skillfully Done Key to His Finicky Work, A Skinfull Down Teeth for a Talulapalooza, The Marx in His Gripes, The Freud in His Feuds, Our Purification and Petrification for Canonization of His Excrementations and Pornographations. Who's Who and Who Cares When Nobody is Everybody, and the exhaustingly exhaustive Myth, Metaphor, Meaning, Symbolism, Morose Delectation and Sneaky Dirty Jones in A Sample Paragraph (3 vols.)

The mummy Osiris rose from the grave.

I am a watchmaker in Amsterdam, he said. The nitrogen cycle.

Ulysses rose from the grave.

I am an advertising canvasser in Dublin, he said.

Stanislaus Joyce came out from under the carpet wearing the Mark of Cain.

Am I my brother's keeper, he asked. Besides, the woman did tempt me. . . .

Oh rocks said the voice of Nora Barnacle.

But Joyce arose from the grave glorified infinitely subtle.

Bad luck to your souls, he laughed, did you think me dead?

Lots of fun at Finnegans Wake, sang the Master Masons.

Merde, said General Canbronne. Age of Reason. Always wear brown trousers in battle.

Dracula rose from the grave.

Don't forget to include me in the I.N.R.I. process, he said. Landlords never die. The other side of the Devil. I never drink wine.

Eduard Einstein and Lucia Joyce were led in, wearing straitjackets, moving with the mindless jerkiness of chronic schizophrenia.

You'll desert my mother, Eduard said accusingly to Albert. You never loved me. All you love is your goddam equations. You are a monster. You live in your head and don't love anyone. Oh I think I shall go mad.

Oh, no, Einstein said sobbing suddenly.

You see, Crowley said to Babcock. Now it's his turn for the *Nun* stage of I.N.R.I. Death on a White Horse.

Lucia Joyce lifted her skirt flirtatiously, showing a blue garter.

Go, damn you, she shouted at James. Hide under the ground. I know you're watching us. Watching, always watching. You know everything—men women boys girls— and you see through it all don't you? You live in your head and don't love anyone.

Shite, Joyce said, sobbing in his wine.

And there's another candidate, Crowley said airily.

You rotten bastard.

It's bloody beastly buggering bleeding hell to be the child of a genius, Eduard Einstein mourned.

Don't I know it, Lucia Joyce agreed.

I am HE, Crowley chanted suddenly drawing their attention again. The Bornless Spirit having sight in the feet Strong and immortal fire Who hate that evil should be wrought in the world He that lightning and thundereth He whose mouth ever flameth He from whom is the shower of life on Earth

A *true initiation never ends*.

Dare to struggle, dare to win, shouted Lenin.

Dare to guzzle Gordon's gin, Joyce added.

Je suis Bovary, Flaubert said looking embarrassed.

Je suis Molly Bloom, Joyce said unembarrassed.
The Master Masons chanted over the Neanderthal fire:

> For of the Father and the Son
> The Holy Spirit is the norm
> Male-female, quintessential, one
> Man-being veiled in womanform
> Glory and worship be to Thee
> Sap of the world-ash, wonder-tree!

I think, Joyce said, that we have somehow been mutated from symbolic verbal consciousness to total body awareness. Is that it?

That is certainly part of it, Einstein agreed thoughtfully. But there is an element also of direct brain consciousness, is there not? It seems to me that you should understand Relativity better now, because *I* certainly understand it better than *I* ever did.

But the table, Joyce said. My God, the table.

What about the table? Einstein asked.

We're inside it, Joyce said.

Yes . . . Einstein said softly . . . that's it. We're inside It and It is inside us. There's a bridge . . .

My God, Joyce said. Yes.

In the material universe, Einstein said happily, the smaller is always inside the larger. But in the mental universe . . . *mein Gott* . . . the larger can be inside the smaller. That's what thought is. . . . We are as big as whatever we perceive and conceive. . . . It's a mobius strip. . . .

Glory to thee from gilded tomb, resounded the voice of Tim Finnegan.

Glory to thee from waiting womb, chanted Molly Bloom.

Glory to thee from earth unploughed, cried Osiris.

Glory to thee from virgin vowed, sang Isis.

The cross becomes a phallus.

The phallas becomes a cross.

The cross becomes a whirling sun.

Two owls and a hen, said King Lear, Three crows and a wren, have all built their nests in my beard.

They were moving toward Zero.

My God it's the Black Hole, Schwartzchild cried.

The entrance to Hell, Babcock said.

The Cup of Our Lady, Crowley corrected them.

It became an enormous pulsating doughnut. Joyce laughed.

Nine months to get out, he said, and the rest of our fool lives trying to get back in again. . . .

The doughnut became the spinning galaxy.

"Have we really been sitting here," Joyce asked finally, "laughing like fools for three or four hours?"

"Something like that," Einstein said.

"Is it over yet?" Babcock asked.

"I don't think so," Joyce replied. "Do you see what I see?"

The earth shook. Cthulhu rose from the Depths waving white-stained garters and stocks bonds currencies of all nations boards and corporations. Governments fell like bowling pins. The stock market crashed. Nameless anarchist hordes stormed the streets, shouting *Up Against The Wall Motherfuckers* as they executed bankers corporation presidents lawyers politicians landlords priests rabbis ministers lady-golfers and anyone with a clean white shirt. Orgies broke out in parliaments, congresses, antique shops, boutiques, business offices, butcher shops, monasteries, trolleycars, hospitals, carousels, universities, academies, laboratories, nunneries, bakeries, cathedrals, law offices, factories; huge brutal cocks were thrust into cunts, assholes, mouths of voluptuous actresses, doddering dowagers, distinguished philosophers, kings, bishops, boys, girls, soldiers, Mother Superiors, bankers, whimpering poets; cunts were fucked, sucked, chewed, licked, kissed; Queen Victoria was gangbanged by 358 Watusi warriors. Madmen defecated in wells, fountains, punchbowls, on streets and in doorways. Drooling farmboys waving signs that said *Bestiality Liberation* charged into pet shops to sodomize dogs, cats, monkeys, birds, tarantulas. André Breton walked about Paris shooting pedestrians at random. The last lawyer was strangled with the guts of the last politician. The Pope appeared in delirium on the balcony facing Saint Peter's Square incoherently chanting *Cthulhu fthagn* while sodomizing himself with a twelve-inch dildo from the Yokohama Sex And Leather Corporation. Housewives murdered their husbands and rushed to the stockyards to fuck goats, howling *Io Pan Io Pan Pan The Goat With a Thousand Young!* Nihilists attacked insane asylums with automatic rifles, murdered the staffs and set the patients free to roam the streets and set fire to psychiatrists' offices. Avant-garde poets seized the newspapers and published strange, unsettling headlines: *Is It a New Electromagnetic Phenomenon or The Heart and Mind of Europe Dying?; Only the Madman Is Absolutely Free; The Star People Are Returning But I Have Lost My One True Love; Where Is God Now That We Need Him?* The next day the women got organized and completed the butchery. And the sky turned into the body of Nuit, black, beautiful, the starmother: and all was changed in a moment, in the flickering of an eye. It never happened. We were just four people sitting on the floor looking past time into eternity.

CROWLEY

[*Solemnly*]:   In my mad and werewolf heart
I have howled thirtynine years away
In laughter and rage: the bread and wine
Of Werewolf Mass

[*Mass dissolves; they float free.*]

JOYCE

[*Liturgically*]:   In my high and mountain heart
I have laughed thirtytwo years away
In folly and scorn: the flesh and blood
Of werewolf Time

[*Time ends; they enter Eternity.*]

EINSTEIN

[*Precisely*]:   In my clear and limpid mind
I have counted thirtyfive years away
In measure and line: the skin and bones
Of werewolf Space

[*Space implodes; they enter Infinity.*]

CROWLEY

[*Furiously*]:   And until defiance builds of its own ache
A truth less tame than the truth of death
My werewolf heart shall howl against
Both werewolf God and werewolf Man

JOYCE

[*Sadly*]:   Yes, until our heartache builds of its own
flames
A truth more wild than the truth of Life—

[*Isis appears. All see Her.*]

BABCOCK

[*Rapt*]:   My werewolf heart is pierced at last
By the silver bullet of the Lady's gaze

CROWLEY

[*Erotomaniac*]: My werewolf heart is pierced at last
By the silver bullet of the Lady's eyes
I am the Beast the Lady rides
I am the stars within her hair

[*Isis and Osiris merge into Apophis.*]

MESCALITO

[*Green, pointyeared, dancing*]:

Glory to Thee, thou sire and dam
And Self of I am that I am!

MASTER MASONS

Glory to Thee, beyond all term,
Thy spring of sperm, thy seed and germ!

[*Pyramidphallus rising again.*]

LOLA LEVINE

Glory to Thee, eternal Sun,
Thou One in Three, Thou Three in One!

MASTER MASONS

Glory and worship unto Thee,
Sap of the world-ash, wonder-tree!

[*The Holy Guardian Angel appears.*]

EINSTEIN

[*Seeing Angel*]: The unified field . . .

JOYCE

[*Seeing Angel*]: The eternal cycle . . .

BABCOCK

[*Seeing Angel*]: 358: My secret Self, my adversary, my devil, my redeemer . . .

CROWLEY

[*Piously, to Angel*]: The Rosy Cross, the eternal embrace!

[*The cock crows; the Golden Dawn arises.*]

JOYCE

[*Intuiting the structure in time*]: Children . . . It reproduces continually . . .

EINSTEIN

[*Reasoning the structure in space-time*]: Unity . . . It's plus one and minus one . . .

BABCOCK

[*Feeling the Force*]: Fucking . . . It's making love to itself all the time . . .

CROWLEY

ARARITA. ARARITA. ARARITA.

[*The* Föhn *stops blowing. These our actors, as foretold, are all spirits and vanish into air, into thin air.*]

JOYCE

The flowers come back every spring. Earth to earth, dust to dust, *merde* to *merde*. Every spring the flowers come back. . . .

EINSTEIN

The nitrogen cycle.

BABCOCK

Through the dark underworld to the Golden Dawn.

CROWLEY

[*Airily*]: 'Tis new to you . . .

Joyce awoke first, hearing a birdsong in the garden. The newday sun on his face told him that it was mid-morning at least.

With tentative step, still coming back from infinity, he rose to look out the window. The garden was green as chemical dye, luminescent: lingering after-effect of the drug. From the street, voices: from a single lark on a birch branch, the song that had wakened him. It was a clear sunbright Swiss spring day, the air no longer stagnant with the wind of witchcraft.

"By *God*," he said softly. It was the same world that Adam saw, naked and astonished: a loving presence.

"Is it morning?" Babcock asked, stirring half-awake in his chair.

"It is the first day of the rest of the universe," Joyce said pensively.

Babcock sat up, eyes wide with mute questions. "My *God*," he said.

"Yes," Joyce said. "It was quite an evening, wasn't it?"

"Did you see the Holy Guardian Angel?" Babcock asked, wholly awake, standing to stretch.

"I saw . . . many things," Joyce said. "I saw, most certainly, how to write this new novel that has been haunting me."

"I think," said Babcock, "that I saw God and died."

Einstein was arising from his chair now, also. "What was it Jones said about the Holy Guardian Angel, long ago?" he asked. "Something to the effect that it might come as a new scientific theory, or a work of art, or just a change of life toward compassion or religion? My *God*," he added.

Joyce turned from the window, his eyes huge and amused behind the thick glasses. "I think we all saw God and died," he said. "Each in our own way."

"When did Crowley leave?" Einstein asked.

"Toward dawn," Babcock said. "You two had already started to doze. I had a few words with him, I remember, while you were both already snoring."

"Oh?" Joyce asked. "And what was the essence of that conversation, if you care to say?"

Babcock arose and smiled at the golden sunlight. "I told him about a doctor I met on the train two nights ago—the doctor you mentioned yourself a few times, named Jung. I said I would like to spend some time here, with Jung, before returning to London and the next stage of my Initiation."

"You intend to continue your Initiation?" Joyce asked.

"When I am ready," Babcock said. "When Dr. Jung thinks I am ready—that is."

Einstein whistled, or sighed, a long astonished breath. " '*For He is like a refiner's fire,*' " he quoted.

Joyce turned. "And what did *you* get out of last night's entertainment?" he asked Einstein.

"It all came together," Einstein replied simply. "I could see all of it, every piece, and how each related to the others. My papers on relativity are just the beginning. There is a unified field that I have to work on, as soon as I finish this paper on relativity of acceleration." He grinned with pixie glee. "It may take me twenty years, or longer, but it will be worth it. Can you imagine? Our ideas about space are as primitive as the ancient ideas about Earth being flat. Space is curved, too. Every movement is a movement in orbit, around a mass: gravity and inertia are reifications of the curvature of space. And that's only the beginning of what I'm beginning to see. . . ."

"So you have no hard feelings about the drug and the incantations and all the other Stone Age shaman's tricks Crowley used?" Joyce asked.

"None whatever," Einstein said. "I think I learned more physics in those hours than in all my life before last night. How about yourself?"

"No hard feelings," Joyce replied, "but if I ever see Crowley coming again, I'll head in the other direction. One night in the caves of Eleusis is enough for a lifetime, as the Greeks knew."

Einstein was pacing again, but more slowly. "It was as if our brains were washed out with soap," he said. "As if—*mein Gott*—we were born again."

"Yes," Joyce said, "born again. That expression comes from the Eleusinian rituals I just mentioned. *Digenes*, the twice-born, were those who had gone through the whole night, in the cave of Demeter, being initiated. No historian claims to know what went on in there, but I think we can all make a good guess, can we not?"

"Those chants Crowley used," Einstein said. "Could they possibly be the same after twenty-five hundred years?"

"Not the same," Joyce said. 'It was very bastard Greek, with Egyptian and Latin fragments here and there. They probably came down through the Gnostics and other heretical sects with a lot of distortion over the ages. . . . But I wouldn't be too surprised if *some* of the words were not

exactly those used in the Eleusinian initiations. Babcock,"
he said suddenly, "I won't ask you to break your Oath,
but it would not be unethical to answer two questions that
occur to me. Does the Mason Word have eight letters?"

"Yes," said Babcock.

"And the Cabalistic value of 72?" Joyce pursued.

"Yes."

"You need tell me no more. I believe Jones was telling
the truth about this Order being forty-five hundred years
old." Joyce smiled. "Just like *Dur* to *Turicum* to *Zürich.*
The word is the clue to everything."

"Well," Babcock said, picking up his briefcase. "I want
to thank you two remarkable gentlemen for everything.
But I really must be off to see Dr. Jung."

"He will find you a delightful case," Joyce said laughing. "Half of your unconscious is conscious already."

"No," Babcock said. "It is not that simple. 'You can
empty infinity from it, and infinity remains,' as Crowley
said—quoting the *Upanishads.*"

"Yes," Joyce said. "Infinity remains. . . ."

"There is always one more hunchback," Einstein said,
smiling gently.

"Good luck, Babcock," Joyce said with his formal manner again.

"Good luck, Sir John," Einstein added, shaking the
younger man's hand as they went to the door.

Joyce stood alone, staring at the bookcase. "Flowers,"
he muttered. "*Blume.* Bloom?"

Einstein returned. "Well, Jeem, what the *devil* do you
think really happened to us?"

"I am no chemist," Joyce said carefully, "but I will
accept your metaphor about washing out the brain. I
suspect that such chemicals are the universal solvents of
alchemy. They dissolve the reflex arcs in the brain, so that
our old ideas and old selves drown in an ocean of new
signals."

"Something like that," Einstein said. "Well, do you really think that impossible novel of yours is finally possible?"

"It is inevitable," Joyce said flatly. "I have at last found the structural groundplan that goes underneath everything else. Under the *Odyssey*, under *Hamlet*, under Moses in the wilderness, under the colors and arts and body organs and all the other allegorical structures. The simple basic human truth that will hold it all up." He laughed again. "And the critics will take decades to dig it out, if they ever do."

"What are you talking about?" Einstein asked.

"The real theme of my book, the theme I've been trying to define for months and years while this was growing slowly in the back of my head." Joyce smiled radiantly.

"So? What is it, for heaven's sake?"

"The parable of the Good Samaritan," Joyce said. "The simple human story that is so ordinary nobody can see it until they have their noses rubbed in it."

"The ordinary," Einstein said. "Of course, to you, it would have to be the *ordinary*."

"Yes," Joyce said. "Listen: we will always remember last night, because it was extraordinary. *But suppose it had been ordinary.* Just four men talking about this and that. And suppose one of us died this morning of a brick falling off a roof? Would not the other three remember last night, in the light of that tragedy, just as intensely as we remember the initiation we underwent? Don't you understand? Nobody *sees* the ordinary until it is too late. I am—by *God* and by *Jesus* and by *Allah*—going to *make* them see it, if it takes me as long as it takes you to work out your unified field theory."

"Well, then," Einstein said, "we all found what we were looking for. But it was different for each of us. I suppose it always is."

"I must be going myself," Joyce said suddenly, "before Nora begins worrying again that I died drunk in a gutter."

"Remember me when you return to Trieste."

"I will, Professor." Joyce stopped on his way to the door. "By the way, what time is it—in this system of coordinates, that is?"

Einstein removed his watch and looked at it carefully. "Exactly thirty-two minutes after eleven."